MW00387420

Hardcover: 978-1-7347634-5-4
Paperback: 978-1-7347634-1-6
Audiobook: 978-1-7347634-4-7
Ebook: 978-1-7347634-3-0

Library of Congress Control Number: 2020940660
First Edition: September 2020

Edited by: Raven Eckman of A New Look On Books
Book Cover Designer: Diana Toledo Calcado of Triumph Book Covers

Hurn Publications | Temple, TX
www.hurnpublications.com

PAIRS WITH LIFE

A NOVEL

JOHN A. TAYLOR

HURN
PUBLICATIONS

To my brother, Steve;

Who handed me a cutlass,
raised the Jolly Roger,
and told me to get onboard.

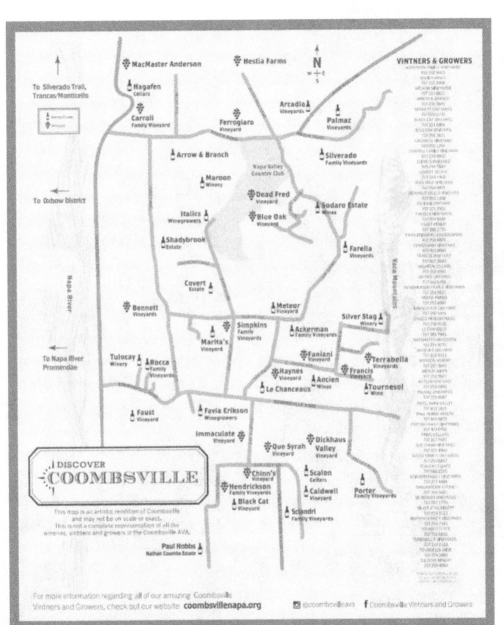

ONE

Let's get one thing clear - I won that bet fair and square, even though I cheated.

I blame the whole thing on Rick Dornin, who was being particularly douchey that night. I used to be able to choose whichever party I wanted to serve without question. That is, until Dornin arrived at Appellation with his anal-retentive online calendar and industrial-grade Napoleon complex.

Yes, *that* Appellation. The most coveted dining experience in all of Napa Valley, and one of only nine restaurants in America awarded three Michelin stars. It took a DNA sample and a copy of your credit report to get a table, and then you'd better be ready to cash in your 401(k) when the bill came.

The evening started out normally enough. I arrived at the restaurant an hour before my shift to check reservations, talk to Chef Dan about the evening's specials, and think of pairings for the *prix fixe*. Dornin was in his office—a modified broom closet next to the staff bathroom that looked like a hoarder's den with one, tiny deer trail leading to his desk. In fact, he was always in his office, even when service was slammed, which drove me batshit crazy. I don't care if you're General Manager or General Patton—when it's time to schlep a plate or buff a glass, you step up and do it.

Anyway, I poked my head through the doorway and said, "Hey, Rick," trying to keep things light and cheery. "What do you know about this Harrison party at eight?"

"Whales," he replied, not bothering to look up from his purchase orders. "Big whales, like Moby Dick whales."

"Sweet!" Visions of stockbrokers trying to one-up each other with bottles of Screaming Eagle at five thousand bucks a pop danced in my head. Tips so big they come in a brown paper bag.

2 | JOHN A. TAYLOR

"Yes." Dornin finally looked up at me and grinned like he learned how to do it from an infomercial. "They'll be in the Veraison Room. With Andrew."

"*What?*" I lunged into the tiny office, nearly tripping over a carton of water glasses. "You can't give it to Andrew!"

"I can give it to whoever I want." He went back to his purchase orders, feigning a *nonchalance* that made me want to smack him. "If I want to move Felipe off of bussing and let him pop some corks, I could do that, too."

Time for a different tack—one that wouldn't involve me going full-on Hannibal Lecter. "I'm just saying that a party like that comes to a restaurant like this to experience the highest level of service in the *world*. I'm the guy they're coming for, not Andrew. I sit for my Master Somm next week, and—"

"You know what you are, Corbett? You're an overpaid bartender." Dornin had thin lips and an Adam's apple the size of Detroit, and it bugged me. "You trained for twenty years to learn how to pull a cork from a bottle and tell people that red wine goes with steak. Whoop-tee-freaking-do. You'll work the floor tonight, and you can have the Jansen party on the terrace at seven-thirty."

My left eyebrow started twitching, which happens when I get stressed out. Apparently, no one can see it, but to me, it feels like a two-year-old is digging tiny fingers into my face and stretching it like saltwater taffy. I considered trying the *No One Has Experience At Up-Selling Like I Do* approach, but this was the third time in as many weeks I'd had such a run-in with Dornin.

I was done.

It was time to talk to Chef Dan.

Most people remember Chef Daniel Foyer from his five seasons on *Elite Chef*, The Food Channel's number one show from 1998 to 2002. With a chin so chiseled it could slice a burnt chuck steak and blue eyes that screamed, "Come taste this gazpacho in my bedroom," he was the prototype celebrity chef. But Father Time had been most inhospitable to Chef Dan, and for the past couple of years the poor soul tried to counteract a rapid aging process by dunking his scalp and Sam Elliott-sized mustache in a fifty-gallon drum of jet-black hair dye. The net effect was so incongruous with the rest of his wrinkled face that I could barely look at him without drowning in the shore break of cognitive dissonance.

Don't get me wrong, I loved the guy. He was a loyal and trusted friend, and straight-up the most amazing culinary artist of my generation. But if I'd had any money, I would have bought stock in Just For Men and eventually retire on my Chef Dan profits alone.

I found Chef Dan at a table with his sous chef, Stacy, looking over some notes.

"Corbett Thomas!" he bellowed. "I'm doing a monkfish for the *prix fixe* tonight that'll go beautifully with this Albarino you picked up."

A near-empty bottle of 2016 Pazo Senorans sat on the table. "Yes, Chef. Sounds great," I said hurriedly. "Hey, can I talk to you for a moment?"

"Sure." Chef Dan handed his stack of papers to Stacy. "Take these," he said to her, adding, "and if you want Geoffrey to be more forceful on the line, then tell him to stop being such a pussy."

Stacy rolled her eyes. "Oh, that's right," Chef sighed. "We can't say 'pussy' anymore."

At sixty, Chef Dan was at least twice as old as everyone else at the restaurant. I was only twelve years behind him, which made us both anachronisms in the eyes of the staff—cautionary tales from a lost generation, something to be tolerated at best.

"All right, rock star," Chef motioned me to sit down. "What can I do for you?"

"It's Dornin," I replied, taking Stacy's seat. "There's a party of major VIPs tonight and he's giving it to Andrew."

"That's his job. He manages the staff. We've been over this."

"I know, but you manage *him* and he's doing a shitty job." I grabbed the bottle of Albarino and poured the last of it in Stacy's glass. It was gorgeous, the color of spring in Barcelona.

"God, you're worse than Stacy." He leaned back in his chair and ran his fingers through his asphalt hair. "Don't take it so personal."

"I'm not taking it personally." I was. "It's bad for the restaurant. It's bad for the brand."

Chef took the last swig of his wine and let out some ghastly noise that sounded like he'd been punched in the throat. "Look, you should know this by now, but every day a restaurant stays open is a miracle—a goddamn blessing. Rick's doing something right, so let him do it. Revenue is up, the place is booked, everything's working. Besides, Andrew needs the experience. What if you get gorged by a deer or something?"

"I'm sorry," I stuttered. "What if I get *gored* by a deer?"

"You know, if you die," he explained. "Randomly. But horribly."

I got the feeling that he might enjoy that. "I just need to know if you're considering my replacement."

Chef Dan grabbed the wine glass from my hand and drank its contents in one gulp. "I'm not considering anything except a monkfish entrée for tonight. And that's why Rick is here, so I don't have to consider you or Stacy or deal with any of the fucking drama in this place." He stared down the neck of the empty bottle like a telescope. "God, this stuff is good. Did you save me a case like I asked?"

"Yes. And you drank it all."

"Save me another."

I got up and walked away from the table. "You got it, Chef."

"Corbett," he called after me. "It's the worst kept secret that if you pass your sit next week, you're out of here."

I swear to God, the rumor mill at a restaurant was like playing a game of Telephone with a dozen drunk, horny sixteen-year-olds. "Look, I've always been honest with you, Chef. This is the best job I've ever had. Why in the hell would I leave?"

Chef Dan lumbered off towards the kitchen. "Why indeed, Rock Star?"

The whole Dornin and The Whales Episode was officially under my skin, so I decided to go out on the terrace and get some fresh air.

Appellation was built into the side of the foothills of the Vaca Range, about a half-mile up a winding road in Rutherford. Our terrace was one of the most stunning places to dine in all of Napa, as it looked out across a 180-degree panorama of the valley floor and was framed by the Mayacamas Mountains to the west.

I leaned against the waist-high railing atop the stone wall lining the terrace and soaked in the view. The vineyards below weaved a delicate tapestry of early fall colors. Waves of vibrant green segued into pale yellow, which then collided with vibrant crimson and an orange so burnt it threatened to steal the glory from the autumn sun.

Twenty years earlier I drove into Napa on my way down to L.A., stopped for the afternoon, and never got back in my car. Now this place was a part of me. Looking out across the acreage of Cabernet and Chardonnay, I could set my watch by the changing of the vines. These colors told me it was the third week in October, the end of harvest.

This sunset told me I was home.

The bucolic scene may have calmed my shit for a moment, until I felt a disturbing presence beside me. A peripheral glance confirmed it, and my grip unconsciously tightened around the railing as Andrew Ridgley moved up quietly next to me, seemingly taking in the view, but mostly standing there just to piss me off.

Andrew was preternaturally thin, to the point where his midsection curved in slightly, giving him the appearance of a flat Pillsbury Crescent roll. A man bun popped from the top of his tiny head like a lonely radish in a barren field, and his face was framed by a freakish red beard, in which every single hair was of uniform length and curvature. If he was going for the King of the Very Polite Vikings look, he nailed it.

"So," I started, still gazing at the majestic scene before me, "might one call those pistachio-colored Capri pants?"

"One might," he replied, faux ignoring me as well. "Might one call that the world's most heteronormative blue blazer?"

I nodded. "One might, if one knew what the word 'heteronormative' meant."

"I rest my case."

I turned to face him. At six-foot-four, I was a foot taller and had at least seventy-five pounds on him. I wasn't going for intimidation, though. Ok, not *a lot* of intimidation. "You getting the Harrison party only proves that there's no such thing as a just and benevolent God."

Andrew scratched his beard mockingly. Not a single hair was displaced. "Harrison? Oh, you mean Harrison-Lowell Partners? The massive private equity firm whose board is having their party here tonight? Those guys?"

I wanted to rip my face off. The truth was, Andrew was half my age, but only a few steps behind me. He was an Advanced Somm, a WSET-3, CSW, and a whole bunch of other mostly useless acronyms. But he had mad tasting skills, which while also hating, I grudgingly respected too.

"Just…get them to do different bottles with each course," I said, trying to mask my aggravation. "No by-the-glass stuff and none of those imports I got on special—"

"Gee, thanks, Corbett," he interrupted. "I'll do my best to remember all of that complex and really insightful information." He walked backwards towards the door, a smug little smirk spreading across his face. "In the meantime, you have an absolutely awesome evening with your bachelorette party."

. . .

On my eighth birthday, my mom woke me up at 3:00 a.m., dragged me out of bed and into the cold backseat of her Datsun hatchback and said, "We're going to Disneyland." I'd never been but leave it to say I could sing all five verses of "Yo Ho, Yo Ho (A Pirate's Life For Me)." She didn't pack anything except a bologna and American cheese sandwich for me, and a thermos filled with "Mommy's Orange Juice" for her. We drove seven hours from Tucson to Los Angeles, got out, and discovered the park was closed.

"Oh," she had said with a frown. She shoved me back in the car and we drove home to Tucson without saying a word.

When I heard that Jansen was a bachelorette party, it felt a lot like that.

I already knew in agonizing detail how the whole night would unfold. Jansen was a party of fifteen, but only thirteen would show up, because the group had been out wine tasting the entire day, and two girls would have already passed out at the hotel, their heads balanced delicately over the edge of the bed to avoid vomit asphyxiation.

Festivities would start with a round of Lemon Drops, followed by selfies, followed by a round of Himalayan Blow Jobs (the shot, not the Sherpa-based sex act), and more selfies. There'd be a polite but stern noise complaint from a nearby diner, which would be met with vitriol and retribution from the maid of honor, and eventually every single customer on the terrace would have to be re-seated with a comped entrée.

By the start of the second course, two more bridesmaids would be "Man down!" and loaded into the limo to be whisked away. This would cause the Bride to launch into Tearful and Wailing Speech Number One: *Don't You Understand This Is My Wedding?* The remedy for this drama would be another round of shots, followed by the meat course, which everyone would secretly *want* to eat but no one *will* eat.

I would then be asked if dancing is allowed. I would say no. This would be met with Tearful and Wailing Speech Number Two: *Don't You* Fucking *Understand This Is My Wedding?*

At the end of the evening, three of the four remaining conscious bridesmaids would attempt to split the check, and they would get it wrong three times. It would be my fault, obviously, and then Drunk Math would result in a three-hundred-dollar underpayment, coming out of the service charge.

"I'll bet you a hundred bucks I sell the most expensive bottle tonight," I blurted. I'm not exactly sure why I said it: Anger at a manager who didn't respect who I was or what I'd been through; or jealousy of a kid who accomplished in six years what took me twenty.

Andrew froze at the door. "Wait, what? Are you serious?"

"Dead serious," I said.

Andrew folded his arms across his chest and stared at me as if I asked him to solve a quadratic equation. "So, you'll bet me a hundred dollars that you can sell a more expensive wine to the Mike's Hard Lemonade Crew than I can to the Board of Directors of the nation's third-largest private equity firm?"

Well, when you put it that way… No matter. I was betting on my ability to optimize potential. I mean, it's not like the Jansens had booked their party at Applebee's.

"You got it."

"You're on." Andrew stuck out his hand and I shook it. He had that kind of non-committal handshake that feels like you're clutching a wet hunk of pork loin. I dropped his hand and brushed past him.

I'll never say out loud that I doubted my potential to win the bet, but it crossed my mind to add Franzia to the system and charge $1,000.00 per box for it.

. . .

Helena was leading service for the Jansen party that night, which was good news. She was awesome—an absolute pro at her job, and mostly unflappable. We met for a few minutes to talk strategy. I didn't tell her about the bet, though maybe I should have, because she thought it was rather odd of me to be so concerned about a bachelorette party.

"Chances are we aren't even going to need you," she said.

"How sexist," I admonished her, practically vomiting hypocrisy. "What if the bride is a director at Google? And all her friends are instructors at the Culinary Institute? What if they're all writers for *Wine Spectator?*"

She wasn't, they weren't, and hell no.

When the bride-to-be finally sashayed into the restaurant atop a wave of millennial entitlement, it was as obvious as the rhinestone tiara atop her head that there would not be a single fuck given to the wine list. I had to admit, though, that the bride glowed; she beamed. She was all shiny teeth, dewy skin and smoky eyes, and radiating with the glorious possibility of a love eternal—a happiness unhinged and unfettered, as ethereal as a dream whispered to the breeze. It was practically contagious, something I could inhale or feel wash over me for one perfect moment as she sauntered by.

Oh, well. Life would drop its fucking jackboot on her heart soon enough.

Helena agreed to let me go in before she asked for an initial drink order, just to see if I could sell them on wine and not something vodka based. I gave the group exactly seven minutes on the terrace before making my entrance.

They were snapping selfies like the paparazzi. I could have been Ryan Gosling riding in naked on a unicorn and no one would have noticed.

"Good evening, ladies!" I bellowed. Mostly silence. "And a special hello to our beautiful bride-to-be, Nicole!" That got a few 'woot-woots.'

"My name is Corbett and I will be your sommelier tonight." Blank stares. "That means I'm the wine guy—"

"Champers!" Nicole screamed, followed by a chorus of twelve other screams.

Champagne was a good sign, and the only indication so far that Andrew was not going to hand me my ass on this bet. The next step was to identify The Decision Maker of the group. Though typically the bride gets what the bride wants, there's usually somebody else lurking on the periphery who foots the bill. I didn't see an obvious candidate as the party walked in, but as I opened the list to the sparkling wine section and brought it over to the bride, I noticed one woman at the far side of the table who was definitely closer to my age than theirs. Her dress was just a tad less revealing than the spaghetti-strap numbers that dominated the herd, and her general demeanor belied a more mature—if not matriarchal—attitude. I made note of her but brought the list to Nicole, nonetheless.

"May I suggest the Nicolas Feuillatte," I offered first. "It's a beautiful, delicious, creamy Champagne." Then I moved in for the kill. "But what I like to recommend is a bottle of the 2007 Cristal for just you and the maid of honor. You know, something to keep under the table, special for the two of you." Sincere smile, friendly wink, and that'll be seven hundred dollars: a solid start, but perhaps not enough to drop the mic on Andrew.

"Yasss Queen!" One of the bridesmaids rushed up, threw her arms around Nicole's waist, and squeezed hard before turning to me. "We need Prosecco! Have you ever heard of Prosecco?"

"Prosecco, hmm, I may have to look it up." I knew I'd have to deep-six the sarcasm, or I'd be a hundred bucks short by the end of the night. A very, very *long* night.

We did have a Cartizze Prosecco at $150, but I didn't have the heart to spring that on them.

On my way into the cellar to grab the wine, Andrew came out, holding two bottles.

"The '14 Edmond Vatan Sancerre," he crowed.

Ugh. Three hundred bucks a bottle, and that's just the first course. "Your suggestion, or does someone know what they're doing?"

"Two collectors. They're completely geeking out."

This was not a good development. "That's all right. The maid of honor is the sous chef at Franglais in Los Angeles," I said.

"No, she's not," Andrew dismissed, walking off.

"Your parents named you after the guy who did nothing in *Wham!*" I called after him.

"I don't even know what that means," he called back.

By the time I got back to the table, Helena's crew had already set up the glasses. Since we were out on the terrace and the mood was festive, I took one bottle and popped the cork like a rocket. That elicited another round of screams, which in turn elicited the first round of noise complaints from the neighbors.

As I poured the wine, I couldn't help but notice the older woman from before. She was alternately staring at me and her phone. This continued the whole time I went down the line of glasses until I reached the one in front of her.

"I know you," she said.

"You do?"

She held her phone up to me, and there I was, guitar in hand, circa 1995. "You're Sensitive Ponytail Guy!" she squealed.

Here's the thing. It never gets old being recognized, and I have an ego-gasm every time it happens. Honestly, twenty years later, it totally makes my day. That said, my brief brushes with fame are exactly the same every single time, so my response has become perfectly crafted over the last two decades.

"Yep, you got me. I was lead singer and guitarist for Reality Star." I smiled. "That was my band. But you have to understand, I was singing *about* Sensitive Ponytail Guy. That's the irony of the song."

"Oh my god!" She went back to looking at the music video playing on her phone. "I saw you guys open for Soundgarden in 1994. I loved this video."

"Thank you, I really appreciate that." I was still smiling like an ego-fueled dork, but knew I had to get back to business. "So, hey, maybe you'd like to take a look at the wine list and see if there's something special you'd—"

A young woman dropped a case of wine on the table beside me. "Ok, bitches! It is ON!"

It was unfortunate to say the least, but it wasn't uncommon for guests to bring bottles to the restaurant that they'd purchased on their wine tasting adventures. I could only hope that Andrew's group did the same, because this turn of events was probably the bet's death knell.

I opened the case and immediately saw that all the capsules were the same. I took out one bottle. Then another. Then one more. My stomach became the Pit of Despair, tied in more knots than a maritime museum.

I read the label aloud, like I was reading my own death sentence. "Rich Bitch Chardonnay."

"Rich Bitch!" the young woman screamed. "You're a fucking rich bitch, Nicole! WOOOOOOOO!"

More screams. All the screams.

Rich Bitch Chardonnay. $12.95 at the local Safeway ("but only $9.95 when you buy six or more!"). There were about seventy-three smartass, wine snob responses I could have said. Instead, I sulked off to find Helena.

One dozen red Solo cups for table eight, please.

Andrew was at the terrace door, waiting. He'd probably seen the whole episode go down and wanted to twist the corkscrew even further into my heart. Silently, without expression, he presented a bottle of 2006 Domain Armand Rousseau Charmes Chambertin Grand Cru.

I found that I was still carrying a bottle of the Rich Bitch, much the same way Jesus had to carry his own cross. I presented it to Andrew in return. He pursed his lips and nodded - I think he felt sorry for me.

"If memory serves," he noted, "that bottle does not cost twelve hundred dollars."

I didn't go back to the Jansen party. What was the point? The servers could pour the case of plonk, and if by some miracle they needed me for something else, Helena would come find me.

I worked the floor for a little while, which typically lifted my spirits when guests needed recommendations or wanted to chat about some extraordinary winery they had discovered that day. On this particular night, it wasn't working.

I hadn't been entirely honest with Chef Dan. No, I didn't want to leave Appellation once I got my credentials. Not because I loved working 3:00 p.m. to 1:00 a.m. six nights a week or dealing with bachelorettes who didn't know their chardonnay from Kool-Aid or losing a bet to a somm who recently graduated from Gymboree.

I wanted to stay for the clout. For the respect. It wasn't exactly like performing before 30,000 screaming fans, but Master Sommeliers were rock stars in their own right. There were only 236 of them in the entire freaking world.

And with that notch on my wine key, I could kiss the world of one-bedroom apartments and Top Ramen goodbye forever. Seamus O'Flaherty, my partner in crime (though attorneys hate being described that way), had been lining me up some pretty amazing freelance gigs over the past year: marketing consultations, restaurant wine lists, that sort of thing. Ten times the money and half the work. As a Master Sommelier leading the wine program at the top restaurant in Napa Valley, well, let's just say I wouldn't have to take out an ad on Craigslist to get more consulting work than I could possibly handle.

I took my fifteen-minute break in the kitchen—a practice that was usually frowned upon. Though there's no such thing as a "slow night" for a restaurant that's fully booked six months in advance. However, I was able to convince Stacy to take pity on me and fix me a double portion of the pork belly course. As comfort food went, it was pure heroin, melting in my mouth like so much pig fat happiness.

And then I saw Rick Dornin.

More appropriately, he saw me, and his face twisted into a perturbed expression that only occurs when somebody yanks on the stick that's been wedged up your ass for thirty-five years.

"You shouldn't be in here," he said. "And didn't you already get your dinner before service?"

"Richard!" I said with game show host enthusiasm. "What, pray tell, brings you out of your shit hole on this fine evening?"

"Seriously, if you have to eat that, do it in your office. But if you've already—" He stopped suddenly, and his lips cracked into some bizarre, smile-like expression. "On second thought, you just stay here and enjoy that. Shouldn't kick a man when he's down." He patted me on the shoulder condescendingly.

"What are you talking about?" I asked, although I already feared the answer.

Dornin didn't reply, but if smarm was a moisturizer, it was slathered all over his sunken face. He gave me one more shoulder pat and walked past me. "Never take a bet you can't win, Corbett."

Freaking Andrew. I could just see him scurrying into Dornin's rat hole to tell him all about our bet, his lips awash with the golden-brown hue of a major ass-kissing. The kid wanted my job in the worst way and was probably willing to be paid even less for it. Worse, Dornin was looking for any excuse to give it to him.

I ran out of the kitchen and caught up with Dornin outside his office. "You're right, I shouldn't take a bet I can't win. So, here's the deal. I'll bet you I pass my sit next week and become a

Master Somm. If I do, you just stay out of my way around here. You can set my hours, but I choose my parties, and I don't answer to you."

Dornin raised a cynical eyebrow. "And if you don't pass?"

"Then Andrew can be Lead Somm. I'll do what you ask me to, no questions asked."

Dornin nodded. "And you won't run off and complain to Chef Dan like a little bitch?"

I glared. "We don't get to use the word 'bitch' anymore. Bitch."

"It's a bet." He tried to do that grinning thing again; it made me want to press my thumbs into his cheeks and guide his face into what an actual smile looks like.

As Dornin slithered into his lair, I felt an uneasy sense of relief mixed with anxiety. A week from now, The Dornin Problem would be settled once and for all. All I had to do was pass my exam.

An exam I had failed the year before.

And the year before that.

It was time for a confidence boost.

I took a deep breath and headed back out to the terrace. Maybe the Rock Mom had gotten drunk enough to order a dessert wine, like a Chateau d'Yquem at $1,500 a pop?

The party was in that loose, transition phase from Not Eating The Meat Course to Dancing On The Tables And Garnering Noise Complaints. I found a half-full bottle of the Rich Bitch Chardonnay and went around the table, pouring it out, listening for an opportunity. I couldn't even find Rock Mom anymore. She probably bowed out an hour ago. I know I would have.

"Hey, are you the wine guy?" It was the girl who brought the case of wine.

"How can I help you, ma'am?"

She held up a bottle of Rich Bitch. "Can you open this for me? It's the last one. I kept it hidden from everyone else," she giggled.

I smiled in resignation as I reached for the bottle and took out my wine key. "So, are you a big fan of chardonnay?"

"Hells yeah!" she said. "Chardonnay is my jam."

I stopped opening the bottle and stared at her for a moment. She had these huge eyes, like something out of a Japanese anime cartoon, but more inquisitive and less vapid.

"Hold on a second," I said, handing the bottle back to her. "You take this, and stay right here, ok? I'll be right back—don't go anywhere!"

"Uh, ok." Her voice was in the initial stages of slurring.

I dashed off to the cellar. I knew we only had one bottle left, and thankfully the price wasn't marked up three times the way we normally do for the rare stuff. I grabbed it and raced back up to the floor, where I found Helena.

"Hey, the Jansen party just ordered this," I said, showing her the bottle. "But they want it on a separate check, so I'll ring it up, ok?"

"Jesus," she said, in sincere shock. "Nice work. You want me to bring out more glasses?"

"No, but thanks." I headed back out to the terrace to find that Powerpuff Girl was still there, in pretty much the exact same position as when I left, holding the unopened chardonnay.

I presented my bottle to her. "This is the 2009 Domain Ramonet Montrachet, Grand Cru, from Cote de Beaune in France," I said. "This is a chardonnay, too, and I want you to try it."

I gingerly pulled the cork and poured a few ounces in each of our glasses. I didn't want to lose her attention or put her off with some long-winded Five Step Program To Fine Wine Enjoyment bullshit, so I just quickly sniffed the glass for flaws and handed it to her. "Now, drink this."

She looked a bit tentative at first but raised the glass to her lips and took a healthy mouthful. And within a few moments, I saw it. By God, I knew it would happen. Her pupils dilated, her cheeks flushed, and a tiny smile pushed at the corner of her lips.

"Oh my God," she whispered. "This is amazing. This is chardonnay? I mean, I can taste it, but it's like…"

"Different? Unbelievable? Unlike any chardonnay you've had before?"

"Yes!"

"Yes!" I screamed. "Yes!" I threw up my arms. "Welcome to my world."

I sat down next to her and filled our glasses. She took another sip, almost greedily this time. "You have taken the red pill," I said. "Nothing will ever be the same now."

She gave me the I Don't Have A Clue What You're Talking About But I'm Not Going To Admit It smile, and kept on drinking.

"Wine is life in a glass." I said, gazing lovingly at the amazing juice in my glass. "It's art, it's history, it's chemistry—like the chemistry of sex." I touched my glass to hers, then breathed in the amazing essence of the wine. It was as though you could take the feeling of floating atop a field of sunflowers and catch it in a wine glass.

"Most important of all, wine is an adventure, a journey without end. Take it. Soak it up like a sponge. Never come back." I took my glass and got up from the table.

"Wait," she called after me, holding up the bottle. "Do I get to keep this?"

"Absolutely. Share it with somebody you love," I told her. "And when you're done, keep that bottle. Remember this night."

I walked back to the servers' station to ring up the Domain Ramonet —$1,542.56 after tax. Paying the rent was highly overrated anyway. I swiped my card and prayed for it to not be declined, then signed the check "Rock Mom Jansen" with a signature so interpretive, no one would ever be able to decipher it.

"You've got to be kidding me," came a voice from behind me. It was Andrew, and I figured I was busted for sure. "The 2009 Montrachet? There's no way."

"Read it and weep," I said, quickly flashing him the illegible receipt. "What else you got?"

"The Armand Rousseau was it," he said.

I wanted to sympathetically pat the top of his man bun but decided against it. "Hey, nothing to be ashamed of." I handed him the glass I poured. "Here," I smirked, "best consolation prize in the universe."

The rest of the night went on as normal, with the last guests having to be politely escorted out the door and put into an Uber at 11:00 p.m. By midnight, most of the kitchen and wait staff were at the bar, and by the time I was leaving at 1:00 a.m., they had worked their way to the top shelf stuff, with Chef Dan taking the lead.

"Corbett!" he shouted. "Come on, come have a drink."

"Yeah, thanks, Chef, but I gotta bow out tonight," I said. "I need to study for my sit."

"What, at one in the morning?"

"No, at nine in the morning, which means no drinking at one in the morning."

He waved me off, and the rest of the crew shouted their loud if not incoherent goodbyes. They were an obnoxious group of incestuous, alcoholic vampires, but the only time I'd ever felt the same sense of brotherhood that I had in the band was when I worked in a restaurant.

"Hey!" Andrew caught up with me at the front door, a hundred-dollar bill sticking up like a middle finger in his clenched fist.

"It's alright. Go ahead and keep it."

"No, dude," he protested. "You won, fair and square."

"So, look," I deflected, "they gave me a fat, cash tip on the way out, ok?"

"Really? How much?"

I took the hundred from his hand and stuffed it in his shirt pocket. "Enough for you to keep this," I muttered. "Good night, Andrew."

I walked out into the darkness of the parking lot. On these autumn nights, the Milky Way smeared across the sky like actual spilled milk.

"You're still the man, Corbett!" Andrew drunkenly shouted across the parking lot. "You're still the man!"

Damn right I am. And yet, even as my arm strained to pat my own back, I knew that a far more important bet—a far more important test— was still ahead of me. And cheating, no matter how I was able to spin it, would not be an option.

TWO

I knew that Remy was in a desperate and manic emotional state when her message said, "It's imperative that we discuss this issue at your earliest convenience." For her, that was as close to a cry for help from the edge of the abyss as I was ever going to hear.

I had turned my phone off while I was studying so it wouldn't be such a temptation. I typically never turn my phone off, just in case there's some kind of progeny/money/sex/wine emergency, but there's something about trying to memorize the primary grape varietals of each of the Chianti DOCG sub-zones that makes me yearn for the crack-like distraction a smartphone can provide. So, I did the right thing and shut it off, and of course that was the time I missed a call from my daughter.

According to her message, there was "an issue" to which she had "applied a considerable amount of thought," and which now was "worthy of a discussion," for which I should "be prepared to give my complete focus." In Remy-speak, this meant the Four Horsemen of the Apocalypse were nigh, and the River of Blood would soon consume us all.

I called her back and suggested dinner. When she said she'd go ahead and make the two-hour drive from Milpitas to Napa, it could only mean that we were already beset by the plague of frogs. Studying for the Practical was shot for the day now, as there'd be no way to concentrate.

For a moment, I entertained the notion that maybe Remy had good news, like she had fallen in love or was considering giving up her stale, due diligence job to fly off to Rhodesia and help leper children. But on second thought, there was no way. Because Remy.

As a little girl, Remy showed signs of following in her daddy's footsteps. She had a genuine musical talent and would sing songs she made up into her *Finding Nemo* MP3 recorder ("You've Got The Freaky" and "Bubblegum Sherbet Face" were two of my personal favorites). By the time she was eleven, however, she was demonstrating an accelerated aptitude in math and it became her new obsession. I was sorry to see the nascent songwriting fall by the wayside but tried to adopt the attitude that passion is passion, no matter what stupid form it took.

I also had visions of making her the world's first child sommelier. With a young, unformed brain, she was in the best position possible to open her mind to the limitless sensory experience of wine.

"What does it smell like?" I'd say, sliding my glass of syrah over to her.

"Like grape juice, only yucky," she'd respond.

"Sure, but what else?" I prodded. "Like, I smell cherries in there. And an oak tree. And the way the backyard smells after it rains."

It only took a few weeks of this before she'd grab my glass of chardonnay, swirl it around, take a whiff and proclaim, "It smells like you got a Hostess Lemon Pie from 7-11 and poked your finger in it to make a gooey-lemon smiley face."

After that, she would rate every wine I drank on the Unicorn Fart Scale, with only the "most un-grossest" wines getting a coveted Ten Unicorn Farts.

Eventually, she lost interest in that as well. Even when she got deep into the teenage years, she wasn't interested in seriously trying wine, or even drinking at all. I honestly don't know where she got that, as I had wine in the house 24/7 and her mother was a Hall of Fame-caliber functional alcoholic.

Remy met me at Pinot, which is the closest thing to a "locals" place available in downtown Napa. Just like anywhere in the world, a great locals place is one where the food is cheap, the drinks are strong, and you know you'll always find someone there you want to talk to. "Cheap" and "Napa" just don't go together, but Pinot found a way to stay in business longer than any place I'd seen in the valley, so it won by default.

As always, Remy arrived freakishly on time. Thankfully, my anxiety had taken the steering wheel and got me there early enough to start on a gin and tonic. As expected, Remy arrived exactly at 6:00PM. She believed that being late was the ultimate sign of disrespect, and I'll be damned if she didn't always, *always* find some way to live by that creed.

"Hi, dad," she said, greeting me with a Remy Kiss.

Even as a baby, Remy dictated the conditions of affection. "Daddy, I want you to hug me," my toddling Princess of Wonderland would say, and my heart would melt into Cream of Wheat as I embraced her tiny frame and breathed in her Johnson's Baby Shampoo yumminess. Then she'd suddenly stiff arm me and say, "That's enough," before walking away.

"Can I get you a drink?" I offered.

"Just a soda water and lime," she said, setting her purse down and sliding into the booth. "It's a school night and I still have work to do."

So did I, until you completely freaked out on me. I could already tell this would be the first of three palliative gin and tonics.

Remy hadn't inherited my lanky tallness, nor my square jaw, nor my untamable, wavy brown hair. She was blessed with more of her mother's features: piercing grey eyes, near-platinum blonde hair, and lips she could have inherited from Angelina Jolie. Remy had grown up being Queen of the Geek Girls, a title she assumed without effort. Even now, with her hair pulled back tight and wearing her dark-rimmed Clark Kent glasses with a Devo T-shirt, she could have come straight from her high school Science Club meeting.

I crossed my hands on top of the table and stared at her in that mocking way that said, "I presume you're now calling this meeting to order?"—which generally ticked her off. I couldn't help it. Remy was Remy and I loved her, not despite it, but because of it.

"So, what's up, sweetheart?" I asked, knowing there wouldn't be anything so cliché as making small talk or ordering dinner first. And yes, I was genuinely concerned.

"It's about mom," she said, diving in with characteristic lack of preamble.

Hey, check it out: a Can of Worms is the featured special tonight. Oh, and it's free!

"Ah," was my non-committal response before I took a long pull of my gin and tonic. The trick to keeping a can of worms closed is to not offer up a can opener.

Remy didn't do things like shift uncomfortably or tap on the table nervously as she considered what to say next. She had thought about every conceivable angle, topic and objection, and knew her responses well in advance. I half-expected a PowerPoint presentation to hit the table.

"I have been trying to process some issues in the wake of mom's death," she continued. "But there are a lot of gaps in the information I have. I want to know more about her. I want to know what happened between the two of you. The truth as to why you divorced."

I waved down our server and ordered another gin and tonic. "Double tall," I requested, "and a soda water and lime for my therapist."

"Dad, I'm serious."

"No shit," I chuckled.

Remy's mother had died unexpectedly. She checked into the hospital for a routine medical procedure, caught some kind of nasty infection, then died of sepsis only a week later.

"Look, sweetheart, you know I've never said anything bad about your mother."

"I know. You don't say *anything* about her. I have no idea how you feel."

"How I feel?" I was genuinely surprised. Feelings? Really?

Remy was unnaturally good at maintaining eye contact. She never looked away during a conversation, which was almost as disconcerting as looking away all the time. "You know, mom wasn't above talking shit about you on occasion. Especially on occasions that involved new business ventures."

"I kind of figured." Behind the scenes, Remy's mom and I fought ferociously, with email as our weapon of choice. We divorced when Remy was barely two. I stayed in Napa, she moved down to San Francisco, and though it wasn't much of a distance—relatively speaking —our custody battle was a war with massive injuries on both sides and no clear victor.

"Honey, your mom died over a year ago. I know it's hard. Is this something you've been holding in all this time?"

"It's been hard," Remy said. "So, how come it hasn't been hard on you? You didn't even come to the funeral."

The server arrived with a tray. *Thank. Freaking. God.*

"Oh, look! Alcohol!" I grabbed the sacred gin and tonic and sucked down half, hoping the magic elixir would transport me to someplace far, far away. The server, who I think was named Penny, also placed a small pour of red wine and a spit cup in front of me.

"This is from Christophe," she said. "He said you have to figure out what it is."

"What, he can't read the label?" I grinned broadly at Remy. She did not grin back.

Christophe owned Pinot and had one of the most amazing palates I'd ever encountered. He was also generous enough to host my wine study groups after hours on Mondays, when he was closed. All he wanted in return was the opportunity to sit in on occasion and learn.

I swirled the wine for a bit and noticed Remy glaring her disapproval at me. I wasn't exactly sure why this dinner meeting was all about spoon-feeding shit into the fan, but I'd take any distraction available to avoid whatever was coming next.

I stuck my nose in the glass and breathed in. "Nice." It smelled like a girl named Ciara, running wistfully through a grove of cherry trees. Of course, that particular analysis would only get me laughed out of my sit the following week. For somms, identifying a wine is all about using the Deductive Tasting Method. So, I dove right in.

"Ok, wine number one is a red wine of medium-minus concentration, a ruby core fading to a garnet rim, medium-plus intensity, day-bright but fairly pale with medium-plus to high viscosity."

In other words, it looked red.

"On the nose, medium-plus intensity, red fruit. Strawberry, cherry, raspberry, red plum, hint of fig. Cocoa powder, mocha, cherry cola, mushroom and baked clay...earth, not like a pinot, though."

Or, it smelled like the aforementioned Italian girl in the orchard. I took in a mouthful of the wine, swished it around for a moment, then spit it in the cup.

"Dry. Medium, medium-plus acidity, medium alcohol, medium-plus intensity. Mix of dried and ripe red fruits, olives, tobacco, brine, dried flowers. Shows age, no new oak. Well, maybe new oak. Damnit."

Christophe, that Belgian bastard, knew that bold Italian reds were still my weakness. He brought this one over on purpose. I took in another large mouthful and swished it around every square centimeter of my oral cavity.

Spit it back in the glass, Corbett, and name the damn wine. You can do this.

They say you don't have taste buds anywhere except on your tongue, but damn it, there was something about the texture and mouthfeel of Italian reds that only became apparent to me when I swallowed. There'd be none of that at the exam next week, so I spit back in the glass.

"1999, *Riserva, Biondi Santi*, Toscana," I offered up.

Possibly Penny looked at a slip of paper in her hand. "Close," she said. "2008."

"Dog fucker," I mumbled. Should have known.

"Still, that was really impressive," said Possibly Penny. Remy rolled her eyes.

"Thanks," I said. "And hey, tell Christophe I appreciate it, and I'll come back and say hi after dinner."

"OK," she said. "Are you guys ready to order?"

"No," Remy said. "Give us a minute. Or ten."

To drive the point home, Remy took the menu and slid it over to the far side of the table: Possibly Penny walked off without a word.

"So, how are things going with that motor deal?" I asked. It was useless to sidetrack Remy, but I had to try something.

"Rotor, not motor," she answered. The firm she worked for crunched numbers for venture capitalists looking to acquire green businesses. She found it to be fascinating stuff. "And it's fine. I think they're going to go public, though."

"Oh!" I jumped at the opening. "That's a good thing, right?"

Remy sipped her soda and lime, looking like an android imitating a person drinking—a really pissed off android that's trying desperately not to reach over the table and commit an act of violence.

"What happened?" she asked. "Why did you guys divorce?"

There was the eye twitching again. I drained the rest of my gin and tonic in two huge gulps and let out an overly dramatic sigh. "Oh, geez, Remy," I whispered.

My brain worked overtime to carefully choose the right words, like trying to pick out a branch from a jammed lawnmower that was still running. "I honestly don't see what possible good could come from dredging all this up."

"Well, that's up to me to decide."

And then, like a Guardian Angel, Seamus appeared. "Shay Money!" I shouted.

He stood near the hostess desk, looking around in a rather bewildered way until I caught his attention and he raced over to the table.

"Jesus, bro. Don't you know how to answer a fucking text?" He noticed Remy on the opposite side of the booth and slipped in to sit down, giving her a quick hug. "Oh, hey honey! Are you fabulous?"

"Fabulous, Uncle Shay." Her monotone gave away how disappointed she was at the interruption.

"I thought I might find you here," he said, unfazed, turning back to me. "I've been calling and texting you for the last hour. Swear to god I'm gonna duct tape your phone to your fucking head."

I shrugged. "I left my phone in the car so I could devote my full attention to my wonderful daughter."

"Seriously?" Remy was genuinely shocked. "In the car? Who does that?"

"Hey, I thought you of all people would appreciate it," I cried.

"Dude," Shay shook his head with obvious disappointment. "If I saw you on fire in the middle of the street, I'd still grab my phone before I got out of the car. But look. Sorry for the interruption and all, but you're not going to fucking believe what's going on."

Seamus O'Flaherty looked like he hadn't aged a day since he played bass with me in Reality Star. He carried himself like a man in his late forties, but there wasn't a single wrinkle, blemish, or laugh line on his smooth, brown face. Not even a random grey hair on his scalp. He credited this to his Filipino heritage and said it was the same for his dad. Apparently, when men in his family turned sixty, it was like *boom!* Definitely sixty.

"What's going on?" I asked.

"So, I get this message from Donna Klopshoff over at Ridley Anders, and I think nothing of it because she works with Peter all the time. And she's all, 'Just give me a call when you have a chance.' No worries, you know? So, I didn't call her back until today."

"Get out!" I said. "That's some crazy shit."

"No, no, no—hear me out. Turns out, Ridley is working with a guy who wants to buy ten acres of vineyard property in Coombsville, and this guy wants us to consult on the development. And you'll never believe who it is." Seamus placed his palms on the table and pushed his shoulders back, like he was about to announce the winner of Best Picture of The Year. "Brogan Prescott."

"No way," Remy said. "Are you serious?"

Never heard of the guy, but his name made Remy the closest thing to excited I'd seen since she won the Northern California Regional Mathalon in 2007, so I guess he was somebody.

"Who's Brogan Prescott?" I asked.

"Oh, come on, Dad, really?" she replied. "4-D Games? *Tom Braxton: Beyond Vengeance?* You don't remember that one?"

I did remember *Beyond Vengeance.* Remy had made me play against her in head-to-head combat mode for years. Mostly I remember my video-guts splaying across the TV screen as she liquefied me time and again with a rocket launcher. I tried not to take it personally.

"He sold 4-D Games about ten years ago for $3.5 billion," Seamus said. "Billion with a 'B.' He's still Chief Imagination Officer, whatever the hell that means, but he's got his hands in all sorts of things now, including restaurants—which is why I think he wants a winery. Did you guys eat already? Are we eating? I'm starving." He grabbed one of the menus and started perusing it.

"Brogan Prescott," I said. "Seriously, his name is Brogan? *Bro*-gan. Is his middle name Mandude?"

"Oh my God, Dad," Remy muttered. "You're being a child. He happens to have a ton of clout in the valley."

"Well, I've never heard of him."

"No, the *other* valley." Remy's shoulders vibrated like she was about to short circuit. "The Silicon Valley."

"Donna didn't bat an eye when I told her it was four hundred an hour and a twenty-thousand-dollar retainer," Shay revealed.

Oh. *Ohhh.* Suddenly, this guy was my new best friend.

Before I could respond, Possibly Penny came back to the table. I ordered the steak frites, which Christophe would cook up for me whether it was on the menu that night or not. Shay ordered the special cassoulet after determining it was the most amount of food available in a single entree, and I waited to hear what vegan abomination Remy would order.

"I'm not eating," she said.

"Honey, come on," I insisted. "You drove all the way up here. You must be starving."

"I'm not hungry," she repeated.

Remy didn't do passive aggressive. When she said, 'I'm not hungry,' it meant she wasn't hungry.

"So, you said he's only getting ten acres?" I asked. "With that kind of money, he could buy the Ponderosa Vineyard."

"Nope, just the ten," Shay said. "The Fogelson Vineyard."

"Hank Fogelson's place? I didn't know he was selling."

"Apparently so."

That was heartbreaking to hear. The Fogelsons had been a fixture in Napa for generations, and Hank had four children. It wasn't unusual for the children of vintners or farmers to seek their fortunes elsewhere, but typically at least one kid returned to the fold and took over the business. Then again, prime vineyard land had never been at such a premium, and maybe it was just the right time for the family to cash out.

"So, is the property already permitted for a winery? I know Hank only has the old house up there now," I said.

"Well, this is all the stuff we need to go over," Shay answered. "And, like, right now, because our meeting is tomorrow morning."

More eye twitching. "Tomorrow? Dude, that's my last full day off of work before the exam. I need that day. Every second of that day."

"So, math." Shay glared at me with his lawyer-y, You're An Idiot look. "Four times our normal rate. That's four times larger than one. What part of this am I not get getting across? Take the fucking exam next year."

"Oh, Shay Money's in the hizzy," I said.

"Don't make me call you a Sucker MC," he warned.

I gasped. "You wouldn't *dare!*"

Remy wasn't finding any of this amusing. She had her grandmother's disturbing ability to unleash generations of Catholic guilt with the single raising of an eyebrow.

"Look, it's a great gig for sure," I said. "But I have to take that exam next week. And I need to have an evening alone with Remy."

"It's alright, Dad," Remy said, grabbing her purse. "You and Uncle Shay stay here and talk."

Remy scooched Shay out of the booth, put on her coat, and leaned over to give me a peck on the cheek.

"Honey," I said sheepishly, why don't you stay and we'll – "

"No." Her tone of finality was unnerving. "You need clients like Brogan Prescott. You get in with a network like that, it's life changing. G'nite, dad."

But I wasn't buying it. Well, I'm not sure if I wasn't buying it or if I felt like a dick for how things were going down. Either way, I stood up before she could get a few steps away.

"Remy, wait. Listen, both of you, none of this changes the fact that I need all day tomorrow to study for my sit."

Remy looked at me quizzically. "Well, it should change the fact. I thought the whole reason you were becoming a Master Somm is so you'll have the credentials to get the 'highest-paying, biggest-profile' wine jobs out there? Well, here it is – here's one right in your lap. And you're just going to say no to it?"

Sometimes Remy's logic was more infuriating than any emotional outburst could ever be.

"You don't understand," I groaned. "With my credentials, I'll get even more of these jobs."

Remy moved up close to me and gently squeezed my arm. "Oh, dad. Do they cheer when you pass the exam?"

She turned and made her way for the exit. I just stood there, watching, knowing that the appropriate response was still four-and-a-half minutes away.

"Did I fuck something up?" I didn't even notice that Shay had got up and was standing next to me. "It feels like I fucked something up."

"Nothing I probably didn't fuck up myself years ago," I sighed. "Hold on."

I sprinted for the exit, then paused on the sidewalk in the chilly autumn air, looking up and down the street for Remy. Finally, I saw her about a half block away, about to get in her car.

"Remy!" I called after her.

She looked around and saw me, then paused beside the open door. I caught up to her, opened my mouth to say something, but then stuck my hands in my pockets and stared at the ground. As a songwriter, I practiced for years to learn how to craft the right combination of words to express just how I felt. On top of that, I could choose from a nearly infinite vocabulary of sounds to augment my words, allowing me to elicit the exact emotional response I wanted from a listener. But standing here in the cold and dark, alone with the one person who meant more to me than anybody, words failed, and silence owned the moment.

I had to try. "So, look, about your mom—"

"My mother is dead." Remy dropped the line with all the sentimentality of a formula in a spreadsheet cell, and I felt a piece of my heart shrivel up. "My mom is dead, and now the only person who can give me the truth is you."

She closed her door and drove away. My baby girl. The only thing I'd ever done right.

The truth is a tricky thing. There was the truth that Remy was named after her mom's favorite cognac, and then there was the Truth. I had hoped that the Truth would be a lot like the 2013 vintage of Napa cabernet: too powerful and concentrated to consume now but stick it in the cellar for thirty years and it'd be a lot more approachable. Apparently, that wasn't going to be the case.

THREE

When I was twelve, I went deep sea fishing with my dad. It was one of three times I saw him before he disappeared completely when I was seventeen. We woke up at 5:00 a.m. and made our way down to the dock, where we picked up rods and reels, bait and tackle, fishing licenses, and a couple of sandwiches.

Dad ordered a cup of coffee. "Want one?" he asked.

I was tired. I stayed up most of the night watching the way my dad slept, rummaging through his suitcase, and gazing at the mysterious figures in the photos in his wallet. For the first time in my life, a cup of coffee sounded good.

The old woman behind the counter with the salt-chiseled face placed a tall Styrofoam cup in front of me. A quart-sized carton of milk and a pink and white box of C&H Sugar cubes sat next to the coffee maker. I reached for a handful of the sugar cubes, but my dad stopped me.

"Drink it black," he said.

"But that's gross," I protested.

Dad was tall. Even at twelve, when I was approaching six-foot, dad still seemed like a giant.

"Here's the deal, son," he said. "One of these days, you're going to be in a war, and you're going to be in a fox hole, and you're going to want a cup of coffee. And there's not going to be any goddamn cream and sugar in the fox hole. So just learn to drink it black."

That night, I stole a picture from my dad's wallet, a snapshot of two smiling little girls hugging a man I didn't recognize in front of a carnival game with rows of grey metal milk bottles. I didn't catch any fish that day, but I still drink my coffee black.

🍷

I clutched a steaming mug of precious Awake Juice as I watched a tiny cloud hug the top edge of Mount George, as though the hill itself exhaled its breath into the cold morning air. Just to the north of the peak, another patch of fog settled like a quilted blanket on the vineyards of the valley floor. Glorious, bright morning sunshine illuminated the rest of the landscape. There was truly nothing quite like the microclimate of Coombsville.

There are sixteen sub-appellations—unique vinicultural regions—that compose the Napa Valley. Coombsville was the last one to get its designation, back in 2011. Comprised of eleven thousand acres on the southern tip of the valley, Coombsville has, I believe, more unique features than any other appellation—not the least of which were these breathtaking sunrises over Mount George.

I was two hours early for the meeting. I didn't sleep much the night before, my monkey mind swinging from branch to branch with thoughts of the Master Sommelier exam, Remy's sudden Truth Crusade, and the details of today's meeting. I gave up at 4:00 a.m. and headed out toward the Fogelson Vineyard around six to watch the sun come up.

I parked on the side of Hagen Road, leaned against the hood of my car, drank my black coffee, and took in the show.

The vineyard was another couple miles east. It was the kind of property that made Coombsville a special and unique appellation: a combination of both valley floor and hillside vineyards, all within the same ten acres. Hank had planted syrah up on the slopes, along with a half-acre of fiano, which was either genius or idiotic, but definitely the only fiano in the entire Napa Valley. The valley floor acreage was pure cabernet—the cash crop.

Though it still bothered me that Hank had to sell the place, the more I learned about this job, the more I liked it. Hank was a farmer, pure and true, like his father and his father's father and his great grandfather. They grew their grapes, they sold their grapes, and it was an honest if not frugal life. But Brogan Prescott was all-in on a winery and a label.

The Fogelson Vineyard would be where the estate grapes were grown, and where the winery—located entirely within a newly-constructed cave—would be built. There were no permits of any kind for all of this yet, but Prescott wanted the project completed in an unprecedented two years. It could be done, but it'd cost a shit ton of money. Money that he had.

I took a page from the Remy Playbook and timed my arrival for exactly 9:00 a.m. The vineyard was right off the main road, lined by a knee-high rock wall that was built in the early 1900s. An unceremonious gap in the wall served as the entrance to the driveway, and directly to the left as I pulled in were some of the oldest cabernet vines I'd ever seen. They had trunks the size of a pine tree. I'd definitely be advising to keep those.

The dirt road went up another hundred yards or so, surrounded by vines on each side, and ended at an exquisite yet small Victorian house. Shay's car was parked out front, which struck me as unusual. I thought I would have noticed him driving by me. Guess the coffee wasn't as strong as I'd hoped.

Shay and Hank were surveying the vines near the house. Hank had to be somewhere in his mid-70's, but it was hard to tell. A lifetime in the sun rendered his face dark and crevassed, but his shoulders and arms were thick and sturdy. He had a broad smile that made his eyes disappear, with unnaturally perfect, straight white teeth. 'Unnatural' because I think one of his sons was a dentist and had reworked Hank's entire grill.

"Good morning, Hank."

He squeezed my hand with a grip that almost turned my knuckles to rice powder.

"Corbett, been too long," he said. "How's your daughter?"

"She's killing me, Hank," I joked.

"Well, that's what daughters do," he replied.

"And top o' the mornin' to you, Seamus O'Flaherty!" I said in my best Irish accent. It was a horrible accent, delivered with all the subtlety of the Lucky Charms leprechaun. Still, I never missed a real opportunity to greet Seamus that way.

"Hup ye boy ye, and God bless all here except the cat." His accent, on the other hand, could have been straight outta Belfast.

"Can I get you a cup of coffee?" Hank offered.

"I appreciate it, but a gallon is typically my cut-off point." Hank flashed that smile of his; it caught the sun and nearly blinded me. In a town full of purple teeth, his grin was disconcerting.

"I gotta tell you, Hank, I was a little surprised to hear that you're selling the place. I mean, this property has been in your family for generations."

Hank poked at the gravely soil with the tip of his boot, the radiant smile fading from his lips. "Well, you know. A time to every purpose, as they say."

A little obtuse for sure, but I took it to mean, *I don't want to talk about it.* The topic was sidelined anyway as a white Tesla Model X pulled up behind our cars. I'm all for Earth-saving practices in general, but the silence of electric cars kind of freaks me out.

The Tesla had those gull-wing doors, which on the one hand look so freaking cool, but on the other hand have all the cheese factor of a 1960s James Bond film. Five people poured out, two of whom immediately started snapping pictures on their phones. The other three headed our way. The guy in the middle stuck his hand out to Hank.

"You must be Hank Fogelson," he said. "I'm Brogan Prescott, nice to meet you."

For a guy in his late thirties, Brogan Prescott had the unhealthy pallor of a sixty-year-old workaholic, and the pot belly of a guy who still ate Totino's pizza rolls by the handful while playing video games all night. His hairline was near extinction, though he sported a full, brown beard—not in the fashion statement way, but in the I Guess I Never Really Noticed That Hair Grows Out Of My Face kind of way.

He wore black Converse, jeans, and a generic brown wool blazer over some kind of 'gimme' shirt. I didn't recognize the name of the company on the shirt, and maybe it was actually hip in some way I was completely unaware of, but it smacked of "this was the shirt on top when I opened the drawer this morning."

In short, it was hard to tell whether this was the way Today's Young Billionaire looked, or if this guy simply didn't give a shit.

I shook his hand next. "Mr. Prescott, I'm Corbett Thomas."

"Dude, call me Brogan," he said. "This is my assistant, Macy, and this is my agent, Dontrell."

More hand shaking all around. I took "agent" to mean real estate agent, and not the guy who made sure Brogan got those coveted film roles.

The Handshaking Parade came to an abrupt halt when Shay got into the mix. "Seamus O'Flaherty," he said. "It's great to finally connect a face with the voice, huh?"

The awkward silence that followed cognitive dissonance slamming into political correctness. Shay had lived at that intersection his entire life, so he knew exactly how to hand them the road map.

"I'm Seamus," he said with a disarming smile. "Long story short, when my parents immigrated from the Philippines, they basically believed every white person in America came from Ireland, so they gave all their kids Irish names. So we'd fit in."

"That may be the most awesome thing I have ever heard," Brogan said. The rest of his entourage chuckled and nodded, the way that entourages do when they're looking for cues on how to behave.

I know entourages; I've seen them a thousand times. Reality Star sort of had one, if you call two girlfriends, a paid soundman, and a guy who came to almost every show and threw weed on stage an "entourage." We never got close to the kind of rich that a true entourage requires for daily maintenance. "Sensitive Pony Tail Guy" hit number four on the *Billboard* Alternative Rock chart, which bought us a ticket to fifteen minutes of glorious fame, but pretty much nothing else after that.

Hank offered to make breakfast for Brogan and his crew, but they declined in favor of getting started with the tour of the property—timelines and meetings and all that, and traffic back to Redwood City. I thought it was a quite a neighborly gesture on Hank's part, and Brogan should have known that food (and of course, wine) is how business is done here. On the other hand, this was going to be the mother of all consulting jobs, so I focused on keeping my opinions to myself unless they happened to be the ones Brogan paid for.

Our walking tour reached a "T" in the dirt road that separated one vineyard block from another. Up to that point, Hank had mostly been talking about the status of the well, and how he was more fortunate than some of his neighbors that it didn't dry up after the earthquake in 2014.

"This isn't it, is it?" Brogan asked, interrupting him. "This isn't the property line?"

"Not at all," Hank replied. "The line goes to the top of those hills. But the hills are only plantable about thirty yards up."

"Ah. Yes. Thought so," Brogan said.

"Just thought you might want to see these syrah vines," I added. "These are some of the oldest producing syrah vines in the entire valley. If you're seriously considering estate wines, you should—"

"That's cool," Brogan cut in, his nose about three inches from his phone. "Really, I'll leave all that stuff up to you. Whatever you think."

I looked over at Shay, whose raised eyebrow conveyed the same thought I was having. *I think we should have charged you four hundred an hour.*

Impressive didn't even begin to describe those syrah vines, though. I knelt down to inspect the trunk of the vine closest to the row post, as it had to be at least the circumference of my lower leg. Even the two arms that came off the trunk were bigger than my own arms. Hank told me earlier that some of these vines were forty years old, and though they weren't as prolific as younger vines, the fruit they did bear was liquid nirvana.

I clutched the post to pull myself back up when I noticed some strange markings near my hand. It wasn't a plaque or any other kind of row tag or marker, but rather something carved into the post itself. Caked-on mud covered some of the engraved letters, which I wiped off with my thumb. "Pikse plagron," it read, or at least that's what I could make out.

"How cool," I whispered. I imagined some little boy named Pike—which is probably one of the most awesome names ever—marking his territory with his pocketknife as he played hide-and-seek amongst the vines. In a place where family wineries were rapidly falling under the corporate knife, this place dripped with love and authenticity.

Meanwhile Brogan raised his phone above eye level and took a panorama picture of the entire east side of the vineyard. Then he took another, this time moving the other direction. "Hey, mind if we head back to the house?" he asked.

"No, certainly," I said, though his request made me slightly anxious. On the one hand, it felt like I wasn't demonstrating enough expertise to warrant my exorbitant fee. On the other, if this guy truly wanted to leave all of "that stuff" up to me, I didn't want to rock the micromanagement boat. Shay's firm had the expertise—and connections—to fast-track the permitting process. I had the expertise to create a winery experience like no other, with a luxury wine brand to complement it. If Brogan wanted all of that done while he went off and did whatever billionaire game designers do, that was fine by me, but I couldn't imagine anyone writing a check that large without rope-size strings attached.

As Uncle Glen used to say, "If you don't want to dig your own grave, put the shovel down." So, once again, I erred on the side of keeping my mouth shut.

There was some kind of history behind the Fogelson house.

Sometimes it's hard to keep Napa legend from Napa fact, so I asked Hank about it as we entered the foyer. "Didn't George Yount live here at some point, Hank?"

Hank chuckled. "Naw, he didn't live here. The house is a replica of his. My great grandfather stole the plans to the house from Yount's son. There've been a few additions and modifications since then, of course, but it's mostly the same place."

Unlike some wineries where the original house has been converted to a gorgeously redesigned tasting parlor, Hank's house was a home: it was a place where people lived, down to the odd stack of books, knick-knacks, mismatched furniture and dishes in the sink. Hank guided us to the main room like a gracious host, but Brogan tiptoed down the hall with the cautious discomfort of a Jehovah's Witness who just knocked on the door during dinner.

"Your home is gorgeous, Mr. Fogelson," he said. Brogan was a good liar. Very sincere delivery. "And it comes with the property, correct?"

"That's right," Hank said. "You can tear it down or do whatever you want."

"We wouldn't dream of tearing it down… But we may move it to another location, right, Dontrell?"

"Right," Dontrell replied. He wore the khaki pants and polo shirt uniform of every real estate agent ever created and donned his can-do attitude like a wetsuit. "It's about twenty dollars a square foot to move the structure, but we'll get you a more accurate bid during the inspection process."

"Oh, that's interesting," I commented. "Do you want to free up this space to plant more vines or were you thinking of building the winery here?"

"It's probably going to be the parking lot."

"I can see that," Shay said, eyeing me cautiously. "If you're going to have visitors, you have to have parking."

"So, what's the master plan, then?" If I didn't know any better, I'd say the monkey had perched itself back on my head and was fumbling its way towards my eyebrow. "Are you going to build the production facility and the tasting room inside a cave?"

Brogan moved to the window and gazed out toward the eastern hills. "Not just a cave," he said. "A unique, subterranean winery habitat." He turned back to face us, and the intensity in his eyes made it apparent that the genius rodent trapped inside his head was currently running a marathon on its little wheel.

"I'm not making a wine cave that's just a bunch of semicircular, granite-covered tubes," he explained. "Think of it more like an ant's nest: it'll be a collective, something intelligently designed, with a cooperative, hive-mind approach."

Alright. Well, at least there was a vision now. A random jambalaya of millennial buzzwords, but a vision none the less.

"Winery, barrel room, tasting room, cellar—all of these things should be integrated with a multi-tiered, utilitarian aesthetic, but also with an Industrial Revolution-era *zeitgeist*. The visitors will receive no instruction and no guidance as to how anything works or functions. It will be a completely subjective interpretation, so that the process is a metaphor for the product."

His entourage was enraptured by this sermon. I was just impressed that he used the word *zeitgeist* in a sentence.

"It will be a colony, but a woke colony. A colony without colonization." Brogan was getting fired up, like he was giving a TED Talk to a crowd that thought he was the next messiah. "The object of the structure will be to find your way down to where the queen would normally reside. But there won't be some arbitrary matriarch there, just a barren cavern. And the cavern will be randomly littered with VR headsets. No explanation, no pattern to it, just visors all over the floor. And when you pick one up and put it on, you'll instantly be transported to the vineyard—soaring like a hawk over hillsides and valleys covered in vines, then twisting through the rows and blocks, leaves slapping against your face, a completely immersive, three-dimensional experience."

I laughed; I laughed loud and hard. I *liked* this guy. He had obviously done his homework, or better still, he'd been a wine guy for years, and was just as repulsed as I was to see how the valley had changed into some kind of Disney-esque nightmare over the past couple of decades. He got it. He was smart, funny and cynical, and it was going to be fun as all get-out working with him.

But my joy was gradually replaced by a horrible, sinking feeling. The look of universal consternation from every living creature in the room made me feel like I was twelve again, when I farted as loud as I could at Joey Barducci's birthday party, but nobody had told me that farting wasn't funny anymore.

"Oh," I said, clearing my throat. "Oh, I'm sorry. This is a thing? This is an actual thing?"

"Maybe we should have that breakfast?" Shay offered in his most cheerful lawyer-voice. "You know, sit down, have something to eat, start hammering out some action items?"

I thought I detected the slightest smile threatening the edge of Brogan's lips, and I wondered if he was testing me in some masochistic way. "Yes," he said. "That's the plan."

"Ok," I said. The monkey was back, alright, grabbing my face with both of its tiny claws and shaking it like some kind of simian bartender mixing a martini. "I just—I just want to get this one little detail straight." My voice shook, and I felt that pressure I get in my chest just before road rage compels me to grab the crowbar under my seat. "People are going to park their car and walk through the vineyard, so they can go into an ant cave, put on a virtual reality visor, and experience what it's like to...*walk through a vineyard*?"

The entourage was practically a dance troupe of uncomfortable shifting at this point, but Brogan maintained that teeny-tiny smile-like thing. "The virtual reality will be a much richer user experience," he said. "There'll be augmented reality as well, like farmhouses from the nineteenth century, or visions of Napa from when dinosaurs roamed the valley."

I laughed again, a short, quick burst this time, and covered my mouth in that fake-polite way my Grandma taught me to do. "Dude. No. Really? You're messing with me, right?"

The tiny cracks on the edge of his lips turned into a full, sardonic grin. "No," he answered. "Not at all."

In 1996, our band played a gig at some dive bar in Austin, Texas. I forget the name of the place, though I do remember it wasn't even on über-hip 6th Street, because by that time, we were on the fast decline to Nowheresville. There were maybe five people in the entire place, none of whom were there to see us perform. And as hard as I tried to get their attention, to get this miniscule crowd involved in the show, there was absolutely nothing I could do or say to get them riled up.

Between songs I made some throwaway comment about Shiner Bock, one of the local beers, and how I couldn't tell if the bottle I took a swig from was the one I was supposed to be drinking or the one I had just used for my enema. *That* got their attention, in the exact same way Brogan now had mine.

"You can't fucking be serious!" I shouted. "What is wrong with you people?" I bolted for the window and threw it open. "Look. Look. You don't need to wear a headset, it's all right there. I mean, I'm sorry it doesn't have any fucking dinosaurs, but maybe we'll have to write-off the five-year-old-boy demographic."

I shot a glance over at Shay, who looked like he wanted to deep-throat the business end of a .44 Magnum. Brogan, on the other hand, didn't look phased in the least. I didn't care. The switch was thrown, the gallows door was swinging. "Listen. No offense to you, your beard, your groupies or your money, but you are everything that's wrong with the wine business right now. You see that guy?" I pointed at Hank. "You see that guy right there? That's a steward of the land, and one by one, men like him are being replaced with idiots like you, and I want no fucking part of it."

I walked over to Hank and shook his hand. "Hank. Always a pleasure. I'm sorry I'm a dick. Have a great day." I stormed off towards the front door, but realized I needed to hammer one more nail in my coffin before the lid was guaranteed to stay shut for eternity.

"You want to get woke, Brooooo-gan?" I said, glaring at him. "Grab a bottle of wine, sit on the back porch, watch the sunset, and shut the fuck up."

Turns out that there are about one million bubbles in a glass of champagne, depending on how you pour it: If you pour it without causing a giant, foamy head, and then let the glass sit there until it's completely still, it has a million bubbles. Amazing.

My gin and tonic had seven bubbles in it. I knew this because I could count every single one of them. It was disgusting and flat, and of course I could tell Oscar that and he'd gladly pour me another one. However, there are two fundamental restaurant rules that everyone should live by, even those of us in the business: One, your server/bartender does not want to have sex with you. Ever. So don't act like they do. Two, don't send back anything you actually ordered. Never mind the contrite smiles and effusive apologies you receive when you complain to your server about your food. Everybody hates Send It Back Guy, and your food will return to you with bacteria of unspeakable origin.

So there I sat, alone at the bar at Pinot at 10:53 a.m., gazing into my seven-bubble gin and tonic, neck-deep in the crushing realization that I'd just screwed up one of the biggest opportunities of my career. To make matters even better, Shay came in, plopped down on the bar stool next to me, and glared at me in silence.

"I'm…just…really sorry, buddy," I eventually said, watching Bubble Four pop into nonexistence. "I can't say it enough."

"No," Shay muttered. "No, you can't." Oscar came over and Shay ordered a Bloody Mary. "At least I don't have to send the check back this time. That always hurts."

"Hey, we'll have clients lining up out the door by next week," I assured him. "We'll be able to pick and choose, and the money shall flow like the mighty river."

Shay was holding back, which meant he had to be really pissed off. Usually in these situations he'd berate me for several minutes straight, so completely wound up he'd unconsciously throw in random insults in Tagalog, most of which roughly translated to, "I'm stuck with you like a mother-in-law." There are also about sixteen different Filipino words for "idiot." Who knew?

But Shay just sat there quietly, eating the celery out of his Bloody Mary. I assumed he was ramping up, taking the necessary time to string together the perfect verbal onslaught.

"You know what, bro?" he finally said. "I think you should buy that vineyard."

It was such a random thing to say that it took me a while to process.

"Buy the vineyard?" I repeated. "The Fogelson Vineyard?"

"Yeah, I really think you should."

I chuckled and took a gentle sip through the tiny, black cocktail straw I didn't want to disturb any of the little bubbles. They were the few remaining friends I had left at this point.

"Sure, man. Let me just stroke you a check for two million bucks."

"We could raise the money for a project like that. Besides, we'd only need thirty percent down."

Bubble Seven met its demise. Sorry, my old friend.

"No one—*no one*—gets rich off a winery," I said. "Wineries are what you do after you're already rich."

"Well, that's not exactly true, and that's not even the point," Shay argued. "The thing is, you'd be good at it. It's a good choice for you right now."

By this point, Shay had eaten every piece of vegetable matter from his Bloody Mary, so it looked like a respectable glass of morning tomato juice.

"The consulting firm is the good choice right now," I countered. "Look at Jordan Naismith. He passed his sit just last year and now his firm can't handle the number of clients he gets. Stay focused, man. Let me just pass the exam and we're on our way. I'll have Dornin off my back, and we'll be perfectly positioned for success."

"On our way." Shay shook his head, then took a major gulp off his adult V-8. "Listen, bro. Our reputation is not on the best footing right now. That little issue with Samuelson. Then the wine bar in the Mission. Then the screw-top fiasco, and the freaking wine capsule monitor—"

"Hey, that's legit," I protested. "That's science."

Shay gave me the Lawyer Smile. It was an expression fine-tuned over fifteen years; it was a smile that said, *you're completely full of shit but I'm going to pretend to listen to your argument.*

"You really didn't help our cause this morning," he continued. "But what you did is convince me of something I've suspected for a while. You'd make a great vintner. It's where your heart's at."

I laughed. I really did have an annoying laugh. A condescending laugh.

"Seriously, bro. We've known each other for, what, almost forty years? That guy who went all self-righteous on Brogan Prescott today was the same guy who convinced me how awesome it would be to throw away my law school ambitions and learn the bass so I could play in his garage band. That's the fire I saw. That's the passion. That's who you are."

"Self-Righteous Guy? Great." I stared into my drink and sighed. Bubbles One and Six were gone, too.

"I get what you're saying, I really do," I said. "And I know I haven't made things easy on you, or this project. But I'm not going to buy a vineyard, ok? Just hang in there. We're almost at the finish line. We're one exam away from everything we've worked years for."

Shay tossed a ten on the bar, got up from his stool and gave me a Bro Hug. "Alright. Stop drinking and go study, then." As he was walking out, he turned around and added, "Hey, I'm just here to play bass."

It was the line he used whenever we showed up to a gig and something was all messed up. Dominic, our lead guitarist, would go completely apoplectic if there was even the slightest malfunction with the PA, or we had to pay for our own drinks, or the freaking sky wasn't blue enough that day. But Seamus wanted nothing more than to deflect the drama: Keep things smooth in Shay World.

The final bubble broke loose from the edge of its ice cube, floated to the top of my glass and popped.

"Hey, Oscar," I said, holding up the glass. "Can I get another one of these? This one's flat."

FOUR

The first messages started coming in at 5:00am, and I was awake to see them all, because I was drinking. Ok, technically speaking, not drinking... Studying.

Remy was the first. She woke up at five o'clock every day to get in a run with that freak of nature dog of hers that was half the size of her apartment. *Good luck,* her text read. *But you won't need it because you've studied very hard.* So sentimental, so endearing. She was also the only 24-year-old woman in existence that didn't believe in using emojis.

More well-wishes followed. An eloquent and understated voicemail from Shay: "For God's sake, bro, don't fuck this thing up," and another from Chef Dan, who was as encouraging as ever: "I hope you fail, you bastard, because I need you here, ha ha."

Around eight in the morning, Trevor Collins also sent me an empowering text: *Obviously the test is rigged and you're going to suck, because they didn't invite me. LOL.*

Sleep was nearly impossible that night, as my brain wouldn't stop obsessing on Italian reds. I finally had enough of it, so I got up at 4:00 a.m. and went through a set of three hundred flash cards on Italy, hoping to avoid the inevitable. But what was the point? Theory wasn't the problem. I had already passed the Theory portion of the exam a year ago. If flash cards could describe how a wine tastes, I'd drink flash cards. They're cheaper.

So, down to my "cellar" I went.

I kept my collection at Napa Caverns Wine Storage, which was a beautiful, temperature-controlled facility that allowed 24-hour access for alcoholics and manic collectors like myself. Gotta say, I had a pretty impressive collection. Not only did I buy my favorites in the years when I had money, but I also allowed restaurant owners to pay me in wine for back wages when they went out of business.

I went through my racks and plundered every Italian red older than ten years. I knew I'd regret the waste, but what the hell? We'd party after I passed my sit, and the remainder of these bottles would be first on the hit list.

Then I carb loaded. Quaker Oats Guy, with his Mona Lisa smile of righteous indignation, glared at me from his cylindrical altar the whole time. *There are only three reds in the tasting. Odds are you won't even get an Italian. Oh, and you're a disappointment to your grandmother, don't forget that part.* Fucking Quaker Oats Guy.

By 6:37 a.m., I had uncorked two different reds from each of Italy's fifteen different growing regions. I went through the entire Deductive Tasting Method out loud for each one, checking my previous notes and creating new ones for the varietals and regions that were the most difficult to differentiate. Yes, it was cramming and yes, it probably did no legitimate good at this point other than to make me feel like I was trying.

I got texts from the other three guys in my study group, all of whom were taking the test that day. It was like being on a group chat with a bunch of twelve-year-old girls before the Big Slumber Party at Stacy's house.

What are you wearing?

Is this shirt too informal?

Do you think Richards will be there? I hate that guy.

I don't want to be early, but I don't want to be late.

I'm nervous AF.

I dressed safe and inconspicuous, yet stylish and sales-y—blue suit, white shirt, solid lavender tie, and brown leather shoes. I would be judged on how I looked during the Practical Service exam, so my outfit needed to give off the "I'm awesome and you should listen to me" vibe without giving off the "You don't look this good, so you suck" vibe.

The exam was held at the Ritz Carlton in San Francisco. I didn't want to freak myself out by fighting traffic the whole way, so I drove from Napa to Lafayette, took the BART from there into the city, then walked to the hotel from the station. I arrived eight minutes before the exam. Fate was on my side.

The rest of the guys from my study group were already there, along with a handful of candidates I didn't recognize. They milled about the hallway outside of the conference rooms in much the same way a convict would mill about the gallery outside the gas chamber, if they allowed Death Row convicts to mill about. There were lots of hands in pockets and eyes gazing the floor. Brad Gerrardi, who was already a high-strung mess of a human being, paced the hall at an uncomfortable speed—like panic attack-speed—mumbling incoherent wine facts under his breath.

There was a legitimate reason to be stressed out though. The Master Sommelier exam has a pass rate of about five percent, and you can only take it if you're among the twenty percent of candidates who passed the Advanced Sommelier exam. It takes all the time, money, dedication and study of becoming a brain surgeon, only it's harder. Most of these guys were on their third or fourth try. Of course, they were nervous.

I, on the other hand, felt rather good. Strangely confident, one might say.

At 9:05 a.m., Anders DeVry emerged from a conference room and approached me. The exams were always given by other Master Somms, and Anders was legendary. I had a chance to meet him in Copenhagen a few years earlier and watching him work was a lesson in humility.

"Corbett." He shook my hand. "It's a pleasure to see you again."

I got all fanboy giddy and shook his hand too long. "Great to see you as well, Anders. Will you be conducting my sit today?"

He led me towards the conference room. "We'll be starting with your Practical Service exam, and you'll have your blind tasting during the afternoon session. Right this way, please."

I was both relieved and bummed that I wouldn't be sitting for the blind tasting first. Relieved in that I knew I'd crush the practical, and it would build confidence for the sit. But disappointed in the respect that I'd rather have gone straight to the blind tasting while the memory of the Italians was still fresh on my palate.

The conference room was small, and dominated by a single, circular table in the center, set for a formal dinner service. Seated around the table were five people, four of whom I recognized—including Jean-Phillipe Marchand, who conducted my blind tasting the previous year… which I failed. Not knowing if we were all acquainted, Anders made introductions, but when he got to Marchand, I jumped in.

"Jean-Francois needs no introduction," I said, flashing a smile that I hope conveyed, *I don't carry a grudge.*

"It is *Jean-Phillippe,*" he corrected. No one can look down their nose at you like the French. They have Disdain down to an art form, and Jean-Phillippe was freaking Picasso.

Solid start to my sit. Just awesome. "Of course. My apologies."

The one person I didn't recognize was a woman whom I took to be one of only twenty-four female Master Sommeliers in the world. She certainly carried herself with all the confident arrogance of a Master Somm, though her smile didn't have nearly the same aura of entitled hegemony.

"This is Sydney Cameron," Anders said. "Ms. Cameron is a volunteer with the Examinations Committee."

"Nice to meet you," she said. "I like men with two last names." It was a weird thing to say, and for a moment I wondered if it was part of the test. Something to throw me. If it was, it worked.

"I like women," I blurted. That was supposed to be followed by something witty. But it wasn't.

"Some men do, apparently," Sydney replied with a smile.

"Ms. Cameron will be joining us as an observer and a mock guest," Anders thankfully interjected. "With your permission, of course."

"The more, the merrier," I said. "And the larger the tip." That got a round of laughs, except from Jean-Phillippe. I got the feeling he wouldn't laugh if he had front row tickets to a Kevin Hart show with a complimentary tank of nitrous.

"Then let us begin," Anders said, taking the empty seat next to Sydney.

"Mr. Thomas," Jean-Phillippe began. "This is the first part of a two-part examination required for your diploma as a Master in the Court of Sommeliers Americas." His accent was thick, really thick, like he wasn't even trying. I've been to France six times, and there are about eight thousand French people more than willing to tell you how much your accent sucks.

"The Practical Restaurant Wine Service and Salesmanship exam is to gauge whether your service and sales techniques are of the highest caliber. The five of us will be your guests for a mock dinner service, at which you will demonstrate these skills. This is all clear to you, non?"

This was all formalities, of course. The Court—and especially the Europeans in the Court —was big on formalities. It was part of the tradition, which was kind of cool in its own way. But yes, I understood what was required of me for this exam and had for years.

"*Oui, Monsieur.*"

"Very well, Mr. Thomas." He handed me a thick, leather-bound wine list. "Whenever you are ready."

I was ready. I was more than ready. I had twenty years of bar and restaurant experience to help me get ready, and half of those years were spent exclusively as a Sommelier. I decided I was pleased that the Practical came before the blind tasting. It put me at ease, and I could already feel my heart rate throttling back a little bit.

"Ladies and gentlemen," I began. "Welcome to the Ritz Carlton, San Francisco. My name is Corbett, and it's my honor to be your

Sommelier this evening." I gently patted the large book in my hand. "Which of you would like to view the wine list tonight?"

"I would, thank you," Anders said, reaching for the list. As I handed it to him, I could see Jean-Phillippe already taking notes.

"Now, may I start you off this evening with a cocktail?" I asked, making proper eye contact with every member of the party. "Might I suggest one from the list of house cocktails crafted by our bartender?"

"It's my birthday!" Sydney squealed suddenly. "We'll definitely need champagne." She snatched the list from Anders, and there were laughs around the table.

"Oh! Well, happy birthday, Ms. Cameron," I said. "Perhaps a bottle of the 2003 Krug—"

"How do you know her name is Ms. Cameron, Mr. Thomas?" Jean-Phillippe interrupted. The smiles and chuckles continued around the table but I was a bit confused. *Was he joking?*

"How do you know my name is Mr. *Thomas*, Jean Francois?"

"I am *Jean-Phillippe*," he corrected, making another note on his yellow pad.

Shit.

"So, champagne it is, then!"

Desperate to leave the awkwardness where it lay, I crossed quickly over to Sydney's chair, noticing she had thick cascades of wavy red hair which spilled onto the pages of the list. "Ah," I said, looking over her shoulder. "I see we don't have the 2003, but the 2002 is a spectacular vintage."

"Well, unless Anders is picking up the tab, how about we start with the Veuve Cliquot?" That was Shane Ossenberg, one of the Masters I hadn't met until that day.

"The Veuve Cliquot. Excellent choice, sir," I replied. "I'll have that for you in a moment."

The wine itself was probably waiting right outside the door. Though the exam was designed to simulate an actual dinner service, the somms giving the test planned in advance which wines I'd be presenting at the table. They obviously wanted to see me uncork a champagne, so they guided the test in that direction.

As I reached the door, Jean-Phillippe called out, "I do not wish to have champagne this evening."

I turned back around and clasped my hands together. "Yes, sir, and what may I start you off with?"

"I would like an aperitif," he said. "Can you explain to me the difference between Lillet and Dubonnet?"

"Certainly, sir." This was also part of the exam. Not just understanding and explaining the differences among wines, aperitifs, and even beers, but staying professional and focused as insufferable French dickheads try to throw you off your game.

"Dubonnet is a wine-based aperitif from France, which typically comes in a *rouge* variety, and has a rich, spicy, port wine flavor, with a slightly bitter accent of quinine. Lillet, on the other hand—"

"LEE-lay," Jean-Phillippe corrected.

"Yes, of course," I said. "Lillet is a—"

"Not LUH-lay!" he admonished again. "*LEE*-lay."

Something was wrong. Something was terribly, terribly wrong. I knew the correct pronunciation—that was child's play. But for some reason, my mouth and tongue were not cooperating.

"You're right, sir, absolutely," I apologized. I took a deep breath and tried to slow things down. "*Lee-lay* is also a French, wine-based aperitif. But unlike Dubonnet, the *blanc* version is most popular, with notes of citrus and spice, and a delicious honeydew texture."

"I see," he said. His face was unreadable. In fact, his face was kind of…wavy? "Never mind. I will join the others in champagne."

"As you wish, sir."

I took several shaky steps for the door, got myself on the other side, and leaned against it in terror. *It couldn't be, God Almighty tell me this isn't happening. Math. Must do the maths. Fifteen different regions in*

Italy, two samples from each region, one ounce per pour—OK, call it two ounces per pour—so that's...that's...

I drank three bottles of wine. Before 8:00 a.m.

I was hammered.

The adrenaline surging through my veins from the sheer terror of the impending exam must have held off the effects of the alcohol until I let my guard down. I had to get this under control. I focused on the four empty chairs across the hall. Or was it twelve chairs?

Ruh-roh.

No problem, Corbett. No problem at all. Most of this Practical Service shit is on autopilot anyway. Take a deep, calming breath, go back in, be slow, careful and methodical, and just get through it. You've got this. You've got this.

I strode back into the exam room, greeted with happy and eager smiles. I smiled back, confident that charm was still my most powerful weapon. But their smiles faded, replaced with shifting glances between the five of them, until finally, Shane Ossenberg spoke up.

"The Veuve Cliquot?"

Fuuuuuuuck.

"Yes!" I said. "Yes, of course. I just wanted to make sure you had flutes." I looked around the table like I was taking inventory.

"The table has been pre-set with all the necessary stemware," Jean-Phillipe said. He scribbled down some more notes. I wanted to rip that pad out of his hands and slap his smarmy face with it.

"Ah. Of course. Be back in a moment, then."

I grabbed the bottle and came back to the table, presenting it label-forward to the party. *Deep breaths, calming breaths, hold the bottle steady for the love of Christ...*

"The Veuve Cliquot," I announced. "Brut...uh...Label." *Focus.* "Brut Yellow Label, Non-Vintage." I delicately unwrapped the foil and began to loosen the *muselet.*

"And where is my aperitif?" Jean-Phillippe asked.

I stopped twisting the little wire cage and stared at him. Probably for too long.

"I thought you were having champagne tonight, Jean-Francois?"

"My name is Jean-*Phillippe*. Jean-Phillippe Marchand, and you will address me as Monsieur Marchand. Is that clear, Mr. Thomas?"

"Yes, of course, Monsieur Marchand, but I – "

POP! The cork rocketed from the champagne bottle.

"Whoop!" Sydney yelled. "Party time!"

The cork hit the ceiling with a loud *crack* and then fell like a perfect free throw into Anders DeVry's pinot noir glass. The champagne bottle ejaculated bubbly foam two feet across the table. I scrambled for my towel—the towel I didn't have.

"Where is your *serviette*, Mr. Thomas?" Marchand yelled.

The room began to spin.

"I am so sorry." I turned to retrieve a towel and knocked into the bottle, spilling champagne all over the table.

"Mon Dieu!" Marchand cried.

I clutched the edge of the table to keep from falling over. The room spun like a carnival ride out of a Tim Burton nightmare. My knees buckled. I watched helplessly as the bottle of Veuve *glug-glug-glugged* its contents all over Marchand's notepad.

"Mr. Thomas!"

"Um, give me a moment here," I whispered. I had a death grip on the table. It was my anchor to the Earth, without which I'd surely spin off into space. I tried to focus my eyes on my right shoe, but it was nothing but a rotating, brown blur.

"Mr. Thomas!"

"I just need a moment here, Jean-Francois," I said a little louder.

Marchand flew from his chair. "It is Jean-Phillippe, you idiot! Do you understand? My name is—"

"EAT A DICK, FRANCOIS!" I screamed.

When I was a junior in high school, civics was one of my required
courses. My teacher was Mr. Klein—this old, Birkenstock-wearing
hippie guy. We spent at least a full month on the civil rights movement
of the '50s and '60s. Every day that month, Mr. Klein would show us
these black and white movies of protesters getting the shit beat out of
them by police in riot gear. And there were these scenes where the cops
whipped out a fire hose and blasted the protesters with it. Bodies would
fly across the sidewalk and smash into cars; people would tumble down
the street for yards, helplessly, head over foot, limbs askew. The fire
hose was like a weapon of mass destruction. It could clear out an entire
city block.

When I puked at the exam, it was a lot like that.

The first wave completely took out the stemware. My head spun so
badly that I couldn't really see the effect of the blast, but I could hear
the jarring sound of shattering glass and breaking plates mixed with
screams of horror, kind of like a vomit version of the Rodney King
riots. A tornado of motion surrounded me—plates and forks flew across
the room, blurry figures scrambled in panic, chairs tumbled.

The second wave was what Strategic Air Command would call an
"air burst." I lost my grip on the table, my legs gave out and I fell
backwards to the floor, releasing a massive, unfettered, chunder-arc
skyward. Red rain showered down from one end of the room to the
other, coating the Degas prints on the walls and creating a permanent
issue for the mocha-taupe window dressings. And there were innocent
civilians caught in this effluent hurricane, people who would need
months of counseling to handle their inevitable PTSD.

The next ten or fifteen minutes are still fuzzy and piecemeal to
me. I was led or dragged or carried out of the room, propped up in a
chair at the end of some distant hallway on the mezzanine, and given
a one-liter bottle of Cool Breeze Gatorade. My jacket and tie were
missing in action. I still had my brown leather shoes, but they were
black now—pitch black—which I was finally coherent enough to

understand was a result of mixing brown with red. Lots and lots
of red.

As the fog cleared, I could make out the image of Shane Ossenberg
sitting in a chair opposite me. He didn't have his jacket on, either,
which was a telling sign. I figured he was going to present me with a
dry-cleaning bill larger than the gross domestic product of Venezuela. I
also noticed he sat far enough away to be outside the blast radius, but
my empty stomach assured me this cannon was no longer loaded.

"Are you gonna die on me?" he asked.

"No," I mumbled. "Unfortunately."

"So, here's the deal, Corbett," he started, "under most
circumstances, you could claim you got a terrible stomach flu, find
some doctor to write you a note, and take the exam again next year. But
with the whole 'eat a dick' thing…you know, Jean-Phillippe is the Head
of the Education Department for the Court in Europe, right?"

I didn't know. But I nodded my head in agreement, slowly.

"So." Shane took a deep breath. "So, the thing is, you're out."

I felt ill again and clutched the edge of the couch with sweaty
palms. "You're not going to let me retake the test?"

"You're out of the Court, Corbett," he said. "No tests, no
credentials. You're banished for life."

I stood up, which was definitely a bad idea, but I couldn't help it.
"No, you can't do that. I'm still an Advanced Somm, I still have that!"

Shane stood up as well. "Listen, bud, there isn't a somm out there
that doesn't want to tell Jean-Phillippe Marchand to eat a dick, here or
in Europe. Hell, you'll probably become some kind of urban legend for
it." He sighed. "But I'm sorry, Corbett, I really am. It's not up to me.
Your credentials are revoked, and you can't have any affiliation with the
Court."

He moved toward me slowly, and I could see on his face that he
wanted to make some kind of sympathetic gesture—a Bro Hug, a pat on
the shoulder, a handshake. But I reeked of bile and Sangiovese, and he

probably didn't want to touch the piñata, as it were. He instead made a kind of awkward waving motion and headed down the hall. "Good luck, Corbett."

I never knew the last show I'd play with Reality Star would be our last show. We were headlining Danny's Pub, an absolute shithole on the west side of Los Angeles in the spring of 1997. The band that came on before us were some local heroes; I don't even remember what their music was like, but they had a crowd of about a hundred who all evacuated from the place like rats when their set was over. We played our show to a couple of waitresses, the bartender, and Weed-throwing Guy, who still followed us on the road like we were the Grateful Dead.

Dominic played his guitar like a zombie. I could read his thoughts because they were my own: two years earlier, when we played Los Angeles, we headlined the Universal Amphitheater. Five thousand fans, singing our songs back to us, creating an intoxicating feedback loop of love and adulation.

When we got to the portion of the set where I'd yell, "See if you can recognize this one!" and launch into *Sensitive Ponytail Guy*, I just counted off the song like it was any other in the set. But as I did, Dominic took his guitar off and placed it gently on the stage.

"Show's over," he said.

Shay and I exchanged the confused look of, *what the hell is going on?* as Dominic crouched down next to his guitar. It gave off some awful feedback—horrendous, screeching waves so painful that even the waitresses took notice. We stopped playing. The feedback grew so loud I had to cover my ears. Dom just stared at his guitar, laying there on the floor, emanating this death wail, until he slowly raised his hand to the volume knob and turned it off. He let his fingers languish on the body of the guitar, as if it were a beloved family pet he had just put to sleep.

"Show's over," he whispered, then walked out of the bar.

I never heard from him again.

FIVE

I sat alone in the chair at the end of the hall in the mezzanine, gazing out a window that looked down on Market Street for several hours. At least, I think it was several hours. I'd left my phone in my jacket pocket, which I figured by this point was removed with the rest of the toxic waste to be incinerated. My head was thankfully pain-free, but my stomach felt like I'd just gone five rounds in the octagon with Connor MacGregor.

Enough time had passed that the final results of the exam had been announced, and the other guys had either received their diplomas, or slinked off to a bar to medicate their rejection. Either way, I didn't want to risk the grueling embarrassment of running into any of them, so I waited until after dark before I made my way down to the lobby and into a restroom.

I looked like shit in the mirror. Sunken eyes—the eyes of failure and disgrace.

Banished. It was laughably Shakespearean, but I wasn't laughing.

The hotel bar was to the left of the restrooms, so I turned right and made my way down to the far exit doors.

"Hey, I know who you are."

It could have been anyone talking to anyone, but there was something familiar about the voice; I stopped and turned around.

"You're the Eat A Dick Francois Guy," she said.

"Sydney," I answered. "The Birthday Girl."

"It was two months ago, but I'll forgive you because I lied about it."

"I should probably be the one apologizing," I muttered. "Though it appears you made it through the storm unscathed."

She looked down at her outfit and then back at me. "I was literally the only object in the room that wasn't touched by your vomit. I think that's kind of magical."

"Well, glad to hear it." It was time to make my exit before my stomach considered a repeat performance. "Now, if you don't mind, I'm going to go find a rock to crawl under." I turned toward the glass exit doors.

"Hey, wait a sec," she called after me. "I have a present for you."

It sounded like the setup for snark at my expense, but I stopped and turned anyway. She took a cell phone from her purse and offered it to me.

"Oh! My phone!" I took the device from her. It seemed relatively puke-free. "I would have been screwed without this."

"I figured it was yours... Because it has a picture of you on the screen."

"Well, there's a story behind that—"

"Let me guess!" she interrupted. "It's a story about you?"

I nodded, frowning. "I don't suppose someone grabbed my jacket as well?"

"Somebody did grab it." She smiled mischievously. "Somebody in a hazmat suit. Looks like there's another trip to Ross Dress For Less in your future."

I sighed and held the phone up. "Ok, well, thanks."

I got three feet away from the valet stand before the thought hit me, colder than the night air: *no jacket, no keys.* My shoulders sank. I just wanted to take this day out back and shoot it in the head. I could have taken an Uber, but a Saturday night trip to Napa would have cost at least $200. I could have called Shay, but that would be like riding home with mom after getting busted for drinking Crème de Menthe under the bleachers at the football game. I had some friends in the city that would let me crash at their place, but I'd just be facing the same problem in the morning.

"You look like an angry man." It was Sydney again.

I hadn't really noticed earlier, but she was quite attractive. Alright, I totally noticed earlier, like in the first second and a half, but I was trying to focus on other things. She had translucent skin that was freakishly flawless, the kind of unblemished that can only be obtained by vampires. Her face did not betray in any manner that she was in her early forties, but her attitude did. I've found that around age forty-three, most women take their giant bucket of fucks and pour it down the toilet, so that they have none left to give. In Sydney's case, she had thrown the bucket itself out as well.

"I'm not angry," I snapped. "I'm just stranded."

"You are angry. I can tell. I'm extremely empathic." Her eyes were like shiny emeralds, which is something a 7th grader would put in his creative writing essay, but I swear her eyes made Looney Tunes cartoon-style green light rays.

"My clothes. You hurt their feelings. You must be sensing that."

"Oh, I'm sorry," she cooed. She reached out and gently smoothed my collar. "I only said that because I didn't know what brand of suits they sell at Target. Come on. Do you need a ride?"

"Nope. I'm good."

She handed her ticket to the kid at the valet stand. "No, you're not. You're drunk and suicidal."

"I'm not drunk."

"Where do you live?"

"Florida."

"That's perfect!" she squealed. "I'm from the Bahamas. I can drop you off on the way."

I rubbed my face. Though the moist, evening air felt rejuvenating, my head was still a bit groggy. "I live in Napa, which is totally out of the—"

"No kidding?" she said. "I'm in Napa, too. Yountville."

I still didn't know if she was serious, or if I even wanted to take a nearly two-our drive with someone so annoying. Genuinely funny and seductive, but annoying.

"My Uncle Glenn told me never to get into a stranger's car. Unless they pay upfront."

"I am not a stranger," she scolded. "You sprayed your fluids all over me. We're practically going steady now."

"I sprayed fluids all *around* you. I never touched you with my fluids."

"Well, that's even more intimate in its own freaky kind of way, don't you think?"

The valet pulled up in a shiny, silver Lexus RC. Sydney took a five from her purse and handed it to the kid as he walked over to the passenger side and opened the door. I got in and he closed the door behind me with a nearly silent *woosh.*

The leather seat folded around me like a cocoon. New Car Smell washed over me like a money shower. "Whoa," I said. "Nice car."

"The red leather is totally whorish," Sydney remarked. "But it was the only car on the lot with a manual transmission."

Within moments, I was sucked back into the seat like a giant octopus was trying to devour me. Sydney weaved between cars with the speed and effortless grace of a Grand Prix driver at Le Mans, her movements on the pedals and gearshift almost Zen-like in their subtlety and purpose.

We dodged cars, people, and busses by mere centimeters, while Sydney kept up a quiet, conversational, almost pleasant monologue about her fellow drivers.

"Apparently a rectum doesn't come with peep holes."

"The pedal on the right, *compadre,* on the right."

"Oh, now you can win a driver's license at Chuck E. Cheese's? How nice."

I was at once terrified and impressed. Her skills were insane. It was art, it was ballet—if ballet was something where, if the dancer missteps, everyone dies horribly in a maelstrom of fire and twisted metal.

After a while, it became too stressful to watch anymore. Since my life was pretty much over anyway, I resigned it to her hands and decided to check my phone. I turned the notifications back on and the device beeped like a toy robot. I'm sure Remy was curious about whether I passed or not—certainly not *anxious* about it or anything—and there were apparently voicemails from the other guys in my study group. But it was still too soon to talk with any of them. Probably stay that way for the next decade or so.

There were six blue dots for new text messages, with Shay's on top. The snippet of text next to the dot read, *For the love of Christ and all that's holy...* I guess *he* was anxious. I took a deep breath and opened up his text first, figuring Shay of all people deserved to know that I took his future, set it on fire, then tried to put it out with the sharp side of an axe.

For the love of Christ and all that's holy, tell me this isn't you, the full message read. Below it was a video. Just the sight of the still frame was enough to make my face sweat.

"No," I whispered. "No no no no no..."

"What is it?" Sydney asked.

It was me in the picture, alright. Me, with my arms outstretched and my head tilted back cartoonishly. My mouth was open so wide you could fit a cantaloupe in it, and my eyes looked like a flounder's, with each one on polar opposite sides of my head.

My thumb shook nervously over the little grey "play" arrow silhouetted on the image. But I had to see.

"Eat a dick, Francois!" the clip began, and then the vortex ensued. It was so much worse than I knew. It was the oatmeal. If there was a Monday Morning Quarterback-type of cable show for this kind of thing, the analyst would say that the real magic behind this clip was the oatmeal. Combined with the three bottles of red wine, it formed a type of plasma that rivaled the energy blast Godzilla used to destroy Tokyo.

And wow, did I ever blast. I remembered two bursts, but it was more like ten. My head craned back like a human Pez dispenser, and the resulting crimson fountains made the "Red Wedding" from *Game of Thrones* look like a paper cut. At one point, Jean-Phillippe grabbed a serving tray and tried to use it as a blast shield, but whether consciously or not, I looked right at him and unleashed a full-force discharge. He may as well have been walking under Niagara Falls with a newspaper over his head.

At the end of the clip, I fell to the floor in shuddering spams, making this *guuullargh* sound reminiscent of a dying narwhal.

When I watched the clip for the fifth time, I thought I heard someone crying in the background, though that might have just been my soul.

I stared out the passenger window, watching hills, homes, and shopping malls buzz past at about a hundred miles per hour. I could just open the door, be sucked out onto the freeway, and this ungodly nightmare would be over in a flat moment.

Sydney broke the silence. "Well, you do have to admit, it's an epic performance. A tour de force, really."

I thumbed through the other ten messages Shay had left, the last one being, *Bro, this clip is practically viral right now. What the fuck HAPPENED?*

I took a deep breath and thumbed the keyboard. "Events unfolded in a manner that was not consistent with the plan," I wrote, saying it aloud under my breath. "More later."

"So, hey," said Sydney. If I was doing anything similar to paying attention, I would have said she sounded sympathetic. "If it's any consolation, I've got a story for you that'll blow your mind."

I went back to staring out the window; Sydney filled the silence with what I suppose was her life story. I switched to Listening Autopilot, unconsciously mumbling the occasional "uh huh" and "oh wow" so she would just keep talking and I wouldn't have to. My phone beeped like R2-D2. I turned it off.

It's a funny thing, losing everything you've worked for over the past twenty years. And by funny, I mean incomprehensibly tragic. I felt old. For the first time in my life, I felt like a middle-aged man. I'd be fifty in two years. Fifty was the freaking life expectancy of a human being in America up until the 1920s. If I devoted myself to a new project that took another twenty years, I'd be almost seventy by that time. No one hits their peak success at seventy unless you count changing your own diaper and getting an erection without mechanical assistance as "success."

I was pushing a half-century with nothing to show for it. Nothing. A rented apartment, a shitty car, three suits that had been in rotation for the last seven years (that I bought at fucking Men's Warehouse, Sydney). I lived week-to-week on a grossly inadequate paycheck that I accepted mostly for the clout behind it. Not a penny saved, and except for three cool guitars and a decent wine collection, not an asset to my name.

What I did have was a dream. A dream I could count on every single day. It was the dream that was my side dish when I couldn't afford groceries, the dream that enjoyed the candlelight when the power was shut off, the dream that whispered, "You're more than this," when customers called me an idiot and sent back their perfectly good wine.

The amazing thing about having a dream is that you can lean on it with your full weight and it never snaps, never breaks. It never walks out of your life when you're four years old, it never forgets your 15th birthday, it never has an affair with another dream.

And now it was gone, too.

I hadn't really noticed we were all the way through Jamison Canyon when I finally tuned into Sydney again, who was asking, "Do I take 29 or go up Soscol?"

"Soscol, like you're going to Silverado Trail."

"I want to give you a quiz on everything I said but I think you'd fail it, and that would break my heart."

"Sorry," I said. "A little distracted, I suppose."

"Well, you missed one hell of a confession." She smirked at me. "And an amazing life story. It was probably so intense and shocking you just couldn't process it."

"Probably."

A Potato Chip Moon, as Remy used to call it, hung in the night sky over Napa. Though it was frosted by a bit of haze, the marine layer still hadn't crept in from San Pablo Bay. By morning, there would be pockets of fog throughout the valley, unless that storm they were talking about came in from up north and—

We sped right past Stonecrest Drive. "Oh shit, I'm sorry. We were supposed to turn back there. Here, just go right on Hagen Road and we'll loop back around."

Locals complained about how dark and dangerous it was on these roads in Coombsville, but I liked it. It was only three minutes from downtown, but it felt like a world away. Nights like this made the wineries along the road seem more like simple homes, and in many ways, some of them still were. There were a few lights on at Arrow & Branch, making it feel like the family was there, just having a glass of wine and watching TV. All the lights were off at Hank's place as we passed by the Fogelson Vineyard, though there was a swarm of fireflies playing over the vines.

"Stop the car!" I shouted.

Sydney screeched to a halt; if I'd had anything left in my stomach to puke, it would have painted the inside of her windshield.

"What's going on?"

Fireflies? I had never seen or even heard of them in Napa before. I rolled down the tinted window and, sure as hell, there they were, dozens of them, twinkling around the vines. I thought I could make out colors as well: they glowed light green or blue, almost like Christmas lights flashing in the sky. They were brilliant, gorgeous and absolutely compelling.

"Oh my God," I whispered. "Check that out."

"Check out what?"

I got out of the car but didn't shut the door, afraid that the sound might scare the tiny creatures away.

"What are you looking at?" Sydney had gotten out of the car, too, and tried to follow my gaze across the vineyard.

"There." I pointed towards the south-west block, near the hillside. "Unbelievable. I used to see fireflies in the south and northwest when the band was on tour, but never here in California."

"Wait, where?" Sydney said. "I don't see anything."

Without thinking, I grabbed Sydney's hand and pulled her with me into the vineyard. I walked as quickly and quietly as I could down the dirt road towards the vineyard block where the tiny insects danced. They couldn't be all that tiny, though—I could see them from the main road, and the vines were still a couple hundred feet away. The lights swayed in gentle circles, flashing on and off. Well, maybe not all the way off: they dimmed a bit then suddenly became brighter, bright enough to cast their iridescent glow on the leaves below. They were gorgeous, and I was consumed with a single-minded desire to get closer to them.

"Um, what exactly are we doing?" Sydney asked.

"Shhh! You'll scare them off."

"Scare who off?"

With each step forward, the swarm seemed to move further away, so that they were always just out of reach, almost as though we were invisibly pushing them back. We kept moving towards them, until I stepped on a thick, dry branch, which broke with a loud *snap!*

Only it wasn't just a *snap*, there was a *click* too. A familiar and very terrifying *click,* one which accompanied the feeling of cold steel against the back of my head.

"You two just move your hands up where I can see them," a voice behind me instructed. "Real slow."

I glanced sideways at Sydney, careful not to turn my head too much.

Sydney stared back at me, wide-eyed and terrified. I did just as the man told me. No sudden moves, all happy and calm-like.

"Hank, is that you?" I asked, trying not to sound like a guy about to pee himself.

I felt the barrel move off of my head. "Turn around," the man ordered.

I eased around slowly to see Hank Fogelson standing there with his .22.

"Corbett?" he said, lowering the rifle. "What the hell are you doing out here? I nearly blew your head off."

"It would have been the high point of my day," I said.

"You could have knocked." Hank's voice trembled. "Would have saved us both a goddamn heart attack."

"I'm sorry, Hank, it's just that I saw these fireflies and – " I turned around to point them out, but they were gone. "Oh. Well, they were right here. Just a second ago."

"Fireflies?" he said. "In Napa?"

I nodded sheepishly. Sydney had the same confused look on her face as Hank. I could not have felt more like an idiot.

"You drunk, Corbett?"

"No," I said with a sigh. "No, I'm just running around your vineyard at ten o'clock on a Saturday night, chasing fireflies that don't exist."

"Chasing fireflies." Hank grinned, then produced a flask from his pocket and handed it to me. "Well, sounds like you should be drunk."

More alcohol was probably the worst idea ever, but I apparently had a thing for bad ideas. I took a swig from the silver and leather vessel. Very good whiskey.

"Who's your lady friend, Corbett?" Hank asked.

"Oh, I'm sorry," I said. "This is Sydney. Sydney...um..."

"Sydney Cameron." She moved forward, extending her hand

towards Hank. "And I'm sorry if we trespassed into your vineyard, Mr.
—?"

"Fogelson. But please, call me Hank. A pleasure, Miss Cameron."

Hank shook Sydney's hand, but even in the near-blackness of the
autumn night, I could see that she was flustered. Hank must have
noticed it, too.

"You alright, ma'am?" he asked.

"It's been a pretty weird night for both of us," I said.

Sydney forced a laugh. "You could definitely say that."

I put the cap back on the flask and handed it to Hank. "Sour mash.
Aged in Port barrels. The real deal."

"A man reaches a certain age, you just stop messing around." He
took the flask back, drank a healthy swig, then offered it to Sydney.

"Oh, no thank you." Sydney looked at me the way Mrs. Saboda did
when she caught me defacing my Pee-Chee folder with myriad phallic
symbols. "And I can't believe you're drinking again."

Hank laughed. "I like you, Miss Cameron. You remind me of my
wife, God rest her soul."

Sydney gave a resigned smile and shook her head. "This day," she
murmured to herself. She grabbed the flask from Hank and tilted it
back. She didn't even wince. Impressive.

Hank turned to me. "That Prescott fella's quite a character."

Just the sound of his name started the twitching thing. "Yeah," I
said. "I'm sorry about that whole episode. I hope I didn't do anything to
torpedo the deal."

"Naw," he said. "Looks like it's full steam ahead on the ant hill." He
cracked a trained half-smile and drank another shot.

"Jesus," I said with a laugh. I took the flask from Hank and had
another sip. This time, I let it linger on my tongue for a while. Swished
it around. The sting felt good. "It's a farm. No one gets that anymore."

"Tell me about it." It sounded more like a question than a statement of agreement. And with the whiskey beginning its warm, unrestrained ascent to my brain, I just went ahead and told him all about it.

"*Terroir*, you know? We keep forgetting there's a name for it. For the land and the weather and the soil and the grapes that grow best in it. There's no need to push it or coax it or do anything like that. We just need to listen. You listen to the land, it tells you what grapes to grow, what wine to make. It tells you what the seasons are, what time it is. It's all right here. There's no need for anything else."

"You want to build a winery? You want to build a world class tasting room? That's great, that's awesome, but it has to be part of the land, too. It can't be detached. They can't be separate ideas." I looked back towards the flat part of the property. "You start right in the middle of the vineyard, and you build an open-air tasting room. A ceiling, but no walls. Each side opens up to a different block of grapes. And not just Cabernet, either, but crazy shit like Garganega and Souzão. And the tasting experience moves from side to side, varietal to varietal, so you can see the vines and the earth as you drink the wine that comes from there."

I drained the remains of the flask. "It's all open air, so if it rains, it rains, and if it's windy, it's windy, and if it's hot as hell, that's the way it goes, because if it's going on in the vineyard, it's going on in the tasting room. And there's no tour, there's only work. Here are some clippers, go prune that vine. Here are some ties, go set those branches up on a trellis. Pick the grapes during harvest. Get your hands dirty, get 'em in the soil. And we wouldn't have some kind of gourmet dinner and wine release party, either. We'd have a Festival of Dionysus, a true Bacchanalia, with food and wine and moonlight and people running through the vineyards all naked with goats' heads on."

Hank laughed. "Can I come?"

"Of course!" I said. "You can be Bacchus."

"I'd like that." His grin was genuine and warm. "I would like that indeed." Hank took another flask from his pocket and twisted off the cap.

I laughed. "You always come out here with a shotgun and two flasks?"

"You always chase make-believe fireflies?" he asked.

I smiled. "I suppose I do."

Hank drank from the flask, but never moved his eyes off me. "Corbett," he said. "You should buy this vineyard."

Apparently, the whiskey was going to his head as well. "What, have you been talking to my lawyer?"

"I'm serious," he said. "The kids don't want it, and I don't want to see someone like Prescott take it over."

"What about Gemma?" I asked. "Of all the kids, I'd have thought she'd want to keep it in the family."

Hank took another sip, leaned up against a trellis post, and gazed out into the night sky. "I thought so, too. But they got different dreams, and I'm just...I'm," He pinched his nose like allergies were the problem. "It's just time. And you're the guy."

Hank offered the flask to Sydney, but she refused with a head shake and a polite little smile.

"Hank, honestly, I'm mostly just full of shit," I said. "What do I know about running a vineyard?"

"Everything that's important? You already got that down," he answered. "Francisco and his crew do all the real viticulture. They'd stay on."

I took another large hit off the flask, mostly to try and quiet the insane little voice in the back of my head that was seriously thinking this through. "I don't have anything even close to that kind of money."

Hank nodded pensively. "I put the property on the market for two million. Prescott's gonna offer two-point-five. I'll give you a ninety-day option to purchase it for one-point five."

"Hank, no, you can't leave that kind of money on the table," I said. "What about the kids?"

"It ain't the kids' decision."

I couldn't believe I was running the numbers in my head. It was a bad choice, a particularly dumb thing to do, but as the King of Stupid Decisions, I was drawn to it like...like...

Fireflies. They'd come back, only this time they were dancing around one of the vineyard blocks in the west. Swirling gently, twinkling perfectly.

"It'd still cost another four million at least to start the tasting room," I said. "And then there's—"

"Don't worry about all that," Hank interrupted. "Start with the property. You said it yourself: it's about the land. Get the land first, build up from there."

Both Hank and Sydney were looking right at me, which meant they had to see the fireflies. I waited for them to say something about it, but neither one did. I turned around and watched as the swarm floated gently about two acres away, on and off, on and off, hypnotic and ethereal.

"Hey, you see that guy?" I looked back and saw Hank grinning and nudging Sydney with his elbow. Then he pointed at me. "You see that guy right there? That's a steward of the land."

Steward of the Land. It'd be a great name for my first wine.

SIX

After dad took off, the only semi-consistent male in my life was Uncle Glen. Uncle Glen came by for Sunday dinner almost every week when I was a kid. Actually, he *made* Sunday dinner every week, as mom typically drank her juice and fell asleep on the couch by six o'clock.

Uncle Glen was one of those Uncles of Unknown Origin that weren't blood related. Mom called him "Uncle Glen," so he was "Uncle Glen," and that was pretty much that. He was a Vietnam veteran, which I only knew because of the black "Vietnam Veteran" baseball cap permanently affixed to his head. The one time we talked about it, he told me he volunteered for three tours of duty.

When I asked him why he went back to the war so many times, he said, "When I joined the Marines I was a stupid, angry kid. After my first tour, I stopped being a kid. After my second tour, I stopped being angry. After my third, I stopped being stupid."

He was also a diehard Cardinals fan, even before they became the Phoenix Cardinals (and then the Arizona Cardinals). So on Sundays during the fall, Uncle Glen would come over to watch football and make his signature tuna casserole, and he'd scream all these new and amazing swear words at the television while I tried to understand this complicated game he loved so much.

One evening, when I was about seven years old, Uncle Glen and I watched a playoff game while mom had to spend most of the night in the bathroom. In the final second of the game, someone from the "good guys" team scored a touchdown, and Uncle Glen went absolutely nuts, laughing and shouting and clapping in that startling, whip-crack way that adults know how to do. The guy who scored the touchdown slammed the ball into the ground, stuck his hand up and started running around the field. It was weird.

"Why is his hand in the air?" I asked.

Uncle Glen stared at me that way that grown-ups who don't have kids stare at kids. "Well, he ain't waving hello, if that's what you're asking." He then held up his index finger. "He's number one, get it? He's taking a victory lap."

I looked back at the TV and, sure enough, the guy had his finger extended to the sky like he could poke holes in the clouds. He'd taken his helmet off, too, and his smile reminded me of the Cheshire Cat.

"Why's he doing that?" I asked.

"Because he's the man!" Uncle Glen clapped again. "He just scored the winning touchdown. The crowd's going crazy for him, and he's soaking it up. That boy's gonna get laid tonight, let me tell ya."

The TV showed different shots of the crowd in the stadium jumping and screaming and hugging, while the football player rounded the big, yellow slingshot thingy and headed back down the field again. The announcer with the wig rattled on about how he'd never seen anything so amazing in his life, and Uncle Glen put an arm around my shoulder and mussed-up my hair, laughing and whooping.

At the few parent-teacher conferences where my mom was sober enough to show up, my teachers would ask her why I always raised my hand with my index finger pointed. She never had an answer.

Shay didn't return my calls or texts the next day. I didn't push it too hard, though I was genuinely excited to tell him more about the vineyard. I left him some details on a voicemail, and tried to sound upbeat, but I imagined he first had to grapple with the reality that our consultancy was dead, and he needed a period of mourning. And as much as he was probably ignoring me, he was also just as likely to show up at my apartment with a machete, so I went down to the riverfront and hung out there, running some preliminary numbers and putting down business plan ideas.

It didn't even occur to me that Shay wouldn't want to be involved with the winery, or that there was a way to get to "there" from "here" without him. He was my oldest and closest friend. We'd met in the fourth grade, on the first day of school, and we were inseparable ever since.

I had transferred to Desert Heights Elementary from a school across town, so I was the new kid, just ripe for some bullying, and Billy Ratner was more than happy to oblige in that respect. Billy especially didn't appreciate that I was taller than him, so he had to get all prison bitch on me and prove he was tougher than the big new guy.

I remember that he was saying something really asinine, like calling me a tree or something while pushing me hard against the chest, when Shay came out of nowhere and smashed Billy's nose in with one punch —laying him out on the ground with screams and blood and crying and everything.

Mrs. Brocklin was there in a heartbeat, and as she dragged Shay off to the Principal's Office, he yelled out, "Hi! I'm Seamus! Want to be friends?"

Shay fled Tucson for Seattle with me when we were eighteen. He was with me before, during, and after the band. He was my partner in crime. Really foolish crime. Crime that never, ever, ever pays.

Why would he duck out now?

I got a bit more nervous on Monday. Appellation was closed Mondays, so I didn't have to go into work, and though I figured Shay would have to go into his office, I thought he'd reach out at some point.

Nothing.

Then, at 5 p.m., I heard a knock on my door and there stood Shay with a shit ton of Indian takeout, like seven bags of it. He stood motionless in the doorway, glaring at me, and holding all these white plastic bags.

"That goddamn video. I swear. It looks like you threw up food you ate, like, fifteen years ago," he said. "So, I got seconds of everything."

"You got seconds of everything because you always eat seconds of everything."

"Hey, you got any wine?" He always thought that was funny.

"I'm never drinking again," I said.

"Oh, I'm sorry, I thought this was Corbett Thomas's apartment."

He strolled past me and set up dinner on my table as I popped open a bottle of Kale Vineyards Grenache Blanc. We filled our plates, clinked our glasses and started eating.

An uncomfortable silence enveloped us like a rash. God knows I didn't want to bring up the death of our consultancy, or the lost clients, or the freaking viral video, but I didn't want to live in denial either and just launch into the vineyard project without addressing the proverbial eight-hundred-pound gorilla (who was eating all the vegetable Korma). I could have started off with yet another apology for yet another massive screwup, but I knew at this point it would only come across as insincere.

"The winery is going to be fifty-fifty," I finally said. "Just like our firm."

Shay nodded but didn't take his eyes off his plate. I topped off his glass.

"I've got some ideas about how to raise the capital," I said. "I know it'll be a bit tricky, what with…everything. But I think it'll work."

Shay nodded again but didn't stop shoveling food into his mouth.

"You know, you're the one who said I should buy the vineyard in the first place. You thought it would be a good idea before—"

Shay dropped his fork on his plate with a resounding *clank!* and glared at me. "Here's the deal, bro, OK?" he said. "I'm a shark. I'm like fucking Jaws over here. I just glide along, eating fools. And I don't stop. I never stop. If I stop, I die. Do you get it?"

"Um, no." I replied.

"If I stop, I die."

"Alright," I said. "No stopping."

He dove right back into his chicken tikka masala. "You're going to need thirty percent as a down payment for a land loan, so about four hundred and fifty thousand." His eyes narrowed on me. "I take it you have about thirty cents to your name?"

"Something like that," I admitted. "But we're going to need money for the tasting room, too."

"You really want to build a winery?"

"Well, probably just a tasting room to start," I said. "We'll custom crush, at first."

And thus we dived in. One bottle of wine turned to two and Shay consumed the vast majority of the Indian food as we worked out the specifics of the plan. I took out my laptop and showed him the one I'd been working on, then he took out his phone and showed me his. It made me feel a little bit better to know that he had already been giving this some thought, aside from, *wouldn't it be nice to murder Corbett and just take him out of my misery?*

Four hours and a third bottle later, we had settled on the soul-crushing number of $600,000 to start, plus another $1.5 million within the next twenty-four months. After the failed wine bar and screw-cap-that-looks-like-a-cork fiasco, finding investors would be next to impossible. We also knew it'd be better to try and get the money outright than take on another business partner, and that wasn't going to be easy, either.

"I think we should sell the wine capsule. If we gave an exclusive to one of the bottling companies, we could probably get a good chunk of change."

"We don't even know if it works yet," Shay replied. "Your stony fucking aunt in Texas sent us incomprehensible test results."

"My cousin," I corrected. "In New Mexico."

That foil covering at the top of a wine bottle? It's mostly there for decoration, though the story goes that it was originally created to keep mice from nibbling on exposed corks. Shay and I developed a wine capsule with a tiny chip at the top that measured the moisture content of the cork and the oxygen level of the wine. If the wine was seeping into the cork or up the edges at an alarming rate, the top of the capsule changed color, indicating it was time to either drink the bottle or throw it away.

"Either way," Shay dismissed me. "For a scientist, she's a fucking idiot, and we haven't made progress on that in over a year. There's only one way I think we can get the capital. We're going to have to sell the app."

We both regarded the app as our ace in the hole, and once the consultancy had more money and clout behind it, the plan was to unleash it on the wine world to riches and acclaim.

Pocket Palate was a mobile app that used the flashlight and camera lens in a smartphone to detect flaws in a glass of wine. Simply open the app, select the varietal and vintage of the wine from the scroll down menu, then point the camera over the top of the glass and press the button.

The app created a spectral analysis of the wine, measuring the type and quantity of specific chemical compounds in the juice. Using that information, the app then determined if the wine suffered from most of the common wine faults: cork taint, oxidation, heat damage, etcetera. Pocket Palate was developed, tested and proven to be accurate over 80% of the time.

"How are we going to make any real money on that now?" I asked. "If we release the app without any marketing behind it, we'll maybe get ten downloads a week or something. That's hardly enough to raise six-hundred thousand in ninety days."

"This is why you're the front man," Shay said, opening bottle number four. I politely bowed out, but Shay could store alcohol in his system like a warehouse. It was especially impressive for a guy who topped out at five-foot-seven.

"Here's the thing. When you look at it as just an app, Pocket Palate only has an audience of wine geeks like you. The real value isn't in the app, it's in the patent, and the magic of the patent is the algorithm that converts the phone into a spectrum analyzer." Shay poured a taste of wine in his glass and swirled it around. "Bro, check this out."

I watched him from my prone position on the couch as he swished the wine around his mouth, chewed it a bit and then spit it out in the sink.

"It's a little trick I learned from a somm I know," he said. "You spit the wine out instead of swallowing it. Did you see that? That way, you don't get wasted when you're tasting through a bunch of wines."

"Eat a dick, Francois," I mumbled.

Shay smirked, grabbed the bottle and his glass and plopped down into my leather recliner. "A decent, handheld spectrum analyzer is about a thousand bucks, but you can pay upwards of thirty-grand for a mobile unit."

He poured himself a healthy glass and swirled it unconsciously. For a civilian, he had an excellent swirl: barely discernable wrist movement, and an instinctual ability not to over-swirl and spill the contents.

"The algorithm in the app has applications way beyond what we're using it for. If we sign the licensing over to another company, I think we could potentially ask for a million up-front, but we'd either get a small or potentially no per-license fee."

I sat up, suddenly a bit more sober than I was before. "Wait, wait, wait," I said. "We were looking at numbers in the neighborhood of six million over four years, and that didn't even include advertising on the social component."

"I know. But we don't have four years. And if we do it ourselves now, we're not going to have any marketing or advertising money behind it. All we have is the technology, so we need to—"

"That's not my point," I cut him off, then leaned over and grabbed his wine glass. It was no time to stop drinking. "The point is we're leaving potentially millions on the table, and I can't do that to you."

"There is no table, bro. You puked all over the fucking table, OK?" Shay took his glass back and took a giant swig. "Is this a GSM blend?" he asked. "If so, the M is for 'manure.'"

"It's got a bit of that barnyard funk that you get in Rhone blends.".

"No, it just tastes like shit," Shay said. "I shouldn't have opened it anyway. I've got an early day tomorrow." He took his phone from his pocket and clicked on the screen. "I'm gonna get a Lyft."

"I thought the app was hung up in the patent process?" I asked. "I thought it was going to take, like, another twenty grand and a year to push it through?"

"Something like that," Shay mumbled. "Closer to forty thousand." He leaned forward in his chair. "So, here's what I'm thinking. I talked to Mason about it. He said he could pull some strings to help rush the patent. And I'll put up the forty-grand."

"Oh, hell no, Shay," I snapped. "I can't ask you to do that. You're practically as broke as I am."

"No doubt about that." He shifted around uncomfortably in the recliner, pulling at the sleeves of his shirt. "But it comes down to this. Everyone we know here in the valley or any of the contacts we thought we could lean on, they're gonna want nothing to do with us really soon. No offense or anything, but we need to secure this funding before the entire world knows what a terminal fuckup you are."

I may have been offended if he didn't have a point. I didn't think the Court would send out a mass email or take out a full-page an ad in *USA Today* proclaiming, "We have revoked Corbett Thomas' credentials as a sommelier. Renounce him accordingly." Nonetheless, the restaurant community—and the wine community specifically—was a small, small world, and word would get out soon enough that I not only failed the exam but lost my credentials entirely. With my street cred toast, we needed to get this money before the singe marks were visible.

"I don't know, man," I sighed. "I don't know if I can let you do that."

"I let you put your house up for the screw cap project," he replied.

"Actually, you told me *not* to put my house up because I'd lose it. And I did."

"I just wanted to hear you say it again." Shay grinned and got up from the chair. "My Lyft's almost here. Thanks for dinner, bro."

"You paid for dinner."

"God, that's right!" he said. "Damn, you're lucky to have me."

I was lucky to have him, luckier than I knew and definitely luckier than I ever told him. "You know this winery is going to be the coolest thing in all of Napa," I said instead. "It's literally going to redefine the way tasting rooms are imagined."

"It's a hit song!" he cried, opening the door.

"It is!" I laughed. "Dude, seriously. It's going to be great. I believe in this thing, I really do. If you could have been out there that night and seen the way—"

"Look, I get it, it's great, and I don't want to talk about this shit. I'm a fucking shark." Shay took a few steps towards the sidewalk, stopped, then came back and gave me a quick hug. "I'll follow you, bro," he said, then he walked out into the rain.

The day I left Seattle, I played with Remy outside our tiny rental while her mom finished packing the moving van with all the last-minute items. Her mom and I were already neck-deep in marital problems, and the only consolation of the move to Los Angeles was the idea that it might be a chance for her and me to start over again. At least, I hoped it'd be that way, as the day started off with yet another Suddenly Hanging Up The Phone When I Walk In The Room episode.

As Remy chucked her Nerf ball at my head, a U-Haul pulled up alongside the house. Shay got out of it, casually leaned up against the back of the truck, lit up a cigarette, and just stood there quietly smoking. Remy's mom came out of the house with the last box and we loaded it into the back of our van, buckled Remy into her child's seat, and got in up front.

As I made a last-minute check for wallet and keys, I noticed Shay standing at my window, and I realized I'd forgotten he was there. I rolled down the window without saying anything. He looked around nonchalantly for a moment, then bumped his fist twice against the door of the truck.

"I'll follow you, bro," he said, then he walked back and started up the U-Haul.

Maybe it was the demise of the band sinking in, maybe it was the latest phone episode, maybe it was not hearing from Dominic or leaving Seattle or a dozen other things, but I broke down and cried. Just bawled like a child as I steered the van on to the freeway.

But there wasn't a moment, not a single moment, that I couldn't see Shay in my rearview mirror.

SEVEN

I figured the best course of action was to lay low when I went back to work the next day. I understood that if Dornin hadn't already heard about the outcome of my exam, he'd eventually corner me, and I'd be forced to confess. That didn't mean I had to burst through the front doors, broadcast my failure for all to hear, and embrace the humiliation of being demoted to Andrew's bitch. That nauseating moment would come soon enough.

What I was really concerned about was having Dornin or Chef discover that minor point about completely losing my sommelier credentials. So, I'd just come in, be cordial, do my job, eat a steaming pile of crow, and in about three months, walk out to go build the coolest winery that Napa Valley has ever seen.

I entered through the kitchen, like always, which meant in all likelihood that Chef would be one of the first people I'd run into. I kept my head down and walked past the guys on the line as fast as I could. Of course, I bumped right into Stacy.

"Oh, hey, Corbett," she said.

"Hey, Stacy."

I glanced over my shoulder as she strolled past me, looking for some kind of sign: an expression, a tone. But I didn't read anything. She'd said, "Hey, Corbett," not, "Tough luck, asshole," or "Andrew put your shit in a box and he's sitting at your desk." That had to be a good sign.

But it got me thinking. Of all things, I'd miss my little cave the most, and I hadn't steeled myself for its loss. I decided to go straight there. If Andrew hadn't already taken it over, it would be a good place to hide.

I opened the door, strolled halfway in and realized I had entered the wrong room. This place had some kind of floor to ceiling wallpaper instead of the natural brick of my office. Disoriented, I turned to walk out, when it hit me like a punch to the throat what was going on.

My entire office—every wall, every piece of furniture, every inch of visible space—was covered with letter-sized paper, upon which was printed my very own meme, my new claim to fame. Each sheet had that image of my face—the distorted, maniacal, cartoonish still-frame from the video—with the words EAT A DICK in huge, black and grey block letters at the top, and the word FRANCOIS lining the bottom in the same font. There must have been at least three hundred of the flyers littering my office. They even covered the floor like tile.

"You want to know why people come to Appellation?" Rick Dornin said from the doorway. The video blared on his phone, which he held out towards me. "To experience the highest level of service in the world. From *this guy*." Behind him was Chef Dan, and Andrew, and Stacy, and about a half-dozen other staff, all crowded into the hallway. They broke into laughter and applause. I took a melodramatic bow, a half-hearted attempt to be a good sport about the joke, all the while knowing down to the darkest reaches of my godforsaken soul that I would never, ever live this down.

Service started as usual, and Dornin had still not called me into his office. Nonetheless, I couldn't shake the feeling as the night progressed that the other steel-toed boot was going to drop at any moment. I avoided Dornin and Chef Dan like the plague, but kept a close eye on Andrew, looking for any telltale signs of giddiness or other promotion-related enthusiasm.

But as last seating began at ten o'clock, I allowed myself to relax a bit. There had been more than a little good-natured ribbing throughout the evening, and one close call from Chef Dan ("You ever puke like that in my restaurant and I'll mop it up with your face"), but no formal demotion from Dornin or anything to indicate that anyone knew I was no longer a sommelier. I even felt a tinge of guilt knowing I'd eventually be leaving this rare, loyal crew.

As I cleared a set of pinot glasses from table eight, Dornin came up to me. "There's a woman at the bar who says she's here to see you."

"Woman?" My heart pounded hard. "What kind of woman?"

Dornin blinked at me in that condescending way that made me want to gouge his eyes out. "The female kind? Jesus, Corbett, I don't know. A *woman*."

This was it. The Grim Reaper was upon me. The Harbinger of Doom had stopped by to brand my chest and strip me of my soul. I didn't know exactly how the Court of Sommeliers made it official, but I imagined they'd serve me with some sort of scarlet letter-like anti-diploma that was slung around my neck for all eternity—something that read, "This Dickhead Is Not A Sommelier And Never Will Be Again." My fingers tingled in that way they do before a massive cardiac arrest.

The bar at Appellation was subtle and understated, which is marketing-douche lingo for "tiny." It was a place for people to wait for their tables while a "mixologist" named Topher, who looked like he'd hopped in a time machine in 1923, created presumptuous craft cocktails featuring eighty different kinds of handmade bitters. The bar was hardly a place to just hang out and have a drink; the room fit eight people, max.

It was empty save for a woman at the far stool, her back to the entrance. I didn't want to walk in and announce, "I guess you have my execution order from the Court of Sommeliers?" so I slinked behind the counter, pretended to examine the wine bottles in the cooler, and waited for her to make the first move.

"Hey, I know who you are." I recognized the voice. "You're Sensitive Pony Tail Guy," Sydney said.

My response was so Pavlovian that I got halfway through the whole "You do understand the irony, right?" explanation before I stopped myself.

"Did you know that your Wiki claims that *Sensitive Ponytail Guy* is the first Top Ten hit in the U.S. with the word 'bisexual' in it?"

"I did know that. Because I—"

"Because you wrote your Wikipedia page," she laughed.

"I did indeed." I couldn't help but laugh too. "Hey, can I get you a drink?"

"That's very sweet of you, but Topher here has already made me the most unique Manhattan. Tastes like it has everything in it except whiskey."

"Well, in that case, I'll get myself a drink." I filled a tumbler with ice and poured the gin. "So, I have to admit, I'm not sure if I got a chance to say goodbye that night in the vineyard. Things got a little bit fuzzy."

Sydney flipped her hair back across her right shoulder. It was the color of pinot noir rosé from the Loire Valley, and I swear to God it couldn't have been touched by a single coloring chemical in her life.

"You ended up passing out on Hank's couch," she said. "We both figured it was best to let sleeping dogs lie, as it were."

"Good decision." Words cannot describe the horror show that was my hangover that next day. As Shay said, you reach a point with hangovers when you're afraid you're going to die. Then you reach another point when you're afraid you're not.

I poured some of Topher's disturbingly brown homemade tonic in my drink. Brown was authentic, apparently. At least I wouldn't have malaria anymore.

Sydney shimmied closer to the bar like we were about to play a game of dice. "I think it's adorable that you used to be a rock star."

"I am not adorable," I muttered. "I'm a brooding artist, filled with angst."

"Hardly. You're adorable. Like a tribble."

My gin and tonic tasted like gin and dirt. "A tribble?"

"Yes, a tribble," she replied. "Oh my god, don't tell me you don't know what a tribble is?"

"I know what a tribble is." I dumped my gin and swamp mud into the sink. "I'm just saying I'm more like a Gorn. Rugged, determined, capable of lifting really large boulders."

Sydney laughed, then took another sip of her Manhattan and shuddered. "Mmm, well, you get fifty points and a quivering ovary for the Gorn reference, but that just makes you all the more adorable."

Her warm smile soon faded into a much more serious expression. She looked down at her drink and stirred it distractedly. "So, the truth is, I'm here to make a confession."

"Oh?"

She drummed her fingers against the bar, still not daring to make eye contact. "I wanted to let you know that I was the one who posted that video."

"Holy shit," I whispered. "Of course. Who else could it have been?"

That video. That freaking video. 7.4 *million* views to date and a permanent part of the public record until electrons cease to exist. In truth, the irony did not escape me that a forty-second clip of me emptying the contents of my stomach was seen by fourteen times more people than had bought my major label album. Had this been a thing back in 1995, I would have gladly puked the words to "Sensitive Ponytail Guy" on camera and been a lot more famous.

I grabbed another glass and thought about filling it with scotch, but eyed Sydney cautiously. "You're not here to post a sequel, are you?"

"No, no!" she implored. "I'm here to make nice. I came to apologize. Really. I'm sorry."

I glared at her. Figured I'd let her squirm for a while. It felt good.

"I shouldn't have done it," she continued. "Or at least, I should have posted it on YouTube so we'd make a few bucks off it."

I shook my head. "Oh, you were so close. Now you're going to have to start all over."

"Really?" she teased. "OK, OK, I'm sorry. I'm sorry I posted the video, I shouldn't have done it, and it was wrong. I had no idea it would go viral, and I sincerely hope it didn't do any damage."

I went ahead and poured the scotch, then drank it down in a single gulp. The way I saw it, I had escaped the Somm Police another day, and if luck was on my side for once, Dornin had forgotten about our bet. *That* at least deserved a drink.

"Well, I appear to still be employed. And I haven't been famous for something in about twenty years. So yeah, OK. Apology accepted."

"Good!" she said. She reached for her drink but decided against it, then tapped out a quick drumroll on the bar with her hands as I poured another scotch in my glass. A small one this time, as I knew Topher was on the hook for all the missing alcohol the staff robbed. Especially the good stuff.

"OK," Sydney said. She reached for her purse, hesitated for a few moments, then took out a $20. "OK," she repeated, placing the bill on the bar. "Well, I'm glad I got that off my chest." She grabbed her coat and slung her purse over her shoulder. "Well, um, thank you. And, take care."

"Have a good evening," I said as she walked off. I could swear someone replaced the Macallan with something blended. No smokiness, none of that signature charcoal finish. Wouldn't have surprised me in the least if Dornin had pulled some bullshit like that.

"Dude," I heard a voice say. I looked up from my glass to see that Topher was still there behind the bar with me, buffing glasses. His handlebar mustache stuck out a good three inches from each side of his face. It defied the law of gravity so radically that it had to be hot glued into place. More than once, after throwing back a few shots, I'd asked him to sing "Oh My Darling Clementine." He did not find this nearly as amusing as I did.

"What?"

"How could you not want that?" He nodded towards the exit. "She was totally into you."

It took me a few moments to figure out what he was talking about. "Wait, her?" I asked. "Sydney? No, she was not…was she?"

"How fucking stupid are you, dude?" A legitimate question, for sure. "She stalked you on the internet, then came here to see you, then apologized to you, flirted with you, called you 'adorable' about sixteen times. What else do you want, the key to her hotel room?"

That would have been nice and much more in line with how the process usually worked, back in the '90s at least.

I guess I hadn't thought about it. Well, I mean, yes, I had *thought* about it. Every man since the dawn of time thinks about it within the first two-and-a-half seconds of meeting a woman, either consciously or unconsciously. In Sydney's case, though, I had to admit it was rather conscious. So, why didn't I do anything about it? Perhaps I'd been distracted by my relief that she wasn't the Court Tormentor, sent to formally strip me of my somm credentials. Either that, or Topher's eloquent observation about my intellectual capacity was dead-on. The latter having made more sense, I headed quickly for the parking lot.

Sydney stood underneath a heat lamp near the awning, waiting for the valet to bring her car around. "Hey, Sydney," I called out.

"Oh, hey," she said.

Was that excitement in her voice? It sounded like excitement. Maybe.

"Hey," I said. I stuck my hands in my pockets. I thought it made me look cool when I was wearing a sports coat, but mostly it was a tactic I employed to convince myself I wasn't the personification of gawkiness. "So, I was, um...I was..."

I was what? I hadn't thought this out at all. Apparently, I was more attracted to her than I thought, or else I wouldn't have run like a puppy out the front door. But then what? This was so much easier back in the band days, when the only opening line I ever had to use was, "Hello." Since then, I had reverted to my junior high school state. Anytime I was around a beautiful woman, a little voice inside my head screamed, *be cool and don't say anything stupid,* which was accompanied by heart palpitations, the eye-twitching thing, and the inevitable muttering of something absolutely inane.

So there I stood, frantically searching for the most dumbass thing to say. I thought about telling her how good looking she was, but fortunately realized that the Sheriff of 1952 would come and serve an eviction notice on my compliment. It certainly wouldn't hurt to mention how funny she was, because a sense of humor is absolutely the sexiest quality a woman can possibly possess. It'd also be less awkward than a comment about the weather, and not flirty in a Creepy Guy kind of way.

I opened my mouth, and what came out was, "You're funny looking."

"Excuse me?"

My chin sank to my chest like I had every vertebra in my neck surgically removed, and my sigh was louder than a Santa Ana wind sweeping through the valley.

"I am so sorry," I mumbled. "It's been a really surreal past couple of days. No, scratch that, it's been a surreal life, and as a result, I am mostly an idiot." I took my hands out of my pockets, so I could wave them around awkwardly. "I'm not exactly sure what I was trying to accomplish out here, but, um, you are gorgeous and funny and your eyes are like something the CIA would use for enhanced interrogation techniques because when you look at me like that, it's like I would—I don't know—clean the floorboards of your car with my tongue if you asked. And that's totally a weird thing to say, so goodbye and I'm sorry and you're beautiful and your shoes are magnificent."

It was a Cool Implosion of epic proportions, one for the record books. I walked back into the restaurant, headed straight for the bar, grabbed the Macallan and—forgery or not—poured myself a glass large enough to become grain-based Propofol.

"Hey," came a voice behind me. I turned and saw Sydney. She nodded towards my glass. "Look. You want to have that drink at my place?"

"Yes," I said. One-word answers were safe answers.

"Well, maybe not *that* particular drink," she said. "We don't want a repeat of your final exam, do we?"

"No."

Sydney took a pen and a crumpled old receipt from her purse. "Here's my address," she said, scrawling on the receipt. "Why don't you just come over when you're done here?"

"Sure." So far, the one-word answers were quite productive.

She gave me a little wave as she headed out the door. Topher smiled his approval. If only he knew.

It took me only fifteen minutes to finish what usually took forty-five, though I blew off filling out Dornin's insipid "Customer Special Request" spreadsheet in Google Docs. I'd fill it out the next day. Or maybe next year.

I plugged Sydney's address into my phone, and Siri guided me northbound along the Silverado Trail.

As I drove through the late Napa evening, I tried not to overthink, over-feel or over-romanticize anything that was going on. But it was hard not to do, because I'm just so good at it. So, despite my best efforts to the contrary, Sydney had invited me back to her place. Maybe it was just for a drink, like she said. She wasn't an easy read, though it was more likely I wasn't paying as much attention as I should.

On the one hand, she struck me as a woman on a mission, and I'd best resign myself to the idea that she was simply going to take control and direct all facets of the evening's festivities. The night could potentially have all the passion of a board meeting. There'd be a white board in her bedroom, with a Meeting Agenda and Project Flow Chart detailing every position we'd be utilizing. I would become the human Value Proposition, and she would leverage Action Items into Concrete Deliverables with an efficiency cultivated through years of Best Practice Management. It'd be all about recognizing the Bottom Line and Maximizing Shareholder Value, if in fact, shareholder value was a wide assortment of reproductive excretions.

On the other hand, there was something naïve, if not lost, about her demeanor. Perhaps her refined confidence and detached cool were as thick as the delicious candy shell of an M&M. As thick as mine, as it were.

Her place was in a newer townhome complex, just east of Yountville's quaint downtown district. She answered the door with a tentative smile and a quick, "Ah, you found the place," then ushered me in.

"Make yourself at home," she offered. "Gin and tonic, right?"

"Oh, yes. Thanks," I said. "And your home is beautiful."

"Not really my home." She went to the kitchen to pour Tanqueray into two glasses. "It's kind of a temporary thing."

But it was beautiful. I can recognize every MALM bed, EKTORP sofa and POÄNG chair that IKEA ever squeezed into a two-dimensional box, and not a single thing like it adorned Sydney's living space. Whatever brand her couch happened to be, I slipped into it, and it was the kind of gooey marshmallow cloud of immaculate comfort that isn't obtainable with pressboard, polyurethane and Allen wrenches.

Sydney handed me a glass and sat down on the Miracle Couch next to me. "Well, cheers," she said, clinking glasses. I wasn't halfway through my first sip when the nervousness returned—the little hamster in my mind whirling away on its Stupidity Wheel. But I wasn't alone. I could tell by the way Sydney fidgeted on the couch that her Wheel was spinning at the same RPM.

"Hey, are you ok?"

Sydney nodded. "I'm good. I just…"

I waited for her to finish, but she gazed off towards the kitchen like she was a million miles away. Finally, she chuckled and turned to me.

"Thank you for noticing my shoes. Really. Thanks." Her smile was genuine and disarming.

I made the Lean, that universal first motion that signals, *I'd like to come in for a kiss.* The Lean always stops short of an actual kiss, of course, so if it's not met by a Lean from the other party, the initial Leaner can easily duck out of a potentially embarrassing situation, such as Being Offered A Cheek.

But she Leaned, too.

She was an amazing kisser. She did not try and vacuum hose my face into her mouth, nor did she use her tongue as a probe to explore the vast reaches of my oral cavity. She did not come at me like a largemouth bass, nor did she pucker up tight and furious. It was simply all the light, warm, soft, wet, awesome things about lips and tongues.

It wasn't long before we frantically stripped the clothes off each other, which started out super sexy. Shirts are always the first thing to go, and that's über hot, because it's nothing but heavy panting, buttons flying, bras popping, delicious flesh and shoulder curves.

But the sexiness came to a screeching halt with the socks. Socks are never the first thing to go. Socks are, in fact, the last thing to go, so right before the moment of naked truth, you're forced to do this awkward abdominal crunch and try to pry your gross, black, calf-length socks from your feet. It is a mood-destroying break in the action that can't be avoided, because there isn't a body in the universe that looks hot in nothing but business socks.

As I feverishly pulled the last one from my toes, Sydney grabbed me by the arm, pulled me into the bedroom and pushed me onto the bed. But instead of falling down on the mattress with me, she reached down and produced a large, brown-paper grocery bag sitting beside the bed frame.

"Alright," she said, rummaging through the bag. "You've got your choice." She pulled out two large boxes of condoms, each still in their shrink wrap. In her left hand was a box of Trojan Magnums, and in her right a box of LifeStyles Snugger Fits.

"Um, I'll go with the Trojans," I said. I mean, what the hell else was

I going to say? I didn't care if my dick looked like a Chihuahua in a circus tent, there was no way I was going to be all like, "Yeah, gimme them Snuggers."

Sydney handed me the box and then fished around the bag some more. "I got this, too, just in case." She took out a giant, clear plastic jug of some kind of translucent gel.

"Jesus Christ!" I laughed. "Did you get that thing at Costco? I didn't know they made family-size K-Y lube."

Sydney put the jug back in bag, folded her hands in her lap and stared down at the sheets, deflated. "We can either do this," she said quietly, "or not do this."

"Hey," I said, placing my hand gently on her thigh. "I'm sorry. I didn't mean...it's been a while since you've done this, hasn't it?"

"Yes, it's been a while," she replied, still not looking up. "If you feel like a guinea pig and want to go, I'd understand."

I lifted her chin until she looked me in the eyes. "I totally want to be your guinea pig. Unless you have an actual guinea pig outfit in that bag, in which case, I'm leaving."

She laughed and covered her face with her hands. "Oh my god!" she screamed into her palms. She laughed some more, in a way that was so embarrassed as to be endearing.

She put her hands down, took a deep breath and nodded. "So."

"So."

"Yes, so..."

"Maybe I should kiss you again?" I said. "It seems like I should kiss you."

"I know, right? There's so much romance going on right now."

The good news about it having "been a while" was that everything I did was the right thing to do, and seemingly the source of all pleasure in the world. There wasn't a curve I caressed, a part I nibbled, or a motion I made that didn't elicit a series of moans so breathless and desperate that I couldn't have been anything less than the Omnipotent

Overlord of All Things Sensual. Not like my ego needed any help to begin with, but every tremble of her flesh and shudder of delight was like a five-star review on Yelp, if Yelp offered reviews for sex partners.

The downside of it having "been a while" was not bad news, technically speaking - more like a quirk. I've been with women in the past who were, shall we say, verbal during climax, but when Sydney came, she yelled, "I am going to have an orgasm!" She shouted it out loud, like wake-the-neighbors loud, but in an educational, statement-of-fact manner. The second time she did it, I noticed she still didn't use a contraction for "I am." The third time she did it, well, I laughed.

She stopped in mid-thrust. "Are you laughing at me?"

"I'm not laughing at you," I laughed. "I'm laughing with you."

"Oh, my god, you're so mean!"

"I'm sorry!" I said. "No, I totally appreciate the updates, and positive reinforcement is always a good thing in these situations. It's just that your delivery is so...*informative.*"

She rolled me over until I was on top of her. "You're such an ass. You should appreciate that you're getting the job done."

"I do, I do!"

She kissed me. "I think it's your turn. I don't want to be selfish."

"Believe me, you're not being selfish," I said. "But don't worry about me. I'm just...not so good with, you know...rubbers."

Sydney's face went completely blank. "Rubbers? Seriously? I thought you were forty-eight, not eighty-eight?"

"You know what I mean," I chuckled.

Sydney wrapped her legs around my waist and pulled me in tight to her. "Tell me what you want," she whispered in my ear. "Tell me what turns you on."

"That," I said. Because it did. Whoa.

"You like that?" she whispered; her breath hot against my ear.

"Oh, hell yes," I moaned. That was working.

"You like to hear me talk to you? You want me to tell you how hot it is to feel that huge…"

"Yes…"

"Throbbing…"

"Yes…"

"Rubber?" Sydney giggled. "I'm not laughing at you, I'm laughing — "

"With you," I said. "Right."

Her eyes smiled even brighter than her lips. There was something different about her gaze. Her eyes didn't make those subtle movements, those tiny shifts as they switched focus from one eye to the other. Her stare remained calm, as if she quietly but instantly found what she was looking for inside me and was happy to simply watch it for a while.

And in this unforeseen state of vulnerability, one I hadn't felt in years, the best I could come up with was this: "I really like you."

Sydney placed her hand on the side my face and stroked my eyebrow softly with her thumb. "Awww," she purred. "That's the nicest thing anyone's said to me since the third grade."

I eased myself back inside her. She kept up her beguiling eye contact, which left me no choice but to keep going as well. "I'm a self-absorbed idiot with delusions of grandeur and a horrible tendency to self-destruct at just the right moment."

"I'm married.".

I came in an instant. "You're perfect."

EIGHT

I'd been avoiding Remy, and I felt terrible about it. She called me a few times and even when I could take the call, I sent her to voicemail, which was an absolute dick thing to do. She'd leave a friendly and innocuous message like, "Hey Dad, give me a call when you can." I called back a couple of times to make sure she was ok, but when the conversation began to lull, I feigned that I had to go.

She had already chastised me for the viral video: "Do you have any idea how horrifying it is when your friends ask you if your dad is the 'Eat A Dick Guy'?"

What I was trying to avoid was the inevitable conversation about her mother. The one conviction I managed to maintain as a single parent was, "Don't talk shit about your ex to your kids." (Well, the actual advice was a lot more eloquent and scholarly than that, but the sentiment was basically the same). Everything I had to say about the woman was bad, so I never mentioned her—not even the conversational, "How's your mom?" whenever I picked Remy up for her time with me.

I had two decades of weapons-grade avoidance under my belt, and I didn't see what good would come from tossing that aside now.

I did tell Remy about my upcoming meeting with Fractal Equity Partners, and how Shay and I hoped they'd purchase the Pocket Palate tech. So a few days before the meeting, Remy whipped out the big guns and sent me a text that read, *Hey Dad, I want to go to this presentation with you. I know a thing or two about meetings like this, and it wouldn't hurt to have the due diligence expert from McMillan Associates on your team.*

Sly girl. It was an interesting proposal, but she apparently didn't know how these things worked. I had this presentation in the bag. With ten years as the front man for a rock band and twenty years in wine sales, I knew how to launch a major Charm Offensive. I politely thanked her and told her it wouldn't be necessary, but I'll be damned if the day of the meeting, there she sat, waiting for me in the lobby of the company's office in the Financial District.

According to Shay, FEP specialized in funding or acquiring earth science technology companies. Mason Freeman, who worked at Shay's firm, had connections at one of those companies, Continuum Sciences. They expressed interest in the algorithm that gave Pocket Palate its juju and set us up with a preliminary meeting with Fractal Equity Partners. It always amazed me when Shay whipped out his lawyer shit like this, all official-like. This is the guy who designed a bass guitar that doubled as a bong, though I figured I'd leave that little detail out of the presentation.

Remy looked every inch the professional in a grey sharkskin suit. With the black-frame glasses, she looked closer to thirty-four than twenty-four, and could have passed as our lead counsel instead of Shay. She gave Shay and I each a Remy Half-Hug.

"You can't be angry, Dad," she greeted.

It always made me laugh when she said things like that. *You're not allowed to have feelings about this, because that makes everything easier to deal with.*

"I'm not angry, baby girl," I said. "I just didn't want to waste your time. I've got this."

"Then I'm just an observer," she said. "And you may want to be careful with the whole 'baby girl' thing during the meeting. By the way, you look nice."

As a matter of fact, I did look good. Sydney had bought me a new suit from one of those online tailoring companies, which arrived with a note that read, *Sorry I insulted your previous suit.* Her eye was amazing, as the thing fit perfectly.

She and I had been mostly inseparable since that first night together, though there was one evening when she literally pretended not to be at

home so that I would stay in and work on my presentation. I felt
confident, like I had it down—but there was one, nagging issue in the
back of my mind that I knew I had to bring up with Shay. We still had
about fifteen minutes before the meeting, so I sprung it on him while we
were waiting in the lobby.

"Are you sure you don't want to give this presentation?" I asked. "I
mean, especially if we're coming at this from the technology angle, it
might sound more legit coming from an attorney."

"Oh, hell no. No way." He shook his head. "There's a reason why
I'm not a litigator. I hate talking in front of people. No, you're the front
man. You do it."

It was true, strangely enough. Though Shay was with me from my
very first garage band, he never once sang a song. Never even said,
"Hello, Cleveland," into the mic. He'd slink around the back line,
hovering between the bass stack and the drums, his head down in a
perpetual shoe-gaze. At first, it was annoying as hell to me, but he
garnered a rep as the "dark and mysterious" one in the band, and well, it
brought out the girls.

"The goal today is to demonstrate the app," Shay said. "Just show
them it works. These characters can't tell their cock from a Cabernet, so
spell it out for them. Make it easy."

We zoomed up to the forty-third floor in an elevator that could have
been used for astronaut training. I expected the doors would open to
reveal a magnificent, glass and brushed aluminum-trimmed office suite,
but instead we uneventfully exited into a nondescript hallway. We
wandered around in both directions like a pack of idiots, looking for
numbers or markings of any kind on the doors, until Remy called out
from down the corridor, "Here it is."

A young woman with a practiced smile lead us into a small
conference room and told us that our hosts would meet us soon.

The first thing I noticed was that the west wall of the room was all
glass, providing what should have been a breathtaking view of the city

had the entire downtown area not been socked in with a massive, monochrome fog bank. I took out my wine bag and began to set up.

"Good morning." Two young men walked into the conference room, notepads in hand. There were handshakes and intros and pleasantries all around.

It's strange, the impressions we create of people we haven't met yet. I'd imagined that a partner from Fractal Equity Partners had to be at least sixty-five, white and mostly bald, like a 21st century version of the Monopoly man. But these two guys were Bros. Maybe not beer-pong-and-lesbian-MILF-porn Bros, but way closer to Remy's age than mine. One sported khaki pants and a polo, and the other looked like something out of a John Hughes movie in jeans and a pink, button-down shirt. The part of me that just wants to see things burn was tempted to ask them if their parents would be joining us, but thankfully I let the feeling pass.

Maybe that feeling was something more akin to jealousy or envy or regret. How did this kid get into this kind of position? What did he do right? Where did I go wrong? It was strange to think that people younger than I was held the reins of power. When I was thirty-four, I was toting around this wine bag, trying to sell ten-dollar Zinfandel to apathetic restaurant owners. And by 'this wine bag,' I mean the very wine bag I had taken wine out of for the presentation.

"I gotta tell you," said the Bro named Jace, "I was rather surprised to hear that we'd be testing a wine app. It's a bit outside our wheelhouse."

"I hate wine," said the Bro named Keevan. "I'm more of a beer guy." He and I were going to get along great. Shay was already giving me the "play nice" look.

"Well, maybe after this meeting, we'll go see if this app works on a frosty IPA?" I grinded out a smile.

"Hells yeah, I'm down," Bro Keevan replied.

I placed four pinot noir glasses in front of the Bros, two apiece.

They each picked one up and examined it, like it was the first wine glass they'd ever seen. "That's a huge glass," Bro Jace intelligently deduced.

I wanted to sound like an expert, yet not speak above them. "For the purposes of our test, we need glasses that have the greatest amount of surface area," I explained. "This allows the wine to have a high exposure to oxygen."

"Ah, right." Bro Jace nodded. "Group seventeen elements react with oxygen to form oxides, which are the basis of some primary wine flaws."

Oh, well, ok. Science Bros, then.

I took two bottles of wine from my case, uncorked them, handed a presentation packet to each of the Bros, and launched into my spiel. "Well, gentlemen, thank you again for taking the time to meet with us this morning. We're very excited to introduce to you what we believe is an app that will revolutionize the way consumers experience wine."

"Well, we're happy to have you here and we're excited about what we've read so far," said Bro Keevan. "Of course, this is a very preliminary meeting, we're mostly here to see a working demonstration of the app before we get into all the nuts and bolts of due diligence."

"Absolutely, and I'll be happy to show you exactly how the app works. Were you able to download it alright?"

They each held up their device. "All good," smiled Bro Keevan. "Although I think I still need to set up my username and password."

I picked up one of the bottles and moved around to their side of the table. "While you do that, I'll go ahead and pour." I stood to the right of Bro Jace and poured half a glass. He looked on in amazement as I twisted the bottle at the end of the pour to prevent drips.

"Guess you've done this a few times," he commented.

"Twenty years." I smiled. "The last three as Lead Sommelier at Appellation, Napa's only three-Michelin-star restaurant."

"Michelin? Like Michelin tires?"

"Dude, the tire guy!" Bro Keevan cried. "That white, donut-looking guy? That dude creeps me out."

I filled his glass. "It's the same Michelin. The Michelin brothers made tires, then they created the Michelin Guide to feature restaurants that were worth driving to." I picked up the second bottle of wine and poured it into their other glass. "The Michelin tire man is one of the oldest trademarks in the world. And he has a name. It's Bibendum."

"No way," Said Bro Jace. "That's crazy."

"Absolutely cray-cray." That one got a visible shudder out of Shay. I set the bottle down, clasped my hands together, and took a deep breath.

"Wine is an experience unlike any other in our lives. It utilizes and ignites our senses, compelling us to dive deeper and deeper into its mysteries. There's a mystique we want to unravel, yet at the same time we want it to overtake us, to overwhelm us, to tell us its story and enlighten us. And to do so, we must see, and smell, and taste."

Bro Jace and Bro Keevan had their noses buried in their phones. I thought they were trying to log into the app, but they seemed a bit lost in the process – especially since Bro Keevan was doing more scrolling than necessary.

I tried not to let it throw me.

"But our senses can sometimes be misleading," I continued. "As an Advanced Sommelier, my senses are trained to reveal the secrets in a glass of wine. But certainly not everyone can take twenty years to educate themselves this way. Indeed, sometimes even the most trained nose cannot detect flaws that can ruin the amazing experience held in that glass."

The Bros exchanged whispers, then looked back over at me. Good sign?

"That's why we developed Pocket Palate. Pocket Palate's proprietary technology allows you to scan a glass for most of the major chemical compounds that lead to flawed wine. As we show in the handout, there's a social component to the app as well, which compiles every user's results on the wine they've scanned. This allows you to track the trends of different vintages and varietals to see whether there's a pattern to the degradation of the wine. Are you up and running with your app now?"

Bro Keevan set his phone down. "Not so much. Why don't we just try it on your phone?"

"Sure, we can do that." I reached for my phone. The app opened easily, which was a relief, and a moment later the circular scanning target appeared on the screen. "Now, gentlemen, what you have in front of you are two glasses of wine. A 2014 pinot noir from the Sonoma Coast, and a 2014 pinot noir from Carneros in Napa Valley. I'd like you to take a sip of each and let me know if you can taste or smell any flaws in the wine."

"You do it, man," Bro Keevan said to Bro Jace. "I can't stand the way that stuff tastes."

Bro Jace tentatively lifted the Sonoma Coast and gave it a whiff, eliciting a giggle from his Bro. He took a small sip, then did the same with the Napa. He put the glass down quickly. "Man, I have no idea. I mean, maybe it's this one, but, I don't know. Maybe it's not."

"No Michelin Stars for you, bro," Bro Keevan joked.

"Well, no problem, then," I said. "That's why you have Pocket Palate. If you're unsure about the quality of the wine, you select the vintage and varietal from the menu, hold the scanner directly over the top of the glass, press the button, and in a matter of seconds you have your results."

I leaned over the table and positioned my phone over the glass. The Bros stood up and leaned in to get a better look.

"You have to position the scanner over the top of the glass until the wine completely fills the target outline on the screen," I instructed. I brought the phone down until it was three inches from the top of the glass, and garnet-colored pinot noir filled the screen to the edges of the target. I pushed the red camera button.

Nothing happened.

The camera light was supposed to come on, the phone was supposed to make its old-school shutter-*click* and the screen was supposed to blink, just like taking a picture. But it didn't. I pushed the red button again.

Nothing.

"Here, let me try it in a horizontal format." I repositioned the phone, holding each end with one hand. I lined up the target and moved my index finger over to tap the camera button.

No light, no click, no blink, no nothing.

I looked over at Remy and Shay. Remy was an impossible read, the absolute definition of a poker face. But cold sweat poured from Shay's forehead like a shower, and he shifted around his swivel chair like a man about to die of constipation.

Think. Fast. I had tested the app a dozen times without fail. What in the hell was going on now?

"Jace, if you don't mind, I'll hold the scanner steady and you press the button," I suggested.

"Sure, let's give it a shot," he replied.

I held the phone with both hands a few feet above the glass, then brought it down slowly until the wine came into focus and passed the edges of the scanner target. "Ok, now."

I don't know if that guy had a pneumatic index finger, or if my hands were sweaty or what, but when Jace pushed the button, the phone slipped through my fingers and fell into the wine glass with a horrifying splash.

Chaos and anarchy ensued: I screamed something like "Dog fuck the planet!" and scrambled to retrieve my phone but knocked over the glass and spilled wine all over the handouts. Shay shot from his chair and practically jumped across the table to get a towel from my wine bag (which wasn't in there). Bro Keevan hunched over in a full-on belly laugh, the sound of which echoed in my ears like the laughter at the fourth grade talent show, when I froze in the middle of my heartfelt performance of *Saturday Night* by the Bay City Rollers.

"Seamus has the app on his phone," I said, ruining my suit jacket in an effort to wipe up the mess. "We can give it another try."

Bro Jace gingerly picked up his notepad and let the wine drip off the front page and onto the table. "That's OK, I think we have enough information for the time being."

"Honestly, guys," I implored. "We've run so many tests on this application and have shown that eighty percent—"

"Really, it's ok," Bro Jace said, his voice sterner this time. "We've got the information; we'll review it and we'll be in touch." He turned for the door, but Bro Keevan stopped him and whispered something in his ear. They both grinned and turned to me.

"There is a favor we'd like to ask of you," Bro Keevan said.

"Sure, anything."

The Bros looked at each other, grinning like children at Christmas. "You're the 'Eat A Dick, Francois' Guy, aren't you? Can we get a selfie with you?"

If the ride up in the elevator hit warp speed, the ride down felt like an afternoon in the waiting room at the dentist's office. Shay focused intently on the blinking lights as we passed each floor, while I stood there like a perp waiting to get his mug shot taken. When the elevator finally opened into the lobby, Shay darted out, mumbling something like, "I got a thing I gotta get to," and nearly ran into a woman with a stroller as he shot through the lobby doors.

"I think I finally broke him."

Remy squeezed my arm. "It's Uncle Shay. Just give him some time."

We walked out of the lobby and into the grey morning haze. "Where are you parked?" I asked.

"I took BART from Fremont," she replied.

"Can I walk you to the station?"

"No, I'm going to meet some friends for coffee." She gave me a hug, a very un-Remy-like hug, squeezing me tight around the shoulders. "Look, Dad, if it's any consolation, you didn't screw up that deal by dropping your phone in the wine. You lost it the moment you opened up your mouth."

"Hmmm. I'm thinking about it, and no, that's not a consolation."

"These guys care about money, and that's it." Remy flung her heavy attaché case across her shoulder. "You got all weird on them, talking about the senses and the mystique of wine and all that stuff.

All they want to know is how much money they're going to make, how fast they're going to make it, and how long it's going to keep coming."

I sulked against the wall of the building. "No, they have to have a sense of why the app is so unique, what makes it special, the power of the—"

"No, they don't." Remy rubbed her brow. *Jesus, did she inherit my twitch?* "I work with guys like this every day, every single day, and they don't care if you developed an app that creates world peace. If they can't make money off it, they don't want it."

She dug her hands into her coat pockets and shook her head. "I don't get it. I just don't understand how you can be so emotional and eloquent about a bottle of wine, but when I ask you to tell me the truth about Mom, the best you can do is send me to voicemail."

"My God, Remy. Are you seriously going to bring that up now?" I said. "Maybe you didn't notice, but I just got my ass handed to me."

"I gotta go, Dad." And with that, she turned and practically sprinted away.

To hell with it, I thought. I'd been carrying around this backpack of bullshit for twenty years. If Remy wanted to slip it on now, it was all hers.

I ran down the sidewalk until I caught up with her and wheeled her around by the arm.

"When you were eighteen months old, your mother got pregnant with your brother," I said. "Or maybe it was your sister. I'll never know, because she had it aborted. Well, actually, it was only your half-sibling, since the guy she was cheating on me with was the one who got her pregnant. And the only reason I found out was because she started bleeding one night and I rushed her to the ER. The doctor said she would have died if I hadn't brought her in. The next morning, when I left her room to get her a breakfast burrito, she took off with the guy."

Remy stared at me, her face blank and still.

"Your mom wouldn't pay your child support. She refused to. When I told her, I'd petition the court and force her to pay, she threatened to make it her life's work to turn you against me. I bounced a check every month for three years to pay for groceries, until the assistant District Attorney called me personally to tell me to knock it off. Your mom had a really nice Lexus, though, and you guys spent a lot of fun weekends in Lake Tahoe."

Still nothing from Remy. She barely blinked.

"It's not exactly breaking news, but your mother was an alcoholic, just like my mother was. What you may not remember is the time your mother left you in the car. Or when she left you at the park. Or when you were four, and your mother took off on a bender with her boyfriend and left you alone in her house for three days. I finally had to have the police smash her door down to come and get you. And when I asked the court to give me full custody of you, they refused, because your mother had a lot more money to hire better attorneys than I could."

Something clicked in Remy's eyes; the shadow of a memory, perhaps.

I let go of her arm. I didn't feel any better, and if I was indeed handing her my old backpack, it sure didn't look like she was taking it.

"Look," I continued, sighing, "I didn't want to tell you all this shit because, the thing is, the truth isn't always this beautiful thing that people say it is. The truth doesn't set you free. Sometimes, the truth locks you in a dark room and leaves you there for years. I know there wasn't a lot I did well as a father, but the one thing I always thought I could do was protect you. Protect you from the ugliness and the lies and the bleeding wounds that can only be inflicted by a person you love. But, um, I guess…not."

I had no idea what was going on behind Remy's confused gaze. I had broken my best friend and now I'd broken my daughter as well. Without a word, she turned and headed down the sidewalk.

I just let her go, then sat down on the curb like some kind of well-dressed homeless guy. Out of habit, I reached for my phone to check for messages, then remembered that it was dead—a victim of involuntary alcohol poisoning.

I loved karate movies when I was a kid. The best Sunday afternoons of my pre-adolescence were spent watching *Kung Fu Theater* on TV while eating Oreo cookies with a spoon after drowning ten of them in a glass of milk. Of course, Bruce Lee movies were the greatest, but I'd take any cheesy, old, poorly-dubbed martial arts film that I could find. I don't remember what it was called, but there was this one movie where the bad guy had developed this nasty technique where, with one swift blow, he could rip a dude's heart out of his chest and show it to him, still beating.

I never saw the selfie that the Bros took, but I know for a fact that it showed the two of them, me, and my still-beating heart in Keevan's hand, with my best friend and my daughter completely out of the frame.

NINE

I drove straight to Sydney's place. It was only 10:30 a.m., and my shift didn't start until 3 p.m. She asked me to text her when I got out of the meeting to let her know how things went, but that wasn't going to happen with an intoxicated phone. I considered calling her from a pay phone, until I realized there wasn't a single phone number in the world that I'd memorized. That, and I wouldn't even know where to find a pay phone these days. Maybe I could use my cell phone to locate one. Right?

I emerged from the gloom of the City into the cold, hazy sunshine of the east bay. At least northbound traffic wasn't bad at this time of the morning—gave me less opportunity to stew in my own juices. Nonetheless, ninety minutes is plenty of time to sow the seeds of doubt and self-loathing. I switched mindlessly between radio stations, aching for some kind of distraction, but it didn't help. Instead, I found myself testing the engineering limits of all four cylinders of my Nissan Versa sedan to get to Sydney's as fast as possible.

"No one just knocks on someone's door anymore," was her greeting. "What, are you from the 19th century?"

I gave her the brief but depressing synopsis. She flinched when I got to the part about the selfie, and I admittedly felt a certain satisfaction when an expression of guilt came over her. She took my phone and buried it in a plastic bag of rice to help dry it out, then offered me a drink. I declined, but told her, "There is something I want to talk to you about, though."

"Is it intense and emotional?" she asked. "I'm kind of thinking this is going to be intense and emotional."

"Probably something like that," I admitted.

"Then I need a drink." She reached into her fridge and pulled out a bottle of white wine. "You know, I always get nervous opening a bottle of wine around you. Like, you're judging me inside for drinking cheap, grocery store wine."

"Oh, I'd never do that," I said, settling into the immaculate sofa. "I'd totally just judge you on the outside."

Sydney found a wine key in the drawer and went to work on the cork. "Are you too Somm-y to drink this?" She turned the label towards me: Pierre Latrice Rhone Valley Viognier. Not horrible.

"I'm apparently not Somm-y at all anymore," I said. "But, no thanks. It's going to be a late night."

Sydney poured a glass that was completely unselfconscious of the fact that it wasn't noon yet. When she sat down next to me, I leaned over to kiss her forehead, lingering there a little while. Somms usually hate perfume of any kind, but her scent was mysterious, intoxicating and just *her*.

"What finally made you cheat on your husband?" I asked.

Sydney frowned and took a large gulp from her glass. She was quiet for a while, long enough that I wondered if I'd crossed a line.

"'Cheat' is an interesting word," she finally said. "Technically, yes, I am cheating on my husband, though we did discuss a trial separation. Well, I discussed it and he just nodded a lot and said, 'OK.' That said, he has been cheating on me for years."

"Really? He's been having an affair?"

Sydney nearly spit up her wine. "Oh, god no. He'd never. At least, I don't think he ever would, though sometimes I think it'd be good for him. No, he's been cheating in a whole different way."

"Like how?"

"He's been cheating me out of him." She gazed into her wine glass like she was reading the leaves at the bottom of a teacup. "Things really changed for us about five years ago. He started pulling away from me, and there was nothing I could do about it. And believe me, I tried everything. *Everything*." She shuddered and took a gulp that made the last one look like it came from an eye dropper.

"So, I lost interest in him as well. About two years ago, our marriage went completely sexless. We became great partners but little else. I never thought of myself as the cheating type, but um, here I am, right? I don't know."

She gave me an embarrassed half-smile and went back to her glass of wine. A storm raged under the surface of her pensive demeanor. She had given me all she wanted to give for now, thank you very much, and pressing the issue would not turn out well for me.

"So, where's all this unseemly adultery talk coming from?" she asked, flipping her attitude with the ease of an actress. "Truth be told, I was expecting you to bemoan this spectacular flame-out of yours."

"It's Remy," I sighed. "Ever since her mother died, she's been asking a lot of questions. Questions about what happened between her mom and me. She wanted to know 'the truth.' So I kind of told her this morning."

"Kind of?" Sydney asked.

"Well, that's the thing, isn't it? There are three sides to every story: his side, her side, and what really happened."

Sydney nodded. "But all she has is your side now."

Sydney got up from the couch and walked into the kitchen. Since she was practiced at it, she performed the maneuver with grace and ease, whereas every time I tried to extract myself from the dense layers of cushiony softness, I moved like a ninety-year-old after two hip replacements.

"So, what did you tell her?" she asked. "I mean, unless you don't want to talk about it, which I'd totally understand."

I guess I did want to talk about it, or I wouldn't have gone to Sydney's house and basically said, "I want to talk about Remy." But at that moment, my heart was tied in knots and nothing made sense.

"I think it's just that a daughter never knows her mother the way a husband knows his wife, and maybe ne'er the twain shall meet. You know what I mean?"

Sydney grimaced. "Sort of. You told Remy about her mother, but nothing about the person she was?"

I nodded. "Something like that. Jennifer was the Queen of the Scene, back in Seattle. There wasn't a band she didn't know or a club she couldn't get into or a bartender that wouldn't comp her drinks. Everyone knew her and everybody loved her, you know? She was the prototype Grunge Girl, all decked out with her omnipresent flannel and black Doc Martens and disenfranchised attitude. I mean, she basically invented that shit.

"And one day, she started coming to our shows. My shows, that nobody came to. And of all the wannabe rock stars—hell, of all the real rock stars—she could have had, she picked me. *Me*. Of all people."

Sydney opened the fridge and grabbed the bottle for a refill, and suddenly a drink sounded like a good idea. "When the band signed with Geffen Records," I said, "and we started getting a taste of all those juicy, rock star trappings, she loved it. She fed on it. She soaked in absolutely every second of it. Probably more than I did, even. I was her rock star, and she worshipped me, and it felt so validating."

"So, what happened?"

"The band had its fifteen minutes. And then it was over. And one day, I was a just a husband without a job, and the father of a screaming baby, and this walking, talking reminder of what we had and what we lost. What I lost. I used to be Superman, and suddenly I was just the guy who couldn't make the rent. And who wants to have sex with that guy?"

Sydney put the bottle back in the fridge without pouring a glass and came back to the couch. She kissed me in that perfect way, with all the softness and the silence and the feelings.

"That sucks, and I'm sorry," she whispered.

"It was a long time ago." And speaking of storms raging, I decided it was best to abandon ship on the conversation. "You're not having another glass? I'd take half, if you wanted to."

"Oh, help yourself," Sydney said. "I just remembered I have a conference call in about an hour, so that's it for me."

I tried to stand up from the couch but ended up turning over until my stomach was on the cushion, then pushed myself up from the front edge with my arms. Sydney enjoyed the display immensely.

"So," I said, trying to compose what was left of my cool, "is this call about the nonprofit you want to work with?"

"This part should just be a formality, and then the day after tomorrow I interview with the Board of Directors for the position."

"Hey, that's great!" I hoped I sounded enthusiastic and not guilty.

The truth was, I had forgotten almost everything Sydney told me about the new job she was trying to land. It had something to do with raising money for a non-profit organization that did…good things. Damn it all. I didn't forget; I wasn't listening. Again. It wasn't just my joints that needed replacement.

I stared at the refrigerator door and decided a glass of wine wasn't such a good idea after all.

Sydney came up behind me, slipped her arms around my waist and rested her head against my back. "You don't have to be Superman," she said quietly.

Maybe not. But perhaps a better man.

As I drove to work, I decided it was time to stress about something entirely different, just to mix things up: the Vineyard Problem and Shay.

Maybe Remy was right. Maybe Shay just needed some space to figure out our next move. Knowing him, he might have actually had a "thing" he had to "get to," and he was currently blowing up my dead phone with new ideas and next steps.

But probably not.

After obsessing all the way to Rutherford, I decided to forego the usual work routine and taste through some wine samples instead. Tasting was a Zen-like experience for me; it kept my monkey mind still and focused. Wine brokers dropped off a lot of sparkling wine this time of year, so tasting through a bunch of those seemed like a festive kind of thing to do.

I was barely on my third sample, a rather lovely Schramsberg Sparkling Rose, when Rick Dornin walked in. "I said to meet me in my office, not yours."

I looked up at him but kept swishing the rose around my mouth. It coated my pallet with a delicious creaminess that's nearly impossible to replicate in domestic sparklers. I spit it out. "What are you talking about?"

"I said to meet me at 2 p.m. You're late."

"Hold on." I scribbled down some notes. It was potentially a keeper for the by-the-glass program, if I could squeeze the price down. The Appellation wine list was a badge of honor: It was a vanity placement, and bragging rights for the winery, which I used to negotiate price.

"My phone is dead," I muttered. "I didn't get your message."

"Whatever," he brushed me off. "Come on."

Well, so much for Dornin forgetting about the bet. In the relative scheme of things, my demotion probably ranked fourth on the List of Corbett's Current Humiliations. Didn't make it an any less painful a prospect, though. What did that guy say in *Goodfellas*? "Everybody takes a beating sometime." Though taking a beating from someone like Dornin—let alone Andrew—was akin to having your little brother bitch slap you in the middle of lunch at the high school cafeteria.

I resigned myself to it and followed Dornin into his office. Andrew was nowhere to be seen.

Oh, shit.

Dornin took a seat at his desk, picked up a purple file folder and pointed it at me. "We're letting you go, effective immediately. In here is a Hold Harmless Agreement and two checks for two weeks' pay each. Sign the form and you can take both checks. Refuse to sign the form and you get one. Eventually, you'll end up signing the agreement, but you won't get the money if you don't do it here and now in my office."

Remy and I used to watch all the Charlie Brown TV specials when she was growing up. Of course, *A Charlie Brown Christmas* was the best (though there was the year that Remy became old enough to ask, "Daddy, why is Charlie Brown depressed?" and wouldn't accept an Adult Blow-Off Answer). There were these scenes where Charlie Brown is in school and the teacher is talking, and her voice is represented by a monotone bleating from a trumpet: "*Wa-wah, wahwah wa-wah?*" That's exactly what I heard from Dornin after the sentence, "We're letting you go."

I stared at the purple folder like a canister of smallpox. "Wait, that wasn't the bet. I said I'd subordinate to Andrew. You can't fire me."

"This isn't about our bet. I can fire you, and I am." His face was blank. Maybe he wasn't enjoying this, but he wasn't not-enjoying it, either.

"Why are you doing this?" I still wasn't touching the godforsaken Purple Folder of Death.

"How many reasons do you want?" He grew increasingly self-righteous the longer I held his stare. "I could probably list ten to start. But all that matters is that California is an At-Will state, and by law I can fire you for any reason, at any time. So, pick your personal favorite, sign the agreement, and get the fuck out of here."

I snatched the folder from his hand. "We'll just see who's getting fired, dickhead."

Righteous indignation aside, I wasn't particularly surprised that I was being fired. After the fiasco with my sit, I considered it a foregone conclusion. But as the days passed without incident, I allowed myself to think I was safe. Chef Dan gave no indication he wanted me out, and the Sommelier Police never showed up to cuff me and take me to Somm

Gladiator School. This had to be Dornin overstepping his bounds and generally being a tool.

I stormed into the kitchen and found Chef Dan. "Dornin's trying to fire me." I held up the Purple Death Certificate. "I can't believe for a moment you OK'd this."

Chef Dan wiped his face-goo with his apron towel. "I didn't ok it," he mumbled.

"Damn it, I knew it!" I yelled. "This is what I'm talking about, Dan. You've got to—"

Chef Dan took me by the elbow and guided me over to the end of the kitchen, away from the others, I supposed, though it's pretty much impossible to get privacy in a commercial kitchen.

"I didn't want to do it," he said quietly. Even his quiet voice sounded like a radial arm saw. "I had to do it."

"What? What do you mean 'you had to'?" I tried to keep it down, but my filter had pretty much imploded.

"This came from the top, Corbett. From the ownership group." I could tell he wasn't happy with this. "There's nothing I can do about it."

"But it's your decision," I implored. "You get to do the hiring and firing around here, it's part of your contract."

"No, you don't get it." He looked over his shoulder like spies were listening from the walk-in. "I can't take this kind of heat. The entire group wants you out. Fucking Tommy Allen, the top restaurant owner in the country. And Candace Meyer, for God's sake. Brogan Prescott, Felix Campanega—"

The eye twitch pegged a ten on the Richter Scale. "Whoa, whoa, whoa...Brogan Prescott? The video game guy, Brogan Prescott? He's part of our ownership group?"

"Not just a part, he's the majority stakeholder. He bought out Jeni Chen. I'm telling you, buddy, I can't fight this. I begged them to reconsider, but it was no-go."

I took the pen from Chef's apron pocket, opened the folder, signed the agreement and stuck the two envelopes in my jacket pocket. I gave Chef a hug.

"You're a good friend, Dan, and I appreciate the opportunity you gave me here."

Chef clutched me hard. "You're the best in the business, Rock Star. I'm going to hate competing against you."

I handed him the folder and placed his pen back in his apron. "You won't be."

The only good thing about a tiny office is that I didn't have much stuff in there. It took me all of ninety seconds to put my belongings in a wood, six-bottle wine box, take my key off its ring and leave it on the desk. And yes, I stole a bottle of '82 Chateau Petrus on my way out the door, because Brogan Prescott could go fuck himself and I was going to drink a five-thousand-dollar bottle of wine he paid for while I watched him do it.

My anger sent me into a kind of delirium, so I wasn't even conscious of the fact that I drove to the Fogelson Vineyard until I got there. That self-righteous asshat Dornin was right in one respect: there were a million reasons to fire me, but Brogan Prescott pulling his little power trip was the last one I imagined. And though I'm certainly not a conspiracy theory guy, Prescott probably had his stubby fingers in Fractal Equity Partners as well, for all I knew. All those Big Money Assholes knew each other. They all fucked the same polo horses and circle jerked at the same country clubs.

I sped about a hundred yards past the main entrance, pulled my car over to the side of the road, then got out and slammed the door with both hands, eliciting a noise from my beleaguered Nissan that sounded as much like an "ouch!" as anything. I paced back and forth across the sand and gravel, kicking up dirt as I went, watching the clouds of dust get thicker and darker around my fucking Payless Shoe Source imitation Steve Madden chukka boots. My heart surged with adrenaline as I completely ruined those Seriously Professional Douche Shoes. *Fuck you, you fucking shoes.*

I knew what I had to do. I hadn't done it in a long, long time, but I needed to now.

I popped open my trunk. Underneath layers of useless crap that at some point I strongly believed belonged in the trunk was a beat-up guitar case. I jostled it free of the detritus and opened it up. There she was, just as beautiful as the day I could afford to buy her—my Taylor Dreadnaught acoustic guitar.

I felt a bit guilty as I pulled the guitar out and assumed the position on the hood of my car. Not just because it had been years since I'd done this, but because it's flat-out stupid to leave a guitar in your car overnight, let alone for five years. Never mind it could have been stolen; the fluctuations between cold and heat would wreak havoc on the wood of a guitar's neck and body. In fact, I was shocked the poor, abused thing hadn't cracked in two.

It took about five minutes just to get it in tune, and though my ear was still good, I had no idea if I was even close to a standard E-natural. I let a few chords ring out into the cold afternoon air, then unconsciously found myself playing "Requiem for the Rain," the only instrumental song I ever wrote and played in Reality Star. It was pretty much a blatant rip-off of the riff from The Beatles' "Blackbird," but then again, every musician for the last fifty years has been trying to reinvent everything The Beatles did.

I stopped the song about halfway through, partly because I allowed my guitar-mind to wander, partly because my fingers didn't want to cooperate after years of neglect. I settled into a bluesy groove of sorts, kind of a minor-key deconstruction of the blues. Very nineties, very Seattle, I chuckled to myself.

Reality Star hadn't been like most of the bands that came out of that scene, which was one of the reasons it took us so long to get noticed and eventually signed. We put the "pop" in "power pop," even more so than the bands we emulated back then, like The Posies and Big Star. That was the music I loved though, the music I felt. That was the music that came out of me.

I've always thought it pretentious to talk about "my art" or "what makes me an artist" and all that crap, and I know I became downright resentful of the band after Dom bailed and we were dropped from the record label. But what I'd been missing—and needed so desperately in this moment—was the release valve that music gave me.

By the time I was fourteen, I was a fully-loaded RV on the road to becoming a messed-up kid. One day, Shay's father, in the single-greatest attempt to be a Cool Dad, got us tickets to see Husker Du with The Replacements at the Rialto Theater. It was an epiphany—the proverbial life-changing moment. I rushed home, dug out the money I'd been hiding from my mom, bought myself a knockoff Kramer Flying-V and a Gallien Krueger amp from Ricardo's Pawn Shop, and practiced until the tips of my fingers blistered and bled.

And this is what I did for countless teenage hours instead of knocking over school desks, breaking into cars, or drinking 12-packs of Pabst Blue Ribbon with the other freaks. When I was forty-four, I spent a shit ton of money on therapy to find out why things happened the way they happened, but at fourteen, all I knew was that it was *happening*. All I knew was that this fucking emotional tsunami raged inside of me, and I needed something to *do* with it, some way to process it.

Music saved me. The guitar found a way to mutate its wood and wires, sink into my skin, wrap its tendrils around my soul, and release the pressure. It wasn't a matter of "getting it out" by writing songs that expressed how I felt:

Oh, I'm so conflicted
Because I feel all this conflict

122 | JOHN A. TAYLOR

So come and moan with me

It was a matter of opening up the pressure valve and letting the sound and the motion work its medicinal magic. My guitar was six-string, 120-decibel Ritalin. Practicing was ritual. Playing was prayer.

Hagen is hardly a busy road in Coombsville, but the few cars that passed by didn't seem to notice or care about some dude sitting on the hood of his car, playing songs to grape vines. Love that about Napa. I strummed away for an hour or so, with no accompaniment except for a lone finch on a distant vine, auditioning her own song for spring. I knew I was done when I looked down at my shoes and apologized to them for my erratic behavior. I also knew I was done because I didn't feel like sawing off Brogan Prescott's head with a hedge trimmer and FedEx-ing it to the rest of the assholes in the owner's group. I was still frustrated and confused, just not at a felony level. But as the better angels of my nature put the hedge trimmer back in the garage, one thought crystalized stronger than any other: I wanted this.

I wanted this vineyard, this piece of land, this tangible thing I could touch and see and hold in my hands. This thing that wouldn't change with the current fashion or have seconds thoughts or make irrational decisions or leave me or die. This thing that wasn't new or hip or trending, whose value wasn't gauged in impressions, engagements, KPIs or unit sales.

I wanted *this*.

I opened the car door and reached for my iPhone risotto. I held down the power button and prayed, and in a few moments the little apple, the one that looked like some dude missing his dentures took a bite from it, appeared on the screen. I breathed a sigh of relief, even though the wallpaper swirled like a light show from The Fillmore circa 1968. I brought up my text messages and found that there was still nothing from Shay. Just as well, I guess. He was going to be even less enthusiastic about what I had to do next.

I keyed out a message to Sydney, saying, *I just got fired. Angry face.*

OMG, she texted back. *Not to point out the obvious, but you've had a really bad day. Oh, and you do know there's an emoji button for that, right?*

I need to go to New Mexico and see my cousin, I typed. *She may be my last hope now to buy this vineyard.*

Why's that?

I'll call on my way to the airport and explain. Shitty reception here.

I put my guitar in its case and placed it in the back seat. Perhaps I had subconsciously condemned the poor thing to a five-year prison sentence in my trunk, but no more. Now, it'd go back in the apartment and get the place of honor it deserved.

My phone beeped again. It was Sydney - *Wait, do you want some company? I love cacti and margaritas, though not necessarily together.*

That would be great, I texted back. *But I thought you had a thing tomorrow?*

It's ok. Why don't you come back here?

Ohhhh...pity sex? Lascivious face.

No. Dork.

I laughed and plugged the phone into the charger then sat in the car a few moments and gazed out at the vineyard, the brown branches almost bereft of leaves. Within days, the vines would be dormant, snuggling down for their long winter's nap. Maybe some part of my conscience had been lying dormant as well and was now trying desperately to wake up.

I couldn't shake the thought that, if I was going to get this vineyard, I wouldn't be able to hit the snooze button anymore.

TEN

Sydney swung the door open before I could even knock. "I know you!" she exclaimed. "You're Hashtag Drunk iPhone Guy!"

"Jesus Christ." I nearly puked a lung on the spot. "Don't tell me that's a thing now?"

"It's not," she replied, turning back into the house. "But I couldn't resist."

Apparently, in the twenty-five minutes it took me to get to her place, Sydney had already purchased airline tickets, rented a car and got us a hotel room. "We need to be out of here in ten minutes," she yelled from her bedroom as she packed.

"We'll swing by your place and you can pack. Quickly. Oh, and it's going to be about twenty degrees at night in Albuquerque, so plan accordingly."

Her efficiency was not only scary, it was a bit out of left field. But when I told her she didn't have to do all that, she brushed me off with a casual, "I'm a planner."

I leaned against the island in her kitchen. She had an hourglass egg timer on the counter, like something out of the 1950's. "We're not going to Albuquerque," I said. "We're going to Los Alamos."

She peeked out of the bedroom, folding a sweater. "How far is that from Albuquerque?"

"I have no idea."

She shrugged and went back into the bedroom. "Oh, well, we're starting in Albuquerque. Guess we'll find out."

I milled around the kitchen for a bit, wondering if I was hungry and wondering if Sydney had anything to help with that. I'm not one of those guys who doesn't eat during times of crisis. If we were in the middle of a nuclear war, I'd be the one shielding my eyes from the blinding flash, asking, "Hey, does anybody else here want a sandwich?"

An old-fashioned teaspoon sat next to the egg timer on the counter. Like, an actual spoon for tea—a delicate little silver thing that held tea leaves. It was tarnished and nicked and bent in a few places, like it had fallen into the garbage disposal one too many times.

"It was my grandmother's," Sydney said. I hadn't noticed she'd come out of the bedroom. "She died when I was just a baby, but my mom said I'm exactly like her." Sydney took the heirloom from me and held it in her palm. "I'm even named after her. I don't know. We lost every picture Mom had of her in the fire."

She placed the spoon next to the egg timer, paused a moment, then adjusted spoon again about a quarter-inch closer to the timer.

"I'm sorry," I said.

"You should be." She smiled and returned to the bedroom.

"That's not what I meant—"

"I know what you meant, goofball," she shouted back. "Oh, and hey, I'm sorry if you were hoping for some tragedy sex, but we just don't have the time."

"Well, not 'tragedy sex,'" I said as she emerged from the bedroom with her overnight bag in tow. "That makes it sound like I lost my face, not my job."

"Ah, well, consolation sex then."

I sighed and picked up her bag and headed for the door. "That makes it sound like I wanted Amy Adams, but I got you instead."

"Amy Adams?" She laughed. "That's random."

"Amy Adams is hot," I protested.

"Alright, you can call me 'Amy' tonight. How about that?"

I turned and kissed her. "I already do, but very quietly."

She pushed me away playfully and we walked out to the car. I threw her bag in the trunk, and as she climbed into the passenger seat, she seemed to notice but didn't say anything about the guitar in back.

. . .

We drove through downtown Yountville then headed south on 29 toward my place.

"So," she said. "Why are we going to New Mexico?"

"To see my cousin Marnie," I replied.

"And why the sudden urge for family reconnection?"

"She's a chemical engineer at Los Alamos National Laboratory." I weaved in and out between a few cars going about thirty miles per hour under the speed limit. I really didn't like Highway 29 at this time of day. At least one out of three cars were driven by people who'd spent the whole day wine tasting and simply shouldn't be behind the wheel. I think the Highway Patrol made their monthly DUI quota in one weekend between 5 p.m. and 7 p.m. on this ten-mile stretch of road.

"A couple years ago, Shay and I gave Marnie the prototype to a new kind of wine capsule we invented, so she could test it out and see if it worked. The capsule has this little sensor in it that's supposed to tell you if your wine is becoming oxidized. We wanted to develop it to a point where it could send a Bluetooth message to your phone that would say, 'Bottle eight in case number 104 is beginning to oxidize, you should drink it tonight.' But the thing is, it can take years or even decades for a wine to start oxidizing, so Marnie was going to use her lab to basically bake the wine, speed up the oxidation process and get us some results."

"Wow," Sydney said. "You're a man of many talents, aren't you?"

"Say my name, baby." I winked at her.

"Oh my God, did you just wink at me?" Her voice tightened like I'd just touched her No-No Square.

"Yes," I replied cautiously.

"Don't ever wink at me. Winking is creepy."

"It wasn't a creepy wink!" I protested.

"Winking is inherently creepy. It's a patriarchal dog whistle and the ultimate physical representation of mansplaining," she retorted. "Trust me. I've put some thought to this."

"Apparently so."

"Anyway, cousin Marnie…?"

"Right. So, a couple of months went by and she didn't say anything about it. She wouldn't return calls or emails, until finally she emailed this like, ninety-page report with all these diagrams and formulas and shit that Shay and I couldn't even begin to decipher. So, I tried calling and emailing again and still got nothing back from her.

"The thing is, around that same time, Shay was starting to line up consulting gigs for us that took up a lot of spare time and paid really well, so the capsule project kind of went to the back-burner as we started ramping up our consulting firm."

We hit the usual traffic congestion around downtown which stretched tortuously to the intersection of Highway 12 and beyond; I said a little prayer that we wouldn't miss our flight. "Anyway, now that I'm a jobless deadbeat and the app is pretty much dead, the capsule may be my last hope of raising enough capital to start the winery. And if Marnie isn't going to return my calls, then I'm going to have to just knock on her door."

"I was going to ask you about that," Sydney said. "Did they give you any reason for firing you?"

"You mean, besides the obvious?" I shook my head. "No, get this shit: You remember me telling you about that guy Brogan Prescott, the one who wants to turn the Fogelson Vineyard into some kind of video game? He bought out a member of Appellation's ownership group, then pressured the rest of the members into firing me."

Sydney's eyes widened in genuine shock. "Are you serious? Why would he do that?"

"My only guess is that he thinks that if I don't have a source of income, I won't be able to get a loan to buy the place, and I'll lose my purchase option. So, again, this is why I have to talk with Marnie. If I can't put together an all-cash offer now, I'm sunk."

Sydney turned and stared out her window. "What an asshole."

"Tell me about it," I grumbled. "It's not like the guy doesn't have a gazillion dollars. He could go buy any freaking vineyard for sale in the valley. Hell, he could buy any vineyard *not* for sale."

Sydney began to say something, but my phone beeped, and I scrambled for it. My heart sank when I saw it was a voicemail from a number I didn't recognize, and not a call or a text from Shay. As much as I loved having Sydney with me, it should have been Shay sitting there, plotting and scheming and planning and generally being his usual cross between a drill sergeant and a cheerleader.

I couldn't bring myself to believe he just walked away, though I wouldn't hold it against him if he did. At the same time, I felt too guilty to reach out to him yet again:

Good Sir Knight, I see that you have a lance through your heart, but if you wouldn't mind getting up on that horse again and charging the horde just one more time? I'd already put him through enough.

When we arrived at my apartment, an oversized manila envelope, frayed and torn around the edges, sat on the doormat. I opened it and discovered about a thousand pages of documents: Real Estate Transfer Disclosures for the Fogelson Vineyard. I figured it'd be appropriate if not completely tedious reading for the flight, so I threw the package in my carry-on with the rest of my stuff.

Once at the airport, I was surprised to see we were booked on a United Airlines flight and not a more regional airline like Southwest. Sydney grabbed the tickets and ducked into the gift shop while I checked my phone again. Still nothing from Shay, and nothing from Remy, either, whom I hadn't heard from since she left me on the sidewalk. Part of me wanted to chalk it up to a malfunction with my wine-bathed mobile device, but the other part of me knew better.

Surprise number two came when they announced First Class

boarding, and Sydney told me it was time to go. "Holy shit, are you serious? I haven't flown First Class in, like, never."

Sydney cracked a huge smile. "Well, I'm glad you like it."

"I love it, but it's not the sort of thing I can…I mean, I only got four weeks' severance—"

"Oh, just hush. This is a mini-vacation for me, and I'm going to do it right."

When we got to our seats, I took out the giant package of documents and then placed my bag in the overhead bin. Sydney plopped into the window seat, reached into her shopping bag and took out a box of Bose headphones.

"I've always wanted to try these," she said. "They're supposed to cancel out airplane noise."

As I took the giant tome of papers from the envelope and placed them on my tray table, the flight attendant came by for a drink order. It was awesome enough that I fit in the chair without having to break my shins in half and store my legs under the seat in front of me, but a drink order before we even left? I started to wonder if tray tables had to be put up for takeoff, or if that was just a burden for the *hoi polloi* in Economy Class. They'd probably let me keep my seat tilted back, too. First Class was apparently a libertarian paradise of limitless potential and personal freedom. And free freaking alcohol. I didn't care if I had to sell meth for the rest of my life, there was no going back from this.

"Hey…hey, hey!" Sydney said with increasing volume. "Hey, say something to me." She had the headphones on, and a look on her face like she was tasting chocolate for the first time.

"Testing, one two three," I said a bit softly, just to mess with her a little.

"Oh my God, these things are amazing," she said, again too loudly. "It's like I can barely hear you speak, and I can't hear, like, the hum. You know what I mean? *The hum?*"

"I know what you mean," I laughed. "I'm glad you like them."

"What?" She sounded like my Uncle Glen, who needed hearing aids in his later years but refused to wear them because they made him feel old.

I shook my head and turned back to the pile of documents. There was a handwritten note on top:

Mr. Thomas,

I wasn't sure if you had an agent or not and Mr. Fogelson didn't know either, so I'm delivering these to you directly. Please review the enclosed documents and sign the attached form, which states you've read and understand them. If you have any questions or need an agent, I'd be happy to help!

Sincerely,

Janis Mandel

Funny I hadn't thought of it yet, but I probably would need an agent, and one with expertise in land purchases. I'd met a handful of good ones through my consultation work, though I wasn't familiar with this Janis Mandel. Contemplating the ominous pile of paperwork in front of me, I figured I'd probably need a team of experts. There had to be at least eight hundred pages of title reports, zoning reports, geological maps, surveys, and soil reports. It was daunting just to look at, even with a free gin and tonic in hand.

"Hey, I got you a birthday present," Sydney said suddenly. She still had the headphones on, and her voice sounded like she was trying to get my attention from the other side of the beer stand at a football game.

She reached into her shopping bag and produced a brand-new iPhone X.

"Oh my God, really?" I felt like I was stealing as I took the box from her. "You know, it's not my birthday…"

"Happy birthday!" she squealed. Really loud.

"Babe, you didn't have to do this, and—"

"I know it's not your birthday," she laughed. "But I do know your current phone is completely fucked."

Toxic White Business Guy sitting across the aisle from me gave me that slight, sideways glance that says, *Walmart shoppers like you don't belong in First Class.* Ignoring him, I reached over and pulled the headphones away from Sydney's ears.

"You're a little loud when you have these things on," I whispered.

"Oh," she said, pushing my hands back against her ears. "The difference with these things is incredible." She immediately went back to inappropriately loud.

I gave her a quick kiss and mouthed *thank you,* putting the iPhone back in her bag. I turned back to the stack of paperwork and sighed. *Where once there was a forest...*

Oh, and I was right: I didn't have to put my tray table up when we took off. I swear, First Class was like being ushered into the Golden Chamber of Revelations and being told that all that Illuminati shit is totally real, or having Jesus walk up to you with a flask of wine and say, "Hi, I'm Jesus, what can I do for you?"

The Title Report was at least a hundred pages itself. The Fogelsons had owned their piece of land longer than I even realized. It was originally ten times its current size, and apparently there was a ton of legal hassle back in 1891 surrounding the Quitclaim of Title from the original spelling of their name, Foggleschoen. By the time I got to the geological survey, my eyes—and my brain—had glazed over. I was done.

I looked over at Sydney, who was merrily thumbing through the pages of *Us Weekly,* her headphones now permanently affixed to her ears. She smiled blissfully when she caught me staring at her, then suddenly leaned into me.

"Do you want a hand job?" she asked. She said it like she was trying to clarify her Jumbo Jack order at the drive-through window for the third time.

Mortified but still amused, I started to reach for her headphones, but she pivoted around in her chair.

"Here's the thing, that whole 'Mile High Club' stuff is a myth. I've tried having sex on a plane before, and believe me, it doesn't work."

It was like listening to the town crier in 18ᵗʰ century London. The two passengers directly in front gave us the Universal Half-Head-Turn of Disapproval.

"But what I *can* do is throw a blanket over your lap, you know, like we're cold. Then I can give you a hand job underneath it and no one will even notice."

No one, that is, except for everyone down to row twenty-two, who just heard her announcement.

"Tell me what you like, baby." She switched to Sexy Voice, only it was the Hundred-Decibel Sexy Voice.

At this point, there was nothing left for me to do except bury my face in my hands and laugh in horror. I didn't even notice that the flight attendant had crouched down next to me until he spoke.

"Ma'am," he said in his most practiced-polite voice, "I need to ask you to try and keep your voice down."

"I would absolutely love another vodka soda," Sydney replied. "Thank you!"

The attendant rolled his eyes, stood up and walked off. I looked at Sydney like a fifth grader who just got busted for cheating on the spelling quiz. She smiled and went back to her magazine…

And winked at me.

It was nearly midnight by the time we picked up the rental car and got to the hotel, but I was still pretty amped up. I never really understood it when people said, "You must be tired from all that traveling." Installing a quarter mile of drainpipe makes you tired. A ten-hour shift at a restaurant makes you tired. Sitting on a plane sipping free gin and tonics doesn't make you tired, unless they're really, really heavy gin and tonics.

Sydney had reserved us a suite at the Hotel Andaluz, and it was magnificent. I was going to protest the cost again, but she was apparently a woman on a mission for fun, so I just rolled with it.

The room was bigger than my apartment, and the bed was whatever size is larger than King Size, like Oligarch Size or Benevolent Overlord Size. Whatever size, it was a vast savannah of softness and comfort, and I wanted to be buried in it.

Sydney straddled me as I sank into the mattress. "Seriously, what is it about hotels where you just have to have sex in them?" she asked. "Is it like, marking your territory or is there some kind of hormone that's released by the fresh sheet smell?"

I wrapped my hands around her waist and flipped her over. "It's like, 'you paid cash money for a room with nothing but a bed in it. Now what are you going to do?'"

She reached for my pants. "Corbett Thomas. Now what are you going to do?"

And thus we had All The Sex. Sex on the bed, sex on the couch, sex on the little table with the old school phone on it. Sex on the floor, sex next to the window, sex on the semi-pointless armchair that lives in every corner of every hotel room on the planet. Loud sex, quiet sex, positions that failed and others that were now committed to memory for future reference. There was intimate sex, slow sex, tender sex and even a fair dose of confessional sex ("You are the most," "I have never," "All I want is…")

It ended in one of the purest moments of physical and emotional release that I'd ever experienced. We lay in the breathless, sweaty, foggy daze of afterglow, and the fact that it was almost 2:00 a.m. on one of the craziest days of my life hit me upside the head like a handful of Quaaludes. Maybe it was the delirium, or maybe it felt like there was nothing left to lose at that point, but I rolled over on my side and faced Sydney.

"So, what if I was to say to you, you know, something about love, and perhaps, the idea of being or wondering whether or not one is in a state similar to something...like that?"

Sydney chuckled. "Oh, you romantic artist types. Such a way with words."

I leaned in and kissed her, but as I pulled away the look on her face had changed completely. A small stream of tears trickled from the corners of her eyes. She didn't weep or make any kind of crying sound, and thankfully she wasn't a snot-crier, either.

"Why would you possibly love me?" she whispered.

"What's there not to love?" I told her. "You're smart and funny and gorgeous and you offer me hand jobs on airplanes."

That made her laugh again as she pulled me on top of her. "Right answer."

"This is actual pillow talk, you know."

"And you've got about ninety seconds before the coma starts."

It was true. One of the many discoveries we had made together was that Sydney passed out like a guy after sex. She came, she saw, she conquered, and she passed out, like Ambien-with-a-NyQuil-chaser passed out, complete with snoring and drooling. It was sexy in its own weird way.

She did that thing where she traced my eyebrow with her thumb. It was hypnotic. "Here's the thing, I've come to believe that we love a person when they love the part of you that needs to be loved."

"Oh, well, that's easy then," I said. "I love the part of you that's

Sydney Cameron. If one were to use such a word to describe the aforementioned feelings."

I wasn't sure if that was the right thing or wrong thing to say, as it made the tears switch from Class One to Class Three rapids in an instant. She wrapped her legs around my hips. There was no way she could be expecting Round Fifteen.

"Alright," she said. "If one were to start using this word of which you speak, what part of you needs to be loved?"

My elbows, was my first thought; I was getting tired of holding myself up. I scooped my arm under her shoulder and flipped us back onto our sides.

"When I was married, and the shit hit the fan, my wife checked out on me. Emotionally, physically, everything. You came into my life when the shit started hitting the fan again, and yet all you seem to do is help me find a new fan." Her hand slipped from my face and her eyes eyelids drooped. We didn't have long.

"I suppose I would love you because you love the part of me that keeps failing."

Her eyelids finally acquiesced and stayed shut. "Wrong answer," she murmured.

I waited for her to enlighten me with the right one, but none was coming. Sleep had overwhelmed her, though the tiniest smile played across her lips. I leaned in and kissed her forehead, then closed my eyes to let the sound of her breathing lull me to sleep.

But then she whispered languidly, as if from a place of dreams, "I love the part of you that still believes."

ELEVEN

It didn't even occur to me what a half-baked and potentially pointless endeavor the whole trip was until we were about a half-hour away from Marnie's house in Los Alamos. I hadn't talked to her or her husband Greg in almost two years, and for all I knew, they'd moved to Tallahassee or Indonesia in that time. Hell, they could have moved across the street and I wouldn't know. The phone number I had for Marnie worked as of a few years back, and though Marnie never answered it, it was time to give it one more try.

"Straight to voicemail," I said to Sydney, who insisted on driving. "But that's nothing new for like, years."

"Well, we'll see. We'll be there soon enough."

Yeah, because we're breaking the very laws of space and time. Sydney decided to go with a Dodge Challenger at the rent-a-car place, after convincing the manager to let her look under the hood first and confirm the car was packing a 351 Hemi. We rolled out onto Highway 25 under the crisp, winter sun, and the blacktop became her own personal Autobahn. I aged about six years on the thirty-minute rocket ride between Albuquerque and Santa Fe, and by the time we were back out on the high desert flats, I had made peace with an inevitable road death like something straight out of *Mad Max*. At least it would be fast. Like, a-hundred-and-fifteen-miles-an-hour fast.

"I'm sorry if this whole thing turns out to be a bust," I said. "I probably should have thought this out a bit more."

"We're having an adventure," Sydney answered, weaving between two little white cars. "If she isn't there, we'll see what we can do about tracking her down. No worries."

I loved her attitude and wished I could cop it. I only slept a few hours the night before, having spent most of the dark hours staring at the ceiling and stressing out. The capsule idea was pretty much my last

hope of finding a way to raise the money needed for the winery, unless
Shay had some other idea. For all I knew, Shay was halfway to the
Caribbean, having thrown in the towel on his idiot friend Corbett and
the Endless Cycle of Stupid Ideas. Oh, and then there was this whole
issue with Brogan Prescott getting me fired. A seriously dick move no
matter how I looked at it. I guess the Ant Queen *really* wanted her
virtual cave.

Siri directed us through the streets of Los Alamos, a quaint if not
aging town, nestled discreetly in the desolate beauty of New Mexico.
The lab had been around since the 1950s, and my guess was that it
pretty much dominated the growth and economy of the community. I'd
never visited Greg and Marnie out here, though they'd come to Seattle a
couple of times and even joined us for a few Thanksgivings in
California back when the ex and I still thought that spending holidays
together in awkward discomfort was a healthy and productive choice
for Remy.

We wove through narrow, suburban streets until we arrived at a
cute, southwest-style bungalow, complete with brown, faux-adobe walls
and squared-off windows with whitewashed frames. By contrast, the
front yard was a disaster. It was all rock and cactus, as was the water-
depleted style for the area, but the rocks had been overtaken by shoots
of brown, dead weeds from one end of the property to the other. There
was a lone elm tree in front that looked like it had shed its leaves for the
winter completely unmonitored. The whole vibe of the place was that
no one had lived there for at least a year. I felt deflated before I even got
out of the car.

Sydney parked in the driveway and we walked the little stone path
to the front door. Animal poop of unknown variety littered the cracked
concrete walkway. It may have been cat poop, or small dog poop, or
possibly even coyote poop. Whichever animal it came from, there was a
ton of it, as if every local mammal had a meeting one day and passed an

ordinance to make Marnie's front yard the Official Los Alamos Public Feral Animal Restroom.

Sydney and I paused tentatively on the front porch, which was covered with a carpet of dried, brown elm leaves. Before I could even reach over and ring the doorbell, we were startled by a voice that crackled from an unseen speaker.

"Who's the female?" It was a woman's voice. Possibly Marnie's, but I couldn't tell for sure. Sydney peered at me; all I could think to do was shrug.

"Hello," Sydney said into the air, trying her best to seem pleasant. "My name is Sydney Cameron."

"I don't know Sydney Cameron," the voice said.

"Marnie, is that you?" I asked, also trying to sound neighborly despite the increasing weirdness. "It's me, Corbett. Corbett Thomas."

Silence. Now it was Sydney's turn to shrug.

"We just came by for a visit," I said. "Are you inside? Can we come in?"

More silence. I looked around for the speaker, or wherever the camera had to be, but couldn't see anything obvious. The doorbell was one of those old-fashioned, nipple-style brass thingies, so it probably wasn't in there. There was nothing on the front door that—

"Sydney Cameron," the voice intoned, "do you have a cell phone with you?"

Sydney took the phone from her purse and held it up. "Why, yes. Yes, I do."

"Power your phone down and place it in the black pot next to you. Then get back in your car and drive it to the end of the block and wait there."

"What the fuck?" I mouthed silently to Sydney, but she shook her head.

"Sure, no problem," she answered.

A large, black, cast-iron Dutch oven sat next to the door, partially covered in leaves. Sydney took the lid off, put her phone in it, and put the lid back on. She leaned in to kiss me on the cheek and whispered, "See you on *Dateline*," then headed back to the car.

"Marnie, what's going on here?" I asked.

"Do the same thing with your phone," the voice replied.

"I left mine in the car." Wherever that damn camera was, it was really well hidden.

I heard the sound of a *click* and the door opened slowly. At first, I didn't recognize her, but it was Marnie alright, dressed in a nondescript, gray T-shirt with matching sweatpants and a pair of New Balance running shoes that were so sparkling white, there's no way she had run in them.

She scanned me head to toe like I was some kind of FDA-rejected meat byproduct, then turned and retreated back into the house, leaving the door open. I took that as a sign that it was OK to come in, though making a beeline in the opposite direction felt like a much better idea.

The door opened into a large living room, completely devoid of furniture save for a single black armchair with a two-drawer end table next to it. At the east end of the room, next to the kitchen, was a small, white dining table with a single white chair pulled up to it, and a plate, knife, fork and water glass set on top. A portion of the west wall appeared to be decorated with some kind of artsy, corrugated steel window dressing, but as I stepped further into the room I discovered she had simply covered the only window with a thick, metal sheet. The whole scene was an otherworldly combination of Zen utility, anal retentive cleanliness and paranoid solitude.

Yet all that was nothing compared to the display on the north wall. Spread across three hundred square feet was a massive montage of papers, pictures, maps, magazine clippings and newspapers, overlaid with index cards inscribed with various numbers and letters in bold, red pen. Marnie stood just left of center of the bizarre tableau, feverishly sorting through a series of clips. It was like something straight out of one of those cop shows where the obsessed detective has turned his office into a convoluted map of clues.

"What the living *fuck*, Marnie?" I whispered. I knew it was an uncouth thing to say, but it's not every day you take an actual step into The Twilight Zone.

I took a few cautious steps closer to the wall, toward an area that had a bunch of pages torn from a yearbook—maybe a high school yearbook—with certain kids' pictures circled, and handwritten notes on index cards next to them. I leaned in closer to read one of the cards when I was startled by Marnie's voice.

"Four of them were in Science Club," she said. "That's only eighteen percent of all the students that went missing, but fully forty percent of the student counselors, and a third of the entire membership of the club."

Before I could respond with anything—which would have been only a slight variation on the earlier "What the living fuck?" theme—Marnie shoved a newspaper clipping at me.

"Today's date, one year ago exactly," she said. Her voice was professionally conversational, like the way a doctor talks to another doctor when discussing a patient's prognosis. The clipping was from the *Bureau County Republican*, and the headline read, "Sheriff to Reduce Disappearance Briefings."

"They were giving up. Not as much information coming in, they said. One year ago today. But they were ignoring the moon data." She took the clip back and pinned it to the wall where she had initially retrieved it, smoothing the edges out gently, almost affectionately.

"Marnie," I said, trying not to sound completely freaked out, "where's Greg?"

She moved quickly to her left, reached up and removed a picture. "Greg Dougherty," she whispered. "Born December 9th, 1986. Graduate of the University of Illinois, Urbana-Champagne, taught AP History and Literature at Princeton High School beginning in 2015." She turned to show me the picture. "Three of the missing adult chaperones were born in December, but not one of the students. Not one."

I scanned the picture of the wide-eyed young teacher. "No," I said. "I meant Greg, your husband."

Marnie's face twitched just the slightest bit, then she turned and put the picture of the teacher back in its place. "It's the ALAMO data, they didn't want anyone to know. Those weren't meteor impact flashes." She dashed toward me, ripping a sheet off the wall. "I did the spectral analysis. I did it. I confirmed it. Those flashes occurred *above* the lunar surface!"

It finally dawned on me: the mass disappearance in Princeton, Illinois. It was all over the news a few years back. Thirty-three high school kids and teachers, out at some kind of camping retreat, all went missing. No trace, no clue. It was the largest confirmed mass disappearance in U.S. history. At the end of a long investigation, authorities concluded it had to be a horrific case of human trafficking, but of course, the incident brought out the Tin Foil Hat Crowd *en masse,* with conspiracy theories ranging from alien abduction to international terrorism to time travel. And now, it appeared, Marnie was more than neck-deep into this whole thing. I had no idea what to make of it. Or her.

"Marnie, what's happened here?" I tried not to sound pandering or patronizing. "Are you still working at the lab? And where's Greg?"

Marnie took a stuttering breath and nodded quickly. "The Automated Lunar and Meteor Observatory at the Marshall Space Flight Center in Huntsville."

"Greg's there? In Huntsville?"

"They stopped releasing data." She turned back to the wall and ran her finger down a line from a picture of the moon to some kind of chart. "It was crowdsourced data analysis, and then they just stopped releasing it. That's when the briefings slowed down. One year later to the day, you show up."

It felt like the ground, the sky, gravity, and all the Fundamental Laws of Reality decided to go on vacation for a year and leave me without a babysitter. Obviously, Marnie was not well, but I had no idea what to do or say about it, or if doing or saying anything would make things better or worse. Greg was a great guy, an artisan who made patio furniture out of cottonwood trees, and kind of the yang to Marnie's yin. He sincerely loved Marnie, and I couldn't imagine him being a passive party to this craziness.

"Maybe we should go find Greg and like, have some lunch?" I suggested. "We can talk more about—"

"You have to leave," she said. Her strangely professional tone started to crack. "Open the door and close it behind you. Do not remove the phone from the pot. Take the pot with you, leaving the lid on until you drive away."

I didn't want to upset her or make things worse, but it felt wrong to just leave her like that. "Marnie, are you sure you don't—"

"Open the door and close it behind you." Her voice was almost a perfect octave higher than it was before. "Take the pot with you, leaving the lid on until you drive away."

"Alright, OK," I said, opening the door. "Look, you have my phone number. If there's anything you need, you call me anytime. Tell Greg that I came by. Tell him I said hello and would love to see him."

I walked out and picked up the black kettle, which was solid and heavy in that way that things made before 1980 were solid and heavy. Marnie appeared in the doorway, holding a picture at arm's length. It was a photo of a young girl with a Mona Lisa-like smile, shy and tentative. Her features appeared to be Chinese, with a smattering of freckles across the bridge of her nose.

"She was Remy's age," Marnie said. The professional tone was gone, replaced by what memory told me was Marnie's true voice, but soaked in fear and remorse. "She was seventeen, and now she's gone."

I wanted to speak but I was drowning. No, sinking, really; I was drowning without fighting. Sinking in silence and blind confusion.

"She's gone!" Marnie shouted then slammed the door.

I bolted for the sidewalk. I took a wild guess that Sydney drove down the block northbound, but when I reached the intersection and the car wasn't in sight, I realized I'd guessed wrong and turned around. I suppose I looked pretty ridiculous, running down the street with this giant Dutch Oven clutched in my hands—a thought that was confirmed when I caught up with Sydney and she said, "Oh, you brought lunch. How thoughtful."

I set the pot down and quickly opened the lid. "Here," I said, handing Sydney her phone. I scanned the neighborhood quickly, searching in near-panic for God knows what. Maybe a road sign that read "Reality - Next Exit" or something similar.

"Hey, are you OK?" Sydney asked. "What happened in there?"

At the end of the cul-de-sac was a red dirt lot with nothing but an old slab foundation in the middle. An abandoned rehab project, perhaps, or the remains of a home fire. I ran towards it with pure fight-or-flight speed. The way my feet slammed against the pavement and the burning in my quads felt instinctual. It felt right.

The vacant lot ended at the edge of a grade overgrown with scrub that sloped down about twenty yards. I scrambled down the slope until I couldn't run any farther, having reached a fence that separated the property line from the rest of the back country. I clutched an old, wooden fence post and breathed hard. All I wanted was a time machine, but I'd have settled for a brown paper bag I could hyperventilate into.

My eyes stung worse than any desert wind could torment them. The girl in Marnie's picture wasn't Remy's age—she was at least seven years younger. Seven years since Marnie saw Remy. Seven years since we got together as a family, since we talked about something that wasn't my Latest Fantastic Idea, since I hadn't forced the world to look at itself through a Corbett-shaped lens. Seven years that I had my head so far up my own ass that I couldn't read between the lines of Marnie's initial report on the capsule and seen that it was as much a cry for help as anything else.

Beyond the fence the mesa stretched out for a half mile, then dove into a desolate valley that lingered all the way to the highway and beyond. There was a familiar beauty about the panorama, something that reminded me of home. Tucson was even more barren than this, but certainly no further removed from New Mexico's geographic DNA than a first cousin.

But Tucson wasn't the home that came to mind, or should I say, came to heart. It wasn't simply the expansive valley, forged by millions of years of river wash, that reminded me of Napa. It was the permanence. The stability. As a fame and hormone-fueled twenty-something, those two concepts meant little to me: home was a van that stole through the night; time was a loan that never had to be paid back. As a man waist-deep in middle age, I was beginning to see permanence and stability as having a magnetic attraction that called to me in the form of ten acres of grape vines. At the same time, stability and permanence were absolutely terrifying. Not because of the change in lifestyle they demanded—one which I now in fact craved—but because I still didn't know if they could apply to love. They never had before.

I felt Sydney's presence behind me, even before she gently rested her head on my arm. She stood with me in the silence of the high desert. *If one were to start using this word of which you speak...* A cricket chirped his lonely call for a mate.

I turned to Sydney and locked my hand into hers. "Let's go," I said. "There's something I want to do."

TWELVE

First, we needed a bottle of wine. A really, really good bottle of wine. Back at the car, Sydney took her phone out and I directed Siri to find us "the best wine shop in Santa Fe, New Mexico." Of course, that was nearly pointless. We were given a list of fifteen different establishments across the Four Corners region that were somehow associated with alcohol, ranging from Discount Liquor Barn in Santa Fe, Arizona, to The Barrio Brinery, a restaurant specializing in pickles. We settled on a place called Susan's Fine Wine and Spirits and Sydney sped back onto the highway.

As we pulled up to the store, Sydney said, "So, listen. This one's on me. I want you to pick out any wine you want. Any bottle at all. I want to watch The Master in action."

"Former almost-Master," I replied. "Look, that's sweet, but—"

"I insist," Sydney said, getting out of the car.

The ironic thing about wine shops is that they all smell like wine gone bad—spilled wine and old wine, dust and cork taint and humidity and mold. It's practically universal, the Wine Shop Odor, and it filled me with a kid-in-the-candy-store anticipation, which is exactly what I needed at that moment. We strolled down the domestic pinot aisle until we reached the front counter, where an older guy, probably in his late sixties, was peering at the pages of a huge wine tome through wire-rimmed reading glasses.

"Good afternoon," he greeted us. "Anything I can help you with?"

"Absolutely. We need a bottle of wine."

The gentleman took off his glasses and scanned the room for a few moments. "Hmmm." He smiled. "It appears we've got a few of those. Any one in particular?"

"Anything that really excites you," I said.

"Oh!" The clerk brightened up. I guess his name was Doug, because he had a plastic tag pinned to his generic black polo shirt that read "Doug."

"Well, what kind of price range are we talking about?"

"No price range!" Sydney shouted. "Whoop!"

"Something you've brought in recently that made you go 'wow' or 'holy shit that's amazing.' That's what we're looking for," I added.

Doug closed his book and stood up. "Ah, well there's quite a difference between 'wow' and 'holy shit.'"

"Let's err on the side of 'holy shit.'"

Sydney chimed in, "Unless you've got 'da-a-a-amn, bitches!' Then we'll take that."

"Ah-ha," Doug said. I think he got the point if not the humor. "Come with me, then."

Doug guided us to a small room with glass doors and compact shelves of wine racks. He took out a key, unlocked the door and lead us inside, where the air felt dry and a perfect fifty-seven degrees. "I think I've got just the thing in here," he said. "Especially if you like Bordeaux."

So, yes and no. Here's the thing: I have a soft spot in my heart for Bordeaux. It was a 1982 Chateau Lynches-Bages that first opened my eyes to the fact that wine could mean more than a box of Franzia. On top of that, there would be no Napa without Bordeaux. Robert Mondavi, the Patron Saint of All Things Napa, deliberately modeled his wines on the Bordeaux style in the early 1970's. Fifty years later we've got something uniquely different in the valley, but the pedigree is undeniable.

That said, Bordeaux is just not my thing, and it has nothing to do with the French. I love the French and all things France. I love the food and the art and the culture, and I'm not blind to the fact we'd all be singing "God Save The Queen" if they hadn't bailed our collective asses out in 1778. I even love their attitude. If America was fifteen hundred years old and got invaded every two weeks, we'd cop an attitude, too.

I followed Doug down rows of aged Burgundies and Barolos until something caught my eye in the far corner: six bottles on a rack with a familiar but non-descript white label. "Hey, you've got some PNV wine."

"Oh yeah," Doug said, looking over at me. "We just got that in a few weeks ago."

"What's that?" Sydney asked.

I grabbed a bottle and rolled it over in my hand. "It's the 2007 J. Davies Vineyards Cabernet Sauvignon, Tierra Roja Block, from the Diamond Mountain District. One of only sixty bottles made." I held the bottle out towards Doug. "You just got this in? They didn't ship this until now?"

Doug shook his head. "The owners had a couple of cases at some other stores. They sent us a few bottles to see if we could hand sell them."

"This is a Bad Dog right here," I said to Sydney. "2007 was one of the best vintages to come out of Napa, and this particular vineyard has some serious history - one of the first ones ever planted in the valley."

"Done deal," Sydney said, taking the bottle from me and handing it to Doug. "We'll take it."

"Syd, no." I protested. "This thing is probably a car payment."

"More like a mortgage payment," Doug said. His pupils dilated like Frisbees. Not quite the "coffee is for closers" line I'd expect from someone so obviously springing a major Sales Boner.

Sydney had a credit card out faster than a switchblade, and with the same ferocity as well. "Make it happen, Doug," she said. "And throw in a corkscrew as well."

Once Doug left us in the little room, she asked, "Do you want to take this back to the room? Save it for dinner? Mainline it like an IV?"

"You didn't buy any IV bags," I joked. "No, I've got another idea. Let's go."

Doug was all effusive gratitude and giant smiles when we returned to the front counter. He put the bottle in a really nice, wood box that still smelled of fresh pine and even gift wrapped the wine key. He probably would have done our laundry at that point if we'd asked. He shook our hands—though it seemed for a moment he was going to hug Sydney—and walked us to the door.

I remembered passing an exit on the highway during our trip up to Los Alamos that lead to the Santa Fe National Forest, one of the numerous and amazing national parks in New Mexico. When we got in the car, we asked Siri about it and she said it was only fifteen minutes from the store. In Sydney Time, that was about five minutes.

"So, I was kind of surprised at your selection," Sydney said as she tore out of the parking lot. "Well, not so much what you chose, but the way you chose it."

"How's that?" I asked.

"Well, I just figured you'd go through some kind of process. You know, checking all the labels, comparing vintages, using your vast wealth of knowledge, that sort of thing." She smiled. "Instead, you were all like, 'Yo, Doug, what tastes good here?'"

"I pretty much always do that." I took the bottle from its nifty pine box and examined it. "I mean, sure, I know about wine and I know what I like and all that, but Doug knows his store. A sommelier knows her list. I think it's best to just ask them what they like the most and take it from there."

"So, what's a 'PV' wine?"

"PNV. Premiere Napa Valley. It's an auction put on every year to benefit the Napa Valley Vintners, which is the trade organization for growers and winemakers in the valley. It's pretty freaking cool. Every year, about two hundred winemakers create one or two barrels of really unique wine, and then auction it off to members of the trade, like stores and restaurant owners. It's almost become like a competition, in terms of who can get their wine sold for the highest bid. So, the wines that come out of it are insane. Like this one."

"Cool," she said.

I looked at Sydney, and it occurred to me that there was still lot I didn't know about her. People throw around words like soulmate or kindred spirit, and the über-romantic side of me would love to embrace those terms as well. But with Sydney, the feeling was different. There was a passionate normalcy, a fiery obviousness between us. Forty-eight years in and she dropped into the center of my life from out of nowhere, and my reaction to it all was, *Of course. That sounds right.*

"So, you've never heard of Premiere before?" I asked.

"I think I've heard of it," she replied.

"But I thought…"

"You thought what?"

"Well, I don't want to sound like a dick or anything, but I thought you were somewhere up the food chain in the wine world. I mean, at the sit, Anders DeVry said you were part of some committee and—"

Sydney laughed. "I literally met Anders at the bar at the Ritz-Carlton the night before your test. He invited me to attend the fake drinking party or whatever that was. I think he just wanted to sleep with me."

"Did you sleep with Anders DeVry?" It was none of my business, and I'm not particularly Penis Comparison Guy, but I am *male.*

"Ew." Sydney instantly lost all joviality. "Are you kidding? I mean, no offense to the guy, but ew." She reached over and stroked my thigh. "No, I'm more into the tall, confident, self-absorbed type."

"Thank God," I said with a smile.

The Santa Fe National Forest was spread out over 1.6 million acres, so we grabbed a map from the ranger station and looked for the first cool spot we could find. There was a picnic area called "Hacienda Lookout" that sounded promising, so we drove another three miles through thick groves of pine trees until we reached a small turnoff. We grabbed the wine and the corkscrew and two plastic GoVino cups that I believe Sydney pocketed (thinking they were free samples, of course) and headed down a narrow, scrubby walking trail, marked by a sign that read "Scenic Point."

After a few hundred yards of hiking, we were rewarded with what must have been the lookout of Hacienda Lookout. The valley stretched off to the horizon, framed by tall, rocky hills with dots of pine and cottonwood trees. A river cut through the middle of the valley, which I could only discern from the twisting line of trees on either side of the banks and the sound of rumbling water just under the wind, like the bass notes of a song.

We sat together on a flat rock that was so smooth on top that our asses could not have been the first to adorn it. I took out the wine key and carefully removed the top of the capsule from the bottle, relieved to see the cork was still in great shape, at least on top. It even came out in one piece, which I should have known it would, but I'm old and bitter and cynical and it wouldn't have surprised me if some wine store idiot had used this bottle as a window display for the past decade.

I poured the wine into our swoopy plastic wine glasses and stuck my nose up like I was about to smell the cure for unhappiness. It was glorious. Not a hint of cork taint or pruning—no faults whatsoever, though it could have used an hour to open up and reveal all its delicious mysteries.

"How long do we smell it?" Sydney asked.

"Give it some time," I said. "It's a little grumpy right now. Especially with older vintages or rare ones like this, I like to simply smell the juice and not taste it for about fifteen minutes or so, just to see how it develops over time. Besides, the sense of smell is its own highly underrated pleasure. We put too much emphasis on shoving everything in our mouth as fast as possible."

"Amen to that," Sydney said. She took a few tentative whiffs. "Smells like pine trees and high desert air."

I laughed. "You really have to stick your nose up in it. Don't be afraid to invade its personal space."

We sat there in silence for several minutes, smelling, swirling, and taking in the view. Sydney even held off on taking her first sip. Maybe she was getting her tasting cues from me, but I could tell she was in her own head as well.

"So, I've been thinking. Maybe there's a way I can help you. With your capsule idea and all."

"Really? How's that?" I asked.

"You said that Marnie gave you a report on the capsule a while back. A bunch of data you couldn't decipher. I know some people that might be able to make heads or tails of it."

"Really?"

"Sure. I've met a lot of smart people at a lot of different nonprofits, and I'm sure one of them could turn Marnie's report into something actionable. Or at least tell you if you're on to something."

"It's probably just a coded map to an alternate universe or some shit," I mumbled.

"Well, that might be worth a few bucks as well," Sydney joked.

You don't deserve this. As the child (and ex-husband) of an alcoholic, wasn't even close to an uncommon feeling to have. Yet it took me by surprise in the moment. It was one of those demons I thought that my Sword of Blind Ambition had managed to slay. For a while, at least.

I stuck my nose back in my glass. He was a tight little bastard of a wine, that was for sure. Cramped up in a bottle for ten years, so much time to think about all the expectations people would have for him.

"I appreciate it," I said finally. "I appreciate the offer, and you being here, and everything you've done. Really. That's why I wanted to come up here with you."

"I'm rooting for you, baby." She held her glass up, as if to toast. "Now, when do we get to drink this stuff?"

"Right now," I said, raising the glass to my lips. I gulped in a large mouthful, swished it around and swallowed. "Wow. That's really good."

Sydney's face sank in disappointment. "That's it?" she said. "That's all you got?"

I smiled at her. "It's really, *really* good."

"I thought you were supposed to give me a rundown of how it tastes like currants and quince and elderberries and…"

"And all that shit you've never heard of or tasted before?" I asked. "Sure, I can do that. I can analyze all the different sensory elements of the wine and deduce the vintage and varietal and vineyard and winery. But that doesn't tell you what the wine *means*. It doesn't give it context. It doesn't give it perspective."

"I see," Sydney said, nodding. "Ok, no I don't."

I held my hand out to her. "Stand up."

I clutched her hand in mine and we stood up on the rock. "Take all that in. The view, the setting sun, the cool breeze on your face, the feel of my hand. Think of this day. What happened. Who you were with. What you said, what you thought. Think of all that stuff, then take a sip. But not a little sip, really drink it in."

We clicked glasses and had a drink. "You're right," she said. "It's really good."

"Right? And yes, it smells like wet asphalt and cherry cola and tastes like blackberries with a hint of vanilla, but what it means, what the wine means, is this moment. This intangible *now*. From now on, when I think of Napa Cabernets from the 2007 vintage, I'll rank them alongside this moment, this experience. You see?" I took another drink. My God. The finish went on longer than the valley.

I watched Sydney as she drank some more, her wide, green eyes a valley all their own, filled with beauty and depth and love and mystery.

"Mmmm," she purred in approval. "This wine pairs with pushing a hundred and twenty in a badass muscle car on a gorgeous stretch of New Mexico highway."

"That's it!" I smiled. "This wine pairs with finding the perfect place to watch the sunset."

"This wine pairs with making an old guy named Doug jizz himself over selling the most expensive bottle of his life," she said.

"This wine pairs with ignoring my family until I need something, only to discover I let my cousin go crazy."

Sydney slipped her arm around my waist. "It pairs with realizing what's important in this world. *Who's* important."

I pulled her in close and kissed the top of her head. "It pairs with a longing for redemption. And maybe connecting with something that's real."

"It pairs with dreams," she whispered.

Smiling, I answered. "Yeah. Pairs with life."

I couldn't sleep that night. Again. This time, I got out of bed and stressed out on the sofa in the other room for a change of pace. I stressed about Marnie, about Greg, about Remy and Shay, about being unemployed, about the freaking wine capsule and how the hell I was going to buy the vineyard before Brogan Prescott turned it into Virtual Dinosaur Playland.

Then I saw the giant stack of Real Estate Transfer Disclosures, sitting next to the TV like a humungous paper Ambien. About ten pages of that mess and it would be lights out. I grabbed the pile, sat it on the coffee table in front of me, and switched on the small table lamp.

The letter from Janis Mandel was on top, and then the title report, which I had perused earlier. I set those aside and found that the next thing in the pile was a Geographic Survey, which was performed only a few months earlier. Stuck to the first page of the report was a yellow

Post-it note with the words "page six" scribbled in cursive. I figured it was the page of the report I needed to sign. I thumbed through the report until I realized I should be reading every tedious word if I really wanted this thing to send me off to La La Land. I flipped back to the beginning and began reading.

The report verified the elevations of the sections of the vineyard that stretched up onto the hillside. If I was reading it right, there was a lot more hillside property than I previously thought. Apparently, the southern property line stretched all the way to the top of a hill that peaked at 1,093 feet above sea level. That was comparable to some of the elevations in the Howell Mountain AVA. I was surprised Hank wasn't utilizing that acreage more to grow some coveted and pricey mountain fruit.

There was nowhere to sign on page six. In fact, page six was nothing more than an expanded map of the mountains, spreading from Coombsville and Atlas Peak on the south end all the way to Lake County in the north. The map was titled "Known Fault Lines of the Vaca Mountain Range." There were different colored dotted lines that represented four fault lines that spanned various parts of the range, some stretching further eastward off the hills and into Solano County.

There was one fault line, which had been marked with yellow highlighter, that ran from Lake County all the way down the mountain range and ended at the foot of the hills smack dab in the Fogelson Vineyard. Effing wonderful. Apparently, Ms. Mandel wanted me to know that my house was going to be flattened when the Big One hit. Full disclosure, I suppose.

There was yet another Geographic Survey following the one I'd just read, and at first I thought it might have simply been a copy, all the way down to the "page six" Post-it note. Until I saw that this one was dated almost forty years earlier, in June of 1980. I turned to page six and once again, there was the "Known Fault Line" map, complete with its spider web of nasty earthquake faults. The main fault line stretched down the length of the mountain range, again highlighted in yellow.

Only this map was slightly different. There was a little more detail on the north end, and the fault line started at an area marked "Proposed McLaughlin Site." The line then ran across the top of the hills but stopped short of Atlas Peak. I wasn't quite sure what it meant. Was this map disputing the idea that my property would be in an earthquake zone?

I opened the first report again and compared the fault lines side-by-side. It was definitely the same line, no doubt about that. So why was this older report included with the newer one, especially if the map didn't encompass the Fogelson property?

Damn. Now my brain was working. This project was not having the desired somatic effect.

Next up was a Soils Report. Coombsville was known for its volcanic soil and high mineral content, and I expected to see nothing less in the report. But this report was also dated June of 1980, and was created for the "Proposed McLaughlin Site," which if I remembered correctly, was somewhere up in Lake County, forty miles north of…

The McLaughlin Site.

My stomach dropped. A lump formed in my throat the size of a grapefruit and my hands began to sweat like I was asking Monica Rossmessler to the prom. I ripped through the soils report and damn it if there wasn't another one exactly like it, dated just a few months ago, created by the same company as the first one, performed on the hillside portion of the Fogelson Vineyard.

I seriously almost shit myself. I know that's a completely disgusting way to put it, but there's no other way to describe that feeling when every sphincter in your goddamned body simply lets loose because your brain is trying to process implications of reality-altering enormity.

I scrambled for my phone. I'd left it in the hotel all day, hooked up to the outlet, in the hope that a full charge might somehow revive its pinot-soaked innards. I held down the power button and whispered a prayer to Our Mother of Perpetual Technology. When the phone finally turned on, revealing a Jupiter-like swirling cloud layer of residual wine on the display, I keyed in the password, but it didn't work. I tried again and still nothing. Finally, on the third try, the main screen appeared.

I saw that I had missed calls and voicemails from both Shay and Remy. That was good. Even if they just wanted to yell at me, it was a good sign. But all I really wanted in that moment was to text Shay one simple message.

I opened up my text messages and saw that I had missed five from Shay. Each one of them was a variation on the theme of "Where the fuck are you?" But explaining everything to him was not the point, at least not now. Now, I needed to give him the message I had sent him or spoke to him countless times since we were sixteen: it was a message always conveyed with absolute sincerity, even when I knew it was a lie.

A message of hope.

A message of dreams.

We're gonna be filthy rich.

THIRTEEN

I'd laid out the reports and disclosures across Shay's dining room table like the plans to the D-Day Invasion, creating a step-by-step road map to my conclusion. A conclusion so mind-blowing that Shay had taken to walking up and down his staircase repeatedly like some kind of drugged lab rat. At the bottom of the staircase, he'd ask a question, then walk up the stairs again as he processed the answer.

"But you don't know, right?" he asked from the bottom step. "I mean, you don't *know*-know. You're not a thousand percent certain."

"Well, not a thousand percent, no," I said as he disappeared up the staircase. "We'd need to extract our own core sample to be completely sure. But I'd go with ninety-nine percent. It's the only conclusion that makes sense."

Shay turned and began his ninth descent of the stairs. His house was pretty big by Napa standards, located in one of the subdivisions east of downtown and built in the 1970s. Though he had furnished it with some modern-ish IKEA pieces, he hadn't touched a single design element of the place, so it looked like something straight out of an episode of *The Brady Bunch,* down to the shag carpet and the etched, glass tile mural above the fireplace. I gave him shit about it constantly and had an annoyingly good time standing on the landing, yelling, "Marsha Marsha Marsha!" (Truth be told, I was more of a Cindy Brady Guy myself. She was closer in age to me, and she had an aura about her that made her seem, I don't know…above it all).

Shay parked himself on the landing and crouched down so that he was staring at me like a convict through the decorative bars of the railing. "Just because the fault line ends at the property doesn't mean the two parcels have the same mineral deposits," he said.

"Ah, no it doesn't!" I replied. Shay was being all lawyer-y at me, but I was prepared. "It's merely an indicator of soil similarity. That's why Prescott got the additional samples from the hillside at the vineyard." I turned around and, for the umpteenth time, looked over the presentation of maps and reports spread out on the table. "There's nothing else that explains it. There's gold on the Fogelson property."

I grabbed the map from the June 1980 report and held it in Shay's direction. "And check this out. It's all publicly owned land from the McLaughlin Mine, down the mountain range, and into Coombsville. The only privately-owned land along the fault line is the Fogelson Vineyard."

Shay nodded slowly. "Which is why Prescott wants it so bad."

"Exactly."

Shay stuck his face between the metal bars; a prisoner in his own home. "How come I've never heard of this McLaughlin gold mine?"

"Well, I don't know," I said. "Maybe you're just like the rest of the universe and you don't stay up to date on 1980s mining trends near Lake Berryessa?"

I grabbed our gin and tonics off the table and took Shay's over to him in his self-made cell. "The only reason I even heard about the McLaughlin Mine is because of the research I had to do about AVAs in the Napa Valley. The mine had shut down operations by the early 90s, before you and I even got here. But by the time they closed the site down, they'd extracted 3.4 million ounces. Again, that's four-and-a-half billion dollars at today's prices."

Shay chugged the remainder of his drink and shook the glass at me in that silent but universal gesture of *get me another one of these.* I strolled to the kitchen and sat our glasses on the faded, white Formica countertop. Seriously, the entire room was like something out of Epcot Center's "Kitchen of Tomorrow!" display, down to the microwave oven the size of a refrigerator that made scary, radiation-leaking noises.

I grabbed the bottle of gin and poured, my hands shaking so wildly that the lip of the bottle clinked repeatedly against the rim of the glass. The only feeling I could compare to this sudden and unexpected windfall was watching aliens step out of a spaceship in my backyard. Not just life-changing money, but world-changing money. *What are you going to do now that you can do absolutely anything?*

In 1993, the band got its first advance from the record company. We decided to go to the ATM together, withdrew a whopping hundred dollars each, then headed down to Coconut Charlie's and went nuts, buying beers for anyone and everyone. (Even though this kind of blatant rock star excess was completely frowned upon in the grunge scene, no one—*no one*—said no to free alcohol). Our advance was nothing even close to life-changing money, but for four guys in their early 20s who lived together in a crappy ass apartment, survived on Kraft macaroni and cheese and stole coffee filters from work to use as toilet paper, it was enough to quit our day jobs for a year.

Dominic had laid his ATM receipt ceremoniously on the bar and smoothed it out like it was the Magna Charta. He ordered a shot of Jack and a Bud, and from what I could tell, he silently drank a toast to the receipt. "Time to practice," he said.

"Practice?" I said. "Dude, it is time to celebrate! This is what we practiced so hard for!"

"Not what I meant," he said, smiling. He wrapped his massive arm around my neck and hugged me tight, then let go just as quick and slapped a twenty on the bar. "Next round on me!" he shouted, and everyone screamed. We drank too much, and I completely chalked up the moment to Dom saying cryptic shit because that's what Dom did.

Facing down a billion-dollar pay day, I finally got it. He didn't mean "time to *practice*," he meant "*time* to practice." Money buys all sorts of expensive and awesome things, but it can also buy time—that precious, elusive, rarest of commodities. Time to do what you want, when you want, is the ultimate freedom. The ultimate power. And now it was mine.

What in the hell am I going to do with it?

"Did you see this?" Shay shouted. He had apparently freed himself from his staircase jail cell and found his way to the dining room table, where he examined a document intently. "Per client's request, core samples were extracted at depths of fifty feet, one hundred feet and two hundred feet. Results will be provided in a supplementary report."

"I wonder if we can get our hands on that report?"

"No way in hell," Shay said. "Doesn't matter, we already know the results. Prescott made the offer, which means he found the gold. Oh, shit! Wait."

Shay rummaged through the documents until he found the title report, then riffled through the pages until he stopped about halfway. "Yes," he sounded like a Bond villain. "You see? The deed shows that mineral rights come with the property, but there's no way the City of Napa would allow mining." Shay dropped the report on the table. "God, that smart son of a bitch. That's where we came in, get it? He wants to build a wine cave. An intricate wine cave with all sorts of long, deep tunnels, like an ant colony, right? That's the front. Constructing the cave was just a legal way to extract thousands of tons of earth from the hill. Fucking evil genius."

"Wow," I said. "I love it."

"Me too." Shay grinned.

I went back to pouring the gin and tonics. My hand hadn't steadied much. "Do you think that Hank knows? I've been wondering whether he's known all along or if Prescott made this discovery himself and he's been keeping it a secret."

I handed Shay his drink and he guzzled half of it. "I gotta think that Prescott came up with this on his own. There's no way he'd tell Hank, either, and since the core sample findings weren't included with the soils report, I don't think he plans on sharing his discovery."

Somehow, someway, out of some horrific and demonic place I wish never existed, my conscience came sniffing around. "We should probably tell Hank."

Shay sounded as disappointed as I felt. "Thing is, what if we're wrong? Then there's no gold *and* we've lost our vineyard project."

"I don't know." Shay was right: these decisions required much more rapid drinking. I sucked down my G&T like the cure for Alzheimer's was at the bottom of the glass. "How about this? We buy the place and when we find the gold, we give half back to Hank."

"Half?" Shay nearly spit through his nose. "What the fuck, Pope Corbett?"

"Dude, what are you going to do with two billion dollars that you can't do with one?"

"Twice as much," Shay countered. "Two Cheeseburger Theory, bro."

Well, that was pure logic right there. The Two Cheeseburger Theory was straightforward and inarguable: if one cheeseburger is good, two cheeseburgers must be *awesome.* This is also the rationale behind threesomes, and though threesomes never, ever live up to their fantasy promise, the Two Cheeseburger Theory left no debate as to why they at least sound like such a fantastic idea.

"Alright, an equal share then," I said. "A third."

Shay waved his empty glass at me again, although this time in that universal gesture of *you're my server, bitch, get me a drink,* because he knew it pushed my buttons. I grabbed his glass anyway and headed back to his Retro Kitchen.

"When I walk into your kitchen, I suddenly want to be Andy Gibb," I said. "I want to put on Angels Flight polyester pants and wear a gold medallion across my hairy chest and have sex with Victoria Principal."

"Bro, Andy Gibb was the coolest of the Gibb brothers," Shay said. "He got all the money and probably bagged Marie Osmond but didn't have to sing embarrassing Bee Gee shit like 'New York Mining Disaster 1941.'"

"It is a universal truth that Barry Gibb is the coolest of the Gibb brothers." I handed Shay his drink. "Andy Gibb is the deadest Gibb brother."

"There's a place in hell specifically for you," Shay scolded.

"There's nothing in the Bible that says it's a sin to point out just how dead Andy Gibb is," I replied. "However, the Good Lord doth frown upon things like greed."

"Alright, alright, a third," Shay conceded. "But we need to get our own core samples, and as soon as possible. Can you set that up?"

"You know what? I could call Alan Cauldwell over at BTG. He's one of their junior engineers and could probably get it done pretty quick. We could have him pull the samples and give them to us, then we'll take them somewhere else for testing. That'd keep things under wraps."

"Excellent." Shay was fully into it now, rearranging the documents on the table into his own jigsaw puzzle. "Getting capital for the purchase won't be a problem now. I've got investors who'd give their left nut to – "

"No, no way," I interrupted. "We can't do that. If word gets out that there's gold on the property, we'll be pushed out of this deal faster than you can say 'fuck those two idiots.'"

"Don't worry about that, bro. I got us covered." The only time Shay looked older than thirty was while wearing his reading glasses. They made him seem downright respectable, in fact. It was disconcerting. "We'll be good. These are people I trust."

Trust. Like the mighty Tyrannosaurus Rex, my trust went extinct about a hundred million years ago. I trusted my parents and that got me abandonment issues and an alcoholic, philandering ex-wife.

I trusted the record company, my agent and my manager, and that got me a full-blown Ten on the Rectal Violation Scale. In fact, I did not possess an orifice that had been un-plundered in my four-plus decades of trusting people. So, what? Like, things were going to be different now? Now that there was a *multi-billion-dollar gold mine* involved?

"Listen, Sydney thinks she can help us out. She has some contacts that are looking through that first wine capsule report that Marnie gave us, and if it all looks good, they may have investors that could be interested."

Shay took his glasses off and set them on the table. "You're really into this woman, aren't you?"

I nodded.

Shay nodded too. "Well bro, I'm happy for you, I really am."

But I knew that nod. It was the nod gave before delivering news like *your house is on fire* or *you have flesh-eating bacteria.*

And he definitely delivered this time, too.

"That said, it doesn't change the fact that you're a total douchebag for fucking some other guy's wife."

Shay and I had an honesty that ran deep. Back in Reality Star, Shay was quality control for the songs I wrote. I'd play him my latest work, he'd listen intently, then pass judgment with a simple, "That's a hit song, bro" or a, "That sucks, bro, try again." He was always right.

And it wasn't like I hadn't given this moral conundrum some thought myself. Not a lot of really conscious thought, but just enough subconscious thought to keep my guilt muscle in fine shape.

"Dude, it's not like that. She's on a trial separation."

"Oh, she's divorced?"

"No, they're just sort of testing it out."

"Then you're fucking another guy's wife."

Shay was certainly *not* the Quaker Oats Guy. I could have reminded him of a thousand breeches of protocol from our days on the road, but it wouldn't change the fact that he had a point. A point that had been nagging at me in a manner I didn't particularly want to face.

"So, you're telling me this is some kind of violation of The Bro Code?" I asked. "Even though I'm not the one doing the cheating, it's still morally reprehensible of me to be seeing her?"

"Yes," Shay replied. "No." He sighed and stuck his finger in his drink, gazing at the glass as he twirled the ice around. "Look, I'm an attorney. I specialize in ambiguity and subjective morality. For three hundred an hour I'll give you a really convincing argument that the Earth is flat and up is down. But I gotta tell you, man. Living like that's getting kind of old."

Was that sincerity I heard? *Regret?*

"The Bro Code is bullshit, I get that," he said. "But what about the Golden Rule? Do unto others and all that? I mean, shouldn't there be at least something?"

The earnestness in Shay's voice told me he couldn't smell the elephantine irony dump he just laid out on the dining room table.

"This from the guy who didn't want to give Hank Fogelson half the gold under his own property?"

Shay extracted his finger from his glass and flicked it at me. "I'm trying, ok? And you should be, too, of all people. God only knows that the universe never lets you get one over on it, bro. You always pay for your mistakes, every time, and frankly, it's kind of painful to watch."

"Thanks for the heads up, Deepak Chopra," I muttered. "Don't worry. I'm fine."

Well, sort of fine. I knew from the very beginning that my relationship with Sydney was akin to having a sliding glass door on a submarine, and that at any moment either of us could decide to open that baby up half a mile underwater. And though breakups hurt—much like drowning under a 50,000-pounds-per-cubic-foot wall of water—I could rationalize the pain away by saying, *well, Corbett, that's what you get for having a submarine with a sliding glass door.*

"Alright, I gotta get some sleep on this," Shay announced. "And by sleep, I mean staying up all night freaking out. Are you OK to drive?"

I flashed back to my sit for my Master Somm, and how being nervous and excited could tragically mask the effects of alcohol consumption. I felt pretty sober in the moment but knew this squadron of drinks was going to drop its payload on me in about two hours. "I'm good."

"Would you mind leaving all this stuff here?"

"Sure, that's fine," I said. "Though at some point pretty soon I should sign the Disclosure Acknowledgment and give it back to Janis, so we don't raise any suspicions."

"Good point." Shay came in and gave me a hug, slapping me sharply on the back. "And since I'm already being a big pussy, I also owe you an apology. I freaked out after the meeting with Fractal Equity Partners and I shouldn't have. I'm sorry. That wasn't your fault. If the damn app had worked to begin with, none of that crazy shit would have happened."

I grabbed my keys, wallet, and phone off the counter. I hate having things in my pockets, so I drain them immediately wherever I go. Yes, it's weird.

"You of all people don't owe me an apology. The shit I've put you through, it's a miracle you let me in your house."

"I only let you in because you came with four billion dollars." Shay opened the door and turned on his 1973 porch light with the chartreuse mosaic glass sconce. "Do you really think we can trust Sydney on this?"

Trust.

Damn.

I went to a shrink once a while back. Ok, I went to a bunch of shrinks a bunch of times, but there was this one I really liked. He would say "Wow!" after every gruesome story I recounted, which made me feel like my problems were interesting. I started seeing him after I began dating again, a few years following my divorce. My issue came down to this: how do you tell the difference between baggage and wisdom? How do I trust that little voice inside my head saying, *this girl's crazy,* when in fact, she could totally have her shit together and I'm the one who's screwed up?

After a few sessions, Dr. Interested concluded that it came down to this: Baggage Voice is a screamer, but Wise Voice simply whispers. The voice that's yelling, *Oh my god, no! Get away!* That one's probably coming from the Baggage Place. But if it's quiet and still in your head and you hear, *this is probably not the right situation for you,* then that's more than likely the voice from the Wise Place.

So, I stopped and listened. And what I heard was very, very surprising to me.

"Yeah," I said. "I trust her."

I was also surprised, as Shay closed the door behind me, to find myself thinking not about the massive fortune falling into my lap, but whether or not it was too late to order modifications to my submarine.

FOURTEEN

Sydney gently untangled herself from my arms and eased out of the bed without so much as the sound of sheets brushing against covers. She tiptoed to the bathroom, closed the door with the gentlest of clicks, and turned on the shower. It was very sweet and thoughtful of her to try not to wake me—as she had tried for the past couple of mornings—but it didn't matter. I was a light sleeper. Which is all Remy's fault.

Back in the band days, sleep was a rare and precious commodity. When we were on tour, the typical day ended at 3:00 a.m. and fired up again around 7:00 a.m., or even earlier if we had a morning radio show appearance. "Sleep" was not an adequate verb to describe the state of consciousness that occurred under these circumstances: I basically went narcoleptic whenever I could. I learned how to go from zero to coma in ten seconds, and executed this trick on buses, in restaurants, in broom closets, and even side-stage during the opening band's performance. However, on a coveted day off, I could fall asleep while a pack of feral hamsters nibbled at my flesh and still get eighteen straight hours of uninterrupted, death-like slumber.

But all that changed when Remy was born. Becoming a parent is like a Faustian bargain with Father Time, where page four, paragraph two, subparagraph B states, "Your circadian rhythm will be completely fucked for the rest of your life." Though the contract was ratified around the third trimester ("Honey, I'm uncomfortable and I can't sleep, *so neither will you*"), it really kicked in the moment we brought home our precious issuance of devoted love, who launched into one of three patented screams every two hours—I Am Starving, Oh My God I Have Soiled Myself, and Come Entertain Me.

I held on to the hope that sleep patterns would return to normal after the first year or so, but there was an insidious and ironic side effect of this Manchurian Candidate-style conditioning: when Remy stopped crying at night, I'd wake up in a panic every two hours anyway, wondering if she was quiet because she was dead. This continued for a few years.

As time went by, things didn't get any better. There was the seven-year period where the only antidote to Remy's bad dreams was to sleep in my bed. "Sleep" in this context meant, "Let me sprawl out on your bed horizontally and dig my razor-like toenails into your back." There were nights I invariably ended up sleeping on my own bedroom floor. ("Daddy! Did you have a slumber party last night?" "Yes. A party. Precisely the word I was looking for.").

For two glorious years between the ages of ten and twelve, I was neither awakened by crying, nor by the terrifying apparition of my daughter standing in the darkness two inches from my face. But by that time, the damage was done. The mere creak of a door hinge or the rush of a flushing toilet or even the barking of a goddamn dog eight miles away would snap me out of my barely-alpha brain waves. Things took an even sharper turn for the worse when Remy turned fifteen, and boys came skulking around like a boner with two legs and a half-developed hippocampus. Many were the nights I lay sleepless in bed, Remy ostensibly "at a girlfriend's house," knowing full well that some acne-crusted jizz machine was perpetrating testosterone crimes on my daughter, the exact same way I did with numerous girls when I was her age. *For the love of God, make sure they* laminate *that freaking thing before it gets within thirty yards of you.*

I gazed out the hotel window at the San Francisco dawn, the myriad glass rectangles of downtown silhouetted against the pale, gray light. Sydney had spent the last several nights commuting between Marin, San Francisco and San Jose, reconnecting with old friends that had been sidelined during her marriage. On the nights she was available, we met at a hotel and racked up a room service bill for nachos and champagne that rivaled the gross domestic product of most third world countries.

She had mentioned when we first met that her trial separation was supposed to be thirty days. Despite the fact that she avoided the subject, I knew a major decision was looming. I found myself growing increasingly disenchanted with the sliding glass door on our submarine and wondered if I would throw myself in front of it if she made a move for the handle. Either way, it was beginning to feel as though the palliative effect of rationalization would to do little to ease the pain of a world without Sydney.

The great thing about pain, though, is that you can fill a hotel room with nachos, sex and wine, lock yourself in it, and it's as good as a shot of lidocaine—as long as you're in your little cave, at least. In the quieter moments, the reality of our situation lay between us on the bed like a wine-soaked, eight-hundred-pound gorilla, licking the plate of nachos and throwing empty bottles across the room.

Sydney emerged from the bathroom wearing nothing but a towel in her hair. I still got nervous looking at her naked body. Not one of us gets past the age of forty without some kind of wrinkle, roll, stretch or scar to account for, but all I saw on Sydney was perfection. Her confidence was a flawless second skin.

"Oh, I'm sorry," she whispered. "Did I wake you?"

"No, you didn't." I smiled. "Again." I stretched out across the Verdant Plain of Coziness that was the hotel bed. Every bed in the world was more comfortable than mine. I don't know why this was so. "So, what's on tap for today?" I asked. "Is this the meeting with the Moesby-Stiller Foundation?"

"Stiller-Moesby," she corrected. "And that's tomorrow." She took a small makeup bag from the bathroom and dropped it in her suitcase. "I'm heading up to Sacramento to see my friend Jeannie, and I was hoping to beat the traffic."

"Oh, that's right." It was hard to keep her schedule straight. That, and the fog in my head was not dissimilar to the wall of grey outside our window.

"The bummer is I need to keep this place one more night, but I don't want to drive all the way back from Sacramento tonight." She threw a few more items into her bag, frowned at it, then threw in a few more. "I'm hoping Jeannie will just let me crash at her place."

I watched as Sydney grabbed her bra and panties from the bag and slipped into them. She somehow made putting clothes on just as sexy as taking them off.

"Well, don't you worry, babe," I said. "In a little while, I'll just buy this hotel for you."

Sydney glared at me. "I told you, I don't mind paying for this. I know you're in a tight place right now."

"Yeah, but I won't be for long." I looked over at the end table and reviewed the damage from the previous evening—two empty bottles of Mumm Blanc de Blancs. I picked one up and shook it in her direction. "This time next year, it'll be nothing but Krug."

Sydney's glare turned into a full-blown scowl. "So, you're mining the gold?"

"Four billion dollars' worth," I said, smiling. "God, I still can't wrap my head around it."

"Neither can I," she mumbled.

Sydney stormed around the hotel room. She picked up clothes and threw them in the suitcase, then took clothes out of the suitcase and threw them on the floor again. She grabbed her lipstick from the bathroom counter and smeared it across her lips, then rubbed it off furiously and reapplied it.

I sat up against the headboard. "What? Why are you so upset?"

Sydney ripped the towel from her hair and pulled a dress over her head. "I don't get it. How does this make you any different than Brogan Prescott?"

"It makes me totally different!" I admonished. "I'm not just some rich douchebag trying to get richer. I'm going to use the money to do really cool things, like support the arts or start a record label, or…buy another vineyard." I rubbed my hands across the trillion-thread-count bed sheets. "Then I'm going to buy a real goddamned bed and get out of that freaking apartment. And I'm going to buy a Humvee, run over my Nissan with it, then give the Humvee to a homeless guy and buy something even cooler. And I'm going to get you anything you want. Anything."

Sydney yanked back her wet hair and pulled it into a tight ponytail. It was pretty obvious I pushed some kind of button, but I couldn't figure out which one.

"I'd have thought that you of all people would know better," she said, staring into the bathroom mirror. "I mean, sure, I can afford a hotel like this and tickets to New Mexico and all that, but the only reason it has any meaning is because I can share it with you. You get it?" She hurried out of the bathroom and slipped on a pair of black flats, then slammed the suitcase shut. "Money means nothing when you're practically dead inside."

I rubbed my twitching eyebrow. "Well, I'm not dead inside. In fact, I'm a guy whose problems would completely disappear if his bank account wasn't as empty as the vacuum of space."

Sydney laughed humorlessly and zipped up her suitcase. She took her purse from the TV stand, checked the contents for a moment, then placed it on top of the suitcase.

"No, you're not dead on the inside, Corbett. But you are corrupted. Something infected you. Some little lie that got under your skin and festered."

Sydney went to the closet and put on a black wool jacket then returned to the foot of the bed and waved her outstretched hand at me.

"This guy?" she said. "I'm not really sure who he is. What happened to the guy in the vineyard that night, the one who waxed poetic about love and beauty and history and tradition? Where's that guy with the dream and the passion and the vision? The one who still believes?"

Sydney put her purse around her shoulder and grabbed her suitcase but stopped and turned to face me once more.

"I'm going to be back at my apartment day after tomorrow. I'd love to see Corbett, but I'd prefer if this guy just forgets the way there."

All hotel room doors, by their very nature, slam shut. But the sound of that particular door was something that echoed in my head well into the day.

♗

By 1991, the band had developed a small tour circuit around the northwest that we rotated through every couple of months. We road tripped as far as Ashland to the south, Spokane to the east and Vancouver to the north, hitting a handful of cities in between. Within a few years, we sold out the smaller clubs and bars in these towns, and even some of the larger venues that fit up to three hundred people.

But of all the clubs, bars, and dives we played in our circuit, none was more fun than The Boom Boom Room in Eugene, Oregon. It was a hole-in-the-wall place about two blocks from the University, and a haven for the lunatic fringe of the student body. The place was done up like an old 1920s burlesque club, or at least, like a really stoned college kid's version of a burlesque club, with red velvet curtains on the walls, black vinyl bean bag chairs the size of king beds, and the coolest wood and brass bar to ever serve me a gin and tonic.

Best of all, the stage was bookended by two giant metal cages hung from the ceiling, in which go-go dancers gyrated the night away to the beat of our music. I figured that any wasted co-ed could jump into the cage and do their thing, but as it turned out, the dancers were mostly pros. Some were MFA candidates in modern dance at the college, some were waitresses that had perfected a routine, and some were straight-up strippers; like Candy.

By our third gig at The Boom Boom Room, I noticed that Candy was a regular in the cage. It was hard not to notice. She was all freakishly hard body, big fake boobs, tattoos and enormous, blonde, haystacked hair. She moved with a purpose, and that purpose was tips, which came raining down on her like confetti at a ticker tape parade.

During the few songs where I played the guitar solo instead of Dom, I'd race over to Candy's cage, stick my foot up on it, and do my best Hair Metal Guy moves, jerking my guitar neck like some kind of rosewood fertility symbol. Candy, in turn, stuck her ass cheeks against the cage, then licked the metal bars. It was rock cliché taken to the extreme—and downright unhygienic—but it drove the crowd freaking nuts.

After a particularly raucous set, I found Candy at the bar and bought her a drink. She told me that she worked her own circuit, dancing in high-end strip clubs between Vancouver and San Francisco, and like us, she just enjoyed performing at The BBR because the crowd was so into it. One drink led to another, then another, and then to me paying Dom twenty bucks to sleep on the floor in Shay's room so that I could have the motel to myself. With Candy.

It was everything I hoped it would be. She knew how to move, how to perform, how to seduce, and she had no problem going totally marathon on me all night long. Afterwards, as I lay in bed in a fog of general depravity, I saw Candy gazing out the window at the first rays of sunrise.

"I guess I should go."

"Sure," I replied. "See you next time."

Next to the day we signed with the label, I'd never had more of a Rock Star Moment in my life. I had arrived. Legit rock stars have sex with strippers and I'd just joined The Club. I checked one off my Rock Star Bucket List and moved on to the next item—throwing a television out a hotel room window.

I was downright giddy when we came back to Eugene three months later, hoping that Candy would be there and that carnal delights would follow. I didn't see her until halfway through our first set, when she unceremoniously took to the cage and just kind of shifted distractedly from one foot to another. I tried to make eye contact with her a number of times, and when she finally glanced in my direction, there was neither a genuine smile of recognition nor an entertainer's smile of manufactured sexual fervor. I stuck my foot up on her cage during my solo, but she turned away, clutched the bars, and continued her uninspired swaying.

When we finished the set, she jumped from the cage, and as soon as I could get away I went looking for her. I couldn't find her at the bar or in the tiny backstage area or anywhere in the crowd. I asked one of the servers, who said she thought she saw her leaving through the stage entrance. I ran through the back doors and another hundred yards down the alleyway until I could make out Candy's distinctive blonde haystack in the haze of a distant streetlight.

"Hey, Candy!" I shouted. "Hold up a second!"

When she turned around, I thought maybe I had the wrong person. There wasn't an iota of makeup on her face, and she wore an expression that was somewhere in that grey zone between desperation and determination.

"Karen," she said. "My name is Karen." She turned back around and walked into the night.

I stood there for a while, watching her segue between darkness and the orange glow of the streetlights, until she was almost out of sight.

"Bro, there you are," Shay said from behind me. "Downbeat in five minutes."

I wanted to run after her. No, not run after her: I wanted to run to her and run away from everything else. Go to her and share my own truth, and just scrub all of reality to a blank slate and start over again—resurrected in obscurity, free of the masks we adorn to hide ourselves from the world. It truly felt like there was this genuine moment in my grasp, and it was walking farther and farther away.

I watched as Candy-Karen waited for the light at the corner to turn green. She ran her hands through her hair, pulling out huge clumps of it. Extensions, I realized. She tossed them in a trash can and crossed the street, and if I wasn't mistaken, she did a little twirl in the intersection.

It wasn't my moment. It was hers. My moment occurred three months earlier, at a Motel 6, when I checked one off my Rock Star Bucket List.

My genuine moment.

"Hey, man, are you good?" Shay asked.

I turned and opened the door back into the club. "No."

FIFTEEN

It was an unusually sunny day for mid-November. Typically, November signaled the beginning of the rainy season, but things weren't typical these last ten years or so. The drought in California was a constant source of worry in Napa, especially its long-term effect on the aquifer. Thus, every beautiful November day came with its own price tag, which I suppose is the case for all beautiful things.

I arrived at the Fogelson Vineyard early that morning to have a cup of coffee with Hank before the soil engineer arrived. As I pulled up, Hank's eldest son, Stephan, stood on the porch with his father, flailing his arms in animated conversation. When I walked up to the steps, Stephan stormed off with little more than a nod in my direction.

"That boy is wound up pretty tight," Hank commented as his son drove away. "That boy" was also about my age. Funny how parents always see their children as children. Remy was still around ten years old in my book.

Remy. I hadn't spoken with Remy since she confronted me about her mom after the FEP meeting. I'd been straddling the thin line between "being sensitive to her need for space as she worked things out" and "totally avoiding any more of this shit at all costs." Remy was certainly prone to retreat to her Fortress of Solitude, hidden deep beneath the emotional frozen tundra, but more than a week had gone by with nothing so much as a text. I resolved to make the first move if I hadn't heard from her by the weekend.

Hank made coffee in his Jurassic-era, faded beige Mr. Coffee coffeemaker, scooping in heaping tablespoons of Folgers from a massive plastic container. The resulting brew was something akin in both texture and taste to liquid asphalt, but *damn* did it get the job done. I sipped the magical, black elixir gingerly, monitoring myself against what could become a fatal caffeine overdose.

Hank leaned against the stained Formica kitchen counter and stared into his mug. "Are you gonna keep the house, Corbett?" His tone suggested it was something that had been on his mind since our first meeting with Brogan Prescott.

"Definitely keeping the house," I replied. Which was true. There'd be no need to move or raze it, and it would be an excellent home to live in until I could afford the Taj Mahal.

"I know it ain't much," he continued. "But it's been a home for a good long while."

Hank didn't take his eyes off the coffee, his face bereft of the deep laugh lines that typically defined it. He was apparently more ambivalent to the idea of moving the house in favor of a parking lot than he had let on earlier.

"Hey, don't you worry about that. I've been stuck in a six hundred square foot apartment for five years. I can't wait to call this place home."

Hank just nodded, gazing into his cup like a black crystal ball. And then I understood. He'd raised four kids in that house and had grown up there himself. The memories in that place had to have been as visceral as the paint peeling from the door trim.

"So, where are you going to live after this?" I asked. "Are you moving in with the kids, getting a new place, or…?"

Hank chuckled humorlessly, then took a long swig from his coffee. I wasn't sure if he was going to answer me or not, but the conversation was sidetracked by the rumble of a flatbed truck pulling up alongside the house. I didn't expect the truck to be so huge, but its bed held three drilling rigs of various sizes and configurations. Maybe it was overkill, but we had to get this right.

Allen Cauldwell, a rather bookish-looking young man for a heavy machine operator, jumped from the truck and joined us on the back porch. Shay arrived a few moments later.

After a round of introductions, Allen asked if he could go survey the hillside for the best spot to extract the samples. Hank seemed rather confused by the whole thing.

"If you're looking for a soils report, Francisco's got 'em all at the office," he said. "No reason to be spending that kind of money."

I exchanged a glance with Shay. A guilty glance. "This is the last one that needs to be done," I said, trying to sound reassuring.

We watched from the porch as Allen maneuvered his truck between the vineyard blocks and up towards the hillside. I asked Hank if he wanted to join us up at the site, but he declined and went back to his coffee. I thought about reassuring him again or at least saying *something*, though it was becoming more apparent that I was the one who needed reassurance.

Shay and I walked up the small road, and though I could see my breath in the cold morning air, I felt like I could no longer see anything else clearly at all.

"You know, we could have just moved forward with the purchase and done these tests afterwards," I said.

"Moved forward with what? We still don't have the funding secured, and I'm not convinced that we don't need a partner in this. Drilling a cave is expensive."

"Hank's practically giving this property away to us," I said. "He's gotta have zero idea what's going on here."

Shay stopped walking and turned to me. "Look, if there's gold on this property, Hank's going to be a billionaire, alright? So stop worrying about Hank. But if we go spouting our mouths off about this, we'll lose the vineyard for sure. Gold or no gold."

"I know." But something still wasn't sitting right with me.

We caught up with Allen at the base of the two hillside syrah blocks. "I don't know how far up the hill I can get," he said. "I guess I could carry the Twenty-Five-TS between those rows, but I don't know if the base would be stable, and it only drills to sixty feet."

"We need to go to a hundred and fifty," I said. "Both on the hillside and the floor."

"We'll need the Thirty-Five for that." He pointed at his truck. "I've got it hitched to a John Deere. I think there's room enough to drive it up between the blocks, but there's no way I can get it up the hillside from an east or west approach."

He was right. Most of the hill was dominated by jagged, volcanic rock. I know that some vintners had used dynamite to turn their big rocks into little rocks and then pronounced it "soil"—like they did across the way at the Collinetta Vineyard—but Hank simply planted all the parts with easy access and left the rest untouched.

Allen scrambled onto his flatbed and released the tie-downs on the largest machine on the truck. It was a bulky, green tractor, with a fifteen-foot-tall steel drill lashed to the front. It seemed like the whole thing was impossibly balanced and could tip forward at any time. Allen jumped into the driver's seat, revved it up, and drove it down the tailgate.

"Damn," said Shay. "How much is this costing us?"

"Costing *you*. I'm as broke as fuck."

"Write him a check," Shay said with a smile, "and postdate it two years."

Allen backed up the rig until he was next to Shay and I. "Might take me a while to find the right spot," he told us. "And then, if we're lucky, we're looking at maybe ten feet an hour. Once we get started, you gentlemen are welcome to watch, but it's going to get boring pretty quick."

I figured I'd stick around long enough for Allen to find the right place to drill the core sample, then once the project was underway, he could text me as he was finishing up. Some irrational part of me was excited to poke a bit at the samples, maybe find some giant nugget of gold stuck in there, but I knew it didn't work like that. Even at the

McLaughlin mine, all that was dug out was dirt and specks of gold dust…several thousand ounces of gold dust.

Just as Allen went back to work, Hank pulled up behind us in a battered old golf cart. "I thought I had a copy of this lying around somewhere," he said, clutching a manila envelope. "This is that soils report I was talking about. The one that Prescott's agent ordered in June."

I looked through a few pages of the report and then handed it to Shay. It was exactly the same one included in the disclosures. "They had a drill like that out here, too," Hank added. "They weren't drilling right between the blocks, though. Don't know if I'm too keen on that, Corbett."

"I'm sorry about that, Hank," I mumbled. "But, well…" Shay gave me a sideways look that I immediately recognized: *We talked about this, damn it.*

"We'll get this done just as quickly as possible," I said. "I promise, Hank. This will be the last test."

Hank wasn't paying attention to me. He stared up the hillside, with his hand over his eyes to shield the sun. "What the hell is that guy doing?"

I looked over and saw Allen crouched down by the base of the drill. As if on cue, he stood up and shouted, "This ain't gonna work! I'm going to need to go a little further up!" He got back on the tractor, put it in gear, and lunged up the hill, the back tires spewing out a plume of pebbles.

"Jesus, careful up there," Hank said, though not nearly loud enough for Allen to hear. I knew it was more for me. "Those are thirty-year-old vines."

We watched as the drill rig bounced slowly up the hill, swerving to the left and right on the slim, rocky path.

Hank turned and glared at me. "What the hell are you guys doing?

You've got the report, you know how to read it. I expected this kind of foolishness from Prescott, but I thought you knew better."

"Hank, it's important," I pleaded. "I swear to you, I wouldn't do this if I didn't think that —"

"Oh, shit!" Shay cried.

I looked to see the drill rig veering right into the vines, crushing two plants with a horrific *SNAP!* that echoed all the way down the hillside. Allen tried to move the rig out of the vines, but rolled backwards a bit, crushing more plants underneath the giant rear wheels.

"Shut it off!" Hank screamed. "Shut it off!"

But Allen over-compensated and the tractor lunged forward, crossed the width of the small path in a mere second, and smashed into the vines on the other side. Branches exploded in succession like the sound of automatic gun fire.

I sprinted across the row of vines and up the hill. "Stop, stop!" I screamed. "Shut it down!" Allen shut the engine down and the tractor was finally motionless. Motionless and sitting atop vines that were older than my daughter and as unique as a Monet painting.

Allen climbed off the rig and surveyed the damage sheepishly. "Hey, I'm sorry, man. I was trying to—"

"It's not your fault," I said. Because I knew exactly whose fault it was.

It was worse than destruction: it was robbery. The world had been robbed of a one-of-a-kind treasure, of a connection to life and history that could never be duplicated. And I was the one who held the gun during the stick up. I was the one who tried to stuff money into a canvas bag and get away.

But god damn it all, who in the world wouldn't do it, even if there was only the slightest chance of finding gold? This was an opportunity for generation-changing money. This would set up Remy, her kids, her kids' kids, and on and on. This was legacy money. Who in the world wouldn't do it?

The thought shriveled my heart like the twisted, dying branches at my feet. *Who in the Napa Valley wouldn't do it, even if there was only the slightest chance of finding gold?*

I owed Hank more than an apology—I owed him a confession. A confession for a sin that only he could absolve. I turned to make my Walk of Shame, and as I looked down the hillside, every nerve in my body became frighteningly alive with the sixth sense that something was wrong.

I took off at a dead run for the golf cart, the words, "no, no, no," escaping my lips like a magical incantation that could wipe away the ugly reality in front of me. I didn't want to see it, hear it nor even process it. I just wanted to drag it all back in, as though I could slam the door on Pandora's Box and hold it shut with the weight of my body.

Hank lay crumpled on the ground, as Shay crouched next to him, screaming his name over and over.

The very first manager that Reality Star worked with was this guy named Johnny Slammer, who swore up and down that "Johnny Slammer" was his actual, God-given name and not a moniker he picked up in some kind of porn career. He heard us play at a club one night, said he was sure he could get us a record deal, and being young and stupid and naïve as we were, that was good enough for us. We took him on as our manager with a handshake deal.

Johnny Slammer had a shit ton of street cred, honed through years of hair-raising experience in the music business. He was a founding member of Betty & The Blasters, the seminal '80s Rockabilly band from Los Angeles. He got The Stray Cats their first record deal, and wrote the song *China,* which was a hit for The Red Rockers in 1983. As such, Johnny had a bottomless grab bag of fascinating and hilarious stories about rock stars and the rock life, which he'd regale us with as long as we were buying the drinks.

Unfortunately, Johnny Slammer turned out to be a pretty lame manager. He didn't get us any particularly great gigs, and the A&R reps he brought to the show were little more than interns, most of whom he was just trying to sleep with. His one lasting legacy to the band was introducing us to Ethan Mankowicz, who became our attorney and kept the role until the band broke up. To this day, Ethan was still a trusted friend. Shay considered him a mentor.

In the summer of 1994, years after we'd parted ways with Johnny Slammer, we got a call from Ethan, who let us know that Johnny had died suddenly of a heart attack. It was as sad as it was scary, but when you burn your candle at both ends, it turns out the wick is only half as long as you thought.

Johnny had a ton of acquaintances and associates, but practically no close friends except for Ethan. So, Ethan took it upon himself to write Johnny's obituary, and had it published in both *The Seattle Times* and *Billboard.* It was quite a thoughtful tribute, and rather impressive as well, listing most of Johnny's major accomplishments in the music business.

Within a few days, however, Ethan received a series of phone calls from people who disputed the accomplishments spelled out in the obit. A member of The Red Rockers called to say no, in fact, Johnny Slammer did not write the song *China,* and if you'd just look at the credits you'd see this for yourself. The manager for The Stray Cats called to say Johnny wasn't involved in the slightest in the band's career, and not a single person in the organization had ever heard of the guy. Betty of Betty & The Blasters even set the record straight that Johnny Slammer was a member of the band for all of one week.

I was flabbergasted, and "flabbergasted" isn't even the kind of word I'd let come out of my mouth. When Ethan told me the news, a sense of disappointment settled over me like a case of mononucleosis. It was just a heavy, depressing, soul-sucking feeling of disenchantment, not because Johnny turned out to be a pathological liar, but because his stories were the tangible evidence that the life of adventure I craved was obtainable.

Ethan, on the other hand, just chuckled and waved it off. "Well," he said, "that's rock n' roll."

"I suppose," I said. "Just an illusion."

"Don't underestimate illusions. Illusions are like teddy bears for grown-ups."

I'd been at Queen of the Valley Medical Center for six hours, alternately pacing the corridors, fidgeting in a hard, plastic waiting room chair, or fetching another cup of the free coffee they offered at the ICU nurse's station. Shay finally had to leave after four hours for a deposition he couldn't postpone again but made me swear I'd call him when I got an update on Hank.

I hadn't heard anything so far. I couldn't tell which doctors were taking care of him, and the nurses told me that they couldn't release any information until the family was made aware of the situation. I'd seen some of his kids come in. Apparently, Stephan and Gemma were still local, but I'd either missed or hadn't seen the others. At one point, Stephan stormed out of Hank's room, his head bowed and his face pinched tight. As much as I wanted to, I didn't approach him.

I tried calling Sydney after Shay had left but had to leave a message. I didn't want to entertain the thought that she saw my number and sent me straight to voicemail, but it had already put its feet up on my coffee table and asked for a glass of cabernet. I also called Remy and had to leave her a message as well. I felt guilty about it after I hung up, since she was probably at work and two hours away, and children shouldn't be responsible for making their selfish and stupid parents feel better about themselves anyway.

Finally, I saw Gemma emerge from Hank's room, and even from down the hallway she looked like a woman who had cried out every tear she held in her body. As much as I needed to know Hank's condition, I didn't want to disturb Gemma in her fragile state, nor do any more harm to her and her family than I'd already done. So, it was with a sense of surprise—and relief—when she came directly to me and wrapped her arms around me in a tight hug.

"The nurses said you rode with Daddy in the ambulance," she said. "Thank you."

I didn't know what to say. I thought of starting with an apology, but even with six hours to think about it, I still didn't know how to put one into words. "How's he doing?" I asked instead.

Gemma let go of me, then placed her purse on one of the chairs. "Not good," she said, her voice barely above a whisper. "Not good at all." She took me by the arm as she sat down, guiding me into the chair next to her, then clutched my hand with both of hers. It took me a few moments to realize that, after all I had done, *she* was trying to comfort *me*.

"Daddy has brain cancer. Stage Four Glioblastoma." She practically choked on the words, and the tears began flowing again.

"Oh my God," I whispered. "Gemma, I had no idea."

"None of us did," she said. "Apparently, he was diagnosed over a year ago, but he didn't tell anyone about it. He started treatment, but his insurance only covered eighty percent, so he just stopped going after a while. He didn't want to trouble us. God, it's so him. I can't believe this."

"Gemma, I'm so sorry." It was awful, but she was also right. Hank was old school, like my Uncle Glen: Stoic and stubborn right down to the bone. He probably got a bad prognosis after his first round of treatment and decided to stop so he wouldn't leave the kids a giant medical bill. Or maybe the bills had piled up, so he decided to sell the vineyard to pay for them. Either way, Hank probably saw his decision as simply the right thing to do, and the closest thing to an 'I love you' the kids would get.

"I'm glad you were there when he passed out," Gemma said, squeezing my hand. "The doctor said he had a series of micro-strokes, and probably would have died without immediate attention."

"Were the strokes a result of the brain cancer?" I couldn't help it. If I had any blame in this, I'd never forgive myself. Chances were, I wouldn't either way.

"Probably," Gemma replied. "I don't know."

"Would you mind if I went in and saw him?"

Gemma searched her purse for another Kleenex, and used ones spilled out of the top. "I'd appreciate it if you would. I need to go get the baby and set her up with Doug. Probably an hour or so? I don't want him to be alone."

She stood up and tried to compose herself, straightening her blouse and dabbing the smeared makeup under her eyes. "God, I'm a mess," she mumbled. "Listen, Dad's pretty out of it right now. Between the strokes and the drugs they've got him on, he's kind of incoherent. He might just sleep the whole time."

"I won't disturb him," I promised. "But I would like to sit with him until you get back."

Gemma leaned in and kissed my cheek. "You're a good man, Corbett."

No. No, I'm not.

I watched as Gemma disappeared into the elevator, then headed to Hank's room. I tried again to think about what I was going to say. What to tell him. What to tell myself.

Hank lay motionless in bed, his eyes half open, his head tilted toward the window. A nightmare of machines and tubes and plastic bags invaded his body. The room itself seemed more alive than he was with its flickering lights, humming machinery and occasional bells and tones. I walked in quietly and sat in the chair facing the bed. I was surprised when he turned to face me. He opened his eyes a bit wider, but they were empty and distant.

He blinked a couple of times and croaked, "Who dat say dey gonna beat dem Saints?"

"Hank, it's me, Corbett," I said. "How are you holding up, buddy?"

He blinked a few more times. There was no sense of recognition on his face. "You coming over for the game?"

I reached over and took his hand. "Yeah, man. Of course." Hank turned and stared at the ceiling.

"Listen, buddy," I said. "I want you to know that everything is going to be alright. I'm going to take care of the vineyard, ok? No more digging, no more drilling, no caves, nothing like that. Nothing but beautiful vines and plump, luscious fruit, just like it's always been. I'm going to see to it, ok?"

He turned back and gazed at me, or perhaps through me. It wasn't easy to tell.

"We think there's gold on the property. That's why Prescott wants it so bad. And why I wanted it, too, when I found out. But I get it now, Hank. I promise you, I get it. The treasure isn't under the soil. It *is* the soil. And it's going to stay that way forever. I swear to you."

Maybe it was wishful thinking, but I thought I saw a slight smile spread across Hank's lips. "Steward of the land," he whispered.

I didn't even try to hold back the tears. "Steward of the land," I croaked.

"I see an angel," Hank said, and admittedly my first reaction was, *Wait! Don't go towards the light!* but then I heard the door behind me and saw Remy.

I got up and gave her a hug. "Thank you for coming, sweetheart," I whispered before turning back to Hank. "Hank, you remember my daughter, Remy?"

Hank smiled broadly. "Gemma. Gemma, you came back."

Remy moved over to the chair and sat down. "No, Mr. Fogelson, it's Remy. Remy Thomas? Corbett's daughter?" She not only sounded calm, she sounded practically nurturing.

"Gemma, my angel heart."

"Gemma's not here yet, Hank," I said, though I wasn't sure I should have. "She'll be back in a little bit."

Hank reached over and took Remy's hand. "Gemma with the angel heart. Want to know something funny? Corbett chased the pixies. Just like you did. He chased the pixies right through the vineyard."

Remy looked to me for some kind of cue and I shook my head slightly. At this point, it was better to just go along with it and not upset the poor guy in any way.

"That's why you have to," he said. "Your brothers never understood, but you have an angel heart."

I moved to stand beside Remy. "Hank, maybe you should try and get some rest? We'll stay right here with you, but I want you to get some sleep now, OK?"

Hank smiled and closed his eyes, but never let go of Remy's hand. We sat there with the corporeal sound of the machines around us for maybe another half-hour, watching Hank, until Gemma finally arrived. I didn't tell her how her father had mistaken Remy for her, or about my pledge to take care of the vineyard. She had enough on her plate, and all that mattered in this moment was that Hank was in good hands.

Remy and I said nothing as we walked out of the room, and even stood in silence in the elevator. Only when we reached the parking lot, did she finally speak. "Are you OK, dad?"

I hugged her tight, and when I started to let go—so as not to push the boundaries of the Remy Hug—she held on a little longer. "I'm OK," I said. "The question is, are you OK?"

"I'm OK."

The awkward pause that consumed the space between us was like the event horizon of a black hole.

"Are *we* OK?" I finally asked.

"We're fine, dad," she sighed.

"Alright." I nodded, though I wasn't sure if I believed her. "You want to go get some dinner and about eight gin and tonics?"

"Sure."

"Look, hun, I'm going to need your help." I stared at the ground and shuffled around nervously, like suddenly she was the parent and I was the child. "I'll explain all the details at dinner, but the thing is, I need to raise the money for this vineyard, and I can't blow it this time. You were right. I lost the pitch with Fractal Equity Partners before it even came out of my mouth, but I can't let that happen again. If it's all about business and money, then so be it. But I'm going to need you to help me with that part, OK?"

"Sure, Dad," she said. "Whatever I can do."

I gave her another quick hug and headed off towards my car. Then I heard her shout, "Hey, can we go somewhere besides Pinot? Like, anywhere besides Pinot?"

"Sure," I called to her. "But you risk having the servers ask if I'm the 'Eat A Dick Francois Guy.'"

"Pinot it is."

After I got in my car, I turned my phone back on and got an alert that Sydney had called and left a voicemail. As happy as I was that she called me back, I was too nervous to listen to her message, afraid that she might not have said what I wanted to hear. So when in doubt, go with the one-sided conversation. I typed out a text message: *Hank is conscious now, but the prognosis is still unknown. Leaving the hospital, going to have dinner with Remy. I would like to come over afterwards if that's OK by you?*

When I was eight years old, some kids from the block and I played our own version of the classic game of "chicken." We'd ride our bikes over to a section of Tully Avenue, where the road curved around the hillside before straightening out again. The three of us would lie on our backs in the middle of the street just south of the curve, and then watch for the headlights of approaching cars. The first one to stand up and run away before getting squashed by a truck was the chicken.

One evening, Scotty Wilson was the first to make a run for it as an AMC Gremlin rounded the bend. Having proven our courage, Craig Peters and I bolted a millisecond behind Scotty. The three of us got tripped up, and Scotty twisted his ankle, crumpling to the asphalt. Craig and I watched in horror from the side of the road as the car locked its brakes and screeched in a cloud of burning rubber and diesel fumes, missing Scotty's head by only a few inches.

The most frustrating thing about a bad idea or a stupid decision is that, at some point, it felt like a *great* idea and the *right* decision. As I sat in my car and sobbed in the concrete darkness of the hospital parking structure, the thought of ripping up sanctified land to find gold —much like lying in the street and getting my head pulped by a Goodyear Radial—was obviously and instinctually a terrible idea. So when was that clarity going to become the norm for my decision-making process? I was nearly a half-century old. When was I going to have the insight to say, "Hey, maybe I shouldn't do that," without doing it first—and subsequently either flushing my soul down the toilet, or hurting everyone around me? When was the right thing to do just going to come naturally?

I honestly didn't know.

I reached for my phone and typed another message to Sydney: *In case you were wondering, this is Corbett. And I remember the way.*

SIXTEEN

Sydney had really come through for Shay and me. One of her contacts was a player in California's new legalized pot industry, and he lined us up with this guy named Robert Kannison, a gray-goateed, stoner-genius type that Shay dubbed "Dr. Strangebob." He examined the data Marnie previously provided and agreed to meet with us to exchange some ideas.

"I get the gist of what you guys are trying to do," he said, referencing the report. "But, um, this stuff here is from another planet." If he only knew.

Dr. Strangebob came up with a few suggestions that would make the capsule sensor even better than we'd imagined, and with a substantially lower production cost as well. One of his truly brilliant ideas was to coat a wire filament with an oxidizing agent, then stick the tiny filament a millimeter through the bottom end of the cork. The filament would contact the wine (as long as the bottle was stored properly on its side), and feed data to the chip at the top of the capsule, which could be monitored via an app on your phone.

Shay and I agreed to give him 20% of the company in exchange for his ideas and a schematic for the device, as long as he could provide it within two weeks. We were already halfway through our 90-day option on the property, and I was anxious about our deadline—and the fact that I had zero income. Even before we had the plans in hand, Shay was chumming the cork-manufacturing waters for an interested party. However, the wheels of wine business grind slowly, if not drunkenly, and it looked like getting our revolutionary device in front of the Deciders was going to take more time than we had.

And then, for once in my godforsaken life, luck was on my side. Shay got a call from L'Enceinte, a French cork producer I hadn't heard of before. They had been developing a similar technology but had run into a wall. They agreed to sign an NDA, check out our schematic, and if all was to their liking, they'd buy the technology outright. They apparently weren't interested in a licensing deal or a partnership of any kind, and since I needed cash yesterday, the arrangement suited me fine.

Remy cleared out her evening schedule for a week and agreed to meet with me each night to grind out valuation spreadsheets and basically school me on the finer points of an effective investment pitch. Our first evening together was like giving birth, and I don't mean the spiritual, joyous, otherworldly exhilaration of bringing another life into the world—but rather the screaming, sweating, horrendously painful nightmare of pushing a watermelon-sized thing out of a dime-sized hole. I'd never done anything so counterintuitive in my life.

It also made me want to take a swim in an Olympic-sized pool of disinfectant. Planning the presentation put a giant mirror in front of my face and forced me to have a nice, long look. For most of my life, I wanted to think of myself as Enlightened Artist Guy, so above these money-grabbing tools like Brogan Prescott. But when fate had put the opportunity in front of me, I was as ready, willing, and able as he was to blast that vineyard into dust, and then take that dust straight to the bank.

While I could rationalize all day long about why I deserved it more than some rich asshole—how I'd been teased with success all my life, had it dangled in front of me time and again like some sweet, delicious Cronut, only to have it yanked away before its decadent sugary awesomeness hit my tongue—that was bullshit. I was bullshit. And that's never an easy thing to face.

Uglier still was the realization that this whole thing was much bigger than me, or even Brogan Prescott. With all the cave digging, the dirt hauling, the smelting and refining, word would eventually leak that there was gold in them thar vines. There was simply no way to keep that genie in the bottle, and then how long would it take for every farmer in Napa Valley to start digging? It wouldn't matter that the Planning Commission disallowed it. Moneyed interests would move in, a more "friendly" Planning Commission would be installed, and what was once hundreds of square miles of beautiful vineyards would become a massive, festering, toxic hole.

So I focused on the task at hand. Remy was patient with me, in much the same way that prison guards are patient with convicts. If I said, "I don't get it" enough, she'd grab an index card, write something down on it, and slide it over to me. "Just say this." Then she'd scribble on another card. "And if they have any objection to it, then say this."

She eventually taped all the index cards up on her living room wall, creating a flow chart for the presentation. I tried to add one about the history of cork, and how the Trappist monks were the first ones to—

"No," Remy said flatly, stripping the card from my hand.

By the third night, we had created a pretty comprehensive battle plan, and I was starting to feel optimistic about my chances in the board room—so much so that Remy even allowed us to indulge in a single glass of wine as we did our nightly review. Remy didn't drink much, but at least she had excellent taste when it came to wine. Of course, most of the bottles in her collection were ones I gave her, so maybe it wasn't quite a matter of the fruit not falling far from the tree.

I slowly paced the length of Remy's living room, recited my pitch, and answered the volley of random questions Remy threw at me, all the while stepping around Fredo, Remy's massive Bernese Mountain Dog and Whippet mix.

Now I know that all dogs go to heaven and that the internet would be devoid of content if not for pets, but this thing was an abomination straight out of Leviticus. Fredo was more equine than canine, had wiry fur the color of snot at the peak of a head cold, and was so colossal that Remy gave it its own couch. Like all dogs it just wanted some affection, and the fact that Remy could love the beast despite the unholy union that created it was proof that a genuine heartbeat in her chest.

As I gave my rote answer to Remy's objection over the perceived market value of our assets, I noticed a picture in a small, wood frame on the middle shelf of her bookcase. It was a Polaroid of Remy's mom, circa 1991. She was dressed in her uniform of the era—a Clash T-shirt from the London Calling tour, a red-checkered flannel tied around her waist, ripped up Levi's 501 jeans, and purple Doc Marten boots. But what really drew me into the picture was the look on her face: it was a genuine, warm, unguarded moment, free of all the Scene Queen Pretense she typically emanated.

"Oh my God," I whispered, taking the dusty frame into my hands. "I haven't seen this picture in years. I think I took this picture."

It's strange how feelings linger like ghosts, haunting a moment in time. The afterimage that remains from every era of our lives isn't the people, places, or things that surrounded us—it's a coda from the emotional soundtrack.

Staring at that image of Jennifer, that unknowable soul preserved in shades of Ektachrome blue, I was overwhelmed by the waves of desperation that came back. We shot through the world at a million miles an hour back then, manically desperate for everything. Desperate for life, for answers, for any kind of feeling that could penetrate the sickness in our hearts. Desperate for a love that we'd never witnessed in our lives.

I looked over my shoulder, expecting Remy to be there, sharing my little soiree into the past. Instead, she was at her small breakfast table, thumbing through a packet of spreadsheets.

"Hey, did you get this from your mother's house?"

Remy didn't look up from the pile of notes. "I don't know."

"Wow." I stared at the picture again. "She's younger than you are in this."

Remy nonchalantly scribbled something on an index card. "You can have it if you want."

I placed the picture back on the shelf, then rested my head against the edge of the bookcase. *God almighty, Corbett. What have you done this time?*

I took the seat across from Remy at the table. She still didn't look at me, pretending instead to be entirely focused on her cards and notes. "Remy, are you angry at your mom? Because of what I told you?"

"No," she replied, pushing her glasses farther up the bridge of her nose with the end of her pencil.

As I said, Remy didn't do passive-aggressive. If she said no, she meant no, though that certainly didn't rule out something else simmering beneath the surface.

"Alright, so, not mad," I said. "Then what is it?"

Remy dropped her pencil and leaned back in her chair. She looked more annoyed than anything else. "I don't know. It's just that, when you're a kid, your parents are never really…people. You know what I mean? They're not like normal people, who do normal people things. They're more than that. They're above that sort of thing, they're larger than life." Remy picked up her pencil again and tapped it against the binder, the cadence growing faster and faster. "But I guess not. Apparently, Mom was just a bitch."

I have to confess, it was hard not to simply agree with her and sweep this under the dog couch once and for all. But I couldn't. The Corbett Thomas Great Reckoning Tour was in full swing now, with stops at Hank Fogelson, Sydney Cameron, and now Remy Thomas.

"You're right, she was a normal person," I said. "And like all normal people, she was flawed. She made mistakes. Everyone does, honey."

"Right, so, you forgave all the shitty things she did to you, and you want me to do the same? I don't think so." Remy held up a spreadsheet. "I get it, everyone makes mistakes. I screwed up this formula and miscalculated production costs. Mom miscalculated and screwed up my *life*."

That monkey I mentioned? The one who sits on my shoulder and yanks on my eyebrow in these situations? Well, he just burrowed his way into my chest cavity and started ripping my pulmonary artery from my right ventricle.

"Look, I spent a decade trying to figure out why things went down the way they did," I said. "I don't want that for you, I never have. That's why I avoided all of this." *God, did she actually put that bottle of wine away? Who does that?* "It's just that…you've got to understand, honey, these things don't happen in a vacuum."

Remy stopped tapping her pencil and glared at me. "What does that mean?"

My voice lowered an octave. My pulse was so fast I could feel it in my earlobes. "There were things I did. Things I'm not very proud of."

Remy didn't say a word. She just kept staring at me; only now I recognized the look in her eyes. It was the same look she gave me when I had to tell her I couldn't get off work and watch her 3rd grade performance of *The Nutcracker*, or when I missed her record-shattering 50-yard freestyle race because my latest shitty car broke down on the way to the swim meet.

"When the band was dropped from the label, and we started running out of money, I racked up fifty thousand dollars in credit card debt. I didn't tell your mom. I was sure we were going to sign with a new label at any moment or get picked up for a major tour. But it never happened. Eventually I lost everything, including the house."

Remy shrugged. "So, that gave her the right to have an affair? Or to use me as a pawn in your divorce battle?"

I shook my head. "No. But, I mean…geez, Remy, these things aren't all black and white like that." I rubbed my eyes hard, like I was trying to wipe stains off a memory. "Look, I cheated on your mom as well. While I was on the road. More than once."

Every psychologist, every relationship expert, every freaking life coach out there is wrong. I came clean, and it was not a load off my chest or a burden from my conscience. I felt like shit, plain and simple.

"I don't know if your mom ever knew," I said. "She must have suspected, but I never told her."

It was a rare occasion to take Remy off guard. She was a planner, a detail person, a woman who sought preparation for every contingency. Her face was an empty canvas, but I could see that behind her eyes, deep down in a place she tried to keep hidden, she was desperately trying to process all of this.

"And you left all this out so that mom would be the bad guy?" Her voice was flat and lifeless.

"No. Maybe. You know how you said that parents are supposed to be larger than life? Well, we know we're supposed to be, too. I just didn't have the courage to tell you anything that would make me something less in your eyes."

Remy slowly stood from her chair and began removing the index cards from the wall.

"Remy, you've got to understand," I implored. "Your mom and I, we were young and stupid and completely ill-equipped to be married, let alone parents. We ended up doing a lot of really horrible things to each other. We just…we didn't know better. We didn't know *how* to do better."

She unpeeled the last of the cards from the wall and placed them in a pile on the table. She then meticulously compiled all the spreadsheets and notes into a single stack. I didn't know what else to say. I could have apologized for not telling her the whole story upfront, but I was as torn apart as she was, and opening my mouth at all risked unleashing anger at her that needed to remain solely directed at myself.

I watched in silence as Remy took a large manila envelope from the desk drawer and placed all the notes, cards, and spreadsheets inside. She sealed it up, smoothing out the small metal clasp at the top with both thumbs, and then handed the envelope to me without looking at my face.

"Drive safe."

I took the envelope without a word, walked to the coat closet, and grabbed my jacket off the white plastic hangar. As I reached for the doorknob, Fredo fell from his couch, hit the floor with a resounding thud, and scurried over to me with double-Y chromosome abandon. I opened the door and stepped onto the porch, then heard the sound of the beast's churning, mucoidal breathing behind me.

I turned around and knelt down. I swear, that animal was so gargantuan it could look me directly in the eyes when I was on one knee. Its tongue dangled from its slobbery mouth like a pound of three-day-old flank steak as its tail slammed excitedly from one edge of the door frame to the other. I tentatively lifted my hand and scratched the side of its head, a thing so malformed it must have been drawn by H.R. Geiger for the *Alien* movies.

The animal licked my face with one tremendous slurp, confident down to its insane heart that it loved me with the searing intensity of the heat-death of the universe.

"Thanks, Fredo," I said. "Maybe there's hope for me yet."

SEVENTEEN

I don't text and drive. It's stupid, dangerous, and truth be told, I don't have the skills for it. Although I have the font size on my phone set to "Extremely Old Person," and I'm unrepentantly Voice Text Guy (the second most annoying person in a supermarket aisle), I'm more dangerous than a blind NASCAR racer if I try to text and drive. So, I don't do it.

Sort of.

I text at red lights. Along with, it seems, every other person on the planet. The thinking goes that you can text to your heart's content while your car is stopped, as long as your eye's peripheral motion sensor sees the car in front of you start to move. Then you set your phone down and start driving as normal. The trouble is, what if the first person in line at the light doesn't see it turn green? She doesn't move, so you don't move, and neither does anyone else, and the street turns into a parking lot-*cum*-office.

So, there I sat, in my semi-mobile cubicle, trying to send Sydney a text and getting frustrated out of my mind. What I said into the phone was, "On my way now for the meeting. Wish me luck. Can't thank you enough. I'll call you when it's over!" What appeared on the screen was, *On a day now for the beating. Fish me luck. Placenta enough. I'll call too when it's over. Exclamation point.*

The whole message was an atrocity, but *placenta*? Seriously? I hadn't even said the word 'placenta' since ten minutes after Remy was born, and God knows I'd never typed the word into my phone. I thought I had pretty good diction, too. I mean, I was a singer, and not in the way Bob Dylan was a singer.

Deciding not to fix the text, I just sent it as-is and followed it up with, "Siri fucking hates me," which came out, as always, as *Siri ducking hates me,* which only proved the point. Sydney texted me back a moment later: *Placenta enough, indeed,* along with an upside-down smiley face emoji, which I think meant, *You're on Lithium.*

I'd spent the last forty-eight hours trying to piece back together the presentation Remy and I had plotted. Some of it made sense and some of it didn't. There were spreadsheets she had created that could have been written in Sumerian for all I knew. I figured she was going to go over them with me at some point, but I wasn't about to bother her for more help. Instead, I did my best to memorize the concepts that didn't make sense, hoping I could just spit them back out by rote if the need arose.

L'Enceinte, the cork company, didn't have an office in wine country, let alone the United States. However, they did have an Account Manager whose territory was all of North America (apparently, they did a vast majority of their business in Europe), who agreed to meet with us at an office near the Oakland Airport. The Director of Business Development would be joining us via Skype from Lyons, France.

Just the mention of France hurdled me into anxiety mode. What if this honcho knew Jean-Phillipe Marchand? Because, you know, all sixty-seven million people in France know each other. What if I was known as *"Le Criminel Notoire,* Corbett Thomas," the infamous *Manger Le Zob Francois* Guy? If that were the case, then Shay should do the pitch while I hid in the lobby: Of course, Shay wanted no part of it. At all. He didn't even want to show up, saying that he'd prefer to hide in his office and wait for a call. Thanks, buddy.

The meeting took place in an office building with a stepped terrace design and gaudy, fake Boston fern décor like something out a science fiction movie from the 1970s. Remy instructed me that the key to being on time was to plan to arrive a half-hour early; hence, I got there a half-hour early and took a seat on one of the unpleasant turquoise benches that lined the atrium. Apparently, people from the 24th century will have evolved past such mundane desires as butt comfort.

As I extracted the stack of flash cards from my satchel, my throat clenched in an anxiety attack I could only attribute to PTSD. For more years than I care to remember, I compiled several thousand flash cards for my sommelier studies, with the last thousand or so specifically for the Master Sommelier exam. I could not afford a fiasco like that today. I had never thought of my life in terms of last chances, but I was face-to-face with one now—a face already flush with cold sweat. At least there wouldn't be alcohol involved, which is typically the reason for ninety-nine percent of all disasters.

L'Enceinte rented a conference room on the third floor, which in terms of its *Logan's Run* esthetic, was right on par with the rest of the building. Even the desk chairs had that swoopy, eggshell-like back support. Oval was simply the shape of the future back in 1975. It took every fiber of my being to not make some kind of comment, but snark doesn't save the world.

The Account Manager for L'Enceinte stood as I entered the room: I totally pegged that she, too, was French before she even opened her mouth. Her slight frame was perfectly contoured in an understated white blouse and black skirt, with her hair pulled back so tight it made Botox unnecessary. But the dead giveaway was her quintessential Gallic face, complete with a nose that screamed, *Rome was here, circa 51 B.C.*

"Mr. Thomas, such a pleasure to meet you," she said, smiling. "I am Michelle Lamont. Thank you for agreeing to come here today." Her English accent was truly impressive, but a slight, French lilt was still there, just beneath the surface.

"*C'est un plaisir de vous recontrer,*" I answered with a smile. Sure, this was a serious meeting, but no reason not to kick things off with a major dose of charm.

Ms. Lamont laughed. God, I love the French. Seriously, there's no other culture on Earth that can laugh so joyously and still have it mean, "Fuck you, peasant."

I took a seat at the opposite end of the table to Ms. Lamont, who settled in her chair with a rigid posture honed through centuries of believing you're the Center of All Culture in the Universe.

"You'll have to forgive me," she said, placing a single earbud in her left ear. "I am having some audio troubles with my co-worker on Skype. If you don't mind, I will just relay to you what she says to me."

It was a hiccup, but one I could deal with. About ten thousand club gigs taught me all about how to handle audio problems: Shut up and let the engineer figure it out.

"That's fine with me, Ms. Lamont."

"Please, call me Michelle." She turned to a briefcase at her feet and took out a wine bottle and a package of papers, which I recognized as the capsule schematic. She placed them on the table in front of her laptop. "Well, let's just dive right in, shall we?"

Sure. Like diving into a volcano. I was wound up like a slinky, and with each passing second, I could feel every bit of information I'd absorbed over the last week leak out my pores and dissipate into the atmosphere.

"The problem we encountered in our own design was creating hardware that did not require a change in the bottling process," Michelle said before I could speak. "The sensor cannot be inserted during the bottling, it must be a part of the capsule."

This was not starting well. I was under the assumption that this meeting was about negotiating the purchase of the tech and supporting our valuation. Michelle was heading into dark territory about the capsule's functionality. Shit. Dr. Strangebob should have been here, too. *Shit, shit, shit.*

Michelle put her finger against her earbud and looked down at her laptop. She nodded a few times and looked back up again. "And, well, the truth is, Mr. Thomas—"

"Call me Corbett." I smiled a smile that held back the fact I was about to pass out.

She returned a hesitant smirk with strained politeness. "Yes. The truth is Corbett…"

That you suck. And your invention sucks. And your plan sucks and your dreams suck. Oh, and your music? That sucked, too, which is why you're caught up in this perpetual Suck Vortex that defines your Life of Suck. You need to give up and go away. Far away. Far enough where your Black Hole of Suck won't threaten the very existence of life on this planet. Oh, and in case I hadn't made it clear enough, you suck.

"…that we think your idea has found a way around this problem."

"Yes! Say my *fucking* name!" I screamed.

I didn't even realize I had bolted upright as well, knocking my chair back about six feet. I even made this awkward motion with the fist I had raised, as if maybe I could use my hand to scoop all the stupidity out of the air and shove it back into my idiot mouth.

Michelle spoke into her headset, and if my French was still up to par, I think it translated to, "Mr. Thomas was expressing his enthusiasm for the project." She gazed above her laptop screen for a moment, and when her eyes met mine, I detected the slightest glint of a smile. A very French, very condescending smile, but a smile, nonetheless.

"We are impressed with the technology, Corbett, but there are a few issues we need to address before we can move forward."

"Of course," I replied, hoping my newfound professional tone would erase the memory of the last fifteen seconds. "Please, go ahead."

Michelle reached for the bottle and pointed the capsule toward me. "The first issue is placement. The chip is right in the center of the foil. If a consumer were to use a Coravin or a similar device to open the bottle, it would pierce the chip and render it useless."

I did not say the words *Corbett, you dumb fuck*, but I thought them very, very loudly. How could we not have thought of that?

"Perhaps the chip could be smaller?" I suggested. "Then it could be placed off-center of the capsule?"

Michelle shook her head. "No, not smaller. But it can be made with a flexible silicone material that would allow it to be placed under the foil, but on the side of the bottle. However, this would create a significant increase to bottling costs."

She placed the bottle to the side and typed something into her laptop. I took the opportunity to scramble through my note cards, looking for anything that resembled a response to an objection over higher bottling costs. I got through maybe two cards before Michelle spoke again.

"Secondly, we have concerns about liability from an end user perspective. The ultra-luxury wine collector market is worth over a billion dollars annually worldwide. If the device doesn't work properly after all, it leaves us exposed to a class-action lawsuit.

"If we create a disclaimer that the product is used on an at-risk basis, it could harm the brand or decrease the adoption curve before it reaches a crest. How do you propose we reconcile this?"

How the hell do I know? was the first answer that came to mind, but fortunately not the answer I gave. My hands shook as I groped for my index cards again. Adoption curve? What the hell was that? I didn't think Remy and I even covered it.

"Well, that's a good question and I have a good answer." I started laying out cards on the table, scanning them for any kind of keyword that sounded like whatever the hell Michelle was talking about.

"The...the luxury market has proven that it adopts new stuff, new technology." I shifted nervously in my chair and knocked half a dozen cards off the table. I lunged for them, but they fell like confetti to the floor. "Just like the Coravin itself," I added. "Boy, that thing's really taking off."

"I'm not talking about adoption of the technology," Michelle said, her impatience reflected in the increased thickness of her accent. "I said it was a liability problem."

"Liability, of course." I thumbed through about fifty cards in twenty seconds, looking for the word *liability* on any one of them, as the cards slid across the table like some kid just dumped out his Hot Wheels collection from a giant cardboard box.

I was done. It was over, and I knew it. I set the remaining cards on the table and closed my eyes. I sat like that for God knows how long, but I didn't care. The blackness was a welcome respite. The world was shut off for one precious moment. And I stayed that way, with nothing but the dark and the sound of my own breath, until I could feel myself flying.

Not falling. Flying.

"Wine goes bad, Michelle." I opened my eyes. "It always has, and it always will, and even the richest, most knowledgeable collectors understand this. Collectors will take any measure available to reduce this risk, from temperature control, to light control, to vintage information. But even under the best conditions, the wine can still go bad. As long as the sensor is a value-add to the capsule, and as long as L'Enceinte assumes the pass-through cost and offers the app as a free download, the brand perception will be that the sensor is simply another tool in the arsenal to reduce risk. It will not be perceived as a liability when wine spoilage occurs. It will be perceived as a differentiator between your capsule and the competition."

Michelle said nothing. Instead, she took her earbud out and closed her laptop. I couldn't read her, but I defaulted to, *Pack up your shit and leave, Mr. Thomas.*

"Or something," I added. "Something like that."

Michelle reached into her briefcase again and produced a large, white envelope. "We are prepared to make you an offer." She extracted documents from the envelope, then walked over and placed them in front of me. I thumbed through them with quivering hands, afraid to open my mouth lest all the nervous stupidity fall out.

"As we discussed, any offer we put forward would be for the sale of the technology, along with all copyrights, patents and other proprietary material," Michelle said. "A complete buyout."

And there it was, on page three, paragraph two. The Bottom Line. I took a deep breath, like a breath so deep it could have filled eight pairs of lungs. I couldn't believe I was about to say what I was about to say, but out it came anyway.

"Two-point-one million? Our valuation came in at six million."

I couldn't help it. Maybe I was looking the proverbial gift horse in the mouth, but anything under six million and I wouldn't have enough to build the winery on the property after I got prison raped on taxes.

"A valuation based on little more than projected sales and other hypotheticals." Michelle pushed aside a few index cards and sat on the edge of the table. "Plus, there are the issues we discussed."

Issues. I got the feeling they had done more research on me than I had done on them. "Five million for the whole company," I countered. Maybe we'd end up with a smaller crush pad, but it'd be a start.

Michelle placed the tip of her middle finger on one of the index cards and flicked it across the table with a wry smile. "Mr. Thomas, there is no company. No company, no sales history, no purchase orders. You are selling your technology. Two point one is extremely generous in this case."

"What kind of time frame are we looking at until funds are received?"

"If we sign the MOU today, we'll have a purchase agreement to your lawyer within sixty days."

I'd like to think I had a poker face, something impossible to read, but I'm sure it was more like *Fun With Dick and Jane.* That timeframe wasn't going to work. We'd blow past our deadline, and Prescott would swoop in.

"If you can deliver a purchase agreement in seven days with a guarantee of funds five business days after signing, I'll take one-point-eight."

Michelle nodded pensively, tapping her finger against another card. She looked at me quizzically, and I knew in an instant what was coming next. *Aren't you Sensitive Ponytail Guy? Aren't you the Eat A Dick Francois Guy? Aren't you any number of completely ridiculous guys who haven't done a single, serious thing in their lives deserving of reward or recognition?*

"We have a deal."

It took about ten seconds for what she said to sink in. It was as though she said it in Japanese, and I needed time to translate.

"Oh," I eventually said. Then another, "Oh." And then finally I wheezed, "Oh, excellent!"

We made rounds of congratulations, and handshakes abounded, and I even hugged Michelle, which I knew was awkward if not downright inappropriate, but there was no one else around to hug and damn it, the situation called for a hug. We made modifications to the Memorandum of Understanding, with initials and signatures galore, followed by more glad-handing and a final attempt on my part to speak French to Michelle, who laughed it off as she waved goodbye.

I ran like an eight-year-old boy down the hallway, then once inside the elevator, pointed at myself in the mirrored panel about fifteen times mouthing, "Who's the man?"

I then strutted out of the elevator and into the lobby to the soundtrack of Rupert Holmes' "Escape," which was drifting out of some speaker hidden among the fake ferns. "I am not into yoga," I sang along with Rupert. "I am into champagne!"

I was Conan the Barbarian and Warren Buffet rolled into one. I had pecs the size of toasters and my penis had grown six additional inches in the past fifteen minutes. I had slayed the woolly mammoth using little more than a cue ball in a tube sock.

"I *am* into champagne," I said to myself. I decided to call Shay and Sydney and anyone else who might listen, order a freaking case of bubbles, and go absolutely insane.

As I walked back to my car, I allowed myself for the first time ever to truly think of myself as the owner of the Fogelson Vineyard, and what that life would look like. I pictured myself in the springtime, watching bud break on the vines; I'd witness clusters of beautiful grapes go through the magic of *veraison* as they turn from chartreuse to lavender to luscious purple. I imagined the biting cold on my bare fingers as I harvested grapes at 2 a.m. on an October morning, then riding in the truck to the crush pad to watch my little babies take their first step into becoming wine.

And I loved every moment of it. Even the mundane was sublime.

I reached for my phone to call Shay and let him know the good news, and to tell him to meet me at Pinot with corks popped and glasses flowing, and that's when it hit me: I was a millionaire now. Sure, I was only a paper millionaire, and I would never physically touch a single dollar of the money, but...after thirty years of wanting it so bad, I had done it.

What struck me even harder—what was most surprising of all—was that finally becoming a millionaire wasn't the first thing I thought of. It wasn't even the reason to celebrate. The money was simply a means to an end. I had no desire whatsoever anymore to define myself as being rich, but I had every desire to define myself as a vintner. As a steward of the land.

I clicked on my phone and saw that I had a missed call, a voicemail, and a text message from Shay. Poor stressed out guy. He'd probably clawed through the drywall in his house like a caged Siberian Husky. Well, that's what he gets for leaving me to do the meeting on my own, the rat bastard.

I opened his text: *Hey bro, left you a VM as well. Sorry if this timing sucks but after thinking about it I figured you may need this news during your meeting. I'm really sorry, but I just heard that Hank Fogelson passed away last night.*

EIGHTEEN

Hank was laid to rest three days later at the Tulocay Cemetery, which I thought was beautifully appropriate. He had given his soul to Coombsville, and now his body would become a part of it as well. It was a private service, family members only. There was a memorial service for the rest of us the following day at Baron's Ridge Winery, up near Atlas Peak. The crowd spilled from the ostentatious barrel room into the parking lot. It was my one moment of happiness that day to see so many people paying their respects. Hank deserved it.

I'd asked Sydney to come with me to the service, but she sheepishly had to refuse. She was afraid to be so obviously in public with me, the questions that might arise and such. I understood, I suppose. It didn't make it any easier, though. I needed her and she wanted to be there for me, but she couldn't, and I didn't want to put her in an uncomfortable position. She felt guilty enough about how she made me feel - it was a twisted situation that left both of us unhappy.

Gemma came to the service and said a few words, and by "a few" I mean she spoke maybe three sentences, thanking everyone who came for their love and support. She couldn't make eye contact with the crowd, couldn't get close enough to the microphone to be heard very well, and didn't have the willpower to make it past a word or two without sobbing. Daughters love their Daddies in magical, messed-up, mysterious ways, and Gemma's profound vulnerability touched me as much as Hank's loss.

A dozen more took to the podium after Gemma to spill their hearts. Many of them were people who had known Hank and his family for decades, including friends of Hank's late wife, Corrine. It hadn't occurred to me until that moment that Gemma and her brothers had now lost both their mother and father. My heart broke for them even more. You're never officially a grown-up until both your parents are dead.

212 | JOHN A. TAYLOR

I decided to say a few words myself. Half the people in attendance were like me: they were folks who knew Hank as this semi-iconic figure in the valley, as part of its tradition and its deep roots. And yet this figure, this man who was a symbol of a way of life, saw something special in me of all people. He saw beyond the layers of narcissistic bullshit, perhaps saw some bit of himself down there. Something good. Someone who could make a connection that mattered. I couldn't say Hank was the father I never had—we didn't get that much time together —but he was what I hoped a father would be like.

As I tried to connect my scattered thoughts, a man who appeared to be around Hank's age stepped up to the mic. I didn't recognize him. He wore a sleeveless, black fleece vest over his plaid shirt—the official uniform of the Napa Winemaker—with thick, grey hair brushed back in a way that made him look like Andrew Jackson. He stood for a moment, gazing out at the crowd, then pursed his lips tight and looked away. I recognized that look. This was a man who was digging deep for the right words and trying not to completely lose it in the process.

"Hank was a good man." He hit each word like it was its own novel. He gazed solemnly at the top of the podium, as if he was staring into some magic TV screen, replaying a lifetime in high definition. "When I die, all I want is for someone to stand up and say, 'Don was a good man.'"

The gentleman nodded a few times, opened his mouth as if to add something else, but simply nodded again and turned and walked out towards the parking lot.

I didn't go up to the podium.

After the service, Toni Fonseca—the genius winemaker for Baron's Ridge—opened three magnums of their 1975 Cabernet Sauvignon, the first vintage made from grapes sourced from the Fogelson Vineyard. Shay managed to snag a few pours, and he brought one out to me on the terrace. We raised our glasses, and probably for the twentieth time that week, drank a toast to Hank. The wine could have used about two more hours to open up: I drank the whole thing down in one glorious, disheartened gulp. Sometimes we don't get another two hours.

Shay and I stood on the terrace in silence, watching the storm clouds lumber across the top of Atlas Peak, feeling the occasional raindrop blown over by bitter winds from San Pablo Bay. Guests began to leave, which was my signal to go back into the barrel room and say some goodbyes. But I didn't. The icy wind, the impending dark, and the silence of the clouds was far better than what inevitably awaited me.

Shay knew it, too, and we shared a few minutes of quiet anxiety before he finally spoke. "Gemma's still here. You need to have a talk with her."

"Gemma? Are you kidding?" I felt a few more drops on my forehead. The storm would be on top of us soon. "Poor girl would probably lose it completely."

"OK, well, Stephan's here, too. You could try talking with him."

"I don't know," I said, sighing. "At the service and all? The whole thing feels like something out of *The Godfather.* I'll call him next week."

"Don't make me be the dick in this thing." Shay sounded less lawyer-like and more panicky. "We don't have until next week."

I just nodded, wishing there was more of that '75 Cab left in my glass—though that fine, sour mash whiskey that Hank carried around might have been more appropriate. If it was enough to numb the pain in his head, it'd be enough to numb the pain in my heart.

I barely caught up to Stephan before he reached his car. He turned as I shouted his name, his shoulders hunched against the rain, which had started in earnest. He squinted as though he didn't recognize me at first, or maybe the wind was whipping into his eyes. "Oh, Corbett. Thought I saw you here earlier."

"Wouldn't have missed it," I said. "It was nice to see so many people here. Your father really touched a lot of lives."

Stephan said nothing. He just squinted at me, his shoulders nearly up around his ears.

"So," I began awkwardly, "I know this isn't the best time or place to discuss this, but I wanted to let you know that I'm ready to move on the vineyard. I can have the cash wired to escrow in two days, and we can sign the papers anytime that's convenient for you. I don't want to make this any more difficult on you or your family, so—"

"You're welcome to submit an offer," Stephan interrupted. "The Members will be looking at all offers on the 14th."

Damn it all, I knew it. I had hoped against it but knew I could never be so lucky. "Well, that's the thing, Stephan." I tried not to sound as desperate as I felt. "Your father and I had a deal. He agreed to give me a ninety-day option on the property for one-point-five million. I've got the money now, all cash, and I can—"

"Do you have a contract?" The interruptions were throwing me off. I didn't know how to respond fast enough. "You have a purchase contract, right? I didn't think so. The purchase price is three million. You can bring your best offer with everyone else on the 14th."

He turned towards his car and I instinctively clutched his arm.

"Hold on." Stephan glared at my hand and I immediately let go. "Look, your father and I shook on it. You of all people should know that he was a man of his word. His handshake meant something, and I think you should honor that."

Stephan took a step towards me until we were almost nose-to-nose. Well, nose-to-chest is more like it. He looked more like his mother than his father with thin, brown eyes and sunken cheekbones that made him appear much older than he was.

"I know exactly the kind of man my father was," he spat. "He sold his grapes for five thousand a ton when he could have gotten eight thousand. He sat by and did nothing while prices on the wine he supplied went from twenty dollars a bottle to a hundred and twenty dollars a bottle. This great man of his word always honored his contracts, and what did it get him? Well, guess what? He's dead now, and no one can take advantage of him anymore. Including you."

Stephan opened the car door but paused before getting inside. "Brogan Prescott is offering three-and-a-half million. If you can't beat that, I'd just prefer that you didn't show up at all."

I didn't really notice that Stephan drove away. I didn't notice that the rain had soaked me to my skin. I didn't notice that I was the last person at the service, standing in the middle of the parking lot like some kind of misplaced traffic cone. I didn't notice when Shay drove up, silently guided me to the passenger seat, and drove off into the night.

Nothing good happens at 3:00 a.m. As a person who used to specialize in 3:00 a.m., I know this firsthand. 2:00 a.m. can still be rationalized: Last call, get a taxi, drive home, and pass out, though not necessarily in that order. But if the "pass out" part hasn't occurred by 2:30 a.m. tops, then you're purposely and deliberately buying a ticket to Troubleville, the Land of Shenanigans. Expect recrimination by loved ones at best, law enforcement at worst.

At 3:00 a.m. the next morning, I went ahead and purchased my ticket.

I lay in bed and thought through the whole scenario like a fifteen-year-old girl. There was no way he would simply take my call at his office. And then what, leave a message? No way he was going to call me back. No way. I could go to his office and make a scene, but he probably had more gatekeepers than Pope Francis, and the scene itself would defeat the purpose. And his Facebook page was probably monitored by some six-figure social media wonk, so messaging him wouldn't work.

Messaging.

I scrambled from bed and tore through the documents still scattered across my table. I knew it was there, on a Post-It note, stuck to a manila folder— the one I took to that very first meeting...

...which I dumped in the trash because I was so freaking pissed off. Damn.

Shay would have it! Of course. He was the one who gave it to me in the first place. I knew I shouldn't call him at 3:00 a.m. for something that could certainly wait until 7:00 a.m., but I was well beyond such mundane considerations as manners or even rational thought. I was making a Hyperactive Mistake Cake here, with a thick, creamy layer of Desperation Frosting.

I expected swearing, and plenty of it. I expected he wouldn't even answer. But not only did he pick up, he handed over the digits with a kind of quiet resignation. "Are you sure about this, bro?" was the only comment he made.

"Dead sure," I told him. "It's the only option left."

And thus, I had it in my grubby little hands (well, on my grubby little phone, really). I thumbed out the message, pure, simple and clear:

"I know about the gold."

I added the word "motherfucker" to the end, but it struck me as slightly confrontational, so I deleted it at the last moment. Then I realized he may not know who was sending him the message, so I added, "This is Corbett Thomas." Maybe that didn't have the Jason Bourne *schadenfreude* I was looking for, but I had to go with it.

He didn't text back. Of course, he didn't. It was 3:17 a.m., and I was texting from Troubleville. By nature, those texts are timed to be delivered at the optimal point of Sender Regret. But I had no regrets. I knew what had to be done.

But maybe he didn't. So, I sent him the same text forty-seven times.

At 7:05 a.m., I got a message back. It was nothing but an address in

Sunnyvale, about two hours away. Nice. He saw my Jason Bourne and raised me a James Bond. I was out the door in two minutes.

Want to know why every wonk in Silicon Valley wants to invent driverless cars? Because traffic. San Francisco is apparently the fifth worst city in the world when it comes to the bumper dance but crawling southbound down the 101 freeway at two miles an hour, it felt more like number one. Slogging through this time suck every day would be enough for me to dedicate my million-dollar Stanford education to the utter annihilation of this lunacy as well.

The address Brogan sent me was for a place called Bean Scene Café, a coffee shop in the Heritage District of Sunnyvale. He didn't include a meeting time, so I hoped he would still be there when I showed up about three days later. Google Maps lady told me I would arrive at 8:43 a.m. when I left Napa, but then she kept pushing that number forward with agonizing updates. I thought of texting Brogan my ETA but stopped when I realized I had the upper hand here. Let the bastard wait, hopefully in a pool of caffeinated sweat.

Almost three hours after jumping in my car, I exited the 280 freeway and began the final mile to my destination. Swear to God, I passed three Starbucks on the way. *Three*. Note to self: open a Starbucks in Silicon Valley if this doesn't work.

With its chalkboard menus, potentially real indoor plants and mahogany chairs, the Bean Scene Café looked a lot less corporate than the typical coffee place. As usual in these circumstances, I stood in the doorway just being tall, like a human signpost that simply reads, "Here I am." Not a single patron looked up from their laptop, and my jaw clenched at the thought that maybe Brogan got tired of waiting and left.

Then I saw him, sitting at a small table near the corner window, wearing the exact same outfit he wore that day we first met at the vineyard. Maybe the shirt was different. Maybe. But he still hadn't discovered the joys of personal grooming. He was engrossed in his phone, his face a canvas of both awe and frustration as he randomly poked and swiped at the screen.

I took the seat across from him. For the entire three-hour trip down there, I thought about this conversation. I rehearsed all the best lines I could think of, blurting out select phrases and sharpening my righteous indignation until it became a Verbal Sword of Virtue, ready to hack and maim all argument and objection.

But sitting down with him now like this, in the Zero Hour, the words that came out of my mouth were, "Do you want some coffee?"

"I hate coffee," he answered, not taking his eyes off the screen. He made a slight head gesture towards a 40-ounce, neon yellow can of Blast Off energy drink that sat nearby.

"Ah," I replied, apparently sheathing the Verbal Sword of Virtue. I was so anxious that a coffee would have only been a Cup o' Stroke, so there I sat, nervously waiting for him to stop doing whatever the hell he was doing on his phone.

Without looking me, he finally said, "Have you played this yet? *Empire of Elites?* This thing is book."

"I don't play games on my phone."

"Damn. Guess I don't get your ninety-nine cents." He suddenly tapped the screen rapidly, his face smashed into a grimace of determination. The spasm stopped almost as quickly as it started, and he went back to casual poking and swiping.

"Well," he said. "Your meeting."

I opened my mouth but all of it was gone. All the great opening lines, all the beautiful turns of phrase, all the epic and convincing tirades. So, back to the basics then. "I know about the gold."

"I got that," he said, smiling.

"I'm here to ask you—to beg you—please, just don't do it. Don't mine the property."

"No one's mining anything. Mining isn't allowed in Napa County."

I reached over and pushed the phone down from Brogan's face, the same way I used to push a book down from Remy's face when she wasn't paying attention.

"You know what I mean," I said. "If you do this, word is going to get out, one way or another, and soon you're going to have everyone in the valley digging. It's going to destroy the place."

Brogan took a swig off his giant can of hellacious, antifreeze-colored chemical brew. "You're being way too dramatic. We did the research. The Fogelson Vineyard is the only property on the entire southeastern side of the Vaca Range that has gold deposits. No one else is going to find anything."

"They're going to look anyway. They're going to dig. They're going to rip up every vineyard in sight. There's a human nature element to this that you don't understand the way I do. People are fucking greedy, Brogan. They get the sniff of money and all sense of discretion goes out the window."

I immediately regretted that last part. It was a jab against people like Brogan, but I was trying to get this guy on my side. I don't know if he took offense, though. His face wasn't easy to read, especially under that Amish-like explosion of face hair.

"Like I said, we're not mining. We're digging a cave."

I scooted my chair in closer to the table. *Read the need.*

"Well, what if I proposed something that got us both what we're looking for? Instead of digging that cave, use the money to build the most unique, most magnificent, world-class winery in Napa? If you agree to do it, I'll be your General Manager. I've got the experience, the connections, and the know-how to oversee the entire project and create the kind of cult wine that fetches thousands of dollars per bottle. Swear to God, you give me five years on this, and I'll generate millions per year for you."

And just like that, my deal with the devil was out on the table, ready for Brogan to ratify at will. Having heard the actual words come out of my mouth, I didn't feel as slimy as I thought I would. In truth, Brogan might have made a pretty good boss. He didn't strike me as much of a micromanager and given that the virtual reality winery thing was just a cover, he'd probably let me steer the ship the way it needed to go. Best of all, no mining.

Brogan stared out the window. The storm from the previous day must have moved south to north, as warm morning sunlight reflected off the wet streets like a postcard picture.

"You're a dreamer, aren't you Corbett?" I couldn't tell if it was a rhetorical question or not, but he spoke again before I could answer. "You dreamed of becoming a rock star. You dreamed of becoming a Master Sommelier. You dreamed of having your own vineyard and starting your own winery. Big dreams, am I right?"

"Yeah," I said hesitantly. "I suppose so."

"Well, maybe you can't tell, but I'm a dreamer, too." He turned from the window, and for the first time he seemed serious. "When I was five, I created my very first card game, *Goblin Go*. It was awesome. Drew every card myself. By the time I was seventeen, I was one of the first people ever to use Java to write my own computer games. And all I ever dreamed of was having my own business, my own company where all I did was sit around and make up games. And you know what? I did it. I dreamed it, and I did it."

And now it was his turn to lean in, read the need, and go for the close.

"You see, I do get it. I'm a dreamer, too, just like you. But the dreams I have, they're huge dreams. Dreams that will change the very way our society functions. World changing dreams. Dreams that are going to benefit you and your family for generations to come. But these dreams are going to cost billions of dollars. Not millions. Billions."

"And you think you've got the right to decimate the entire Napa

Valley for this? Just destroy this unique, magical place that's been around for millions of years for whatever new techie idea you've got?"

Brogan tapped is index finger on the table rapidly, like he was still playing his game. "I'm not destroying the valley. All I need is one tiny vineyard," he said. "In fact, one section of one tiny vineyard. And yes, I'm sorry that we'll have to sacrifice a few vines to do it, but that's nothing compared to the good that's going to come out of this project."

I tried desperately not to raise my voice, but I don't think it worked. "Listen to me. Mike Alizen is a grower who lives right on the other side of the hill. Sells his grapes, manages his vineyard, gets by decently, but is always just one or two bad seasons away from losing it all. What do you think a guy like that is going to do when he learns that his neighbor found gold on his property? What do you think they're all going to do? They're going to dig the place up and go for the money."

Brogan turned back towards the window.

"Go for the money." he said quietly.

His tone made me feel like he was considering it, like my argument was making a difference. But I couldn't leave anything to chance, so I went in for the kill.

"I can't allow this to happen, Brogan. Either accept my offer or I'm going to tell the Fogelson kids about the gold."

Brogan chuckled. "What, you think Stephan Fogelson wouldn't be out there himself with a shovel if he knew?"

"I think he doesn't have your resources. It'd take him three years just to get permitted to build a cave, which would buy me enough time to tell city officials what's really going on out there."

A young couple passed by on the sidewalk, and as they approached the café window, the young man hurriedly took out his phone and snapped a picture of Brogan. The man waved like a six-year-old waving to Mickey Mouse at Disneyland. Brogan lifted his palm in detached acknowledgement, then reached around and fished out a small slip of paper from his back pocket. He flipped the slip of paper on the table in front of me.

It was folded in half and crumpled around the edges, but something about its size made it immediately recognizable. I turned it over and unfolded it, and in a split second my face became hot and flush—first with excitement, then with guilt. It was a handwritten personal check, made out to me, for five million dollars.

I guess it was such a surreal moment that my brain's filters overloaded and shut off, because the first thing out of my mouth was, "You kept a five-million-dollar check folded up in your back pocket? What are you, twelve?"

"If you want me to make it out to your company name or send it to your lawyer, I can do that."

I couldn't take my eyes off the thing. I'd never seen a check for anything near that amount, let alone held one in my hand. Especially not one *that was made out to me*. Even my biggest royalty check back in the band days was only five-figures.

"So, I believe in the vernacular they call this 'Hush Money?'" I said.

"I prefer 'Dream Money,'" he replied.

I don't think we're in Kansas anymore, Toto. The thin paper shook between my fingers, and I slumped onto my elbows to keep the vertigo from spinning me out of my chair. Brogan, sensing the confused animal before him, wasn't leaving anything to chance, either, and it was his turn to go in for the kill.

"Think about it, Corbett. What are you, fifty years old now? Empty nest, right? You're unemployed, you've lost your credentials and your reputation, and now you've lost this vineyard. What are you going to do next? Go work at some wine bar in the suburbs, pouring Cougar Juice for minimum wage? How much money do you have saved for retirement? Let me guess—none. You gonna move out of the state and live on Social Security in a mobile home park? Hope that maybe your daughter comes around sometimes and kicks down a few bucks for groceries? Is that your plan?"

I wanted to hate him. I wanted to reach across the table and wrap my hands around his goddamn throat. But you can't squeeze the life out of the truth.

"But look what you've got now," he whispered. "Now you've got a chance. Now you've got freedom. Enough money to do anything you want. Go buy some other vineyard, start your own winery. Or go be a rock star again. That's your true calling, isn't it? You never should have stopped, and you know it. Just think of the creative freedom you'd have, knowing that your music doesn't have to pay the bills. Do anything. Do everything. This is your chance to be the authentic you, for the first time in your life."

Spinning, falling, dying, I didn't know what you'd call it. I couldn't make a sound, form a word, put together a cohesive thought. I watched myself from outside my own body as I stood up, legs pushing the chair back slowly across the tile floor with a horrible screeching noise. I didn't even notice that I'd stuffed the check in my coat pocket. I could see a dog through the window at the café across the street, its leash tied to a chair, barking in confusion for its missing owner. I shuffled towards the exit, or at least towards where I thought the exit was.

Brogan called out just before I reached the door. "Oh, and Corbett," he said. "You really shouldn't worry about the vineyard. I still plan on building a winery there. My wife, Sydney, is going to run it."

NINETEEN

I have never blacked out before. This may come as a surprise, seeing as how I've been a professional drinker since before I was legally able to be. Yet I've never inflicted on myself that curious malady where one does not remember portions of the evening, nor the untoward behavior perpetrated therein. This has nothing to do with responsibility and probably everything to do with genetics or good fortune but suffice to say the good, bad, or ugly, I remember it all.

Except that morning when I drove to Sydney's apartment.

I don't remember the drive. I don't remember racing through her townhome complex. I don't remember sprinting up the stairs. Fortunately, our brains are gifted with a mechanism to wipe away the pain and the tears and the screams and the snot and the betrayal and the dry heaving and the slamming of a fist so hard into the dashboard that the radio shatters.

I wandered out of a coffee place, and then I was in Sydney's living room. That's about it.

"You know exactly why," I heard myself snap.

She had said something a moment earlier, something when I first came through the door, but I wasn't fully back from my visit to Nowhereland.

"What's going on, Corbett?" She held something strange in her hands. Some kind of tool maybe. Something else that didn't connect.

"I'm talking about Sydney Prescott!" I screamed. "Sydney fucking Prescott!"

I'd hoped that line would have the effect of a bullet through the heart: Sydney would stumble backwards from the brutal force of my shocking revelation, and the tears would stream from her eyes and the apologies would fall off her tongue as she drowned under the weight of her guilt.

Instead, Sydney sighed with impatient resignation, tossed whatever it was she was holding into a cardboard box at her feet, and sat slowly on the edge of the couch. "I really hoped it wouldn't come to this," she said.

"Well, pardon me for finding out," I replied sarcastically. "I hope you enjoyed your little spy game, or whatever bullshit this was."

"What are you talking about?" Sydney sounded indignant, which angered me even more, since I was the only one who deserved a monopoly on that particular emotion.

"Did you and your husband plan this all along? Been meeting in secret all these nights when you were supposedly with your old friends?"

"Whoa, whoa, whoa." Sydney stood up. "You've got this all wrong."

"The fuck I do!" I shouted. "You've been playing me since the night we met."

"Oh, since that first night?" Her indignation swamped mine like a kayak in the North Atlantic. "Since that very first night I met you?"

"Oh, so you always start flirting with a guy who nearly pukes all over you? You practically begged to give me a ride home so you could—"

"So I could what?" Sydney got up in my face. She stood on her tip toes and went nose-to-nose with me.

"So you could...could..."

"So I could what?!"

Oh. Holy. Shit.

Legend has it that Isaac Newton first thought of the law of gravity when an apple fell on his head. My epiphany struck me more like a bowling ball from a third-story window. And when it hit, I almost wished it was an actual bowling ball, because then I'd be put out of my misery. And everyone else's, too.

"You told me everything," I whispered. Turns out, I was the one who stumbled back from the brutal force of shocking revelation. My legs buckled under me like my knees had been abducted, and I sank down onto the living room carpet.

"That night, in the car. You told me your whole story. You said your husband was this rich game designer, that he'd become obsessed with buying some vineyard, and um, it was the last straw for you, so you asked for a trial separation."

Sydney sat crossed-legged in front of me and put her hands on my knees. "It was like some weird karmic thing or twist of fate or God knows what when you had me stop the car at the vineyard that night," she said. "I didn't connect the dots that it was the same vineyard Brogan wanted until you introduced me to Hank. I tried to bring it up again the first time you came back to my place, but it didn't come out right. And after that, well, that's when I started getting too deep."

"Too deep into me, or too deep in this whole…thing?" I asked.

"Well, both."

The bowling ball stuck in my cranium jarred a few things loose.

"You're the one who made sure the disclosures got in front of me," I said. "You wrote those Post-It notes and put them on the reports, right? You were trying to point me in the right direction."

"Yes," she whispered, looking down into her lap.

"Wow. And what else? I suppose that Dr. Strangebob is a personal friend?"

Sydney nodded slowly. "Yep." She looked back up with me. "And…?"

"And?" I asked.

The final revelation made the previous bowling ball feel like a pea.

"Oh. Oh, no way. You're the home office in Lyon? I'd never heard of L'Enceinte because there's no such company. That was all you. Including the money."

Sydney just nodded; I took what some shrink of mine called "a deep cleansing breath."

I did not feel cleansed.

"Syd, did you do all this just to spite your husband? Was I part of some twisted game the two of you were playing?" Though my brain bits were scattered all over her apartment, I could still tell there was genuine love and concern in her eyes.

"No. No, it wasn't like that." She leaned in closer, resting her arms on my shoulders. "I did it because I wanted this for you. I believe in you. I believe in what you're trying to do."

I guess it made sense in its own completely messed-up way. It was the most loving, dysfunctional, generous and fucked up thing a person had ever done for me.

I tucked my face into her thick hair to breathe in her scent, to feel her warmth, to take my mind off the objects I saw around me and how they now made sense. It only worked for a few moments.

"You're packing," I said.

She pulled away gently. "Yes."

"Are you going back to him?"

Sydney stood up and went into the kitchen where she pulled a small, bubble-wrapped item from a box on the counter, then came back and handed it to me. I could see through the layers of wrapping that it was the antique teaspoon she had kept on the counter.

"When I was seventeen, my mom grounded me for taking the car without asking," she started, sitting down next to me. "So, one night, I snuck my friend Teri into the house after my mom went to sleep and we hung out in my bedroom. Teri smoked these awful smelling clove cigarettes, so we kept the window open to try and air out the place so my mom wouldn't know."

Sydney took the spoon from me and cradled it in her palm. "Teri fell asleep with a cigarette burning and the house caught on fire. We woke up in time and got out the window, but my mom...my mom didn't. This is, um, this is all I have left of her."

I expected more tears—hell, even I was welling up—but Sydney stiffened. She'd gone down this road many times before and had apparently learned to navigate it.

"So, seeming as how I'm in high school, everyone kind of freaks out about the incident and no one knows how to handle it, including me. All my friends distanced themselves from me, even Teri, who finally moved away. I became the Weird Girl with the Dead Mom, and no one wanted anything to do with me.

"And then one day, I open up my locker and this piece of paper falls out. It was a drawing of me, really detailed, but like one of those Japanese anime cartoons with the knee socks and the super short skirts. And every day, one of these pictures would show up in my locker, and they always looked the same. But after a few days I started to notice these subtle differences, until I figured out that it was a flip book, and I was getting one page at a time. So finally, after about four months of this, I put the whole thing together, and it was this cartoon of me holding a red balloon. The balloon slips from my hand and I start to cry, when suddenly this guy runs over, grabs the balloon out of the sky, and hands it back to me with a kiss. The very last page was signed 'Brogan Prescott.'"

She was making it really hard to hate this guy.

"That's just the kind of guy he was. He used to make me a game every year on my birthday." She smiled; a genuine smile for a genuinely nice memory. "And I mean, all the way up until just a few years ago. Board games, card games, these funny little dice games. His passion for it was so real, so sincere.

"Anyway, he was this nerdy little freshman kid and I was a senior, but it didn't matter. He was my savior. I went off to UCLA, he eventually went to CalArts, and he was my boyfriend the whole time."

Sydney stood up and took the spoon back to the small box in the kitchen. There were half a dozen boxes scattered around—more stuff than someone would bring for a short-term rental. I realized then that the place was probably one of several vacation homes she and Brogan owned.

"I got an opportunity to go work in Washington, DC, and Brogan said he'd come with me. But after a couple of years, he still hadn't moved out. He decided to start 4-D Games in San Francisco, and he begged me to come back and be with him. So, I put my career on hold and came back. I supported him for years—took a job I didn't want, stuck it out through two bankruptcies. And then, one day...boom.

"For the first few years after the money came in, it was like, 'Holy shit, look at all this money!' and we just *partied.* Then suddenly everything changed. Brogan had always been a man-child, albeit a loveable and mostly engaged man-child. But after the money came in, he became this weirdly obsessive, completely detached man-child. And I became...me. This me I'd never known, who wasn't defined by the pain and guilt of this tragedy I went through as a kid."

"The authentic you," I whispered.

Sydney cocked her head to the side. "Wait...did you talk to Brogan?"

"Yeah," I said. "We had coffee and bribes. You didn't know?"

Sydney laughed morosely. "Of course, you did. 'Authentic you' is the big catch phrase he uses all the time. It's kind of ironic, really, considering the authentic him is mostly a dick."

I stood up and came close to her. "Then why are you going back to him?"

Sydney buried her face in her hands. "Oh god, Corbett, don't you get it? I'm not going back to him." She reached into a box and pulled out two glasses, then grabbed a bottle of Maker's Mark from another box. Gliding past me, she walked out to the balcony, and I followed her.

The balcony had the best view in the complex, facing out towards Yountville Crossroads and across the glorious acreage of the Second Son Vineyard. The recent rains turned most of the soil to mud, but with the sun finally peeking through the billowing storm clouds, the scene looked like something out of a Visitor Center postcard.

Sydney poured two overly-generous glasses and handed me one as she simultaneously drank from the other. She made this sighing noise that sounded like a turbo jet before saying, "I'm not going back to my husband, and I can't stay here with you."

She didn't even bother to use the handle. She magically pulled out some kind of Thor's Hammer from her pocket and chucked it at the sliding glass door of our submarine: A wall of water blasted into the submarine and pinned me up against the bulkhead. *This is what you get for buying a submarine with a sliding glass door*, I kept trying to tell myself, but all I heard was, *This is what you get for trusting someone.*

Drowning was neither fast nor painless. As hard as I treaded, I couldn't keep my mouth above the water line—that line between me and four-year-old me who watched his dad slam the door behind him. Between me and twenty-four-year-old me who waited in bed alone at 2:00 a.m. for his wife to text him if she'd be coming home that night.

"Why?" It was the best I could manage.

Sydney poured more whiskey in her glass. "Don't you see what's happened here? I gave my life up for my husband. My plans, my dreams, my career—hell—my very identity. So, I left to go discover Sydney Cameron again, to really be *her* for the first time in my life, and what's the first thing I did? I lost myself in another man. Same old shit, same pattern. I put my life back on hold and started helping you."

"Well," I said. "It's not like that's a particularly *bad* thing – "

"Not for you! Not for him!"

"No, no, that's not what I meant." *What the hell do I mean? And how come the ballast pumps aren't draining this damn water?* "I mean, you could have done this with me. You could have just told me. Like that night in Albuquerque."

Sydney stepped in close to me and rested her head on my chest. "I know. But by that time, what we had was so amazing that I didn't want to take the chance of losing it."

I stroked her hair. "Ah. Selfish," I said. "I totally understand selfish."

She pulled away and looked up at me. "I did what I did because no one had ever loved me or accepted me for the person that I want to be. And I know it sounds screwed up, but I have to start doing these things for me, now. Sydney Cameron really deserves a Sydney Cameron."

What's that old saying? If you love something, lock it in a cage and never let it out of your sight? Something like that. I wanted her to stay, plain and simple. We'd run off together and everything would switch from black-and-white to color like *The Wizard of Oz.*

Though I felt totally sorry for myself that this absolute Goddess would no longer be bringing me her free-pizza-delivery-by-unicorn brand of love, I knew it had to be like this. And if the knife wasn't twisting in its *seppuku* irony enough, I realized it would only push her away more if I asked her to stay.

When it comes to crying, I really only have two speeds—Light Weeping and Ugly Wailing. The moment warranted the latter, but I rallied my inner Marcus Aurelius for the sake of preserving what was left of my dignity. Or at least, I tried to.

Sydney raised her hand to my face and gently wiped a tear with her thumb. "You have to find some way to buy that vineyard." Her own tears were only slightly less the caliber of a garden hose. "You have to."

"I'm not sure how at this point," I said. I looked out over the landscape. Weird how the winter sun hangs in the sky like it's always 3 p.m. outside.

"I'd offer you more money, but—"

"But you wouldn't really offer it and I wouldn't take it," I said. "I do happen to understand what you're talking about. I have to get this vineyard on my own. I need a god damn victory lap."

"A victory lap?"

"You know." I raised up my index finger. 'We're number one' and all that?" I looked at my empty glass and reconsidered filling it. Two more like the last one, though, and there'd be the aforementioned wailing and a truly pathetic style of begging.

"The band used to have this tour circuit we played all the time, before we got signed," I said. "Little clubs, dives, hole-in-the-wall joints. If we got fifty people in the room we thought it was incredible, a real blow-out. And we did this for years. Then when we got signed, we hooked up with a big-time agent and he put us on the road with Soundgarden, who were this really huge band from Seattle that was—"

"I'm from Earth," Sydney cut in. "I know who Soundgarden was."

"Right. So, one night we're playing for about fifteen people at this nowhere bar in Moscow, Idaho, and the next night we join Soundgarden on tour in Madison, Wisconsin. Veterans Memorial Coliseum. Twenty thousand people. And when the lights went down and they cued us to take the stage, the crowd went absolutely nuts. Cheering, screaming, I mean they hadn't even heard us yet and they just...I'd never felt anything like it in my entire life. It felt like...like..."

"Validation?"

I shook my head. "Vindication."

"Vindication? For what?"

"For being different." Fuck it. I grabbed the whiskey bottle off the railing, filled my glass and shot it down. "The point is, I've spent the last twenty years trying to get back to that moment. The way it felt. The pain it washed away. The sins it redeemed. I know now that I'll never get back to it, that I'll never be able to duplicate it, and that's OK, really.

"You see, what I never understood at the time—what I never realized when we took the stage in Madison that night—is that it would end. That one day, it would all come to a screeching halt. And that's the thing. A victory lap is as much about acknowledging the end as it is about celebrating what you've done."

Sydney placed her hands on my waist. "Brogan is a master strategist. Seriously, he's playing four-dimensional chess while the rest of us argue over the rules to Candyland. But you have a distinct advantage that he doesn't have."

"What's that?" I asked.

"This isn't a game to you."

I set my glass down and pulled her in tight.

We held each other for borrowed moments, listening to a murder of crows argue in a nearby sweetgum tree, watching the occasional car make its way up the crossroad, and feeling our breath move into synchronicity.

I over-romanticized a lot of moments in my life, mostly in a well-intentioned but misguided attempt to give my mundane existence some deeper meaning. God and I were never really BFFs: I already had one father in my life who acted like a dick. And love seemed like an answer, or perhaps *the* answer, but the real deal was constantly elusive, which was my fault as much as anything else. My Emotional Toolbox contained all of two Allen wrenches (both metric and mostly incompatible) and a Phillips-head screwdriver that was stripped at the top.

My last moment with Sydney could be interpreted a million different ways, but never over-romanticized.

"Lock the door on your way out," she said.

She let go of me and ran back into the apartment.

As parting lines went, it wasn't even close to *here's looking at you, kid*, but as she took a quick right down the hallway and slammed the bedroom door behind her, I understood.

I thought about going after her, but Sober Voice, that little guy inside your brain who always knows the right thing to do but is typically drowned out by Less Sober Voice, had his way instead.

I considered a final drink but decided against it. A semi-sober breakup might be a refreshing change of pace. I went to the front door and found it was still slightly ajar; I walked out and closed it behind me. I took Sydney's key off of my keychain, but as I stuck it in the deadbolt, Less Sober Voice—along with his second cousin, Futile Gesture Voice —told me instead to leave the door unlocked and put the key back in my pocket. Futile Gesture Voice won out.

TWENTY

Shay twisted his entire torso over the top of the bar, his arms folded against his chest, and his nose maybe six inches from the check laying on top. His body language reminded me of Remy when she was eight years old and would find a banana slug on one of our hikes. She was fascinated by it, wanted to see it as close up as possible, but there was something repugnant about touching the thing.

"Bro," he whispered.

"Dude," I replied.

Shay tentatively extended two fingers, like a pair of tweezers, and picked up the check by its top right corner. He held it up to the light for a moment, inspecting it like some kind of archeological artifact, then placed it back on the top of the bar. He took a Family Sized swig off his gin and tonic and shook his head.

"Bro," he said.

"Dude," I replied. "Right?"

The lunch crowd was starting to wrap up at Pinot. The customers were still mostly tourists—people spending time in Napa for Christmas break, shoppers from San Francisco, and the occasional local hosting relatives from out of town. A young couple at the far end of the bar sniped over some political topic while Oscar robotically chopped limes and other garnishes, prepping for the dinner crowd.

Shay and I were lost in our own world: it was a bizarre, quantum universe that centered on a handwritten, multi-million-dollar personal check.

Shay's distorted body and sudden inability to mutter anything aside from the occasional 'bro' made it clear that he was more lost in this world than I was. And this created yet another problem. I simply didn't know if I had the heart to pull this six-by-three-inch rug out from under my best friend once again.

"What if we take this money and use it to bid on the Vineyard?" Shay cracked an insidious smile. "Buy it with his own money? That'd be some Shakespearean-level shit right there, bro."

"I thought of that, too. But if we offer five million, he'll just offer six. Or seven. Or ten, or whatever it takes."

"I suppose." Shay un-twisted himself from the bar top and settled into his chair, then swirled his gin and tonic with his little black cocktail straw. If one could swirl a cocktail existentially, Shay was doing it.

How many times had we been in this exact position? How many times had the ultimate payoff been in our grasp and I'd either ignored it, dismissed it, or flat-out ruined it? How long had I been dragging Shay through this nightmare of disappointment and unfulfilled promises? Well, *thirty freaking years*, if you want to be precise. I honestly didn't know if I had the right to do it anymore.

"Look," I said, clutching my glass like it was my only anchor to reality. "If you want to take the money, we can."

Shay stopped stirring and turned to face me. I met his gaze and prepared for the worst. And there it was, the fury behind his eyes in all its roiling glory. It wasn't easy to get Shay worked up like that, unless you're me, in which case it's pretty simple.

"I can't keep doing this to you anymore," I continued. "I know there needs to be a payday, and if this is it, then so be it."

Shay clutched the brass rail of the bar as though he was going to rip it off the edge. *"Putang ina naman! Bakit ba parating sira ang ulo mo?"* I thought I recognized a word or two from previous tirades. Something about my questionable genetic pedigree and my intellectual capacity, I believe.

After what felt like an eternity, Shay released his Vulcan death grip on the bar rail and unleashed a random and disconcerting laugh, one that lacked social grace and didn't care where it was or who else was listening.

"Bro! Bro. I gotta tell you this story." He slid his chair right up to mine. His face was almost maniacal, a canvas of caricatured enthusiasm. "Seriously, seriously this is the best story ever." He gesticulated with his hands all splayed out like he was grasping for some giant, invisible ham. "This is absolutely going to blow your fucking mind. Ok, are you ready? Are you ready? I don't think you're ready for this."

I didn't know if I was ready for this, either. "Sure man, lay it on me."

"Alright, then." He looked over his shoulder and then back at me, as if to be sure the Department of Homeland Security wasn't listening in. "Alright, now get this. So, last Wednesday, around 2 p.m., I was sitting in my office, you know, over on Soscol Avenue. And Carol comes in and says, 'Your 2 p.m. deposition is ready,' so I get up from my desk and go into the conference room. And the plaintiff is sitting there, across the table from me, so I start asking him the questions I had prepared with my client. We went through these questions, one by one, and he answered all of them. I took notes. Lots of notes. After the deposition, the plaintiff leaves, and I have a brief conversation with my client before I packed up some documents and went home."

I waited. Then, I waited some more. I was afraid to ask but I did anyway. "That's it?"

Shay silently mouthed the word *boom* and made an explosion gesture with his outstretched fingers.

"That's the lamest story I've ever heard."

"Of course it is!" he screamed. "It's the lamest goddamn story of all time. Who in their right mind would ever want to listen to a story like that? You know who's going to buy you a drink with that story? No one." Shay scooted up even closer to me.

"But here's the thing. If I tell the story of our first performance at Lollapalooza, that gets the drinks flowing. If I tell the story about the time I kicked Eddie Vedder off our couch for being a deadbeat, the crowd all gathers 'round to listen to that. When I talk about how we got in the face of a Silicon Valley billionaire, or how you flunked your Master Somm exam by blowing chowder all over the place—people go crazy for that shit."

"Aw, geez," I moaned. "You've told people about the exam?"

"Well, only the three people left in the world who didn't see the video. But yes, of course! That's the reason for all of this." Shay pushed off from the bar rail and spun his barstool in a circle like a merry-go-round for buzzed adults.

"I'm going to tell you a see-cret," he sang in that annoying "Neener neener!" kind of way. He grabbed hold of the bar to stop his carousel ride, took another quick glance over his shoulder, then looked me straight in the eyes. "I don't give a fuck about the money," he whispered. "Never have, never will. The way I see it, you and I are like pirates. I'm just in it for the adventure. Hoist the Jolly Roger, motherfucker, steer this ship straight into the storm and pass me a bottle of rum."

Shay raised his drink in salute and downed the remainder in one gulp. "Though gin will do just fine. Now, would a little buried treasure every now and then be nice? Of course it would. But it's not the treasure that keeps this ship afloat."

He poked me in the chest with his stubby index finger. Several times. And it hurt.

"And that's the part you don't fucking understand. *We* keep the ship afloat. You and me. Every day we weigh anchor and sail into the unknown is a day that I feel alive. Truly, honestly, deeply alive. And I will not give that up. I refuse to. I will not accept a future where I'm eighty years old, reliving stories about when my life peaked sixty years ago. No fucking way.

"When I'm eighty, I'll be the one telling hair-raising tales that start like this: 'When I was seventy-five, Corbett and I, dot dot dot.'" Shay pirouetted off the bar stool and grabbed his coat. "So, raise the main sail, you ignorant son of a bitch, and pay for these drinks while you're at it." He slapped me on the back and headed for the door.

"Whoa, whoa, whoa!" I called after him. "Where are you going?"

Shay flashed a carnal grin. "I'm off to plunder booty."

"Wait a second." I slid off my bar stool and went to him. "Listen, not to pummel the hell out of your metaphor, but what if I want to steer this ship into port for a while?"

Shay gave me a hug. Not one of his perfected Bro Hugs, but a warm embrace that he held for several moments. "My friend, some of the best adventures happen in port."

I watched him as he left the restaurant. He gave Sarah, the hostess, a quick peck on the cheek and waved at a party he recognized, then merrily strolled out the door.

I sat back down on my barstool and made eye contact with Oscar, whom if I wasn't mistaken, was the only bartender ever to work at Pinot. "Hey, buddy. Last one, if you don't mind."

"I don't mind." Oscar grinned. "It's what I do."

I laid the check out in front of me for the seven millionth time. Only this time, the first thought that came to mind wasn't about the potential this tiny slip of paper held, but of Sydney. 176 minutes and two gin and tonics had done nothing to fill the emptiness so far, and God only knew what quantity of time and alcohol ever would.

Yet at that moment, what echoed through my head and into my heart wasn't the hypnotic curve of her tiny nose, or the randomly Canadian way she pronounced "O." Rather, it was something she said, something I easily dismissed at the time as a feeble attempt to make me feel better about the cascading failures of my life:

You've got one distinct advantage he'll never have. This isn't a game to you.

Oscar picked up my empty glass and placed the fresh drink in front of me. "Hey, Oscar, you want a check for five million dollars?"

Oscar folded his arms, took a deep breath and looked to be giving the offer some serious consideration. He frowned suddenly and shook his head, then walked back to his chopping block. "Naw," he said, taking up his knife, "I'd only blow it all on cool shoes."

I tore the check into four pieces, then crumpled the pieces in a ball and executed a perfect three-pointer into the trash can behind the bar.

I sighed. "Me too."

So, here's a tip: read the freaking contract before signing it. As it turns out, Napa Caverns Wine Storage is more than happy to pick up your wine purchases and store them at their facility, but if you're clearing out your locker for good, it's "Screw you, Charlie. Come get your shit out of here and don't let the door hit you in the ass on your way out." Oh, and when you're bringing wine in, there's a special power-assisted hand truck at your disposal. When you're loading out, there's a dolly with two flat tires.

I had to rent a truck from U-Haul, complete with shelves and tie-down straps and other pricey add-ons. With each case I loaded and strapped into place, I pictured myself driving the rig slower and slower, until finally I was doing all of six miles an hour down the middle of Highway 29. One broken case could be the difference in thousands of dollars. Several shattered cases would ruin everything.

With that horrifying thought in mind, I decided to mix up some of the cases, so that the irreplaceable first growth Bordeaux, for example, weren't all packaged together. This meant creating a whole new inventory manifest, which was an epic pain in the ass. I numbered each case with a Sharpie, then referenced from the previous manifest which bottles were in that specific case. I figured if the new system didn't confuse me, it wouldn't confuse anyone, but if worse came to worst I could rearrange the cases back to their original composition when I dropped them off.

"Seriously?" came a voice from behind me. "I had to see it for myself to believe it."

"Oh, hey sweetheart." I almost didn't recognize Remy. She was bundled up in one of those puffy, quilted rain jackets that made her look like a marshmallow, and her hair was tucked up into a Gimme Hat. I had neither seen nor heard from her since the night I'd come clean.

"Not like it isn't wonderful to see you," I said. "But what are you doing here?"

"I talked to Uncle Shay."

I don't know what it was about my daughter that made her think she could say next to nothing and expect me to understand everything. But, well, I understood everything. "Honey, this is the only way I can—"

"I can't believe you're doing this, Dad," she said. "This is the only asset you have. There's nothing left after this."

"There's a couple of really bad ass guitars," I reminded her. "But I'm selling those, too."

"Uncle Shay said that Brogan Prescott offered you five million dollars to walk away. And you didn't take it."

Gee, thanks, buddy. "It's not as simple as that." I tossed the clipboard onto one of the cases littering the room. "If Brogan gets his hands on that vineyard, it's going to mean the end of Napa as we know it. I can't let that happen."

She grunted, shoving her hands in her jacket pockets. She meandered over to one of the wine cases and tapped it with her foot. "And how much are you getting for all this?"

I really didn't want to say. I felt embarrassed just hearing the number in my head. My collection was worth three times what I was getting for it, easy. But I had to sell fast. "Fair price, for my situation."

"And who's the buyer?"

She had to have known or she wouldn't have asked. She just wanted to see me squirm.

"Rick Dornin," I mumbled. "My old GM over at Appellation."

Remy continued her mock inspection of the cases, not bothering to look at me. "So, Brogan Prescott is going to come in and offer, what? Three million? Four million? And you're going to offer...?"

"I have a plan, Remy," I said. I knew where this was going, but I suppose I wanted her to get there herself.

"Ah, a plan," she said, nodding. "There's always a plan, isn't there, dad? Another plan, another scheme, another big idea, the *best* idea." She tapped her foot against another case, only this time it was hard enough to make the bottles rattle inside with a nerve-wracking *clink!* "Another shiny object. Because that's what you do, isn't it? You scurry from one shiny object to the next, blinded by the beauty of the next new thing, the next half-baked adolescent fantasy."

"Wow, you're really getting worked up about this," I said. "Like, getting worked up the way people who give a shit about things get worked up." It was a dick thing to say, but it felt like she wanted to snap. Since that was something new for her, it was going to need a little coaxing.

I got my wish. Sort of.

"Fuck you, Dad." She blurted the epithet like Christopher Walken reading a cue card he'd never seen before.

"That's a good start."

"This isn't a joke, Dad!" she shouted. "You're about to throw away the last thing you have for another pointless dream."

"That's how you see this?" I asked. "A pointless dream?"

Remy stripped the cap from her head and ran her fingers through her thick hair. "Worse than pointless. I mean, how's this whole dream thing working out for you? Seems to me like its left you with no job and no credentials and no prospects and no money. And you can't see that it's over. You're about to flush your very last dollar down the toilet because you just don't get that it's over."

I shook my head. As dispassionate as she sounded, she was starting to push my buttons. "It's not over, Remy. The whole point of having a dream is that it's never over."

"Well, maybe it's time for it to be over. Maybe it's time for you to just grow up." Remy put her cap back on and started backing down the hallway. "Because all of this—all of this here? It's all just a mask. You try to come across as so high and mighty with these ideals that are so much more insightful than everyone else's, but it's all just to hide the fact that you're incapable of living in the real world."

Remy turned her back to me and walked out, slamming the bulky metal door behind her with a jarring explosion that echoed through the concrete hallways. I went straight to case number fifteen, ripped it open, grabbed bottle number 154, and ran after her. I caught up with her just as she was about to get into her car.

"What did you do with it?" I said.

"Do with what?" she asked.

"With the truth. What did you do with it?"

Remy stammered. "I-I don't know what you're talking about."

"Of course you don't. For weeks you begged me to tell you the truth, and maybe I didn't give you it all at once, but I bared my soul. I stuck a fucking knife in my heart and spilled out the whole dirty, ugly, nasty thing at your feet. So, what did you *do* with it?"

Remy was silent. More than silent, she was lost.

"You see, this is exactly what I'm talking about!" I was yelling. Maybe as much at myself as I was at her. "You can't take the truth and stick it in a spreadsheet formula or try and predict its market value. This is who I *am*, Remy, and if you understood the truth, you would understand that. Your mom and I did a lot of really messed up things because we were really messed up people, but at the heart of it—at the truth of it—was passion. Whether we were using it for sex or weaponry, she and I dealt in raw, bleeding, immaculate passion. We spoke its language, a language that's only understood with the heart. And you've got a heart, Remy, I know you do. But until you figure out how it works, the truth won't mean shit to you."

I unceremoniously shoved the bottle in her direction. "Here. That's a 1992 Moet & Chandon Grand Vintage. That's the champagne your mother and I drank at our wedding. I'm selling every freaking bottle I've got but this one, and it's all for you. When I die and you come back from my funeral, that's the bottle I want you to open. You drink a toast to me from that. And if that doesn't crack open your lifeless soul, I don't know what will."

Daddies aren't supposed to make their little girls cry, but when I turned around and headed back into the storage unit, it wasn't because I was afraid I would see her tears. It was because I was afraid I wouldn't.

TWENTY-ONE

I have a serious love-hate relationship with the rain. Though I only lived there for the first eighteen years of my life, Tucson runs in my bloodstream. The relentless, beating sun and skin-sucking heat of the desert became my baseline definition of normal weather. When I graduated high school, I wanted nothing more than to escape the furnace, so Seattle, the city that invented Seasonal Affective Disorder, seemed like the perfect choice. But I guess I didn't stay there long enough for the constant rain to alter my weather DNA. One would think that an additional twenty years in rainy Northern California might change my perspective as well, but it didn't. Though I inherently understood that rain meant life and growth and the promise of a potentially good harvest, it also meant, well, no sunshine.

The bottom line that hadn't changed in thirty years was that the rain bummed me out.

Huge droplets tapped on my windshield like a cop wanting to ask me for my driver's license and registration. The windows fogged up quickly as I shut off my engine, clouding my view of the Fogelson residence and surrounding vineyard. Obscured by the haze, the house appeared to be floating atop one massive mud puddle. Item Number One if I get the property: build a better pathway to the house—one that doesn't flood during the rain.

When you get the property, Corbett. *When.*

The fact that I hadn't slept much in the past three days didn't help my mood, either. It was crunch time—time to fill in a lot of the financial gaps that I never had to consider on the marketing side of winery consultation. Stuff that Remy had been trying to pound into my skull over the last several weeks. Stuff that made the list of Things I Regretted Not Listening To More Closely.

The net result of my work sat on the passenger seat next to me.

Funny how four hundred cases of wine, three vintage guitars, and a lifetime of experience can be transformed into a half-ream of paper and a few clear plastic binders.

The windshield fogged up to the point where the outside world was little more than a best guess. There was a surge in the back of my eyeballs, some kind of pressure that threatened to become tears if I wasn't mindful of its power. I wanted to be Braveheart. I wanted to be MacArthur at Normandy. I wanted to be King Henry V, rallying his men with an epic St. Crispin's Eve speech: "This story shall a good man teach his son!" I wanted to slog through that Olympic-sized mud puddle accompanied by an orchestral soundtrack so epic it made "Cry of the Valkyries" sound like the theme song to *Mr. Roger's Neighborhood.*

But I just sat there, breathing, my ass glued to the cracked, imitation leather seat, fully and explicitly conscious of the fact that I was at the end of the line. Jobless, penniless, with no other dream or scheme to pull out of my Briefcase of Bad Ideas.

I couldn't be King Henry, but maybe—just maybe—I could be George Harrison. The Cool Beatle. The one who hung out quietly in the background while John and Paul bitched at each other, stepping up only to tear off a signature guitar riff that would blow minds for the next five decades. The guy who dragged the band to India because he believed in that Krishna stuff. The guy who let Eric Clapton steal his first wife because, you know, they loved each other so that's cool. The guy who had a garden the size of a city block that he loved and tended. The guy who didn't fear death.

Stuffing the proposals in my satchel, I grabbed my umbrella and lunged out of the car like I was taking the stage at JFK Stadium in 1966. Screams everywhere! Pandemonium! *Give me hope, help me cope with this heavy load.*

I was startled by the presence of a figure at the front of my car, clutching an umbrella. The edge of it masked half her face, but a father can recognize his child with far less.

"Remy? What are you doing here?"

She came around to my side of the car until the lip of her umbrella touched mine. She had that humongous bag slung across her shoulder again. It made my satchel look like a fanny pack.

"Dad, you've got to convince Gemma to take your offer. She's the critical one." I could tell she was trying to shout over the noise of the rain, but her voice also belied an anxiety I wasn't used to hearing out of her.

"I know," I said. "I feel really good about this offer, and I think she's going to—"

"No, that's not what I'm talking about." Remy shifted her tremendous bag further up her shoulder. "You remember that day we visited Mr. Fogelson in the hospital, and how he was all delirious and thought I was Gemma?"

"Yeah?"

"There was something he said and it's been bugging me ever since. I was up most of the night thinking about it, and it finally hit me. He said, 'That's why you have to, Gemma. Your brothers never understood.'"

I tried to think back to that afternoon. "That's right. He kept calling you 'Angel Heart.'"

"Right, right!" Remy said excitedly. "I kept thinking he was saying something like, 'that's why you *have to*, Gemma.' But what he was really saying is, 'That's why you have *two*, Gemma.'" Remy held up two fingers. "You get it?"

"No."

"Gemma gets two votes. She gets the tie-breaking vote, you see? There are four members of the LLC that holds the property, Gemma and her three brothers. But Hank saw something in Gemma that he didn't see in the rest of them, so he gave her a second vote to break any ties."

Here comes the sun, doo doo doo doo...

"You've got to focus on Gemma," Remy said. "She's the key to all this."

I wasn't sure if it was true, let alone if this new information would be that much help, but I could see in Remy's eyes how important she thought it was. How important it was to tell me, even after the way I treated her.

"So, listen, sweetheart," I choked up. "About the other day, in the parking lot, what I was trying to—"

"Don't worry about it, Dad." She turned away: It was the third time I'd seen her do that recently, and for a woman who never breaks eye contact, it was a disconcerting new habit.

"Look, it's just that I have no idea how I came from you two freaks," she said. "But, apparently I did. And though I don't really understand why you do what you do, I'm going to try to open my heart to it more."

And like a comet that only blazes through the night sky once every fifteen years, a single tear streaked across Remy's cheek. She probably hoped I thought it was just the rain. Or maybe, finally, she didn't.

"Will you come in with me?" I asked. "I couldn't have put this offer together without you and what you tried to teach me, and it only makes sense that you, well…"

That damn thing behind my eyes was coming back, despite George trying to beat it down with some perfectly-crafted guitar licks.

"Can we just let this die right now and get inside?" Remy said. I wanted to think there was a smile threatening her lips.

"Great idea."

As I turned towards the house, Shay pulled up beside us in his black Mercedes sedan. He got out of the car, holding a copy of *Rolling Stone* above his head like an umbrella.

"Hey, I couldn't let you go in there without your lawyer," he greeted, smiling.

"Alright," I smiled back. "Looks like the gang's all here."

"OK," Shay said. "Well, now that we've had our little *Full House* moment, I just want to say that I fully expect this to be another dumpster fire, so I popped a Xanax on the way here, and I'm just going to sit in the corner and try to keep my shit together."

"Fair enough," I said.

The march through the mud was even worse than I thought it would be. The puddle surrounding the house was about the size of Lake Erie and avoiding it would have required cutting through several rows of vines, which felt to me like sacrilege. So, through the middle we trudged, abandoning all hope for our shoes or a semblance of dry feet.

I knocked on the door and was greeted by a man I didn't recognize but whose sharp, Nordic features divulged his Fogelson heritage. "Hi, folks," he said with an eerily familiar voice. "Are you here to submit an offer?"

I stuck my hand out. "Corbett Thomas. And yes."

"Ah, OK," he said, shaking my hand. "Hank Fogelson." He must have seen the look of shock wash across my face, as he quickly added, "Henrick Fogelson, the third. Won't you come in?" He looked down at our feet. "You can leave your shoes on the porch, if you'd like."

Remy slipped hers off. "These pumps are completely jacked." She shook Hank's hand. "Remy Thomas, McMillan Associates. It's a pleasure."

"Seamus O'Flaherty," Shay said, brushing past Hank. "I'm on tranquilizers."

I opted to keep my shoes on in a bizarre display of defiant optimism. By the end of the day, I'd own this house, so I'd track mud all over if I wanted to. Hank III led us into the dining room, where the rest of the Fogelson clan was seated at the table. I recognized Stephan, of course, and assumed the one I didn't recognize thumbing out something on his phone was the third brother, Jonas. Strange that after all these years, I never knew that Hank was actually Hank Junior.

Gemma was there as well, staring intently at some notes on a yellow legal pad.

And seated at the head of the table was Brogan Prescott.

He sat with his hands folded in his lap, smiling contently, like he was a member of the fucking family or something. I tried not to betray my utter disappointment or let his presence shake me, but George Harrison would have needed to bring Vishnu himself to the party to calm my shit down at that moment. Was Brogan part of the decision process now? Was my offer just a moot point?

Play some fucking chords, George. Right now.

There were two other people in the room as well, one man and one woman, both dressed to the hilt in formal business attire, sitting in plastic chairs just behind Brogan. I took them to be lawyers or agents or some other kind of Brogan groupies of the Not Fun variety. There were two other empty plastic chairs near the far wall, which Remy and Shay took.

"Corbett Thomas," Stephan said with all the enthusiasm of reading the ingredients off a package of head cheese. "I'm frankly surprised to see you here."

I stepped up to the table and placed my satchel on it, then opened it and took out the contents. "Ladies and gentlemen, I believe you'll be more than surprised by my offer, and more than pleased as well. It's all laid out here, but if you'll give me a few moments of your time, I can walk you through the finer points."

I slid a copy of the offer to each of the Fogelsons, smiling broadly at Gemma as she looked up at me. She returned the smile and opened the package of papers.

"It's nice to see you, Corbett," she said, then gave a sideways glance at Stephan. "I'm glad you came."

"Good to see you too, Gemma." I snuck my own glance at Remy, who gave me the slightest nod in return. Xanax or not, Shay looked like a death row inmate waiting for a final pardon from the governor.

No index cards, no slide deck, no gadgets, no dramatic speeches. Deep breath.

I've been uptight and made a mess

But I'll clean it up myself, I guess

Oh, the sweet smell of success

Handle me with care

"The Executive Summary on page two outlines the offer in a three-step process that begins with acquisition of the – "

"Whoa whoa whoa," Stephan interrupted, holding his palm up like an elementary school crossing guard. "Am I reading this right? Are you offering seventy-five thousand dollars?"

"Seventy-five thousand for a fifty-one percent stake in a new corporation that holds the assets of the vineyard and the—"

"Seventy-five thousand," Stephan interrupted again. He looked over at Brogan and then back at me. Brogan's placid smile was unflinching. "We currently have an offer on the table for three-point-five *million*."

"The offer I'm proposing will net you five times that much over a ten-year period," I said. "What I'm proposing is a business venture that creates an ongoing revenue stream as opposed to a—"

"We're not looking for a business venture," Stephan snapped, flipping my proposal closed and tossing it across the table. "We're looking for an offer on the property. That's all."

"Jesus, bro, just chill out." That was Jonas. If I thought that Hank III had a voice like his father, it was nothing compared to Jonas. It ran shivers even through my already-frozen feet. "Let the guy talk for a minute."

Stephan sighed like a fifteen-year-old girl who just got her smartphone taken away and folded his arms across his chest. There was a family dynamic going on there that I didn't even want to touch. But thank you, Jonas.

Another deep breath.

"Basically, the offer comes down to seventy-five thousand dollars for a fifty-one percent interest in a new ownership group that encompasses all the assets of the current LLC: the vineyard, the house and the equipment. The new group will build a winery and tasting room by year four, hitting a ten-thousand case production level by year five. Earnings before interest, taxes, depreciation and amortization reach six million dollars by year six, and approximately seven-point-five million dollars annually after that."

"How come we don't get a controlling interest?" Hank III asked. I assumed he wasn't the dentist in the group.

"Frankly speaking," I replied, "you don't want a controlling interest. You all have businesses and families and lives of your own. If you wanted to run a winery, we wouldn't be here today." *Aw, hell, was that too frank? Too harsh? Was that a jab?* "Besides, this is my area of expertise. I know what it takes to compete with other luxury wine brands, and how to maximize margin by focusing on direct-to-consumer initiatives."

I turned briefly to Remy, who flashed me a quick and covert thumbs-up.

"Corbett," said Gemma, her eyes fixed to the page, "it looks here like you're going to mortgage the property to help pay for the winery. Daddy was really careful about never going into debt. Don't you think it's pretty risky?"

Guess you never read the Title Report, Gemma, because your dad mortgaged this property four times in the last two decades.

"That's a really good point, Gemma," I replied and took out my copy of the offer, flipping through the pages. "I've tried to mitigate that risk through several factors. First off, the lien will be an equity line, so we only use as much as is required annually, keeping our debt load to a minimum. Secondly, we start the wine brand almost immediately, but hold off on construction of our own winery until year three. This gives us time to establish a revenue stream in the marketplace while keeping costs at a minimum."

I stole another glance at Remy. She was as wide-eyed as a puffer fish. It was as validating as it was disconcerting.

"But still, these are pretty significant, non-deductible startup costs in years one and two," said Hank III. Definitely not the dentist.

"Which is why you have to take into account the amortization from the vineyard's appellation value," I explained.

Silence from the table. Even Brogan arched an eyebrow.

"It's a little-known tax loophole that applies to vineyards in a designated AVA," I

continued. "In 1993, Congress passed Section 197 of the Internal Revenue Code, providing for a fifteen-year amortization period for certain intangible assets. Seven years later, the IRS concluded that the right to use an AVA designation upon a purchase of a vineyard is considered a license or other right granted by a government unit, rather than an interest in land. Therefore, it's an amortizable asset under Section 197. So basically, we can amortize the entire fair market value of the vineyard over a period of 15 years, even during the period where we're not producing wine."

Nothing but the sound of raindrops pattering against the tar and gravel roof shingles. *Boom, bitches.* I even understood what that shit *meant.* No more rote memorization for this guy.

There were a few glances exchanged between the Fogelsons, some which looked like questions, others that appeared to be plain old confusion as Remy fidgeted like a five-year-old waiting to unwrap a room full of Christmas presents. I decided it was as good a time as any to whip out the keys and drive this puppy home.

"The bottom line is that I'm offering you an ongoing, annual revenue of nearly one million dollars each, subject to a combined state and federal corporate tax rate of twenty-nine percent, whereas Mr. Prescott is offering you each a one-time payment of eight hundred and seventy-five thousand dollars, subject to a combined thirty-three percent capital gains tax. Do the math. Tell me which one you think is the better offer."

If I had a mic, I would have dropped it, so I was really glad I didn't have one with me.

I looked over at Brogan. The unctuous, little *Fuck You* smile had disappeared from his lips, and I desperately wanted to believe that my superior gamesmanship had wiped it from his face...as much as I wanted to believe that he wasn't about to say the one thing that would blow this deal completely out of the water. Instead, it was Stephan who started talking.

"Honestly, Corbett, I'm impressed with your offer and the obvious amount of effort you put into it." I was thrown by his newfound admiration and seeming sincerity. In fact, it was more unnerving than if he had simply told me to go fuck myself. "The problem I'm seeing the 'What if?' What if there's a drought and grape yields go down? For that matter, what if people don't like the wine or don't come to the winery or we get bad scores any number of a million unknowns? Your proposal is entirely speculative—"

"It's not speculative at all." It was my turn to interrupt. In fact, I think I got three turns. "This is a data-driven proposal, based on both trends and established market history with Napa Valley brands."

"OK, but what if the trends change?" Stephan picked up the offer and pointed it at me like a knife. "You've got us producing cabernet and chardonnay through all ten years of these projections. But what if everyone suddenly goes crazy for malbec, like they went crazy for pinot noir in 2005? Dad had to replant, what, six times? And each time set him back another three years."

I had this. I had a response to this. A brilliant response.

But Stephan was too fast. "Look, I'm just going to say outright that I can't buy into this. My vote is no."

Normally, such a declaration would have broken two strings on George's gently weeping guitar, but I expected this from Stephan going into it.

"Well, I totally disagree," said Jonas, my new best friend. "I think we should do this."

"Oh, for God's sake," Stephan moaned.

"Dude, this is exactly what I told dad he should have done ten years ago," Jonas countered. "I know people who pay a thousand bucks a bottle for this shit. It's crazy that we're not getting in on this."

George switched on his Vox amplifier and cranked it up to ten.

"Hank, will you help me out here?" Stephan said.

Hank closed the offer packet and drummed it nervously with his fingers. "I don't know," he sighed. "I certainly don't like the tax bill we're about to get slammed with, but I think I'm with Stephan on this. Your proposal looks good, Corbett, if it'd work. But it's too much risk."

Sproing!

Twonk!

Brogan shifted in his chair for the first time since I entered the room. He uncrossed his legs and leaned forward, placing his forearms on the table. The sly grin dissolved into something a bit more concerned, more curious, and I wondered if he was considering what would happen in the event of a tie vote.

Was Remy right?

That's when I noticed that every single eye in the room was focused on Gemma. She must have been aware of it, too, as she became nervous, uncomfortable—downright scared. She fidgeted through my offer haphazardly, feigning a sense of attention, perhaps hoping that some previously-unseen yet enormously important detail would jump off a page and fall into her lap.

She dropped the package of papers and buried her face in her hands. "Here's the thing, Corbett," she said through her fingers, "I know that Daddy gave you an option on the property. And I know that he really hoped you would take over the vineyard."

"Gem," Stephan said. "You can't be—"

"Hold on, Steph," she said before looking up at me. "But I've got my family to consider now. Not just my baby, but my brothers and their families as well."

"And I get that," I jumped in. "I get it because it's the right thing to do. That's why I structured the offer this way. Not only do we take care of you financially, we keep the property within the family. Five generations of Fogelsons. Your legacy lives on this way."

Gemma Fogelson was not a difficult read. She wore her conflict like a Kabuki mask. She pushed slowly back from the table, lifted her feet onto the edge of her chair, and wrapped her arms around her legs. She then planted her chin between her knees and gazed into the distance with a thousand-yard stare that would have put my Uncle, the Vietnam War vet, to shame.

Stephan leaned over and put his hand on his sister's shoulder. "Gem," he said quietly. "We talked about this. We've already decided, as a family. This is what's best. For everybody."

"I know." She shrugged brother's hand away and turned the stare toward me. It was plaintive, yearning, as if she was begging me to come up with just the right formula that would allow her to say yes.

I dug deep to find it, and what I came back with was Remy's advice: this was about the money. *Stay focused. Think of the financial cues Gemma had given. Don't get emotional.*

"If it's the lack of cash flow in year two that you're concerned about just remember that the property's valuation won't be determined by my purchase price, so we can easily—"

"That's not it," Gemma muttered. I fell silent as she looked away. I could see her lips trembling. "I'm sorry, Corbett. God, I'm so sorry, but I can't do this. I can't accept your offer."

I felt it all slipping away. I wasn't channeling George Castanza, let alone George Harrison, and my ears practically thundered with the sound of amplifiers and sound equipment crashing down around me.

"Gemma, vineyard properties have nearly doubled in value over the past five years. If this plan isn't working by—"

"The motion on the table is to reject the offer from Corbett Thomas," Stephan announced loudly. "All in favor of the motion say 'aye.'"

"Aye," said Hank III.

"Aye," said Stephan.

Years earlier, I'd read an interview with George Harrison's wife. In it, she said that the moment her husband died, the room glowed with a blinding, pure white light.

The moment my dream died - it was nothing like that at all.

The room drowned in a darkness beyond understanding, an emptiness so complete that it sucked the very breath from my lungs. There were no words, no thoughts and no feelings, really. Those mundane things simply weren't designed to comprehend the void into which I had fallen. It wasn't *the end,* because *the end* denotes that a new beginning would take place at some point. This was pure falling, unadulterated and unfettered demise, a silence louder than any scream or cry I could possibly emote.

Yet it wasn't completely silent.

"Daddy chased the pixies through the vineyard!" I looked for the source of the shouting and found Remy standing on top of her chair. "Daddy chased the pixies through the vineyard!" she yelled again.

Gemma unclasped her legs and stood up slowly. "What…what do you mean?"

"I-I don't know what I mean," Remy answered. Her voice was shakier than I'd ever heard it before, and if I was truly falling into the void, Remy was right there beside me. "That night that we went to see your father in the hospital. He was delirious, and he thought I was you, and he talked about how my dad chased the pixies through the vineyard, like the way you used to do when you were a child."

"Gemma, please, tell me this isn't happening," Stephan mumbled.

But if Gemma heard a word her brother said, she didn't show it. Her eyes were focused on me with laser precision. She came around the table and approached me like I was a bunny at a petting zoo, as if one sudden move would make this fluffy, enchanted object bounce away forever.

"Really?" she asked, her voice barely above a whisper. "Did you really see them?"

I recognized the look on Gemma's face. I'd seen it a hundred times before on Remy, when she was a child, and her heart was a tome filled with thousands of unwritten pages, each gleaming with the dazzling brilliance of possibility. It was so easy in that moment to picture Gemma as a little girl, running through the rows of vines, playing hide-and-seek…

…taking out her pocketknife…

"Not 'Pike's Playground," I whispered. "*Pixie* Playground. It was you. You're the one who carved it into the post."

Tears streamed from Gemma's eyes. "Yes, when I was six. The first time I saw them. Corbett, please, tell me you saw them, too."

I knew I could have water colored anything I wanted to on the blank page that Gemma offered—whatever it took to get the deal approved. But I couldn't bring myself to do it. In that moment, Gemma was as much my daughter as Remy, and I'd have to hope that the gray-shaded pencil drawings of truth wouldn't slam the book shut on me.

"I saw…something," I said. "That night. That night I came to the vineyard and talked with your dad. Little lights everywhere. It was…it was…" I sighed and placed my hands on Gemma's shoulders. "I don't know what it was, Gemma. But I do know this. The land, the vineyard, it's not just about the grapes and the vines and the money. It's about love. It's about connection. And yes, it's about magic. I believe that. And you know it, too. Just like your father did."

Gemma threw her arms around me and pinched her eyes shut. "I move that we accept the offer presented by Corbett Thomas." Her voice broke with sobs. "All those in favor say 'aye.' Aye!"

"Seven million dollars," Brogan said. He was all Deadly Serious Gamer Guy face. "Seven million dollars, all cash, no contingencies."

"No!" Remy screamed, still atop her chair-perch. She pointed an accusatory finger at Brogan with Spanish Inquisition flair. "Don't listen to this one! He does not speak the language of passion!"

I had no idea what ninth dimensional alternate universe this Remy had fallen out of.

"Remy, are you OK up there?"

"Yes," she said, though her eyes were about the size of Frisbees. "I kinda like the chair."

Stephan bolted upright and slammed his palm against the table. "Gemma, it's seven million dollars! For the love of God, I'm begging you. Don't do this."

But Gemma was in her own world, or at least her vice grip on my lower rib cage told me so. "Jonas," she said, tears spilling onto my shirt, "tell me you're with me here."

"I got you, sis," Jonas quietly replied.

Gemma looked up at me and smiled. The pencil drawing was beautiful enough. She colored in all the important parts on her own and returned the book to its safe place in her Hello Kitty backpack.

"The ayes have it. The offer from Corbett Thomas is accepted."

All you need is love.

"Yes!" Remy screamed, pumping her fists like a person who had never made a fist in her life. She also started up some weird kind of dance that involved waving her arms straight at the ground like she was trying to stir a cauldron with no hands. I think Shay had passed out.

Brogan Prescott excused himself from the table with an emotionless, "Thank you for your consideration," and made his way out the front door with his minions in tow. There was something that had been bugging me from the moment the proverbial ball dropped into Gemma's court, so I gently pulled away from her, excused myself as well, and went after Brogan.

He stood at the edge of the giant puddle with his flunkies, ostensibly consulting his crack legal team about the best way to navigate it. I came up beside him. "Hey, mind if I talk to you for a second?"

Brogan dismissed his attorneys with a wave. They passed a look between them that said, *Keep remembering we make about a gazillion dollars*, and they marched off right through the center of the massive mud pit.

"This will never hold up in court," a voice shouted behind me. Stephan Fogelson got into a Jeep parked near the porch. "Brogan, we'll be in touch."

Brogan gave a half-hearted wave in his direction, then turned to me. "It'll totally hold up in court. So, what do you want, Corbett?"

"I don't understand. You could have completely blown up the deal. All you had to do was tell the kids about the gold."

"Then I would have lost the long game as well," he replied.

I'm not entirely sure what I was looking for from Brogan. Maybe I just couldn't process that this fight was finally over, and that I had come out on top. But my spidey sense, honed through years of alcohol abuse and mostly getting things wrong, told me something was up.

"I still don't get it," was my rapier-sharp response.

Brogan smiled, and I'll be damned if it wasn't a genuine—if not boyish—smile. For a moment, I could see in his face the kid that

Sydney had fallen in love with. Genuine and caring, kind of self-effacing.

"So, here's the thing, Corbett. You're a failure. You always have been, you always will be. You failed to become any kind of legitimate rock star. You failed at every restaurant you worked in. You failed to become a Master Somm, and you're going to fail with this vineyard. And when you do, I'll be there. I'll be there to either buy it from you, or buy it from the bank, or buy it from the guy you sell it to. Doesn't matter. Either way, I'll get this property eventually."

Ah. Missed that call.

Admittedly, Neanderthal Guy wanted to make some kind of territorial-pissing comeback about how great it was to have sex with his wife. Truth was, I had no idea if he ever knew about what happened between Sydney and me. However, this strange, new Higher Evolved Guy decided against that particular tact.

Still, there was no way Brogan was winning the moment.

I took a step closer to him, not in a threatening way, but in a totally uncomfortable, personal-space-invading kind of way and stood silently while alternately surveying our surroundings. I grinned at him like an idiot, my nose about two inches from his forehead. When he took an uncomfortable step away from me, I casually stepped up close to him again. This went on until the sheer power of awkwardness threatened to rip the very fabric of the space/time continuum.

"Oh, I'm sorry!" I finally exclaimed. "Were you saying something? Because I was too distracted by the fact that I just bought this vineyard out from under you for thirty-seven cents and a pack of gum."

Brogan shook his head and walked off toward a row of cabernet vines, probably looking for the best way around the mud pond.

"Hey, numbnuts!" I turned to see Shay, yelling from the porch. "Get your donut-snarfing ass out of my grape vines!"

Brogan hesitated a moment, probably from the shock of having someone reference his ass in any other manner except to kiss it. He finally turned and made his knee-deep trek through the sludge of Loch Fogelson.

Shay walked up beside me, and together, we watched every unpleasant, glorious moment of it. "I think I'm going to like being a vintner."

Shay and I returned to the house to find Remy in the dining room holding a machete. Of all the otherworldly things I'd seen and heard in the previous fifteen minutes, somehow this one seemed the least bizarre.

Hank III had apparently taken off—or ran for his life—though Gemma and Jonas were still at the table and didn't have the terrorized pallor of hostages.

Upon closer inspection, I saw that Remy held a champagne saber in one hand and a bottle in the other.

"Dad," she said excitedly, "I watched a bunch of videos on YouTube and learned how to do this whole champagne sabering thing. And I thought it would be the perfect way to celebrate!"

"Oh. Wow," I said. It was either that or just being speechless.

Remy inspected the bottle for the seam that ran down the side, then rotated it in her hand until the seam was parallel with the ground.

"Wait a second," I called out. "Is that the bottle I gave you the other day?"

Remy turned the label towards me. "Yes! The '92 Moet & Chandon Grand Vintage. I thought it was a fitting bottle for the occasion. 98 points from *Wine Spectator,* in case you didn't know. I looked that up, too."

She pointed the front of the bottle away from the table and drew back the sword.

"Actually," I said, "why don't we use a different bottle instead – "

"I've got this, dad," Remy said. "I practiced on half a case of Korbell last night. And one! Two – !"

"Remy, wait!" I shouted, but 'three' came anyway.

Remy *swished* the dull edge of the saber across the seam of the bottle and through the glass edge at the top. But instead of the neck slicing off smoothly and rocketing across the house, the top of the bottle shattered into a dozen glass shards, eliciting screams from everyone in the room. And instead of a shower of bubbles streaming three feet out from the neck of the bottle, a poof of grey smoke the size of a golf ball burped from the top, which slowly rained dust to the floor.

"Oh my God," Remy squealed. "What is that?"

"That," I sighed, "is your mother."

TWENTY-TWO

It'd be cool if I could say that the universe, in all its Cosmic and Infinite Wonder, did bequeath unto us a gloriously sunny day specifically for the ceremony. But it wasn't like that at all. Knowing that *El Niño* was forecasted to be absolutely relentless for another eight weeks, Remy, Shay, and I agreed to keep our schedules open enough that when the first sunny day occurred, we'd drop everything and meet at the vineyard.

That day finally happened on a Wednesday in the third week of February. I woke up to sunlight reflecting straight into my eyes off the aesthetically ugly, yet sentimentally beautiful flower vase Remy had gotten me for Father's Day ten years earlier. I scrambled for my phone and typed out: *Strange glowing orb in the sky...I believe it's the Sign. Two hours?* Everyone texted back in the affirmative, and by late morning, we met in the parking lot of the Fogelson Vineyard.

Remy brought her mother's ashes, still contained for the most part in the broken champagne bottle, now encased in bubble wrap. I brought a baby Syrah vine in a small pot of soil, along with a five-by-seven-inch engraved copper plaque. Shay brought a bottle of Cupcake Chardonnay, after much debate about which wine would pair best with the occasion. Remy's mom drank that shit by the carload, so that argument carried the day.

The vineyard was still a mud disaster—a situation that would take a lot more than one random, sunny day to rectify. Fortunately, grape vines go dormant in the winter, so none of the flooding would have an adverse effect on my newly-acquired vineyard, as long as the freakishly wet weather didn't extend too far into March.

We weaved past puddles, made our way up to the base of the hillside, and gathered at the front end of a row of Syrah vines that was thankfully situated on a grade steep enough where the miracle of drainage spared us from standing shin-deep in muck.

I crouched down at the base of the row, produced a trowel from my jacket pocket, and dug a small hole for the little Syrah vine. Remy crouched next to me, took the bubble wrap off the broken bottle, and poured a small amount of the ashes into the dirt. There were still splinters of glass coming out of the bottle as she poured, which I thought was quite *a propos*, given the circumstance.

Mixing the dirt with the ashes, I patted it down, and shared a silent moment with Remy before she rewrapped the champagne bottle and handed it to me. We both concurred that the broken container was still the best and most appropriate vessel for the remaining ashes, which Remy agreed to let me spread over downtown Seattle from the top of the Columbia Center. It'd be the second stop on my short western U.S. tour: the first stop was Los Alamos, to see what I could do about getting Marnie the help she needed.

Shay opened the bottle of Chardonnay while I took a nail from my jacket and hammered the small, copper plaque to the row post. I stepped back to survey my work. It was a little off-kilter, which again was totally appropriate, but I straightened it out anyway.

I put the trowel back in my pocket, smiled at my daughter and best friend, and took a deep breath. "Well, I hereby dedicate this block of vines to the memory of Jennifer Tillison-Thomas."

"Wow, bro," Shay said between chugs from the bottle. "Maya Angelou is like, weeping in the darkness right now."

I frowned at Shay and snatched the bottle from him. It tasted like malolactic cat piss with hints of imitation oak flavoring.

"You need to dig deep, Dad. I didn't feel that at all." I still wasn't sure about this new, more emotional model of Remy. Be careful what you ask for, as they say.

But she was right. I had already told Remy and Shay the story of how I managed to steal Jennifer's ashes: I went to the funeral home and told the creepy sales guy there that my friends, the Thomases, had found what they considered the perfect urn for their mother, and I wanted one exactly like it. I then drove by the funeral home every day for a week, hoping there'd be a service in progress, and after five days I finally hit pay dirt (so to speak) and walked into the service with the new urn like I was supposed to be there. I made my way into the back of the parlor—which is an old band trick whereby you can get backstage almost every time if you just *look* like you belong backstage —and there I discovered Jennifer's real urn. I switched the two and off I went.

Remy had been kind of pissed to find that she'd spread the contents of my vacuum cleaner across San Francisco Bay, but I was quickly forgiven.

Quicker than I'd forgiven myself, really. I had no idea why I'd stolen Jennifer's ashes and then blown off the funeral. It was the most random act of confusion and selfishness imaginable. At the time, it just felt like there was something *not right* about the whole thing—the ceremony wasn't right, the funeral parlor wasn't right, the last twenty years weren't right.

Twenty years. That's the part that really threw me. I had spent three times longer apart from Jennifer than I'd spent with her, and yet there I was, perpetrating criminal activity to secure her ashes. None of it made sense.

Until now.

Remy locked arms with Shay, and the two glared at me with the aura of semi-patient tolerance that one usually affords drunk uncles and kids who come to the door selling magazine subscriptions.

"Jennifer would have hated this," I said, chuckling. "She was all about the city, all about Seattle, down to her bone marrow. Even when we moved down here, she never really left the place."

I nudged a rock out of the mud with the toe of my shoe. "I'm sorry," I mumbled. "This isn't going in the right direction."

Closing my eyes, I turned my face toward the late morning sun. Its glorious warmth soaked into me, reaffirming that I was equal parts cactus, redwood tree, and wildflower. The three had one thing in common, though: they each craved the rebirth of a new season, the equalizing purity of sunlight, and the longing for roots that stretched deep into the earth. I opened my eyes to the ethereal image of my daughter.

"You asked me once if I wanted you to forgive what your mother had done to me, the way I had forgiven her. The fact is, I never forgave your mother. The reason I had such a hard time accepting her death was because I wouldn't be able to hate her anymore. With her gone, what was I supposed to do with this anger? It'd been my companion for the past twenty-five years. It was my crutch, my muse of dysfunction. My all-purpose excuse. I couldn't just let it go.

"You asked me for the truth but what I gave you instead were stories. Maybe not fictions, but history, and history is always open to interpretation. But it wasn't the truth. I can't move forward like that, and it would be unforgivable to pass that on to you."

Unforgivable. Now there was a concept I'd lived with for too long.

"So, here's the truth," I said. "There was a time when I loved your mother. I loved Jennifer with everything in me that knew how to love. And that's it. That's all. In the end, that's the only truth that should live on. The only truth that matters."

Remy exploded into tears, which was this bizarre new thing she had been doing a lot of recently, and lunged at me and gave me the most Un-Remy Hug of my adult life. Shay quickly followed suit, wrapping his arms around the two of us. We were like some kind of unbalanced, three-person rugby scrum, if rugby were a game where emotionally confused adults searched for the answers to life's mysteries by crying and hugging.

I eventually detached myself from the pile. "Hey, guys, if you don't mind, I'm gonna take a little walk. I just need a few minutes alone."

"Don't be too long," Shay said. "Or I'm going to drink all this really exquisite chardonnay myself." He held the bottle at arm's length and glared at it. "Oh, wait. No I'm not."

I strolled off towards the next set of rows, staying up on the grade to avoid the larger mud pits, until I had walked past the house and into the blocks of Cabernet vines. I came down the grade to where the rows were flat and straight, stretching out for another three acres before ending at the fire break.

I looked around. And I listened. And what I didn't see and didn't hear made all the difference. There was no three-hundred-foot projection screen behind me, blazing an image of my face that could be seen all the way in the back row of the arena. There was no deafening roar of joy and adoration from a crowd of thirty thousand screaming fans. There were no amplifiers, no lasers, no spotlights, no fireworks and explosions, no groupies, no entourage, no endorsements, no envelope full of cash from the promoter, no smoked salmon crudité and Perrier on ice in the green room.

There was nothing but silence, sunshine and vines. And these two people whom I loved. It was perfect. I stuck my index finger as far as it would go into the beautiful, blue sky.

And I took my victory lap.

TWENTY-THREE

I swear it's true what they say about being able to feel somebody's eyes burn a hole in the back of your head. It's that strange sense that someone's watching you, or more likely, laughing at you. I felt it as surely as I felt the heat of the mid-afternoon sun on my neck, and I turned to see Francisco's mischievous, Puck-like grin framed by a patch of wide, green cabernet leaves. He tried to not look over at me from the adjacent row as he tied up the vines with practiced precision, but I could tell he was finding this whole thing quite amusing.

"Did you just lap me, Francisco?"

His smile switched from 'mischievous and Puck-like' to 'shit-eating grin' in an instant. "*No comprende*, Mr. Corbett."

"You've never heard the word 'lapped' before?" I asked.

"Does it mean that I've gone around you twice?"

"Not twice," I laughed. "Once."

"Then I have never heard this word before."

Francisco crouched between a gap in the vines and the wires of the trellis and came over to where I was working. He hesitated for a moment, then said, "Do you want me to show you a little trick?"

"Absolutely," I answered.

He stepped up to the vine with a tie strap, but then stopped. "You sure? You're the boss."

"You're the Vineyard Manager," I said. "I'm not the boss here."

"It's not my name at the bottom of the check, *amigo*."

I laughed as Francisco gently took the top branch of the vine in his left hand and kept the tie in his right. "Don't pull the cane," he instructed. "Bring it straight up and wrap it once around the second wire like this. Then wrap the tie around here. That way, the cane isn't pulling against you as you tie it down."

I noticed that the rest of his crew was watching this little lesson go down from the opposite row. No, I wasn't the boss out here, but I also didn't particularly want to look like the amateur idiot, either. I moved down to the next vine in the row, took the cane in my left hand and grabbed a tie in my right.

"Like this?" I asked. I knew in an instant it wasn't 'like this' at all, as I ripped three leaves from the cane in the process, eliciting whoops of laughter from the crew.

"*Aquí*," Francisco said, flawlessly executing the knot with his right hand.

"Ahh!" I said. "*Usted es bueno en eso.*"

Francisco laughed. "Your *Espanol* is *muy* suck, Mr. Corbett."

"Yes, yes, *muy* suck," I giggled, shaking my head. "Thanks so much, really appreciate that."

Francisco headed back towards his own row, then turned around and shouted, *"Pero eres un gran trabajador!"*

He was smiling as he said it, so I took it to mean something other than, "You don't pay me enough for this, asshole."

I turned back to the trellis and gently wrapped the cane against the second wire with my left hand, then made the quick knot with the tie down as per Francisco's instructions with my right. I let go of the cane and it stayed in place, allowing me to finish up the knot with both hands. So much easier. The vineyard would be a disaster without Francisco.

Perhaps I could say I was the soul of the place, but Francisco and his crew were its heart.

I continued down the row, working the canes on both the first and second wire, getting a little bit faster with each one. Not nearly as fast as the rest of the crew, for sure, but it was my first trellising. My heart tinged with a small combination of guilt and sadness for not pitching in the previous year, but financial concerns and Stephan's promised lawsuit had me ankles-to-earlobes at the time. But as even Brogan predicted the suit was eventually thrown out of court, courtesy of Shay's major league-caliber throwing arm.

By 4:00 p.m., we had finished all the rows of cabernet. Well, Francisco's crew had finished all the rows; I was just kind of tagging along, apparently. I had to get to the post office before it closed, so I set up the crew on the porch with a case of *cerveza*, which provided instant amnesia—if not forgiveness—for my lack of vineyard skill.

I still had the freaking Nissan Versa, the ultimate Farmer's Embarrassment. It would be another two years at least until I could afford a proper truck. I didn't need a Massive Penis Truck, some four-wheeled fertility symbol of my agricultural prowess; I just needed something that fit supplies in it and didn't get stuck in the mud during the rainy season. And God forbid I'd ever be pretentious Maserati Vintner Guy, who stuffs fertilizer bags in the trunk of his $150,000 sports car. That said, I'd buy a Maserati in a heartbeat if I could. Some things change, and some things don't.

I made it to the post office in plenty of time, grabbed the Certified Mail slip from my glove box, and waited in line. Like the four other people standing there, I took out my phone and pretended that there was something so urgently important that it required my immediate attention during this two and a half minutes of down time. I scrolled through eight cat pictures, six wine bottle photos, and one unnaturally-chiseled, yoga pants-clad ass shot courtesy of "@wineanddinefitnessgurl4u."

A few minutes later, I handed my slip to the artificially pleasant woman behind the counter and she retreated into the back to get my letter. I didn't recognize the San Francisco address on the notice slip, but nothing fun ever comes via Certified Mail. The previous year, all the legal bullshit from Stephan Fogelson's attorney that wasn't personally served at the house came via Certified Mail, and then there was a bunch of IRS stuff that wasn't directly addressed to me but affected the estate in one way or another.

Thank God for Marnie. After an incident which involved me being on the business end of a baseball bat and a call to the police, I was able to discover that Marnie had been diagnosed with schizophrenia and was supposed to be on a regiment of Clozaril under the supervision of her husband, Greg. But Greg had taken off without a word or a trace.

Marnie got back on her meds, and eventually agreed to come work for me in Napa. She turned out to be an amazing admin, a Remy-caliber detail person who stayed on top of all things legal and financial. She was also fascinated with fermentation and buried herself in the organic chemistry of yeast during her off hours. Which was a far, far better thing than tracking down high schoolers abducted by aliens.

The postal worker came back with my parcel, only this time she looked genuinely pleased. She had me sign for the letter, placed a "Next Window Please" sign on the counter in front of me, then went to work closing down her station for the day. I flipped the envelope over to see which Institution of Pain this particular letter was from and froze.

It was from the Cameron Foundation—specifically, Sydney Cameron, Executive Director.

My hands shook as I scrambled to open the thick envelope. I was as surprised to hear from her as I was at my visceral reaction to it. In the one year, two months, one week, and five days since I'd smelled her Maui Sunrise coconut moisturizing conditioner, I'd tried to fill the empty space she'd left with all the not-her things I could find to shove into it. Holding that letter in my hand only served to remind me that the size of the space didn't matter. It would always be a Sydney-shaped hole.

The envelope was stuffed with pages stapled together and a hand-written note clipped to the top that simply read, "Hey! Look at all the awesome things I've done for this really cool woman I know." The stapled pages were various articles, news stories, features and social media posts about Sydney and her work through the Cameron Foundation: announcements about the foundation's generous gift to the Bay Area Children's Fund, stories of Ms. Cameron visiting the nation's first charter school established exclusively for emotionally-troubled girls in Detroit's inner-city, and pictures of Sydney accepting the UK Charity Award for her work.

In each picture, she smiled more broadly and brightly than I had ever seen before. If her green eyes once shone like Kryptonite, they were a lighthouse now, a beacon powered by her soul. She had cut her hair short, like Tinker Bell short, which somehow made her seem taller than I remembered. Or maybe I'd forgotten, but I doubted that. There wasn't a moment I'd forgotten. Not one. There wasn't a single memory that escaped the replays that occurred on moonless summer nights in the vineyard, late autumn afternoons on the porch, or cold winter mornings alone in bed.

As I folded up the papers, I noticed she had written something else at the bottom of her note:

"P.S. You didn't lock the door when you left. ~S."

"Good news?" It took me a moment to realize someone was talking to me.

"Excuse me?"

"Oh, I'm sorry to pry," said the woman behind the counter. "Occupational hazard. It's just, um, you look like you got some good news."

I nodded sheepishly. The tug against my cheeks was indeed quite the smile. "Yes, you could definitely say that."

The woman cocked her head to the side and looked at me inquisitively. "Wait a second. Don't I know you?"

It had been so long since I'd been recognized that I was slow on the uptake with my rehearsed response. To make it worse, I realized she could have just as easily and even more likely pegged me as the Eat A Dick Francois Guy. I had no idea what to say.

"You're Corbett Thomas," she said. "You're the guy who bought the Fogelson Vineyard."

If I was smiling before, it was an ear-to-ear grin now.

"Yeah," I said. "I'm *that* guy."

THE END

DID YOU ENJOY THIS BOOK?

You can help make a difference for the author by showing your support!

Reviews are the most powerful tool in an author's arsenal when it comes to getting attention for their books. Honest reviews help bring the attention of other readers and spread the word so more people can enjoy the stories authors have to tell.

If you enjoyed this book, please consider taking a minute or two to leave a review on any of your sites.

We appreciate your support!

ACKNOWLEDGMENTS

It's 6:47PM on an unseasonably muggy Monday evening here in the Bay Area, and I'm officially three-and-a-half days late getting these acknowledgements to my publisher. I'm thinking she's not going to burn down my house for it, but I also think pissing off your publisher is probably the last thing a debut writer wants to do.

The truth is, I have been over-thinking this section far too much. I thought it should be filled with profundities and insights and clever, heartfelt words like some kind of awards ceremony acceptance speech. But after this second glass of wine, I've realized I just need to say thank you. A lot. I have been extremely fortunate to have wonderful people in my life who've believed in me and supported me, even during times when they flat-out shouldn't. So, I'm just going to get to the point and thank them all.

First and foremost, my parents, who watched me basically throw away a four-year degree to go play rock star but responded with nothing but hugs and love and support. Miraculously, this did not end when I followed-up with a succession of similarly poor choices. How I was lucky enough to have such amazing role models in my life is one of the Great Cosmic Mysteries of All Time.

I'd like to thank a trusted group of friends who read through various drafts of the book, giving me the honest feedback I needed to get from, "What the hell are you thinking?" to "Wow, this is pretty good." So, big thanks to Malia Miller, Jennifer Case, Steve Taylor, Alyne Hart, Joshua Mertz, Angela McQuay, Kristen Gutierrez, and Kelly Gerard.

And a special thanks to my dear friend Michael Mayhew, whose consistent, valuable, and honest feedback was not unlike a continuous pummeling with the Baseball Bat of Necessary Truth.

A heartfelt thanks to Christine Trice - for her love of this project, and for a heart that always listened.

To Sione Aeschliman, I owe a debt of gratitude, along with my eternal admiration and respect. You gave this book emotional continuity and opened my eyes to a way of writing that made all the difference.

I also have to thank John Talbot, The Agent Who Tried. Though we couldn't quite bring it over the finish line, the fact that you believed in the project when others wouldn't meant the world to me.

Of course, this book would still be just a bunch of ones and zeros on my hard dive without Meaghan Hurn and Hurn Publications. It's seldom that a person will take a chance on you –risk something because they believe in you so much. I am blessed to have your faith, Meaghan, and I'll never forget it.

To the boys in the band: Steve, Bill, Bruce, Ladd and Eddie; brothers in arms forever, partners in crime (that never, ever, ever pays).

And if friends are the family you choose, then a big thanks for the constant support from my Other-Brothers, Sam Helmi and Troy Lininger. There's a little bit of Shay in everything you say…

Finally, I have to say thanks to Sydney, though "thanks" seems awfully inadequate. You came to me during the darkest part of my life, sat on my couch, drank far too much cheap bubbly with me, and helped me wipe the slate clean. I'm not sure if we lit the way out for one another or ended up fumbling and burning each other with our candles. But I am sure this book would not be the same without you.

ABOUT THE AUTHOR

John Taylor is a writer, musician, wine geek, sci-fi nerd and Certified Master of Failure & Redemption. A graduate of the USC School of Journalism, John threw his education out the window to become a founding member of the alternative rock band, The Uninvited. The band enjoyed about nine minutes of its allotted fifteen minutes of fame, including a release on Atlantic Records, movie & TV soundtracks, and an on-going appearance on that "One Hit Wonders of the 90's" station your coworker listens to incessantly.

After a brief but horrifying stint in real estate in the early 2000's, John got wise and made a day job out of his favorite hobby – wine – and has held various sales & marketing positions in Napa Valley since 2011. John's writing career started in earnest at this point, with blogs, essays and short stories appearing in various online and print publications.

The father of three adorable kids and one annoying cat (and sometimes vice-versa), John lives in the Bay Area of California.

Author Links:
Website:https://pairswithlife.net/
Facebook: @pairswithlife
Instagram: @pairswithlife
Twitter: @JATauthor

Leave a review on Goodreads:

BOOK CLUB QUESTIONS

1. What was your initial reaction to the book? Did it hook you immediately or did it take time to develop and bring you in?
2. Do you think the story was plot-based or character driven?
3. What was your favorite quote/passage?
4. What made the setting unique or important? Could the story have taken place anywhere?
5. Did you pick out any themes throughout the book?
6. How credible/believable did you find the narrator? Do you feel like you got the true story?
7. How did the characters change throughout the story? Did your opinion of them change?
8. What symbolism did you find within the book? Did you understand the religious discrimination and sexism the author has experienced and tried to convey in her book?
9. Which character did you relate to the most, and what was it about them that you connected with?
10. How did you feel about the ending? What did you like, what did you not like, and what do you wish had been different?
11. Did the book change your opinion or perspective on anything? Do you feel different now than you did before you read it?
12. If the book were being adapted into a movie, who would you want to see play what parts?
13. What is your impression of the author?
14. Who is your favorite character and why?
15. If you could meet one of the characters right now, what would you say to them?

ABOUT THE EDITOR

A New Look On Books
Raven Eckman, Editor
Raven is a freelance editor by night and fangirl at every other available opportunity.

She always knew books were her passion, well after her grandmother's challenge to read a book a day and obtained her B.A. in English with a concentration in Creative Writing from Arcadia University.

Currently, she is drowning in her TBR list, revising her second WIP, and expanding her freelancing business-all while looking for more bookish things to get involved with.

She is active on Twitter, Instagram and sometimes Facebook when she remembers.

Editor Links:
Website: https://anewlookonbooks.com/
Twitter: https://twitter.com/anewlookonbooks
Instagram: https://www.instagram.com/anewlookonbooks/

ABOUT THE BOOK DESIGNER

Triumph Book Covers
Diana TC, Designer

Diana Toledo Calcado is a book cover designer and an avid reader.

Having an artistic family, growing up she was always encouraged to learn a variety of different types of art, from metal embossing to oil painting. This gave her the encouragement needed to start learning digital art for her own book covers and for other authors as well.

Whether this is your very first book or you're an experienced author with many published books under your belt, Diana TC will help you create a cover that you will love.

Designer Links:
Website: https://triumphbookcovers.com
Facebook: https://www.facebook.com/triumphcovers

Pairs With Life Wine List

As one might expect in a story that takes place in The Napa Valley, there are a lot of different wines featured here. Some of them are as fictional as the characters, while others are not. Here's a list of the non-fiction wines I used.

…And not because someone paid me to do so. But not like I wouldn't. I mean, if you want to stroke a check, I am all about putting your wine in this book. I like paying rent just as much as the next writer.

White Wine List

Chateau d' Yquem

Cupcake Chardonnay

Kale Vineyards Grenache Blanc

Pierre Latrice Rhone Valley Viognier

2009 Domain Ramonet Montrachet

2014 Edmond Vatan Sancerre

Red Wine List

2006 Domaine Armand Rousseau Charmes Chambertin Grand Cru

1982 Chateau Lynches-Bages

1999 Riserva, Biondi Santi, Toscana

2007 J. Davies Vineyards Cabernet Sauvignon, Tierra Roja Block (Premiere Napa Valley)

Champagne | Prosecco | Sparkling List

Cartizze Prosecco

Champagne Nicolas Feuillatte

Mumm Blanc de Blancs

Schramsberg Sparkling Rosé
Veuve Cliquot, N.V.
1992 Moet & Chandon Grand Vintage
2002 Krug
2007 Cristal

Pairs With Life Book Recipes

<u>Lemon Drops</u>

2 Cups Frozen Vodka
½ Cup Freshly Squeezed Lemon Juice
½ Cup Superfine Sugar
1 Lemon, Thinly Sliced
Combine the vodka, lemon juice, and sugar and pour into a cocktail shaker with ice.
Pour into martini glasses and garnish with lemon slices.

<u>Himalayan Blow Jobs</u>

½ oz Amaretto Liqueur
1/5 oz Irish Cream Liqueur
Whipped Cream
In a Himalayan shot glass, slowly pout the amaretto, then the Irish cream and top it with the whipped cream without mixing.
This layered shot is meant to be imbibed hands-free.

<u>Gin & Tonic</u>

2 oz Gin
4-5 oz Tonic Water
Lime Wedge, For The Garnish
In a highball glass, filled with ice cubes, pour the gin and top with tonic water.
Gently stir to combine, but not so much that you lose the carbonation.
Garnish with a lime wedge.

<u>Bloody Mary</u>

1 48oz Can of Tomato Juice (or about 6 cups)
3 Tablespoons Prepared Creamy Hot Horseradish
3 Tablespoons Worcestershire Sauce
2 ¼ Teaspoons Celery Salt
3 Teaspoons Garlic Salt
Tabasco Sauce
Freshly Ground Black Pepper
Pickle-infused Vodka (or regular vodka)

For The Rim

1 Tablespoon Celery Salt
1 Tablespoon Kosher Salt

Mix the tomato juice, horseradish, worcestershire sauce, celery salt, garlic salt and black pepper in a large pitcher. Season with 10-15 shakes of Tabasco sauce, or to taste. Refrigerate until ready to serve.

To assemble drinks, mix celery salt and kosher salt on a small plate. Dip the rim of your glass in a shallow amount of water, then dip into the salt mix and twist. Fill an 8-ounce glass to the top with ice. Add 2 ounces of pickle-infused vodka or regular vodka then top with bloody mary tomato mixture.

Garnish with limes, lemons, celery ribs, blue cheese stuffed olives, bacon strips, pepperoncini, cooked shrimp, hot sauce, pickles, pickled asparagus or green beans, pickled beets, chunks of cheese, and anything your heart desires.

Note: Be sure to have skewers on hand that are long enough to fit the size of your trimmings for maximum loadability.

ABOUT THE PUBLISHER

Hurn Publications is the proud publisher of great writers and gifted storytellers, beloved books and eminent works. We believe that literature can fuel the imagination and guide the soul. There is a book on our shelves for every reader, and we relish the opportunity to publish across every category and interest with the utmost care, attention to diverse inclusion and enthusiasm.

Find your next great read: www.hurnpublications.com

HP Newsletter Signup

Signing up for our newsletter gets you **Book Reviews, Books On Tour, Cover Reveals, Giveaways** and **Book Sales** delivered right to your inbox.
Stay up to date in the Indie Publishing world!

Link: https://www.subscribepage.com/hurnpublications